The Mace Goes In

LLES
NOIZ

Copyright © 2020 LLES NOIZ

All rights reserved.

This book is a work of fiction. Names, characters, businesses, places and events are product of the author's imagination or are used fictiously. Any resemblance to actual persons, living or dead, events or locales is entirely coincidental.

Cover design & images: © 2020 TGC – Email: herokiddystar@hotmail.com

ISBN – 979-8-6394-9480-2

Available as an e-book on Kindle

DEDICATION

I dedicate this book, The Mace Goes In, to my wife, Wendy, who entered my life to show me the light.

CONTENTS

Chapter	Heading	Page
1	The Mace	1
2	Cape Triangle	30
3	Japanese Ship	50
4	Morris Minor	65
5	The Bronze Pump	81
6	Garrison's Gorillas	105
7	1/6d For A Spoon	119
8	It's Because I Love Him	139
9	21 Day Clause	156
10	Glisten Like Gold	168
11	Never mind That Now Bill	184
12	You Treacherous Basket	193
13	Silver Bullion	204
14	Thoughts Of Instant Riches	213
15	Del To Ve	223
16	Ve Suspects	244
17	Going Straight	281

CONTENTS CONTINUED

Chapter	Heading	Page
18	Canal Metals	296
19	To You Bill, £50	326
20	Cottage	339
21	Bang Bang	360
22	Sergeant Griffiths	374
23	It's Not An Hotel	389
24	Condition Purple	405
	About the Author	428

The Mace

CHAPTER 1

"It's Foggy outside," she stated, as she pushed back the curtain.

"Well, let him in," he quipped, "he should have been here at seven o'clock. Anyway Beth, have you made that tea yet?"

A maroon dressing gown clad, attractive dark haired woman, in her mid forties replied, "Of course Vandel, it's on the table."

The 'knock, knock,' on the front door told him that William Foggit had finally arrived.

Vandel drew back the bolt and allowed him to enter.

In walked a grey haired man in his fifties who held his height of six feet boldly, with shoulders tucked well back, clothed in an old shapeless blue serge suit and black shoes. A rugged face, not entirely free from facial scars from flying debris, stemming from continual grenade attacks.

Vandel was clad similarly, but his suit was brown with matching shoes.

"Oh by the way Del, we need a float if we are going to trade," said he, peeling off the bundle of banknotes. "Fifty nicker (pounds) should do it, I meantersay, it's not as if we're going to pay anything is it?" he reasoned.

Del looked Willy squarely in the eye and said, "I don't like this Willy - I don't like this at all!"

"But Del?" he remonstrated.

"No Willy, we'll do it, but I don't have to like it, I'm not keen on the idea of paying for stuff. The day you start educating the clients by offering money - we lose out!" he determined, as he held out his hand, waving it – palm down.

THE MACE GOES IN

Willy handed him the fivers and Del stuffed them into his inside pocket. He motioned Willy into the kitchen where he'd prepared a meal of eggs on toast, which his friend had espied with great relish and commenced to consume as he sat alongside him.

Vandel had a weather beaten face with a typical boozer's nose, which was deep purple and mottled. He still had most of his hair, but it had lost its colour. His expression showed signs of a life of struggle and his ears, the tell-tale marks of Queensbury rules, wherein his youth he had sported golden gloves and stood five feet-eleven inches in his sou'paw stance. Now he bent to five feet-ten inches, round-shouldered and crippled with gout.

Living as he did together with Beth his wife in their concrete home, typical, of the instant erection houses of the 1950s. Its exterior painted in bright light colours, which lent good contrast to the houses with liberal lawns and the arrays of colourful plants, favoured by their occupants and pleasing to the most discriminate eye.

Vandel and Beth Bovis, had attempted many times over the years to produce a family but their fate dealt them a cruel blow when they discovered that Beth couldn't conceive.

Now they were forced to keep their pet dog, Winston, a cross between an Afghan hound and a Labrador with cute floppy ears. It was aptly called Winston, for it always chewed Vandel's cigar butts causing much merriment to the Bovis's, but provided them both with appreciated company.

Beth stopped flipping the bacon, dished it out and then poured some tea for them, which they gulped down gladly. It had been a long walk from Lemon Street to Vandel's house for Willy and he slurped the tea briskly to warm himself.

Del was fascinated by the way Willy ate his food. He chewed his toast thoroughly, in order to glean as much taste as was possible from the butter and washed down the bread pieces systematically. He spent three times as long as the average eater to complete his meal and seemed to regard eating as a serious operation.

Del's plate had long since been made bare, but Willy had

succeeded in replenishment yet again and even two extra cups of tea, much to Del's despair, as he was forced to refill the kettle.

All hopes of an early start to the day were dashed, as Willy pushed the boat out further, by withdrawing his tobacco tin and hand rolling a cigarette. The red nose had left his face, as he sat back contentedly lighting his roll-up.

"Mm, mm," he muttered appreciably, as he exhaled the smoke, "that's better, you know Del, the simple things in life are best, a poached egg between two pieces of hot buttered toast, some crispy bacon, a nice cuppa to wash it down and a fag ter finish - yeh, give me the simple life."

"I couldn't agree with you more Willy, but come on mate, let's get going, it's getting late and we need to be on the road," he urged.

Willy arose, fastening his coat buttons to keep the warmth inside his body. Del in turn donned his Crombie, signalling him to open the front door.

"Ta'ra love," he bade, kissing his wife.

Beth handed Del the plastic bag containing both of the mens' lunches and looked on adoringly as her husband left the house.

He returned her smile as he viewed her five feet-six inch, slim figure, "Keep taking the beauty pills Beth?"

"Away with yer blarney Vandel!" she replied colouring up.

Both men walked toward the old Bedford petrol wagon, parked alongside the lane. Del put the key in the door, opened it and beckoned Willy to enter the now open passenger-side.

As he complied, Del keyed the ignition, 'Rrrrrr, rrrrr, rrrr,' but the old wagon refused to start, 'rrrr, rrrrr'...

"No, don't Del," pleaded Willy, "you'll wet the plugs."

But Del was oblivious to his cries and he continued to run the battery down.

'Rrrrrrr, rrrrr, rrrrr,' and then 'click, click, click,' sounded the starter to the promptings of his key.

"Oh hell Willy, what are we going to do now?" he mouthed despairingly.

Willy reached over and turned off the key, quite angrily by now, scolding furiously, "You won't be flippin' well told will you Del?"

THE MACE GOES IN

He reached for the starting handle in two minds whether to beat Del over the head with it, to satisfy his exasperation, but fought for control and won it, as he succeeded to open the faulty door mechanism.. He inserted the handle and shouted aloud, "Put the key in and turn it - but only to switch on, do you think you can do that Del?" he added sarcastically.

"Okay Willy it's done," replied Del. He was only too glad to assist - if only for Willy to forget his earlier faux pas.

Willy felt for compression and upon location shouted, "Ready Del? Give it the gas!"

Del clogged the pedal and it almost started after the first swing.

"Try it again Willy, I think it's going to fire."

Willy swung the handle once more but although the engine fired, it faltered and stopped soon after. He swung it again and yet again, but to no avail. Finally Willy gave vent to a load of abuse aimed at Del, who promptly came out to the rescue.

"Here," he motioned, with a pun, "give Vandel the handle!"

Willy was puffing and blowing like an old steam engine and past caring about the dilemma. He wearily climbed into the drivers' seat and noticed that the choke had not been applied. Quickly he rectified this and in reply to Del's turning, immediately the engine responded; 'DDDD dom, DDD dom, DDD dom, drummm, drummm, drummm,' it sounded, as he applied the pedal.

"There you are," Del howled triumphantly, "I knew the old girl wouldn't let us down with the right man on the handle. You have to put your BACK into it Willy," he indicated. "You've had it too soft all these years in the army, Serge. Now you're back in Civvie Street, you don't know what's hit you, do you?" he voiced with derision.

"Listen you flamin' sprog, if you had brains you'd be dangerous. Don't you know that an engine needs choke when it's cold, why if you'd been in our corps, you wouldn't have lasted five minutes? You'd have been sacked and I repeat sacked," Willy assured him, adding, "and nobody gets sacked from the army, Nobody, but in your case, they'd make an exception."

"All right, all right mate, anybody can make a mistake - look, let bygones be bygones and we'll get going, it must be near nine?"

Willy's face showed a look of urgency, as he nodded in agreement, as Del, climbed into the off-side depositing the handle behind the drivers' seat once more. They drove away heading in the direction of Birkenhead. Their first stop being made at Wallace's builders' yard, parking the wagon on the opposite side of the road. Del left the vehicle to solicit Mr. Wallace's attention, who was busy in the yard. A man with a weather beaten face, tanned and rugged, six feet tall dressed in an open red necked shirt and bib and brace overalls with black boots.

The main street of Leatham Village was quite sparse of traffic at this time and Del was able to attract the attention of Mr. Wallace opposite, who was busy sorting out his wooden scaffolding frames, used in this pre-health and safety era.

Quite an assortment of remnants remained from previous contracts deposited in the yard of; wheelbarrows in need of cleaning, broken fireplaces, leftovers of various coloured bricks, pieces of guttering, down-pipes, lengths of copper pipes, copper boilers, lead piping, brass coupling, in fact anything connected to the building trade was there.

Obviously distressed by the entangled mass of previous contracts, Mr. Wallace was frantically categorising each item and stacking it, to give some semblance of order, to cope with storing commodities, needed for his newly landed contract of 240 council houses and private homes as well.

As Del approached the yard on Leatham Village Road, the builder didn't look up but when he did and spotted Del, he suspected trouble was in store and pretended not to see him.

Firstly Del surveyed the area noticing at once a large heap of copper pipes and boilers, lying stacked in the far end of the yard. Praying for inspiration, he remembered the timber he had seen at the timber merchants, where he had recently tended for demolition estimates.

Now it was customary for both Willy and Del when dealing with traders and the like, to speak more common like and today was no exception.

"Oh Mr. Wallace, could yer possibly help me out 'ere?" Del queried, enlisting the aid of the quite dubious builder, who'd had dealings with Del before.

"What seems to be the problem?" he asked, still untrusting.

"Well, it's like this sir, I've gorra demolition job to complete in Winsford and I'm at a bit of a loss just where ter get rid of the timber."

"Oh, you mean used stuff?" the man probed.

"Ooh no sir, this is all new stuff - about 200,000 feet of 3" x 2" and a few 'undred door frames and window frames, but I don't 'ave any idea where to sell it?" he lied. He could see the change appear on the builder's face, as the man pretended he wasn't interested.

"Well, I suppose I could sell it for you here, have you got it with you?"

"No sir, I've sent the low-loader out with the coffin planks to a furniture manufacturer in Bristol with the main lot and he won't be back until tomorra."

"Tomorrow?" he asked incredulously, "why such a long time?"

"Well sir," he replied, "he 'as to collect a load of machinery on 'is return – 'ere's my card," he indicated, it read: Vandel Bovis, Machine Dismantler, Salvage Merchant, non-ferrous metals bought. 47, Dock Rd, NEWTOWN TEL: 242 601732.

Mr. Wallace pocketed the card after scrutinising the address and phone number.

"Now about this timber, mmmm, yes," he assured him, "I'm sure that I could find an interested party for you Mr. Bovis. About how much did you have-in-mind, anyway – also, is it spruce or redwood?" he queried, in a put on, pretended lack of interest kind of voice, to keep the price down low.

"Well, I'm not sure sir - perhaps you could tell me, I've gorra a piece in the cab. I'll go and get it."

Del walked quickly away toward the cab and returned just as promptly with the sample which he offered to Mr. Wallace

The builder's eyes nearly popped out of his head as he examined it. It was prime redwood.

"Whereabouts is this timber Mr. Bovis, and how did you come to acquire so much?" he questioned, suspiciously.

"Well Mr. Wallace, I'm really sorry I took that timber yard on," said Del, raising his hands helplessly in the air. "All I know about, is, non-ferrous metals buying - you know, old copper boilers and lead pipes; I think I've gone in over my 'ead with this demolition business," he lied, "still, these days yer have to take what you can get - don't yer? I've sold all of the coffin planks and complete trees - I 'ad to, they don't give you the demolition fee right away and the over-'eads need to be paid."

Mr. Wallace became more avid in his quest to secure a positive agreement, with this new avenue he hoped to exploit, and replied, "Could you possibly bring some of the timber today - I need to show it to my customers?"

This was the opening that Del was waiting for, "Well, I don't know really sir, you see; I've gorra fulfil my quota of scrap copper to the Everton Refineries this morning, in order to complete the contract and I 'ave a call to make in Liverpool. Damn nuisance really, I meantersay, they get five tons a month from me as it is - before I get paid," he rued - with an act that would have won an Oscar. "On the other 'and, if I could locate my quota elsewhere, I'd be able to get back to Winsford straight afterward." Del's head leaned over to one side, looking past Mr. Wallace, "Wait a minute, what's that stuff you've got at the back of the yard?" he asked, pretending discovery.

"Oh that," said Mr. Wallace, dangling a carrot, "it's just a load of old rubbish the plumbers took out of a block of houses we re-furbished."

"Rubbish, rubbish? This isn't rubbish Mr. Wallace this is just the stuff I need to fulfil my contract. Well isn't this a co-in-cidence? Here's me stuck for a load and you've got one right 'ere," he said, "I'll bet you've got close on a ton 'ere?" he spoke glibly, not allowing Mr. Wallace to change his direction. Del knew approximately how much was really there, but determined that he would make an offer, that Wallace could not refuse.

"Let's see, the going rate for copper is £30 an 'undred weight - and you have at least a ton, give or take a few pounds, so that makes it at least £600 that this lot's worth."

THE MACE GOES IN

Wallace couldn't believe his luck, here was a man with a load of timber – more than enough, he envisaged to supply the new contract, he had just acquired of 38 semi-detached houses. Two hundred thousand feet of 3" x 2" would cater for all of the roofs and probably the built on garages too. Greed had got the better of him and he couldn't believe his good luck, "I must handle this carefully," he thought. "I imagine…I could probably pay him a deposit with that old scrap copper- yes that's it, that's what I'll do. I hope I can convince him," he thought worryingly.

"£600 - as much as that?" he queried, "Well Mr. Bovis, it looks as if we might be able to help each other."

"Yeh," Del agreed happily - genuinely this time - "I could take this lot right down to Everton's weighbridge and straight back to Winsford for a load of 3"x 2"…Willy!" he shouted.

Willy looked up from his newspaper upon hearing Del's yell.

"Willy," Del beckoned, "come over 'ere will yer?"

Willy almost started a canter to reach Del and when he arrived, his partner asked, "Give me the cheque book mate, and the £50 cheque card."

Willy reached into his inside pocket for the cheque book. After making a show of entering all of his other pockets and a pre-planned look of dismay on his face to indicate negative results, Del exclaimed, "Oh no, - not again, you 'aven't left it in the kitchen have yer."

"I've left my baccer tin there as well Del!" said Willy ruefully.

"That's it," raged Del, "I've flamin' well had it with you. That's the last time you're letting me down - you're sacked. Get your lunch out of the cab, you can walk home!"

"But Del," said Willy with a long face, "I couldn't 'elp it - I only…"

"Don't sack him," pleaded Mr. Wallace, "he's doing his best Mr. Bovis - really, it doesn't matter about paying me now, we can work something out later today, when you and Willy come back with the timber," he reasoned, protecting his interest in the 3"x 2".

"Well… I don't know…" Del paused but changing the scowl to a half smile. "Ah' all right," he agreed adding, "somebody 'as to employ these old soldiers I s'pose. Okay Willy, get back in the cab and bring the wagon up. We'll load this up now and by half past ten," he said glancing at his watch, "we should be well on the way back to Winsford, and see if yer can do it without 'itting any of these gate posts," he added with derision.

Willy gave a pretended look of joy, as he sped off to bring up the Bedford, which started easily, due to its warmed up condition. He drove into the yard and reversed to the rear, halting by the scrap copper. He descended and reached the rear of the vehicle dropping down the tailboard.

"Put all the scrap copper pipes and boilers on Willy," Del pointed to the skip. So Willy picked up the pieces, fighting off the temptation to throw it all on quickly, before the builder changed his mind. He took approximately ten minutes to complete the task and pretending disinterest as best he could- surveyed the rest of the yard for anything he possibly may have missed. Satisfied that all of the scrap - including the old boilers - were on the wagon, he replaced the tailboard and resumed to drive out of the yard, coming to a halt alongside the road where he waited for Del, who was busily relating with the builder to take his mind away from Willy!

Del, upon catching sight of Willy driving by, cut short his spiel with, "Ooh, it's a quarter to ten, I'll 'ave to be off, if I'm gonna catch the weighbridge before the ten o'clock break," he indicated shaking the builder's hand adding: "About one o'clock do yer Mr. Wallace?"

"One o'clock!" repeated the man.

"Yes," Del replied, "and mind you 'ave enough room to take it!"

"Okay Mr. Bovis, I'll move these building frames - don't worry there'll be plenty of room - I'll make the room," he assured, rubbing his hands avariciously, visions of a huge profit.

Del joined Willy in the cab signalling him to drive away.

"You know Willy," said Del in platitude, "one of these days they're going to wise up to the 'Mace,' ha, ha, ha, ha, but until they do, let's make hay while the sun shines."

"Mind you Del," chuckled Willy, "I'd love to see his face this afternoon when we don't show up with the wood. heh, heh, heh, heh!"

THE MACE GOES IN

Willy slowed up alongside a scrapyard querying, "Eric's place okay Del?"

"Why not?" his partner agreed and stepped down from the cab, after Willy drove into the entrance.

Del wasn't just a con-man in his business but he also cheated his workmates.

Upon acquisition of Eric's office, he met Eric himself explaining that he required two receipts both for the same load and with Eric's agreement on the matter, signalled Willy to move the wagon inside. Willy concurred and drove the Bedford near the non-ferrous scale. Eric made his way to the scale, just as Willy was loading it up ready for weighing, eagerly watched by Del who didn't trust Eric, in case he attempted to gyp them on the true weight.

"Go and get me some Old Holborn Willy, here's the money," said Del keen to get Willy away from the true knowledge of the weight.

Willy was slightly suspicious of Del's ulterior motive, but dismissed it from his mind, knowing full well, he was going to be 'Maced'. He had decided a long time ago, that although he had to put up with Del's cheating, he was happy just to be making a good living for a middle-aged man of 52 with no prospects of a job.

"Half an ounce of Old Holborn and a packet of Job's please?" said Willy, after entering the newsagents.

Meanwhile, Del was arguing with Eric, that he hadn't pushed the counter-balance far enough on the scale, before jamming the fulcrum, thus giving the wrong reading of two hundred weight, five pounds instead of the real weight of six pounds heavier-a true weight of 2 cwt (hundred-weight) 11 lbs (pounds). Del considered that Eric, after weighing the copper in seven separate parcels, had cheated him out of at least 42 pounds of copper, valued somewhere in the excess of £15.

He thought quickly, "How will I justify this much deficit to Willy - surely he'll smell a rat?"

"Eric, I know I'm putting a 'mace' on Willy, but there's got to be honour among thieves - so to speak," he emphasised, "I don't mind being maced myself - but only when people are 'honest' about it!"

Eric couldn't believe his ears and started to laugh with embarrassment, at being caught red-handed giving short weight readings.

"Del, ha, ha, "you take the cake - yeh, p'rhaps I have been a bit hasty about the weight. Yeh, you're right this scale does jump a bit. I could shove another 17 or 18 pounds on the total?" he reasoned, obviously worried about Del taking his wares elsewhere especially since copper had increased in value on the daily stock exchange prices index.

"Now that's something like it," said Del triumphantly - "Here Eric, have a roll," he gestured, handing him his baccer tin.

Eric felt honoured to say the least. Having known Del for most of his working life, which included, a knowledge, that he didn't share his tobacco with anyone, unless they were esteemed 'special' in his eyes. Eric motioned Del into the office where he added up the final weights 14 cwt 11 pounds at £30 per hundred-weight.

"Yes Del, that's £420 and £2/19/11 bringing it up to a grand total of £422/19/11 how's that sound?"

"It'll be okay if you give me two receipts - you remember I told you for my expenses?" reminded Del.

"Oh yes, I'd forgotten about that mate, well let's see now…I'll change that to 13 cwt 11lbs coming to a total of, er" out came his fingers to count, but Del was way ahead of him.

"£392/19/11 and a separate one for £30 Eric!"

"Er right Del," Eric concurred. "Would you put your 'monica' on these two receipts mate?"

Del signed quickly on both dotted lines and motioned Eric to give him the £30 first, in case Willy was returning.

He had just pocketed the £30, when Willy actually did return with the tobacco.

"Here y'are Del, an 'ere's yer change," he voiced, somehow aware of the subterfuge.

"Thanks Willy, and now I've got some good news; Eric here is just about to pay us out. Okay Eric, how much do you owe us?" he

THE MACE GOES IN

pretended.

"£392/19/11 Del, here y'are mate." The trader motioned pushing the money into Del's hands, causing the change to roll onto the floor.

Willy dived downward to recover the money and handed it back to Del. "Well mate, I suppose we could both take one and half hundred each and leave the odd £92 for a good float. How does that grab yer?"

Willy nearly had a heart attack at the thought of £150 for an hours' work and tried to hide his avidity with a disapproving scowl, replying, "If you think that's the best idea Del?"

"Hey Willy," criticised Del, outraged, "if you want to we can go right down the middle and forget the needs of the wagon - it doesn't really need oil - or petrol does it" he mouthed with emphatic sarcasm.

"No, no Del," Willy suddenly got the message, "you're right, we need a good float for emergencies," he agreed, gladly accepting the bundle being proffered by his partner.

The drive home, saw Willy stopping by the newsagents to get himself 20 full strength cigarettes, the packet of which he quickly tore open and stuffed a cigarette into his eager mouth. After lighting the weed, he drew in a large drag of smoke and upon exhalation mumbled, appreciatively, "Ah, that's better."

He wasn't so keen really on tobacco loose, although he carried it around, but Capstan full strength reminded him of Nicosia, where he had spent the last of his army service abroad in Cyprus. Suddenly that's where he was and Del gave him a rude awakening by, "Look out Willy - watch the road will yer?"

Willy awoke quickly to his dismay, to find he'd almost run into the back of a tanker ahead.

"You'll have to get to bed earlier - and leave the women alone," Del criticised, really having a go at Willy now with his sarcasm.

"Give me strength," Willy muttered under his breath, "- to get home without thumping Del," he thought in a fervent prayer.

Finally he steered the old wagon into the disused road by 'The George Public House' and carefully parked it with the nose toward the pub itself, in order to hide the fact that the excise license had lapsed. 'The George' had been built in 1950, with all the designs prevalent with that year. It comprised a large bar and snug on one side, but the other side had carpets and a penny dearer on each pint catering for the discerning customer. It was this side also, which provided the occasional music group and in other times allowed the locals to participate in local talent nights for the would-be singer.

It was this posher side, which was favoured by Del and Willy, due to its easy access to the turf accountant's office availability, situated on waste ground, alongside.

They both left the cab making a beeline for 'Peter Strate's Betting Shop,' - the turf accountant. After entering, Del scoured the board feverishly studying form reading aloud, through the newspapers pinned to the wall.

"Momma's Boy: bottom weight 6 stone 2, three firsts and two seconds in previous form. Today's reckoning 9-4 favourite." He produced £15 and at a later thought changed it to £60 to win. Yes, greed had got the better of him. He paid the tax extra and snatched up his receipt. Del only ever backed the favourites. He had long since learned through past experience, that this was the only avenue which ever paid off.

Willy on the other hand, was not a punter of the turf, but preferred his favourite game of draw poker. For this he had a passion. Both Del and Willy hurried into the best room of 'The George' and Willy ordered two pints of bitter. Del always allowed Willy to buy the first round. Attempting to get a drink out of Del was like trying to get blood out of a stone. He would only comply, if there was no other way out of paying for a round. Although he liked drinking, if it were mid-day - then his first love of racing predominated, and in no way, would he deviate from commuting between the bookies' and 'The George', until the last race at 4-45 which had long since seen the towels go up at the bar.

"Here we are at the start of this great race at Cheltenham," said the broadcasting commentator with enthusiasm. "There's 'Wingate Lad' 11-2, 'Chalmers Prince' 5-1, 'Mommas boy' 9-4, 'Seven Bells' 11-4, 'Quick of the Mark' 13-2 and 'King's Ransom' 5-2....no, I'm

THE MACE GOES IN

wrong, it isn't King's Ransom, it's a newcomer......Oh, I've just been informed that the second favourite has been scratched."

With this revelation, suddenly bustle started in 'Peter's', of punters frantically attempting to change their bets over the counter to Mommas Boy but to no avail. "I'm sorry gents - can't be done, you know the rules on scratched mounts," Peter stated tongue in cheek.

"They're lined up ready now for the off and the newcomer is-yes, I've just been informed is 'Oh Boy' at 15-2."

Immediately silence prevailed to hear the starters' orders..................

"Oh Boy's rider at 15-2 seems to be having trouble controlling his mount. Momma's Boy at 9-4 seems to be agitated too. They're getting ready for the start and the wire's going up-they're off. Quick off the Mark, true to form is leaving them all behind. Seven Bells followed by Mommas Boy, Wingate Lad and Chalmers Prince close on their heels. Oh Boy, still not started-oh yes here he comes now, Oh Boy coursing up to the rest. It's Seven Bells and Momma's Boy with Wingate Lad followed by Quick off the Mark. Wait, Oh Boy is challenging Quick off the Mark - he's passing him, now he's hot on the heels of Chalmers Prince - he's passing him too, now he's passing Wingate Lad so it's Seven Bells and Momma's Boy and Oh Boy whose started to slow down at last. Now Mommas Boy's rider is looking back at Oh Boy. He's started to use the whip and Mommas Boy is coming to the lead - yes, Mommas Boy is now leading Seven Bells and Oh Boy and Chalmers Prince and Wingate Lad with Quick off the Mark behind. It's Mommas Boy leading and putting some distance now between Seven Bells with Oh Boy? Yes it's oh Boy challenging - yes it's passing Seven Bells and now threatening Mommas Boy...I don't believe it - it's actually catching Mommas Boy. What's this Oh Boy made of? It can't keep up this pace, but it is! It's passing Momma's Boy. It's in the lead and at least three lengths in front. Momma's Boy's rider using the whip madly with Seven Bells struggling for second place. Yes Seven Bells is now level with Momma's Boy. Oh Boy still in the lead but starting to show signs of fatigue. Yes a definite lag starting to show with this newcomer. He's starting to drop back and Seven Bells almost level. It's Seven Bells close behind Oh Boy with Momma's Boy faltering but its rider still using the whip without mercy. Seven Bells now challenging oh Boy for the lead, with Oh Boy very close to the rail. Seven Bells almost level now and still moving up. They're very close to each other with Oh Boy being nudged into the rail by Seven Bells-aghh, Oh Boy's rider is plummeting down onto the course. He's lying face down on the turf, he's hurt badly. All of the mounts are attempting to avoid collision. Oh Boy's still galloping on rider-less with Seven Bells and Mommas Boy following and Chalmers Prince behind.

Oh good, St. John's Ambulance men have managed to revive Oh Boy's Jockey" he sighed, "They're nearing the post and it's Seven Bells. It's Seven Bells in the lead with Momma's Boy labouring to pass Seven Bells. Yes Momma's Boy is challenging Seven Bells and almost level. Drawing up now but very close to the rail. Seven Bells' rider using the whip madly to no avail. Seven Bells is falling back but still ahead of Momma's Boy. He's drawing too close to Momma's Boy. Momma's Boy now moving up - yes he's overtaking Seven Bells- yes he's passing him. Seven Bells frantically surging forward to regain the lead. He's too close to Momma's Boy who's near the rail. Seven Bells is moving to the left and forcing Momma's Boy against the rail. Momma's Boy struggling to hold the lead but moving into the rail. He's having to drop back and Seven Bells is taking the lead. They're nearing the finish line and it's Seven Bells. The crowd is going mad. It's Seven Bells and Momma's Boy second and Chalmers Prince third followed by Wingate Lad and Oh Boy. What a race! We're waiting for the official results to appear..."

By this time Del had almost had a coronary through what seemed like a certain loss of his £60 and he angrily screwed up the ticket, until, "Wait, there's been an objection by the stewards..." The commentator compensated for the suspense by waffling, "blah, blah, blah...and, yes, Seven Bells has been disqualified from the race by the stewards' decision, which leaves Momma's Boy at 9-4 the winner followed by Chalmers Prince at second place 5-1 and Wingate Lad at 11-2."

"Wow," said Del, "Let's see now, (he straightens out his ticket) 'er 15 x 9 equals er, er 135 pound, and my £60 back rounds it off to a nice sum of £195," he smiled.

"Right Peter," he commanded, "pay me 195 nicker!"

Peter Strate tried to hide his anger with a false smile as the majority of the punters thrust their betting slips at him for payment. "Always a pleasure to pay out the winners gents," he beamed, seething inside.

Del clawed greedily at the fivers thrust to him, but before he could resume his study of the form, was intercepted by Willy who whispered, panic stricken, "The law Del - looking for you!"

Del's face paled, "Are you sure it's me Willy?"

"The tax mate, he blimped, it's out of date."

"Go home to Beth and tell her to give yer the postal order receipt Willy - come back 'ere and pass it to me before the 'Old Bill' sees me."

"Okay Del," breathed Willy flying out of the side door.

It wasn't that Vandel couldn't afford to pay his excise license all year round, he just didn't want to, so in order to fool any enquiring constables, he would produce the Counterfoil of a postal order, which would represent three months road tax. The postal order was cashed each month and renewed afresh, to keep its issue current to that particular month, and this system proved to be viable, even if it wasn't entirely honest.

Willy arrived at Del's home enlightening Beth of the dilemma, who immediately took the existing postal order to the sub-post office, to replace it with a fresh one with that day's date on the receipt, so that Del could be deemed as covered from that date in time. He arrived back at Peter's betting shop and handed Del the new receipt just prior to Sergeant Holding's entrance.

Into the best room strutted a very large man in a police sergeant's uniform weighing up the patrons, who all carefully looked at the floor to avoid his gaze. He scrutinised all of the patrons who pretended they hadn't seen him in the hope he'd just go away, but that wasn't to be. His eyes suddenly rested on Del, who was reading the Mirror's racing tips when, without even giving eye contact, the policeman spoke:

"Mr. Bovis?" he boomed.

Del looked up - unwavering, "That's me!" he replied.

"Could I see you outside sir?"

Del nodded and walked outside followed by the sergeant.

"What can I do for you officer?" queried Del in a smug voice.

The sergeant smirked thinking, "I've got you at last, bang to rights, you miserable beggar, you've led us traffic cops on a merry dance over the years and now it's pay back time. I'm going to throw the book at you! - today!" Then he spoke out, aloud, "This your motor sir?"

"Yes, that's right!" he answered glibly, "is it for my insurance," handing the policeman his MOT certificate and insurance, adding, "you'll find the postal order receipt there also, I posted it today," he lied.

"Postal order?"

"Oh, I'm sorry - yes, I should have said - it's for my road tax." The sergeant looked slightly sickened as he realised everything appeared in order, "and this is for your excise license sir?" he queried holding up the counter foil, making a note of the number, adding: "I'll have to check this out sir, by the way, at what police station can you produce your excise license?"

"Undermere," Del replied and the officer gave him a chit along with the return of his papers. To sicken Del even more, the sergeant then commenced to examine closely the tyres of the Bedford, but said no more and returned to his vehicle driving away slowly.

"Phew, that was a close call Willy," breathed Del, "let's go for a few scoops." They walked into 'The George' and Del ordered two pints of bitter and two chasers of Scotch, Willy nearly swallowed his false teeth in surprise. They both walked toward a table and sat down. Del upended the pint glass and washed it down with the whisky smacking his lips to signal Willy it was his turn to buy a round.

Willy looked up at the cue and countered with, "Er, none for me Del - I can't drink as fast as you, just get one for yourself!"

Del felt frustrated by this new ploy of Willy's and walked up to the bar to re-order a pint. He returned to the table only to be confronted by Willy who said, "Hey Del, can you answer me this?"

"If I can," he said.

"Why is it that you muck about getting a postal order for the tax if you're not going to use it right away?"

Del was exasperated, "WILLY, I thought you were a wide-boy," holding his head in his hands, "Listen - and I'm going to explain this only once. If I buy a postal order for the price of three months tax and I don't get stopped by the police for that month, it means that I've got away with no tax for that month, Now Willy," he patronised, "how much do you think that a months' tax is worth?"

"Er, er - about £2 odd," he guessed.

"Right, and how much do you think I'd pay for the postal orders?"

"Er....about..."

"Exactly," concurred Del with glee, "So Willy, if I don't get stopped for a year how much am I saving?"

Willy's head was starting to nod as he commenced to smile but suddenly turned to a frown,

"Yeh, but what if you do get stopped Del?"

"Then I have to tax the motor mate."

"But then you wouldn't be savin' anythin'" pleaded Willy.

"Course I would - what about all the other months' tax I've had free?"

Willy's face suddenly brightened up, as the point became clear.

"Oh aye, yeh!" he murmured and quaffed down the rest of his pint in one gulp, feeling rather foolish by his lack of understanding, as a result of which, he made an excuse of needing to ring his dentist for a future appointment, leaving Del to study the racing form.

The next night Willy decided to have a drink at his local and to his surprise Del was there...

"Hiya Del, how are yer?"

"Not so bad Willy, not so bad."

Willy looked at the table noticing only a quarter full glass saying, "D'yer wanna refill mate?"

Del's eyes lit up so he said, "Oh thanks Willy."

So Willy approached the bar and ordered two pints of bitter.

Then returning, placed down both glasses on the table, handing one to Del saying, "Hey Del, I've been thinking about that Coopers Builders yard, where all those old copper boilers are kept and thought if we offered them a deuce a piece, we could make a nice little profit there?"

"No Willy, it's no good trying to cheat them on the prices. Don't yer think that others have tried the same," he refuted.

"Well how can we get them off them then?"

"Hah, hah, dead easy mate, we'll offer them top bat."

"But how can we make a profit then?"

Del guffawed and then said, "We'll Mace 'em Willy."

"I don't understand Del, what is this 'Mace'?"

"Oh Willy, I thought you were a wide boy?"

Willy had a puzzled look on his face, as Del continued. "Don't you know what a mace is Willy, after all this time?"

"I er, I er… I honestly don't know Del, I just don't get it."

Del smiled and explained: "In the old days, in battle, folk used to swing a club called a mace, which is a rounded globe shape with spikes on it."

"But what's this got to do with trading?"

"Well Willy, have you ever heard of a dictionary?"

"Er, yeh, what kind of question is that?" he said in an offended voice.

"Ok, ok, right, now to get to the point I'm making, we have to think about just what a mace entails, 'cos if we take the word 'case', which sounds just like it we can…"

"'Ang on Del, what are we talking about?"

"Well Willy, have you ever wondered why the coppers just hate to see people in groups hanging around?"

"Oh, I can see what yer mean Del, 'cos they call this loitering, don't they. Yeh, they can lock you up for it, can't they?"

"Well Willy, what we call this action, is to 'case the job', we have in mind, don't we?"

Oh aye, yeh."

"Now this word 'case', its definition means to surround something by an outer covering. So if you've been cased or…

encased is more like it, means you've be secluded by the covering with no means of escape."

"Yes, but what's this got to do with mace?"

"Well mate, both 'case' and 'mace' are, almost the same by their actions. For example cased means enclosed to prevent retaliation, whereas maced means to stop someone from retaliation, by using violence with a club to knock him down."

"Yes, I can see the similarities Del, so really what you're surmising is that the proposed party is prevented to retaliate by whatever means?"

"Yes Willy, exactly."

"Well Del, just supposin' we are to use this tactic on some poor unsuspecting blighter, whose got what we want, then how do we use it?"

"With the mace!"

"What, you knock 'em down?"

"No Willy, we con them inter thinking that they'll get a fortune for this commodity."

But how Del?"

"Well, we promise them the earth but they receive nothing, just like we did with Mr. Harry Wallace yesterday, remember…?"

"Oh I see Del, I get it. We offer them some outlandish price, but say we'll pay for it on completion. So this means Del, that as we load up the wagon, we make sure that we agree to pay on completion, but promise to come back for the rest, only don't 'ey Del? Yes I can see just why you used encased and maced. 'Cos if we con them, they are powerless to ever retaliate – yeh? Well it's got merit Del, I'll give you that, but to arrive at this desired situation, then all we need is bait."

"Yes Willy and I've got just the ticket."

"What's that Del?"

"Remember those valves, we found, in that old skip last year."

"Oh y'mean those, used ter fit three quarter copper tubing? Oh aye yerse, we had half an hundred weight of them. So, have yer still got them Del?"

"'Course I 'ave, I meantersay, who in his right mind would be daft enough ter weigh them in for scrap, just for the brass price? Well as a matter of fact, I happen ter know that Coopers Plumbing, has just landed the contract to install all the three quarter copper piping, in those new council houses, that Peter Smergin's building – up the road in Newtown."

"Well, you're well informed, Del."

"Actually Willy, it took a few pints I gave to their contracts manager, after he had lost is shirt on a bet."

"Not Coopers, that big plumbing outfit?"

"Yeh, the very same. Appears he's got a gambling problem like me."

"You turf punters are all the same!"

"Now don't be like that Willy, it's just a preference we have."

"I understand Del, with you, you spend your money on gambling, whereas I spend mine on pretty women - yeh?"

"You've got it Willy, anyway mate, George Cooper, he's the boss's son, but he's always broke - like today. Oh here he comes now…."

In came a largish man with a short cigar, almost burned away. Looking round he spotted Del and his eyes lit up.

"Hello Del."

"Hiya George, a pint is it?"

Before he could reply, Del whispered to Willy, "Give him your pint, I'll explain later."

Grudgingly Willy gave George his pint and added a smile to hide his scowl, he then arose to order another drink for himself. After paying for it, he slowly made his way, through the crowded pub, back to where Del and George sat, who were now, so deep in conversation, barely notice Willy sitting back down.

"…Well George, soon after completing that demolition of the bronze casting's company, I found myself with a rubber check for payment of our services rendered. I 'adn't gorreeenough cash flow to pay the men their wages and so I went back to the bronze bloke an 'e said they'd 'ad a wage snatch that day, with police everywhere and 'e couldn't pay me my dues. So I was in Queer St. and so I asked Mary if she'd lend me the dosh ter pay the men their wages and she went up like a bottle o' pop."

THE MACE GOES IN

"So 'ow did you pay the men Del?"

"Well George, lucky for me, my pal, Willy here, 'ad been poker playin' and came off best and was able ter lend me a coupla grand…"

Just then Del glanced at Willy and gave his knowing eyewink, indicated a scam, just as Del came out with it, "Oh speak of the devil, I wuz just tellin' George about your good luck with the cards Willy."

"Oh that, well… lady luck was with me that day."

So Del, glad that Willy had recognised his intentions and to play along continued: "Aye George, when I got back ter the bronze bloke, all 'e could do was pay me in kind. I played 'eck with 'im saying, "What the 'ell am I gonna do with eight gross of castings?"

"Well, I'm sorry Del, 'cos since this last robbery, it's made us all flat broke, to even pay our own workers - never mind yours!"

"What were the castings Del?" George asked, with curiosity.

"Oh the usual rubbish George, y'know, them what they use on the three quarter pipin'. 20mm I meantersay, 'ow am I going to get rid of these flippin' things," pulling from his pocket the three quarter elbow used in plumbing. Saying, "I've gorra fifty pound sample bag of 'em in the car, I just don't know 'ow to offload 'em, 'ey George, you're in plumbin' 'ave yer ANY idea where I could sell dese, I've got at least four cwt all told," he lied.

George's face was a picture, for by just merely the appearance of the bronze elbow, was having on him. For his face turned red as he said, "Er, erm, can I have a look at the bag you got in your car Del?"

"Er, aye George, 'ere come out and 'ave a look at 'em." And he sauntered out of the pub to its car park, followed by an excited George, keen on accessing a bargain. Then Del opened up the boot of his Austin Cambridge, where the Hessian sack had spilled out its contents (purposely by Del earlier) to present their worth in its best way.

One look at the gleaming bronze elbows had an alarming effect upon George for a fortune in elbows now lay here. So he tried to pretend he might be interested, saying, "Oh well Del, p'raps you could sell 'em for scrap mate, 'ave you got many more?"

"Oh, about sixteen more bags George, p'raps you're right, p'raps I should'a turned 'em into scrap, I meantersay I could get the goin' rate for gun metal, couldn't I?"

"How much is bronze these days?"

"Erm, well, it's about £30 an 'undred weight."

So you 'ave about four hundred weight then at 120pounds, well…p'raps I could take 'em off yer 'ands, so's ter speak?"

"So 'ow much are yer willin' ter pay George?"

"Oh let's see now, erm, p'raps we could use 'em on that job ter come, Coopers 'ave landed?"

"'Ow much George?"

"Well Del, seein' as it's you, and you are a good friend, p'raps Coopers would take 'em all off your hands - Yeh?" George nodded his head smiling and quoting, "We'll pay you… lets see… say, two-times the scrap value, 'ows that grab you?"

Del's head was nodding with glee, just as Willy brought him down to earth with, "No, no, no, George, Del we've got a contract with Everton refiners to fulfil with at least one ton of copper per month, No Del, I'm not lettin' you just offload these bronzes, just so's to be, 'good friends' with George, no mate, can't yer see, 'es takin' yer to the cleaners with this offer."

"Now wait just a minute…"

"No George, you wait – just a minute. Let me tell you, that unless we fulfil our monthly contract for scrap copper, then our contract is void."

So as they all ambled back in to the pub, Del spoke up.

"Now 'ang on Willy, don't I 'ave some say in all of this, 'cos we are business partners, when all said and done?"

"Now you know I'm aware of that Del, but can't you see that 'es tryin' to con yer out of these elbows and after all, they are fifty percent mine as well, don't yer see?"

"Now hang on Willy," intervened George, "I'm not trying to con you out of anything, Del offered me these mouldings at a fair price and…"

"Wait a minute George, we're not that desperate for the price of a good drink and bookie fodder, no mate, what we have to remember is, that we deal in tons, not merely hundred weights."

George looked on thoughtfully before he spoke, but when he did,

THE MACE GOES IN

it stopped Willy's criticism.

"What if I could offer your partnership, a possible answer to your copper problem?" And he quaffed his beer.

"In what way George?" But Willy knew already, for judging by George's reaction of the bronze elbow bait, he now played right in to Willy's piece de theatre.

"Supposing I knew, just where I could lay my hands upon one ton of scrap copper at least?"

"Well George, that would be good for starters and if this would be made so, then we could negotiate a deal with the bronzes later, but only if there is at least a ton?"

"It's a deal Willy, I'll tell Pater to expect you at the yard, first thing Monday morning - OK?" he smiled, saying, "I propose a toast, a toast for Monday morning." So they all raised their glasses and gulped down the beer, stating, unitedly, Monday morning." Where they all drank heartily until the towels had gone up – to signal drinkers to leave.

Del said his goodbye to George, of whom he promised again, that Pater, would be at the yard on Monday morning, to give Del's 30 CWT wagon access to it.

So now, Del drove Willy back to his home to where Willy had parked his Morris Minor.

Upon entering the Austin he said to Willy, "Hey Willy, well done for coming in on the deal, just at the right time mate. But only one thing Willy, I've been thinking of how we could kid him at Coopers, about the true weight of the copper?"

"Well tell me about it Del."

Del looked on excited with a devious smile saying, "Remember that time when we got them doalies, ter place them paves on our wagon's flat?"

"Yeh I do, bur I don't want ter have to do any heavy lifting?"

"Well Willy yer won't have to."

"So how Del?"

"Well mate, with five, forty gallon drums on the wagon for taring, filled with water from the back of our house, with clips on - yeh."

"But how could this work Del, and where could we empty

them?"

"Immediately after we've tared off Willy, we could drop down the full drums which would weigh collectively about a ton, to lose the water. We could then reverse up to our other empty wagon, parked outside and then chuck the empty barrels into that wagon and you could drive back safely to leave it parked up."

"But what good will that do Del? 'cos…Oh I gerrit, you crafty beggar, this means that before we weigh in at the scrapyard, that our load would be a false reckoning on Coopers scale. So, at the scrap yard we could then claim the weight additionally, representing the water, because our tare at the scrap yard would be considerably less, thus we would be getting more copper payment? Oh you crafty so and so, this means we could take almost another ton out as well? Yes, how d'you sleep at night Del, thinking up these scams. Yer must be a flippin' insomniac?"

But Del just laughed.

"Yeh, and this business about the mace, so why particularly do you call it, 'The Mace' Del?"

"Well I'll tell yer Willy, my old dad was the first to use it. Only at first, he was a con artist of the 'first water'. Yes his first specialty was to reconnoitre the landscape for gullible females, whom he would scam for their fortunes, by promising them a sumptuous living, if they would respond to all of his amorous gestures, by supplying him with cheques, to tide him over business ventures and escapades, where he would absquatulate, leaving no trace. Yes he conned most of the aristocracy with these ways of procuring money, for his none – existent gold mines, diamond seams and silver lodes, where he become infamous for his scams. It got to the stage where the police would ascertain those scammed, as being recipients, of the most nefarious man of all time, of 'con, artistry, Del's abbreviation 'conspired at Delvin's', C.A.D. so here we have it Willy. Now can you remember a certain film called…with Allister Sim as its professor of 'One-upmanship'."

"Oh yes, and wasn't that posh sounding star, Terry Thomas, who played the one who accused Ian Carmichael of…"

"Yes that's the one, now what was it Willy?"

"Oh I remember, 'You're a cad sir, an absolute cad!"

"Yes that's right Willy, a cad, or that's what the police called him."

"Well Del, up to now, I used to wonder just what being a cad meant, now it's no mystery. So really…was this down to your dad, who created the cad? Or was it like you said, the coppers?"

"Del just laughed, "Ha, ha, ha, anyway Willy, in answer to your question before, of why I call my action 'The Mace'- is this?"

Willy was all ears.

"Willy, do you ever read the dictionary?"

"'Course I do, you asked me that before," feeling slightly insulted.

"Well mate, if we take the word case, then what does it mean?"

"Well Del, it means to loiter or to reconnoitre, to look at the job in hand, to get the lay of the land for either strength or weakness."

"Oh really, in what way Willy?"

"Oh you know, ter case it, ter see if it could be burgled."

"You mean case it?"

"Exactly Del."

"Trust you Willy, ter think of that, this proves that you're dishonest, ha, ha, ha!"

"No I'm not, I'm just explaining things. Anyway you asked me this all before."

"'Course you are, well my reasons for using the word case, were not just because it rhymes with mace."

"No…what Del?" Willy fished, feeling he'd been put on the spot.

"It's this Willy, case means to surround or to enclose with a covering, like encase, Yeh?"

"I know Del, I 'ave been to school, y'know!"

"Yes Willy, of course you have. Now if we're lucky enough to con them out of payment for the first load, by pretending to go back for the last load, even if we don't go back, they are powerless to come on us, for the first load's payment. Why? Because we haven't finished the load. So this is the catch 22 and creates the paradox in itself. So no payment can be made, this can be termed as a 'Mace'. I suppose it's better, than actually being hit with a globular mace, complete with chain and spikes."

"Oh perish the thought Del. Tell me mate, have you yourself ever been maced?"

"Only once Willy."

"Really! How?"

"By a flippin' judy, Willy, yeh, I was bludgeoned with mace'nry."

"By whom Del..?"

"By Beth of course, yeh tricked in to marriage, I was, ha, ha, ha!"

Willy left Del to go get in his car. Upon glancing back looked at Del, who was still laughing as he walked to his house, Willy thought, "He must never sleep at night, with a mind like that."

So, early on Monday, just before dawn of the day, both of them were taking turns at the rear of Del's house, filling the five, forty gallon drums, which were placed on the bed of the large wagon. They then lifted up the drop sides, which stood just a little higher than the barrels, concealing their presence, of any would be on lookers. Willy climbed in to the cab of the large wagon and started the engine, while Del got in the smaller wagon and got ready to follow behind.

On the way Del started thinking of every eventuality; "What if Pater wanted payment upfront…? What if the barrels were discovered…? What if Pater was waiting at the gates and not in his office…? Will they be able to get the barrels emptied fast enough to avoid suspicion…?" Del's mind never rested, but that was his strength, his cunning prowess and his ability to think fast on his feet, is what had kept him ahead of the game. Yes he thought, "Having the barrels on the wagon meant that if all else failed, he would still walk away with a ton of free scrap." He smiled to himself, satisfied that he had thought of everything.

Willy arrived and pulled up fifty yards from Coopers' entrance. Del, observing Willy parking, quickly turned his vehicle around and reversed up to the back of the large wagon. On his way to join Willy, he dropped the tail gate of the smaller wagon, to save time later, and then climbed in to the cab, where Willy was waiting.

The yard was concealed by a huge wall, which had the name 'Coopers' painted in large white letters on it and protected at one end, by two large iron gates, which from where Willy was, could see

THE MACE GOES IN

they were already open.

"OK Willy, take her in." Willy carefully drove the wagon in and stopped on the weigh-in scales. From the cab they could see the small office and through the window, sitting at the desk was Pater.

Del nodded to Willy and said, "Keep the engine running." Then swiftly climbed out of the wagon and dashed in to the office, before Pater even had the chance to stand up – part of Del's ploy. A few minutes later Del came out holding the tare-off, with the wagon's weight on it.

"Right Willy, I told Pater, we'll just turn the wagon round so it will be easier to load the boilers," Del said, while rubbing his hands together in glee.

Willy reversed out of the yard, on to the street. Within a 'blink of an eye' he had positioned the large wagon right up to the tail of the smaller one. Then with great haste, they both climbed on to the bed of the large wagon and tipped over the five laden barrels, which sent water gushing down the gutter, like a small river. The barrels now empty - they threw them on to the smaller wagon then closed the tail gate. Willy jumped back in to the large wagon, now devoid of the weight and reversed back in to the yard, alongside the scrap boilers, where moments later Del joined him on foot.

Pater was now in the yard checking on their progress, as Del approached the wagon.

"Right Willy, quick as we can, we got another job in thirty minutes."

They wasted no time - Twenty seven boilers all stacked and secured in the wagon. Pater signalled them to drive back on the scales for the final weigh-in – two ton 7 cwt.

Del signalled goodbye to Pater and climbed back in to the cab. Willy drove the wagon out of the yard, stopping at the other wagon, where Del got in and they off with Willy following behind, to go and weigh-in the scrap.

The boilers were much heavier than usual and the weigh-in altogether totalled three ton 14 cwt, from where they deducted the extra weight, thus establishing for themselves at £300 per ton £984 pounds, they split two-ways to be £492's each.

Later that night at Del's home, saw both of them, each with a bottle of scotch, celebrating their victory. Before long they were both out for the count.

When Beth arrived home all she saw were the two men asleep in the armchairs, clutching the empty bottles of scotch. She tried to wake them but couldn't, fuming she said out a loud, "Just wait till you wake up…"

Beth took out two blankets, covered the men up to keep them warm and then retired to bed.

Cape Triangle

CHAPTER 2

Del had managed to develop a system of betting, which he thought, just could not fail and was so intrigued by it that at first he didn't notice Billy Hinchcliffe sidle over to his table.

"Just the fella I wanna see," voiced his friend.

"Hey, what?" Del suddenly awoke from his dreams of affluence.

The punch drunk character, who suddenly accosted him supporting cauliflower ears and a broken nose, dressed in a dapper pin striped suit with maroon waistcoat and tie to match - Del felt a hand on his shoulder after he spoke:

"Oi Del, 'ow y' doin' mate - 'ow are yeh?"

"Sit down Billy, what can I do for yer? Me old pal." he asked.

"I've gorra plan 'ere that'll make yer a few bob Del," he quipped, "but I wanna drink out of it!"

"Let's 'ear it Billy," Del said, his interest roused.

"Yer remember I took that job wi' the brass millers in New Ferry?"

"Yeh!"

"Well mate, I 'ave ter sweep out all the machines free o' swarf, an' a lot of it is just pure brass with not much steel in it at all," he assured him.

"You're talkin' my language," Del indicated.

"Anyway mate, I started ter bag it all ready, ter doss it in the skip an' I guessed, there should 'ave bin about 'alf a ton there in bags....well Del, that sneaky rotter of a foreman 'as bin pipin' me all this time, so when I goes ter shove it in the boot o' me car, 'e comes up behind me with 'is hand on me shoulder and feels me collar!"

"Whar 'appened Billy?"

"I nearly 'ad an 'eart attack - that's whar 'appened," he emphasised adding, "I thought it was the old Bill!"

Del looked across the table sympathetically, "are they takin' yer ter court?"

"No, that's the funny thing Del, it appears that they already 'ave a practice there o' baggin' all the swarf ready for sale - a 'perk' of the job, so to speak, an' the bosses turn a blind eye to it, in fact they encourage it to save payin' money out on the hire of extra skips."

"So where do we come in?" asked Del suspiciously.

"Well Del, the lads 'ave this fella comin' in, a dealer like yourself- all legit 'oo loads 'is wagon up an' takes it across the weighbridge all legal like, an' buys it as mixed scrap for forty quid a ton. 'E always takes no less than 2 ton out every time 'e comes."

"Lucky bloke!" smiled Del, "that's the way ter make money."

"The only trouble is Del, he takes out more than 2 ton, an' the lads feel like they're gerrin' robbed of their 'oliday money."

"Ows' 'e doin' it Bill?"

"I dunno Del - unless 'e's got the weighbridge fella on a dropsie, but nobody can ever prove it, 'cos nobody but the foreman, is allowed out with 'im."

"So what's the foreman doin' about that bagful you were tryin' ter pinch?"

"Nuthin' Del, that's the funny part about it, 'e just ticked me off with a warnin' laffin' at me all the time, sayin' 'e understood an' let me go, tellin' me that 'e wouldn't mention it ter the bosses and I was ter forget all abour it."

"E's definitely bent then."

"Jus' wor I thought," agreed Billy.

"What you need Billy is a new dealer!"

"Yer right Del - that's the problem, if only we could get rid of this one - but how?"

"No problem Bill, now all I want from you is the name of the foreman an' where 'e drinks."

"That's easy Del - it's 'Arry Parker."

"Not 'im 'oo I thumped that time, over that bir o' stuff in the

THE MACE GOES IN

'Black Rabbit'?"

"That's 'im Del."

"A piece o' cake Billy - leave it ter me. Don't worry lad you'll ger a good cut outer this. 'Ere wor are yer 'avin' - a pint?"

"Aye!"

"Bitter?"

"Yeh - thanks Del," he beamed, as Del walked to the bar and ordered a pint each. "There's a pint 'ere already paid for by Willy, Del," said the landlord.

"Okay Bert, well give me another for my pal."

Del carried the two pints back to the table, handing one to Bill who thanked him. "Well Bill," said Del, "I've got to make a move now to the office," joked he, indicating the turf accountants and he upended his pint in a thirsty quaff signalling Willy to follow him.

Willy hurried behind him asking, "What's up Del?"

"We've got a problem Willy," he indicated, "what do we know about Harry Parker?"

"'Arry Parker, 'Arry Park-er, isn't 'e that one you bashed over that birra' skirt?" said Willy.

His awareness immediately in response.

"Besides that," said Del, exasperated by the reply, "What do we know about Parker we can use against 'im."

"Yer mean blackmail?"

"Yeh - well anythin' like that. 'As he done anythin' we could hold on 'im?"

"Er……yeh, I think so, but you wouldn't grass 'im would yer Del - I meantersay, I know he's a bir of a snake, but I couldn't bring myself around to stoopin' that low."

"Noooo, Willy, I wouldn't do that - you know me mate?"

"Yeh, only too well," thought Willy suspiciously.

"No me ole mate," repeated Del, "I need somethin' on 'im, 'cos 'e doesn't know it yet, but we're goin' to be business partners."

"Partners?"

"Yeh," he answered and commenced to enlighten Willy of the plan. At the completion of the scheme Del said, "Now tell me about Parker?"

"Well Del, d'you remember that German seaman Hans Muller, 'oo called the police when 'is wallet got nicked at the bar last week? Well I saw 'Arry Parker slide it out of the Hun's pocket an' shove it into 'is own. 'E shot outside an' gor into his car as quick as 'e could, with me followin' behind in my pick-up truck, making sure 'e didn't see me cos' he pulled up outside 'is 'ouse and shot in."

"That's no good, what proof 'ave we got that 'e did the job?"

"Wait a minute Del, let me finish," said he, "I waited for a good hour for 'im to come out and when 'e did, I gor out of the motor and followed 'im on foot. 'E kept lookin' around ter see if 'e was bein' tailed, bur I was way ahead of 'im and following across the road where 'e couldn't see me. 'Ave you ever followed anybody from in front? - they just don't see yer," he smiled triumphantly.

"Go on," breathed Del impatiently.

"Well, as I observed him through the mirror of the shop winder- 'e suddenly ducks into the 'ock shop," he enlightened

"Ock shop- not Cohen's the pawnbrokers?"

"Yeh!" he agreed, "I waited for 'im to come out and followed 'im till 'e shot down an entry an' flung the Gerry's, wallet out as far as 'e could, ducking into the car park of the Bowling Pub. He went further down and sneaked through the bar-room from the rear. By the time I came in, 'e was spendin' money like water. It was then that I decided to get the pawn ticket off him and later go back to Cohens to find out what 'ed 'ocked," he explained. "I entered the pub and made straight for the counter. 'Arry was so busy yappin' 'e didn't even see me. I sidled up next to 'im an' waited for 'im to pay for the round 'ed just bought, when he put his wallet back, I bumped into 'im quite 'ard and grabbed it out of his pocket as 'e held on to me ter regain 'is balance. I said 'sorry' and went into the toilet where I quickly scrutinised the contents - cash everywhere but there it was, the pawn ticket. I put it in my wallet and went back in the bar, dropping his wallet by his feet remarking to his pal, "Isn't that your wallet Fred?"

"Er no Willy, but it's probably 'Arry's - 'Arry, is this yours?" 'e said.

Harry paled, "Whew, thanks Fred!" 'e said, grabbing it, checking the notes. "There must 'ave been an 'undred in tens at least." he added,

"What about the ticket?"

"Oh yeh, well, after chuckin' out time, I went over to Cohen's with the ticket tellin' 'im a cock an' bull story about winning it in a poker game." 'e said, "I'd need a fortune to redeem the item, so I asked 'im what it was. Would you believe it Del, it was a genuine Cape of Good Hope triangle postage stamp, worth an arm and a leg," he emphasised, "it was in good nick too, I know Del, I used to collect 'em," he assured him.

"Ave yer still got the ticket mate?"

Willy was way ahead of him and opening his wallet produced what looked like a parking stub.

"Bingo," exclaimed Del, snatching the stub, "we're 'ome an' dry Willy," kissing the ticket lovingly.

"£150 nicker it'll cost yer mate," said Willy demonstratively, snatching back the stub.

"Willy - Wi-lly?" he remonstrated.

"And that's another thing - call me 'Bill' in future Del, I'm sick of this 'Willy' business."

"Okay mate - I mean Bill, yeh, certainly Bill, anything you say. Listen mate, give me this ticket, an' I'll go down to the Bowling and put the squeeze on 'im," he indicated.

"No Del, if anybody puts the squeeze on 'im it'll be both of us - or none at all!"

Del suddenly became aware, that 'Bill' was a force to be reckoned with and decided he'd have to play this by ear.

"A pint Bill?" he asked.

"Yeh, and a drop o' rum for a chaser Del."

Del suddenly choked on his pint, coughing to clear his throat - much to Bill's delight.

"Er okay Bill," concurred he, getting up to the bar.

Bill almost guffawed with happiness when Del was out of earshot, "Never thought I'd see the day when Del would buy me a rum," he mused.

Upon Del's return with the beer, Bill noticed that there were more than two glasses' of Rum on the tray, yes Del had bought four doubles accompanied by two pints of Bitter.

"Here you are mate," he piped handing him the pint and two glasses of spirit. I hope you have room for this lot?"

Bill reached for a double and drank it down in two gulps. It warmed him immensely and he hefted his pint and commenced to drink.

"What if I were to make an offer of £75 Bill for the pawn ticket."

"Seventy f…?"

"Wait mate, half way mark - you know 'cos when I do the deal with that snake Parker, we'll both be there in on it and both share the profits."

"If I agree to this Del - I don't let you or the ticket out of my sight and you let Parker know that I'm in on the deal from the start!"

"Now wait a minute. "

"Either this way or the deal is off," ordered he.

"Okay, okay, right from the start," repeated Del, worried that he may not be able to deal at all if Bill changed his mind. "We'll drink on it then Bill?"

"Right Del."

"To the job," toasted Del.

"To our job," corrected Bill.

"To our job," concurred Del adding, "let's 'ave a good drink now mate and we'll go back to our place at half three and leave Beth with the ticket," adding, "in case it gets lost."

"No Del," said Bill. "I've got a better idea....You give me £75 and I'll give you a receipt naming you as an equal partner in the redemption of the pawn ticket."

Del didn't answer, he didn't like the odds. After some time of looking hard at Bill, he finally agreed reaching for the money. Bill removed some note paper from his pocket and wrote out the receipt. He reached for the money, counted it - much to Del's annoyance and handed over the piece of paper clinching the deal. "Hadn't you better sign this Bill, rather than print it?" he questioned.

"Oh yeh, I'd forgotten about that," he said with glee, much to Del's irate look which tickled Bill's humour.

THE MACE GOES IN

They hit with their right hands and shook with their left - a typical 'Diddy Keyes' way of clinching a deal, and Del hurriedly left adding, "I'll see yer ter-morrer at the 'ouse at half past eight Bill, okay?"

Bill nodded and resumed drinking allowing the Rum to slither down his throat to warm it.

"Bill Foggit! Billy Foggit? It is!" hailed the cockney voice coming from a medium sized man with reddish hair and trim muscular figure in his fifties.

Bill turned around to find himself face to face with his old friend Zachary Bleen, with whom he'd served alongside in the Royal Armoured Corps, up to his end of term, but Zach had stayed in the services longer. Bill shook his friend's hand feverishly and gave him a comrade hug.

"I'll get you some rum Zach, are you staying 'til three o'clock?" he asked.

"You betcha."

"Then I'll get a bottle," he answered and strode up to the bar. "Give us a bottle of Lambs Navy, Bert and put it by the snug - don't worry, I'll pay the 'tottage extra' charge. Me and my mate want ter talk over old times," he enlightened. He paid Bert informing Zach of the arrangement and they both sidled around to the smaller room sitting down, where they poured out the rum in large measures.

"Well Zach, what 'ave yer bin doin' with yerself since 1962?" enquired Bill.

"Oh, yer know, this n that," he answered.

"Wor 'appened over that load o' 'Cypros' you shot Zach?"

"What load of 'Cypros'?"

"Wasn't it you 'oo went mad with that G,P,M.G.?"

"Eh?"

Bill was getting frustrated at this point and decided to elucidate......

"Yer know that sprog they sent us from Hipswell - a Lance-jack I think 'e was?"

"Er - oh aye, yeh, I remember 'im, flamin' cream puff if yer ask me!"

"No 'e wasn't Zach, 'e was the feller what rounded 'em all up, 'cos 'e came up ter me, ter ask what ter do with 'em, I told 'im ter go up ter Sergeant Bleen - that's you, ter give 'im an hand ter watch 'em. That was the last I saw of 'em till I 'eard that they'd all bin shot – ha, ha, funny me thinkin' it was you?"

"Me? Oh I see, yer thought it was…… 'ey Bill, how did 'e come ter round 'em all up anyway?"

"Well," said Bill thoughtfully, "I'11 tell yer, Cecil got fed up of us all takin' the mick out of 'is name - I meantersay, Cecil Richards Roguefeller or somethin' like that. Can you imagine bein' stuck with that? Well anyway, old Cec' decided ter go fer a bevvie with them Turks, an' 'e got on quite well with 'em - that is until one of 'em slipped 'im a mickey, so's 'e could roll 'im for his wallet."

Cec' wasn't as daft as 'e looked, 'cos 'e spotted the attempt right away and grabbed the beggar there an' then. I saw it all, as 'e whipped the Turk's arm up 'is back, just as the beggar pulled out a Mauser 3.7, Cec' took it off 'im, and that was when the rest of 'em cum at 'im with shivs. He wounded two of 'em an' forced the rest of 'em against the wall, I was tryin' ter do an 'Alley shuffle' ter get out the way when Cec calls, 'Sergeant Foggit,' I thought - too late, here we go back ter jankers' when the MPs get 'ere. No ruddy fear I thinks - we'll take 'em all prisoners, an' I picks up a Luger what someone's dropped shoutin,' 'Chop chop - hands up against bar.' We frisked 'em for weapons and then frog marched 'em all to your sector by that 'ole 'in the wall."

"'Ole in the wall?"

"Yeh you know that cave where we used ter take the Bints?"(Girlfriends)

"Oh aye," Zach remembered - "I'd 'ad many a good time up there..."

"Nonetheless," Bill added, "Cec ended up takin' 'em into that cave, anyway, wasn't that area covered by your company Zach?"

"Come ter think of it Bill that was the place of all the action," he recalled.

"Well, wor 'appened then mate?"

"As I remember Bill, you were gettin' shipped out that night weren't yer?"

"That's right."

"Oh aye," Zach continued, "it was after you'd dropped 'im off with me at the cave that I showed him where to put 'em all. I gave 'im me 'Right Marker' to 'elp

"'Im - you know, that Lance-jack they sent us from Catterick?- Tall fella with big feet?" he reminisced.

"Yeh I've seen 'im Zach."

"Well, big Georgie poked 'em all with that new issued SLR and pointed 'em all into the back of the cave, where Cecil erected the G.M.P.G. ter frighten 'em."

"Frighten 'em, what the 'ell for?" asked Bill smirking.

"Oh I dunno, p'raps 'e thought it'd discourage 'em trying to ger away?"

"'Oo pulled the trigger?"

"I'm comin' ter that. Georgie was watchin' 'em during the day, while Cecil went ter phone Captain Thomas for instructions 'cos I'd bin called away ter 'elp the MPs in the town with a squirmish and 'e..," he stopped to slurp his rum, glugging it down and re-filling his glass, "...as I was tellin' yer Bill, Cecil came back from the phone and told us 'e'd been instructed ter 'ang fire till 'C' Company arrived."

"Wor about 'F' Company - couldn't you do anythin' to 'elp?"

"No Bill I 'ad no chance - I couldn't leave the main Drag, Archbishop Makarios was comin' at any time an' we 'ad to keep the crowds from the road, 'e was always bein' shot at, an' we 'ad ter protect 'im! As it happened, Makarios arrived finally and we were able to resume normal duties."

"What 'appened then?" queried Bill, quaffing his pint and washing it down with rum.

"Oh, that was when I told Cecil to take a turn on the watch which 'e did," he explained, "I was at the inquest too when 'e gave is evidence. Got right out the service - lucky beggar. They said 'e was nuts (diminished responsibility) or something they called it."

"But 'ow did it 'appen?" asked Bill, frantically.

"Oh that, yeh, well anyway, as I was sayin', he told the court that when big Georgie came out, them 'Cypros' gor up ter some jiggery poke an' came at Cecil sudden - like. I don't care wha' yer say Billy, that Cecil's a cream puff," Zach ascertained, "cos when the 'Cypros' came at 'im, 'e didn't even tell 'em to halt, but just opened up on 'em with the Bren, cut 'em ter pieces, an' when we got to 'im- 'e was still pullin' the trigger. We had a hell of a job ter ger it off 'im. 'e broke down in tears there and then, an' when they gor 'im ter court, he burst in ter more tears - a cream puff 'e is an' no mistake!" affirmed he.

"Wot's 'e doin' now?"

"Crafty devil went right back ter Blighty an' set 'im self up with a restaurant in the north end of Shoreditch."

"Ow der yeh know?"

"I've bin there Bill, I knew a birra' stuff livin' in Pearson Street at E2, an' low 'an' be'old there it stood - this modern 'Cafe Roguefellers' it was unmistakeable - 'is name I mean. I just 'ad ter 'ave a blimp inside, an' there 'e was surrounded by all that crumpet in them short skirts. An' 'oo should be there amongst 'em, but my Doreen - her 'oo I'd come ter see. I saw red - especially when I recognised 'im 'oldin 'er 'and, I went a bit beserk. I 'ammered 'im good style - knocked most of 'is teeth out with this fist," he pointed holding up his right hand. "I kept 'ittin 'im till 'is eyes closed. They 'ad ter pull me ohf 'im. 'E was in an hell of a mess, blood everywhere. Worst of it was, Doreen didn't even recognise me, an' finally after the 'Scuffers' came, I tried to tell 'em why I'd 'it 'im. Y'know what Bill? She didn't even want ter talk ter me, when she found out 'oo I really was. Appears she was plannin' ter marry 'im.'

Tears were welling up in Zach's eyes as he continued, "Gor an 'andful for that lot in the 'Scrubs' an' ter make matters worse, I got court martialled in the bargain. Fifteen years in the Corps down the drain, no pension - I 'ad to forfeit that. All I got was me back pay." Zach took a large gulp from his glass and Bill feverishly replenished it to the brim, which Zach continued to slurp down to choke off the tears.

"Never mind mate," humoured Bill, patting him on the back, "women aren't worth it, yer can't trust 'em an inch. Take my Eva, I couldn't let 'er out of me sight, when I was on manoeuvres in

THE MACE GOES IN

Penang, she up an' left, took up with a tea planter an' filed for a divorce in 61." Better off without 'er. Here I am 8 years later and still happy. Anyway mate, 'ow did yer ger out of the clink?"

"Oh yeh Bill, at first I couldn't do the time an' wanted ter top meself, but they caught me in the act an' cut me down. Ended up 'in the 'ospital ward - thought I was nuts. 'Ad this 'ead shrinker come round, put me right. Clever bloke, gave me a goal ter aim at. 'E'eld a writin' class for blokes like me - 'oo'd of thought I could write - It started with poetry, an' now I'm inter short stories. 'E even taught me to speak correctly - King's English Y'know."

By this time Bill was getting bored and kept looking at his watch.

"Goin' somewhere Bill?"

"No, no," said he trying to look interested.

"The rain in Spain falls mainly on the plain!"

"What, where's your Cockney accent gone Zach?"

"That's what I've bin trying to tell you Bill, I can speak properly now mate. 'Ere I'll show yer som'ink..." He put his hand in his pocket and removed a small book labelled, 'Wormswood Words.' "Ere Bill, read this poetry on page 17."

"Poetry? Er, no thanks Zach," he replied, but seeing the hurt look on his comrade's face changed his tune by saying, "You read it mate it'll sound better comin' from you - the writer."

A look of joy appeared on Zach's face as he feverishly thumbed the pages to find the item.

"I wrote this Bill, in a competition. I call it, 'Deterred' Okay, right I'll start," he drooled:

"Locked within sickened bitter,
Of past crimes - giving much thought,
Coming to sense far in the latter,
Taking part - getting caught.

The root of all evil, we are told,
Is money, kind, silver, gold,
In my case, wanton lust,
Material things to have - a must.

Now the battle fought and lost,
Looking back on better days past,
Methinks this date - be the last,
One visit here deters most.

How I wish a scene of choice,
To have been born of a stupor,
To appreciate of the small and simple,
To love, comprehend, within defines,
And most of all - piece of mind.

Happiness without the strife,
To lead a good enjoyable life,
God, I fear I cannot accept,
For in this life I cannot conceive,
Beyond material concept,
Beyond the air I breathe.

There is no future for others like me,
From being here of this I've learned,
To pirate in this earthly sea,
The only enjoyed is that of earned.

I see now I must love and cherish,
Kin and home - to hell with strife,
For inevitably I'11 perish,
If carried on this way of life.

The moral being for chaps today,
If you can't afford to lose - don't play!"

Bill was hypnotised. Zach had to shake him, "Are you alright mate - Billy?"

Tears had started to run down Bill's face as he looked up to Zach.

THE MACE GOES IN

"That was absolutely ruddy marvellous mate, you could make a fortune if you filled a book up with 'em. I've never heard anythin' so to the point, why, it 'acherly breathes reform. I can see that Old Nick's done you a power of good," he complimented. "Wor are yer plans now Zach, 'ave yer gorra job ter go to?"

"Well Bill, these last three years I've bin doin' a birra wheelin' an' dealin' in the motor trade, doin' quite well too. Made meself a bob or two, norra fortune, bur I'm doin' all right," said Zach reassuringly.

"Sellin' cars?"

"No chance."

"I know, you're in car factors, aren't you?" he probed.

"Well sort of," relented Zach, "let's say that I do the H. P. financiers a good turn."

"Good turn?"

"That's right, hey Bill, can yer put me onter a reputable garage - I need some new business".

"Of course I can, what do yer 'ave in mind?"

"Listen Bill an' listen carefully - how'd yer like ter make yerself some cash, easy like?"

"Well," Bill mused thoughtfully, a bit suspicious, but more disinterested, due to the £150 in his pocket burning a hole there, pointing him to a poker game.

Zach sensing Bill's apathy re-phrased the question, "Real money Bill," he emphasised, "yeh real cash money - in yer 'and, but what we need is a load of old bangers to do it right yer see. D'yer know where we can gerra load of 'em?"

"Old bangers - yer mean old crocs, cars and the like?"

"You've gorrit the first time Bill!" he smiled.

"Course I do, in the sales yer can pick up anythin' yer like if yer got the brass."

"How about this," said Zach waving a roll of fivers which resembled a coffee mug.

Bill's eyes nearly popped out of his head.

"Er, er, er, that yours then?" he questioned, unable to tear his eyes away.

"You could 'ave a bundle like this."

"How's that mate?"

"Well Bill, I'll tell yer, just as soon as yer get,'old of an old banger for me."

"What's wrong with you gerrin' it?" he probed suspiciously.

"Well Bill, in order for it ter work, somebody other than meself needs ter buy the old banger, so's I can set it up. Listen Bill, all you gorra do, is buy the old car an' that's it - no come back. Then yer sell it ter me all legal like an' I goes me own sweet way. I take all the chances, 'cos I does all the signin' an' Lumberin' myself with all the debt. Course, you gets an equal cut 'cos you as ter go an' buy back the banger ter make it work. Now then, if I asked yer ter buy an old croc, d'yer think you could do it?"

"Course I could, but..."

"Don't worry mate all will be explained soon," he assured him, "are you in or out Bill?"

"Well, if yer sure that's all I need ter do, I suppose I'm in, but just one thing?"

"Fire away Bill!"

"Where's the poke comin' from ter buy it?"

"'E'yare mate, here's £25 quid, ger a late model but bad body work, you can pick 'em up cheap."

"Done," said Bill holding out his hand to shake Zach's.

The time was approaching 3.10pm and the towels had already appeared over the pumps.

"Towels are up Zach, we'd berra be going," voiced Bill. "Where are yer kippin' tonight mate?"

"Oh I'm all right, I've gorra workobus with a bunk-bed Bill so yer don't ave ter worry about me."

"Nooo, can't 'ave yer kippin' in a van, come to my place, I've gorra council flat an' I can put yer up on the sofa in front of the fire."

"I can't put yer ter that kind of trouble mate?"

"It's no trouble Zach, if a fella can't 'elp an old comrade at arms - there's somethin' up."

"Are yer sure?"

"Say no more mate," he encouraged as he motioned Zach to the door. They walked through it and out into the car park.

"Where's yer bus Zach - oh is that it, the blue an' yeller top?"

"The very same," he answered proudly, "Yeh mate, me an old Bertha 'ave been tergether fer 2 years now."

"Bertha?" said Bill full of mirth.

"Aye mate, I saw it in the sale room an' thought I'll just 'ave to 'ave 'er, cos yer know 'ow it is when yer've nowhere ter go."

The Bedford based caravanette gleamed with clean paint work as they approached. Zach reached for his keys and opened the offside door, inviting Bill in through the rear side he had just unlocked and started up the engine.

"Which way Bill?"

"Take a left here Zach an' then another an' keep goin' down 'Allport Lane', 'til yer cum ter the lights, then I'll tell yer again. Mmm, 'ood a' thought that you of all people had reformed."

"Reformed - me? Ha, ha, haaa," he chortled, "yer've gorra be kiddin' aven't yer Bill, me, MEEEE, ha, ha, ha, ha, ha,. I kidded that 'ed shrinker good style. When I was ready ter leave 'Winson Green' an' go back ter the 'Scrubs' 'e was the one 'oo recommended me fer remission an' got almost 19 months knocked off me sentence. It would've been more but I 'ad ter lose a month due to tryin' ter 'ang meself.

'E gave me a clean bill of 'ealth and I was a model prisoner - why they even made me a star.

"A star, like on the telly Zach?"

"No Bill, it's a special ratin' in the nick, yer 'ave to wear a red star on the top o' yer arm, ter let the screw know yer a creeper, I played my part well an' bided my time, till they opened that gate ter let me out. Then that were it, I took my National Assistance to a transport cafe an gor' in with this load of conmen 'oo took all me four quid in a couple of 'ands of poker.

I was stuck an' no mistake, couldn't even pay for my bed, but give 'em their due, they 'elped me out, seein' as I'd just cum out the nick."

Zach travelled down the road and took a left, "Yeh," he resumed, they gave me the entrance fee ter the pub an' started ter educate me on 'ow ter put the squeeze on."

"The squeeze?" queried Bill.

"Yeh, livin' on yer wits so ter speak."

"Ay, yer pullin' me leg aren't yeh Zach," Bill guffawed showing his disbelief.

"No mate, I'm deadly serious, it was through these fellers, that I caught wind of this side of the car business," he informed him. "Hey Bill, I want ter tell yer somethin' funny, I was 'avin a drink in the 'Rabbit's 'Ead' on the 'Kingsland Road' with me mates an' we was stuck for a drink. We 'adn't got a shillin' between us for a bevvie, an' contemplatin' whether or not ter gerra job an' 'ave done with it, when in walks a real dope from out of town. When I think about it, he must 'ave bin a country bumpkin. All the eyes light up and we starts arguin' on 'oos gonna con 'im first. They tosses up and Arfur wins."

"Who's Arthur, Zach?"

"Arfur Millington, used ter play at the windmill - magic act an' all that. Been on the palladium in his hay day that is, 'till 'e came unstuck with a show girl, so now he does 'brown uniform' (debtors Prison) for failure of maintenance for the baby - twice a year and 'e won't work at all but spends 'is time in dole queues for is keep and connin' people in pubs for 'is drink and…. Up 'e gets an makes a bee line fer the bar," he said.

"Turn left 'ere Zach," interrupted Bill, "Right now pull up along 'ere at the third block."

Zach complied as Bill said, "Right 'ere."

They got out of the motor and Zach followed Bill after he'd locked the doors. After climbing the steps outside the flat they walked along the corridor until Bill pulled out his key and inserted it in the fourth door.

The block of maisonettes stood proudly on the main Newton Road, almost to the centre and gave a modernistic contrast to the impoverished surrounds.

It had been the pride of Newton's Borough Council's attempts, to house the ever growing population of the post war boom, and showed off tenants in their clamour to secure a flat. Bill had been one of the lucky ones after his demob from Korea conflicts, and had remained there still.

The large spacious windows considered beautiful in an age where 'out went the old' back to back terraced rabbit hutch houses and 'in came the new' modern spacious flats such as this. As they entered Bill's flat he motioned his friend to enter.

"Sit down mate," invited Bill, as Zach entered the kitchen leading to the lounge, I'll get yer a cuppa," he added.

"Oh, ta Bill."

"Eggs on toast okay for yer Zach?"

"Lovely."

"What was yer sayin' about that country boy mate?"

"Oh, I, yeh, Arfur walks up ter the bar hangin' on ter his half a bitter like it was 'is life's blood. He moved up close ter the bumpkin an' sez, 'Mornin' mate - ow are yeh'?"

The lad turns round an' sez "Er, not bad mate, 'ow are you?"

"I'm fine," Arfur pipes, "now that I've mastered me new act!"

"Eh, new act, are you on the stage then?" he asks surprised like...

"Arfur Edwards, 'magician extraordinaire' at your service my boy," he says holding out his hand.

The lad shakes it and replies, "I'm very pleased to meet you sir, what kind of magic do you perform?"

"Sleight of hand, the quickness of the hand deceives the eye," says Arfur, putting his hand on the lad's shoulder then putting on a grave voice whispers,

"All trickery y'know, nothing magical about it, in fact anyone could do it given the right instruction!"

"Really?"

"Of course, a piece of cake," he replies pulling out three aces which he squares up, places in his left hand tapping it lightly and when he turns over his hand the cards have gone.

"Gosh," breathes the lad, "how did you do that?"

"Elementary my dear chap!" chuckles Arfur, sizing him up querying, "would you like to participate within my sphere of talent?"

"Parti-er?"

"Have a go old chap! Would you like me to show you some of my tricks?"

"Oo rather," enthuses the lad, "what would I have to do?"

"Well" Arfur, states, "How would you like to....no, I'll go one better." He starts weighing the lad up and down.

"Hmm, yes, I think you'll have the intelligence for this?"

The lad looks on all smiles as Arfur continues,

"Yes, this trick goes down very well at all the clubs. Firstly, I want to ask you if you believe that the hand could be quicker than the eye?"

"Er, yes I think it could."

"Very well my boy," boomed Arfur, in a loud voice. "Then I shall commence, firstly, let's see what sort of props we need," he indicates, as he searches through his pockets, "ah yes, here it is, my magic wand. Imperative to perform magic," he informs him jokingly as he removes the conductor's baton from his inside pocket. "Now then let's see, what else do we need…ah yes the proverbial glass," he remarks, looking straight at the lad and saying no more.

The young 'un just stares back bewildered, "Glass?" looking puzzled.

"But of course," retorts Arfur, "we can't do the trick without the whisky. Get a single Scotch and 'er, no, I think we have all we need - oh yes, make sure it's in a wine glass lad."

The bumpkin motions the barman who takes a glass to the optic and gives it to him, "Three shillin's sir?" and the kid coughs up givin' the whisky ter Arfur.

"Now for the demonstration," he beams, "I shall now attempt to take this glass of whisky, in front of your good self my boy and drink it down in your immediate view, but with one difference, yes, I shall drink it down without your actual knowledge by Sleight of hand," he indicates, in a voice of melodrama. Then he did his daft 'alicazaoma alicazam' with his hands first at the lad and then at the glass. Then he picks up the glass and downs it in one go, "There," he said, "how's that?" waiting for his reply.

"But I saw you do it!"

"No my boy, you couldn't have!"

"But I did, I did, you just drank it down!"

"B,b,b, but you, er, that is, I mean. Let's see, I said alicazaoma, alicazam, then I put the 'fluence on you and…oh no, I forgot to put the 'fluence on. How could I have been so stupid? I'll never live this

THE MACE GOES IN

down I'll be kicked out of the magician's union if this ever gets out... it's the end, the end...,I know I can make the trick work given another chance? Would you give me another chance?"

The lad looked on not even sure of anything as Arfur went on, "Let's see what have I got here, hmm, my last shilling," he mused with remorse, "I'll tell you what my boy, I'd be willing to bet with this shilling, that I could succeed with the trick were you to give me another chance. If I fail..., then the shilling is yours. What do you say? I couldn't be fairer than that could I?"

The lad took the shilling, examined it and put it back on the bar, "Well," he replied, "I don't know."

"Don't know, don't know, I should say so, where's your shilling lad? - come on, make it worth my while. Put your stake next to mine. You know I can do it don't you, that's why you won't stake a shilling, eh, eh?"

The lad put his hand in his pocket and counted out twelve pence placing it on the counter adding, "This is silly, you'll never be able to do it, it's a piece of cake." He ordered a whisky and put it down on the bar stating smugly, "Let's see you drink this one while I'm watching you?"

Arfur replied, "Right my boy, are you ready?"

"Ready and waiting!" said the lad confidently.

Arfur goes through the old routine, "Alicazaoma," at the lad, "alicazam," at the glass, an' then waves 'is arms at the lad sayin', "You are very sleepy, you are very sleepy, you are going to sleep."

The lad just smiles as Arfur picks up the glass and as 'e downs the Scotch, the lad roars out in laughter chuckling, "I saw you, I saw you!"

"Damnation," said Arfur, "I've blown it again," he says, in an act that was fooling every body. "Let's see," he says frantically, "have I got another shilling?" He roots through all of his pockets and comes up with a few pence, four pence I think, adding, "I know I can do it and I'm willing to stake my last four pence on it."

"But you can't do it, you've had two goes at it, you've lost a shilling already, it's like taking candy from a baby," the lad protested.

"Just let me have another go? I can guarantee you, after this next try, that you will have learned a good trick and the method to do it which can make you a lot of money, I assure you. Are you game? You look like a good sport?"

"Oh well, all right then, here we are," the lad agreed putting four pence on the bar adding: "Really, I don't want to take your money?"

He ordered a whiskey and handed it to Arfur who took it from him thanking him replying, tongue in cheek, "This is the trick, are you ready?"

Before the lad could reply, Arfur quaffed the Scotch down with the terrible truth, "How much have I put on that bar, one and four pence was it? Now then lad, think now, just think about how much the knowledge of this trick has cost you!" he said sympathetically, "nine shillings with one and four pence return so we can safely say you've spent seven and eight pence for the privilege of learning show business."

The lad just stood there dumb founded, mouth agape unable to say anything as Arfur returned to the group.

"Cheapest Scotch I've ever tasted," remarked Arfur, with a smirk.

"That Arfur, he certainly knows 'ow ter con people." said Zach," mmm, that smells good Bill. Y'know mate there's somethin' nice about eggs, especially on toast," he remarked appreciably, as Bill handed him the plate.

Bill sat down with his plate also, handing Zach the butter dish and knife.

Japanese Ship

CHAPTER 3

'Bbbrrring, brrr, brrring,' sounded the alarm clock as it heralded seven strikes.

Bill awoke immediately on the chair in the lounge and Zach who lay face down on the sofa murmured, "Wha' w, what time is it Bill?"

"Just after 7.00 pm, cum' on we'll be able ter gerra game o' poker at Fred's Gym if we 'urry up. Charlie'll be there by now an' he'll 'ave is mates with 'im, just bin paid y'know, them big spenders.

"Oh I?" Zach commented, "yer'll never change Bill, yer know. Still takin' everybody ter the cleaners eh?"

"We'll go down in your motor Zach if that's okay by you?"

"Too right mate," his friend agreed and they entered in. Zach drove out of the road with Bill directing him. After just a few turns left they reached the main drag.

Bill suddenly indicated, "A quick right 'ere Zach, now right again."

"Is this it Bill?" pointing to the council flats.

"Yep, we're right here, now then - see them steps, we 'ave ter go up there an' it's at the top second door."

What at first glance resembled a famous London West End shop's entrance, lay before them cradled by massive glazed white marble like stone pillars holding up the entrance. Along with huge pieces of the same stone occupying consecutive brick courses, exemplifying an age where both labour and materials had been cheap.

Bill had been always intrigued by the shop's gracious splendour and its mere presence caused him to feel good inside. He'd always favoured the upper floor of the shop, which for the most of his teenage years he had frequented to play billiards in the upstairs snooker room. Now alas, it had changed to give vent to Freddie's gym - to cater for the profession of wrestlers who attended regularly until late, when in order to 'pay the table', Fred had turned some of it into a poker school, which proved to pay better than the gym ever did.

Freddie's access lay on the side of the building up two flights of iron railings.

They commenced to ascend just as the figure of a man started to run down them.

Because he was descending so quickly Bill shouted out, "What's up pal?"

The man suddenly saw them for the first time and panic took him over. He stopped indecisive about whether to run back up… and then quite quickly continued to run down once more. Quite innocently Zach stuck his foot out looking the other way and the man went headlong into the side street hitting his head and then lying still. Zach and Bill reached down to pick him up just as the 'bang' occurred and a missile flew past his ear as another man came rushing down the steps clutching a revolver.

The second man took aim and fired again and the man on the ground arched up and then lay still once again. The armed man then reached the bottom step and attempted to brush past them both. Zach gingerly stuck his foot out once more and the second man also tumbled to the ground.

"Gotcha," voiced Zach, triumphantly whipping the man's arm up his back forcing him to cry out in pain and drop the gun.

"Right you nasty little excuse for a man, I'm going to make you sorry you ever picked up this gun," and he retrieved the revolver and commenced to baste about the head, the man whom he was now holding down with one of his knees on his back - the other on his neck.

"Agh, aagh, aaa-ah," the man moaned, "I've had enough, I give you best."

THE MACE GOES IN

Zach eased off him ordering him to get up. Still keeping the man's arm up his back and the gun pointed at his head he bawled out, "Billy, call the ambulance and the coppers."

"O, okay Zach," Bill replied and sped off in the direction of a phone.

"Der-dagh, der-dagh, der," sounded the ambulance as it entered the street stopping by the body of the first man, who was now stirring. A police car rolled up just as the ambulance men were attempting to put the victim on a stretcher. A sergeant leapt out of the car and made straight for Zach who was holding the gunman at bay.

"Here officer," he motioned handing the policeman the pistol, butt first.

The sergeant took hold of the gun and thrust it in his pocket, "Right sir, what is this citizen's arrest?"

"Something like that," nodded Zach.

"Well done sir, we'll take it from here," he indicated and relaxed Zach's grip from the man. "Your friend William Foggit enlightened us of what transpired sir. Are you free to come and make a statement? I'd be glad to give you a lift there and back sir."

"I'm okay sergeant, I have wheels," he pointed in the direction of his workobus, adding, "I'll come right now if you like," he said smiling.

Zach climbed into the cab and started the engine.

"Just follow the constable sir," said the sergeant. Zach complied and tailed the police car all the way to the station.

An hour later saw Bill and Zach leaving the boys in blue with a sigh of relief from both of them for although they knew that they had aided the police make an arrest, the thoughts of getting involved in a court case - even as witnesses for the Crown was disconcerting.

Because of the lack of space to park in the police area, they'd left their vehicle over the other side of the main road. Zach's caravanette was parked in the forecourt of the 'Bullfrog. They crossed over the main road and Zach opened the off-side door motioning Bill, "Here mate, gerra gobful o' this!" He pushed a half bottle of rum to his friend as they both entered the vehicle. Bill opened the bottle and upended it, swallowing rapidly three gulps before handing it back.

"That's better Zach," he murmured appreciably.

Zach glugged the bottle down like he was drinking water and deposited it empty into the waste basket of the forecourt.

"Cor, look at the time Bill, 'alf nine. D'yer think yer'll still be able ter ger in on that poker 'and?"

Bill's face was livid, "Blinkin' scuffers - I 'ate 'em," he said with derision, "They've messed the night up now, we'll just 'ave ter 'ave a bevvie instead," he voiced sadly.

"Never mind Bill, no sweat, night time's fer drinkin' I always say, let's try this ale-'ouse, it looks nice enough."

"Okay mate," he agreed and they both sauntered into the bar.

"Two pints, bitter please, 'an two rums," ordered Zach. The Barman complied and sat the glasses on the bar.

"Six shillings and two pence - thank you," he motioned.

Zach said, "'Ere y'are, 'ave a bevvie yerself."

They sat down at a table and Bill looked up to recognise a friend who had caught his eye, "'Ow are yer Llew," asked Bill.

A short dark haired man with a lined face and rough working clothes – fifty-ish replied, "Oh can't grumble. I dare say," he replied, "yer might be able ter 'elp me out mate?"

Bill went cold - the dismay showed on his face perceived by his friend who re-assured him.

"It isn't money Bill."

The smile returned to Bill's face.

Llew continued, "D'Yer ever get any scrap cars when yer collectin' yer old iron mate?"

"Cars?" retorted Bill, "no chance Llew, why what's the problem?"

"I've been given the chance of a Morris Minor for ten pounds but I can't seem to get it started. I think it needs a new carburettor," he added.

"Well why don't yer get one?" asked Bill.

"'E wants 'alf a quid - that's what!"

"'Oo does?"

THE MACE GOES IN

"The breaker's yard," Llew explained, "that's an 'elluv a lot for a carb,"

"I see what yer mean," agreed Bill, "yeh, yer, can't really make much of a profit if yer've gorra shell out before yer start. 'Ave yer got the car at 'ome?"

"No Bill," he remarked dismally.

"Oh, I see, yer can't really do much to it can yer? Sorry me old pal, I can't 'elp yer on this, what are yer drinkin' anyway?" he queried.

"Er a pint o' mild Bill - thanks a lot."

Bill arose out of his chair to the bar and collected the pint, together with a repeat of their own requirement.

"'Ere yer are Llew," he motioned.

"Ta Bill," he voiced happily and commenced to sup the brew. .

"What year is it Llew?" he asked, for the sake of something to say.

"Nineteen sixty."

"Is it in good nick?"

"Well...."

"Oh it's not eh?"

"It's not that bad," he emphasised, "in fact it's quite good for its year, it's only nine years old and a bit of touching up should make it respectable for some punter to use for his holidays," he enthused.

"That good eh Llew? Well, I tell yer what mate, if yer want ter make a couple of bob out of it - provided it's a good looker of course I'd be willin' ter take it off yer 'ands. 'Ow's that grab yer?"

"Yeh, why not Bill, mind you, I'll want £20 at least."

"Twenty quid, yer jokin' aren't yer? Yer only payin' ten!" pleaded Bill.

"Ay, but it's worth £25 really," he reasoned.

"Tell yer wha', I'll come up ter morra dinner time to 'ave a blimp Llew, okay?"

"Right Bill, I'll be in all day anyway."

Bill reminisced with Zach all night of their army days without noticing the disappearance of Llew and soon it was 10.45pm and the towels were up.

"Well mate, I think we'd better go 'ome with a carry out. I'll gerra

LLES NOIZ

bottle o' Scotch. Do yer want any thin' Zach, I've gorra few bob?"

"Yer all right Bill, I'll gerra bottle o' rum."

They both collected their bottles and made their way to Zach's motor. Finally arriving at Bill's flat, where they sat down in front of the gas fire and gulped their bottles, until they both reached oblivion.

The alarm sounded 6.55am and Bill reluctantly reached over to switch off the bell. A quick wash and shave proved to rid him of the hangover which prevailed and yet he was very careful not to turn around too quickly, in order to keep his headache at bay.

He left a hurried note for Zach enlightening him of his intended return at 11.30 am(opening time) placing it on the table by the side of the sofa.

"Come in Willy, er, I mean Bill," said Del, correcting himself quickly.

Bill walked through the door as Beth turned the kidneys and bacon over in the skillet. Bill sniffed the air in appreciation, "By gosh, that smells delicious," he drooled.

Beth turned the mixed grill over once more and gave the skillet a shake before removing the meats onto two dishes and replenished the now scorching fry pan with eggs, which took only a matter of minutes to cook, which she removed and placed on top of the dishes covering the meats, offering one of them to Bill, who eagerly took the plate from her setting it down upon the table and commenced to devour the contents.

Bill was a decisive eater, firstly he cut the kidneys into pieces and consumed them along with some bread which he dipped in the gravy. He removed all of the fat from the bacon and started to gnaw at what was left. He then cut slices of bread which he dunked into the egg, then he sliced the remains and stuffed it into his mouth, to appreciate the final taste of the albumen. A cup of tea he upended to wash it all down. Out came his baccy tin which he opened with relish to make a cigarette. Compared to Del who was busily stuffing his mixed grill into his mouth, washing it down intermittently with gulps from his tea-cup. At last he came to the end with, "Gorra roll Bill? I 'aven't gor any till I get ter the shop."

Bill obliged Del by offering him the one he'd just made, ploughing back into his tin to repeat the same operation. The reason for this action was all too clear in his mind, for he knew if Del got hold of this tin, then half of his baccy would disappear, so he wasn't taking any chances.

Bill lit his fag slowly, drawing long welcome puffs from it that gave him great satisfaction.

"Right," interrupted Del, "out of the £62 I have left, £6 of this has gone on a full tank for the wagon which leaves £56 for our float."

"Fair enough Del, why don't we ante up a minimum of £50 for the float and keep £6 for future petrol - we could ask Beth to keep it safe, in case we were tempted to gamble it away?"

"Good idea Bill," he enthused, "mind you, I'll have to ask her first."

"Ask me what?" she queried suspiciously, for she knew Del for the con-man husband he was.

"Wondered if you'd 'ang onto our cash Beth, and not give it to us all at once, unless it were for petrol?"

"Oh, I don't know whether I should Del - you know what you're like when you've got a hot tip and no cash to back it, No, I don't think I could stand the trauma, you're hard enough to live with now, without the hassle of eking out allowances. Sorry love, but you'll just have to accept me for the way I am!"

"Well that's put the kibosh on that Bill, now who can we ask?" he said with disgust.

Bill looked at him for quite a long time and Del caught his glance commenting! "What are you looking at me like that for Bill?"

Bill looked him squarely in the eyes replying, "You can leave the float with me Del," he said simply, "and I'll give you back nothing."

"Nothing, what are yer talkin' about Bill?"

"Oh come on Del, I gave you credit for more brains than this, think back to yesterday," he prompted.

"Yesterday," Del repeated, with a puzzled look.

"What was the first thing that you asked me when I came here?"

hinted Bill. Silence reigned for 30 seconds until…

"Oh I yeh!" said Del, as the penny dropped.

"Yeeees!" Bill mimicked, "I did? - Don't tell me you forgot Del?" he remarked sarcastically, "you've still got it haven't you?" he queried accusingly.

"Y, y, y, yes, of course I 'ave Bill, in fact I was saying to Beth earlier on, I'd better not forget to give this back to Bill." Del's face had developed quite a reddish colour by now as he reached into the assortment of betting slips in his inside pocket to retrieve a bundle of fivers which he counted in his blustered state dropping most of them onto the floor.

"Er, 'ere y'are Bill £50, check it's all there," he offered, as he bent down to retrieve the bundle on the floor.

Bill indexed the wad agreeing, "Yeh, it's all 'ere Del," adding, "now I can pay the 'lectric man."

This ploy for the benefit of Del indicating his reluctance to invest anything else.

"And now back to that other cash Del, you said you 'ad £56 left?"

"That's right Bill, I thought…"

"Never mind that now Del, I'll tell you what's the best; carve it down the middle makin' it £28 each," he directed.

"But Bill - what about the float?"

"Well Del, if we both carry cash then there'll be no problem will there?" he assured.

Del's face screwed up as he said, "P'raps you're right Bill, come on we'd better get goin' I can 'ear them eight leggers fillin' up the main jigger so we'd be better startin' out now."

They said their goodbyes and went through the front door.

"'Ow's the battery Del?"

"Gorrit charged up lasts night, purit on this mornin' an' it started - no bother."

Bill entered the cab and pulled the choke. To his surprise the engine started first time.

"See," chuckled Del with glee, as Bill put the motor in gear and turned into the street.

THE MACE GOES IN

"Roll us a cigi Del?" Bill voiced, as he turned into the approach of the industrial estate.

"Certainly mate, where's yer tin?" asked his friend.

"Oh I dunno," he lied, "'Ave you got any?"

The look of derision formed on Del's face as he reached for his packet of full strength.

"Try one o' these Bill," he said, opening the pack trying hard not to show his reluctance.

"Ta Del," he replied, taking one and flicking his lighter quickly, in order to remain in control of the wheel.

"Long time since I've 'ad one o' these," he added, appreciably breathing out with satisfaction, "used ter smoke 'em in Nicosia, that was when I 'ad a few bob. Not like now scratchin' round fer a livin', mind you Del, I'm not ungrateful, no mate, we've 'ad some 'appy times since we've bin at it 'aven't we?"

"Yeh, Bill yer right, I often think that... 'ang on, stop 'ere!"

"'Eh?"

"Yeh, 'ave a look at these gates!"

Above them were the names in wrought iron gates contained between two pillars it read; 'Cobden and Allbright, Chemicals.'

Bill stopped the wagon just passed the gates and Del commenced to spruce himself up, "This is the place," he said, as he straightened his tie.

"Why, what's 'ere Del?" queried Bill.

"Leave this ter me Bill, oh give us half a quid ter tip the gate man with - I've got no change."

Bill dug down in his pocket and gave Del a 10/- note.

"Right, listen Bill, this chief engineer is desperate ter get rid of 'is empty drums of chemical, Eddie Shaw told me, 'e works 'ere on the night shift."

"Oh aye?"

"Yeh, an' if we screw our nuts mate, we 'can' con our way inter gerrin' the scrap contract," said Del, rubbing his gripped hands together with avarice.

"Empty drums don't weigh much...oh I see yer crafty devil, it's not goin' ter stop there is it?" he chuckled.

"Yer talkin' my language Bill," he smiled.

They backed the wagon up and drove to the gate. The weighbridge man came out and asked, "Yes what firm is it?"

"Bovis and Co Machine Dismantlers," boomed Del, getting out of the motor, offering him his card adding, "we need to tare off - before we come in."

For some reason the man was convinced that he was on the level and pointed to the scale which was situated by his hut, "If you pull over there, I'll give you the correct reading sir."

Del waved to Bill and pointed to the weighbridge and Bill turned the wheel over and stopped the motor, "Okay here Del?" he asked?

"Yeh, stay in the motor Bill."

The gateman made a quick note, stamped it and offered it to Del who thanked him and with a gesture which only Bill could see, Del waved the 10/- note in full view of his driver, craftily screwing it up in his other hand and shaking the gateman's hand which all the world would have thought he was tipping with the money. He climbed back into the cab attempting to insert the ten shilling note in his Jacket which was draped over the seat only to find Bill's hand snatching the money back who added: "Really Del, you know I grew up with you! Fancy pullin' a stroke like that?"

Del's face once again acquired that embarrassed, reddened hue, as he nervously tried to laugh it off, "You're some fella Bill, and no mistake, ha, ha, aha!"

But Bill wasn't laughing, yet suddenly he saw the funny side and guffawed with laughter. Then both of them laughed in chorus enjoying the joke.

Travelling into the factory compound, Del said: "Slow down Bill" as they approached the structure.

Bill was driving the motor almost to the end of the building when Del motioned, "Stop 'ere mate, I've just spotted Eddie Shaw."

Bill complied just as 'Eddie' approached them.

He was quite tubby with long blonde curly hair, which he regularly pushed from his eyes.

"I'm on an 'early' this week Del, see that office up those steps, that's where Glynne Evans the chief engineer works. Yer'll find 'im there right now," he Stated, "if yer wait 'til half nine, that's when 'e as is cuppa."

"Okay mate thanks, I'll make sure yer gerra drink outer this."

The man left and Del motioned Bill to pull the truck up under the office and park it.

Del walked furtively up the wooden steps not knowing just what he would encounter, but with the boldness of all the Bovis's, quickened his step. As he reached the top landing, he scrutinised the office window, wherein a man had his back to him. On the desk were a number of objects, including a picture of Don Bradman famous batsman of cricket. The bats, trophies prevalent on the shelves, enlightened Del that the occupier was indeed a fan of the noble art. Del confidently knocked business like on the door ahead.

"Come in," hailed the voice.

He was a well developed man in his fifties, with a bronze sun burned complexion and barrel chested with obvious regular gymnasium workouts. He looked up as Del appeared, and read the heading on the door 'Cyril Evans, Works engineer.'

Del entered with, "Good morning sir, I was told by my business associates that you would be able to help me fill up my Japanese ship with light iron!" he flashed his card.

"Light iron?" the man's eyes lit up, "do I take it you mean tin drums and the like?" he questioned anxiously.

"Anything possible at all," said Del, "in fact, I can offer you four pounds a ton for good clean light iron, old drums, tin cans, in fact - anything which resembles iron sir, I'll pay over the scale for," he assured him.

"I'm afraid I can't help you in that respect Mr. Bovis, you see we already have scrap metal dealers here - two in fact."

"But surely you don't want all those drums located on your tip down the road sir?" he pleaded clutching at straws.

The engineer looked up at Del hopefully, lingered awhile before replying, "Well Mr. Bovis, I must admit we are running out of room for those drums, but they wouldn't be of any use to you. The reason we dump them there, is that the scrap dealers won't touch them, due to the chemical waste within them."

"Well Mr. Evans, I can safely say that I'll buy the lot from you here and now. Perhaps because of the chemical in them I'll have to half my original quote. I'd get one of me lads to clean 'em y'know - wages and all that"

"Well, I don't know really?" he replied, worrying whether Bovis would sue him if any of his employees were to get hurt due to the corrosive action of the chemical.

"Is this yours sir?" indicated Del, picking up the picture of Don Bradman.

"Er yes," said the man, wondering what Del wanted.

"And these?" asked Del, fingering the cricket trophies, "Do you play this noble game sir?"

Mr. Evans was quite impressed at this new ploy of praise and coloured slightly but pleased at Del's interest.

"Yes Mr. Bovis, I did dabble a bit in my youth."

"Really, I've never been lucky enough to meet a famous batsman - it's my favourite sport."

"Oh yes?" enthused Evans.

"Yes," mimicked Del, "I had a chance to be interviewed by Mr. Bradman in the early forties but the navy sent me my call-up papers that very same week and I had to report for a medical," he lied.

"Oh shame," the man sympathised, "have you tried since the war to get into it?"

Del held up his right hand to show the loss of his little finger saying, "I lost this on the 'Kelly' when she was torpedoed. Caught me arm under a load of iron gantry. Lucky to be alive I suppose. Woke up an army hospital in Malaya - minus the finger. Were you in the war sir?" pretending to put on a brave face.

"Oh no, I was deferred, lucky I suppose, the government employed me in research, where I was left until 'V' day," he voiced.

"It's a good thing the government had men like you Mr. Evans, no doubt by your endeavour you helped us win the war."

"Oh I don't know…"

At this point Del put down the cricket trophy clumsily making it obvious that his loss of finger was at fault.

"Damned nuisance this at times sir," he emphasised, "can't seem to get used to it - even after all this time."

"I know what you mean Mr. Bovls, I've had broken fingers and felt I couldn't manage. By the way, how are you at driving?"

"Oh not so bad since the rehabilitation centre fixed me up with a specially made steering wheel - mind you, I have a driver for my wagon, in fact he's right here now. Grand chap, served in the Korean War, got decorated for it but due to his injuries can't get a job now. This is why we're both scrap metal buyers," he lied, drawing sympathy from the man. "Gosh, that reminds me, I've got that contract with the Japanese boat to fulfil… I've got to get 100 tons before the week's out. Anything will do, light iron, any kind of rubbish – the Japanese will buy the lot," he emphasised.

"Well, perhaps you could take these drums Mr. Bovis, but what arrangement could we come to for payment? The trouble is, I've to account for everything that leaves the plant."

"I've got my wagon downstairs sir, tell you what, we could load it up with drums and then use your weighbridge to count the tonnage, this way you could keep track of everything."

"Good man," agreed the engineer, "I'll get onto the waste department right away." He lifted up his phone explaining what was needed and after a few minutes of, "Yes, okay I'll do that," he agreed saying, "did you say your wagon is here Mr. Bovis?" holding open the phone.

Del nodded smiling, "Yes," thinking, he's on the hook?

"Could you start today?" queried the engineer earnestly.

"Right now, if need be sir," he said with a smile.

"Good show, yes Arthur, I'll send him down right away," he assured, "oh, about payment Mr. Bovis, will it be cash or cheques?" Without waiting for Del to answer he added, "You could pay daily or weekly, which ever you think best."

"Pay you on completion sir, this is the usual format with scrap, if that's all right with you?"

"Splendid," he said, "now, if you go out of here, turn left at the top," he pointed, as they moved to the steps, "and then the second right."

"Second right," repeated Del.

"Yes, Arthur Pearson will be waiting there for you to show you what needs to go. Thank you Mr. Bovis," he said, offering his hand.

"Thank YOU sir," emphasised Del, and bade the man, "cheerio sir, I'll see you later this week."

Del nearly fell down the steps with excitement as he rushed to tell Bill the news.

"I've done it, I've pulled it off Bill," he cried, "we're blinkin' well 'ome and dry mate."

Bill looked ecstatic and smiled commenting, "That's lovely Del, I'm made up! 'Ow much 'ave yer got ter pay Del?"

Del looked exasperated, "Pay - pay, yer've gorra be, flamin' jokin' Bill, I've neva 'ad ter pay fer anythin' in the scrap game. No mate," he declared, "we promises 'em the earth but we gives 'em Nuthin. You know the score by now Bill, the 'mace' goes in," he declared happily.

"So we're gonna mace 'em are we Del, I thought for a minute when you came down those steps that you'd seen the light and become an 'onest business man at last, an' left the 'mace' alone, but I see that this was too much to expect, wasn't it?"

"Yer breakin' me bleedin' 'eart Bill ha, ha, ha, listen mate d'yer want in or out? I'm easy, yer can either start the wagon up or gerout of it, but if yer do gerout, don't bother cummin' back," he warned.

"Can't I 'ave a say in the matter without us fallin' out Del? I think I'm entitled to air me views once in a while -aren't I?" he reasoned.

"Well…okay Bill, but we need t'get goin' if we're out ter gera few bob today," he exhorted.

"Okay Del, where d'yer want me ter take 'er?" he asked.

"Right Bill, now as yer go out here turn left and then second right."

Bill keyed the starter and followed Del's directions.

For the next three hours both were involved in supervising the factory's work force to load up their wagon which they drove out fully loaded over the weighbridge and returned twice for removals. At twelve o'clock they resumed to load and drove out for the last time. None of the loads went to the docks Del had implied, but down to the plant's tip every time, which was some considerable distance away from the factory, after which Del mouthed, "Let's get back to Hock Country, I'm starving!"

So Bill complied and headed for home. He drove the wagon into 'The George' and faced the cab toward the wall at the rear of the pub. Del shot straight away into the snug, ordering himself a pork hock and as Bill arrived he added, "Oh yeh, one for Bill too," motioning Bill to pay the woman. Bill paid her for the hocks and they turned to sit down at a table.

"Brought yer a birasalt," motioned the barmaid who had arrived to collect empty glasses, "are yer 'avin a bevvie Bill?" she asked.

"Er…" Bill thought he'd go after eating the hock and replied, "no Rita, I shan't bother, I've gorra go in a minute. My 'oppo wants a pint though, don't yer Del?" he prompted.

"Course I do Rita, I'll 'ave a drop o' Scotch an' all," he indicated. "By the way Bill, where are yer off now - are yer not feelin' well?"

"Bit of business mate," he revealed cautiously, not wanting Del to know about his deal with Zach, for the first time in his life Bill ate quickly and literally wolfed down the meat from the pork-bone. He finished it noisily and lay the bone down on the plate.

"Well, I'll see yer on Saturday Del, about eight o'clock, tara mate," he concluded, and before his friend could question him he was gone.

Del crept out a few steps after him hoping to find the source of his friend's new interest but when he arrived into the car park, Bill was gone. If Del had only taken the trouble to search the car park, he would have spotted Bill hiding behind the scrap wagon. After five minutes Bill emerged hoping the coast was clear and headed for the opposite side of 'The George' bar, where he phoned for a taxi. After four minutes it arrived and sped off in the direction of his friend, Llew's house.

Morris Minor

CHAPTER 4

"Hiya Llew," he mouthed, as his friend opened the door, "I've come to see this car."

"Oh aye, hang on Bill, I'll be with yer in a minute."

He came out with his overcoat on.

"Not cold are yer Llew?"

"No Bill, but I've gorra chill from that draughty bedroom an' knowin' my luck it'll turn inter the flu."

"Yes, yer gorra take care of yerself, at our age," Bill said, with a hint of concern.

After they had walked half a mile Bill asked, "Much further Llew?"

"We're right 'ere Bill," he indicated and motioned his friend to open the small double gate facing him. The house was a tumbledown old cottage in red random sandstone, which for all to see resembled chips from broken stones, which had long since been abandoned for their lack of uniformity. But here it all was joined together and held intact, by some miracle or other, but somehow Bill appreciated the outward appearance of the home.

The windows with their tiny panes in obvious need of repair, but the gardens compensated lending its colour from the rhododendrons in various shades, which adorned the residence. Also compensated by the array of small border colourful plants, which echoed the tender care of the occupant. Roses bloomed also in contrast. A pinkish car stood on the drive and Llew knocked the door. It was opened by a white haired old woman, who said, "Oh hello Mr. Jones, have you come to pick up the car?"

THE MACE GOES IN

"Er, not just yet Mrs. Stevens, my friend's here to see if he can get it going for me."

"Righto Mr. Jones, would you like a cup of tea or something, how about your friend?"

"That would be lovely," he answered, "we'd both like some thanks."

The old woman disappeared whilst Bill commenced to open the bonnet as Llew opened the door.

"Try it!" he requested.

Llew inserted the key in the ignition and started the starter –rrrr, rrrr, rr, click, click, click, sounded the unit.

"Damn," cursed Llew, "the battery's flat."

"Let's 'ave a look Llew, give me a 7/16 AF spanner," voiced his friend.

"Here y'are Bill, sorry, it's only an adjustable Bill"

Bill started to slacken the base plate of the distributor secretly making it appear by all intent and purpose that he was stripping the carburettor.

Mrs. Stevens re-appeared with, "Tea's made."

Llew said, "I'm going in for a cup Bill, I'm a bit cold mate, d'yer want yours out 'ere?"

"No Llew," he replied, "I'll be in soon - you go ahead."

As his friend entered the house Bill advanced the distributor after first removing the cap to indicate the direction of the contact breaker and then he returned the key in the ignition to supply the spark. He then replaced the cap and inserted the starting handle which he had located in the boot. He felt for the compression which was really quite hard now before he reached in and turned off the ignition. Hurriedly, he stripped down the carburettor until he located the jets which he perceived were malfunctioning. He removed both of them and blew them out with his mouth, sighting them through to ensure that no blockage remained. He then re-assembled the unit and re-connected the system but didn't tighten up. Putting his hand down on the manual pump connected to the camshaft he shoved the lever up and down. Just as he expected the petrol flowed up to the carburettor forcing its way thro' the float chamber. Seeing the liquid appear he tightened up the union nut and replaced the handle in the socket. Switching on the ignition, he was careful not to turn the handle by hand. He furtively pushed downward with his foot just as it started to kick back. There was a terrible rattle as the engine fired into action, 'brrrrooooom,' and started to run madly away. He dashed to the choked accelerator connection and frantically toned it down with finger and thumb.

Llew suddenly came running out, "You've done it - you've done it!" he exclaimed excitedly, with a smile.

They let it run for a few minutes before Bill said, "Come on Llew, where's that cuppa?"

Llew directed him to the front door as he reached over to turn off the key. They both sat at the table after Bill had washed his hands in the kitchen sink.

"My Albert used to say to me, "Ethel," the old woman droned suddenly, "the day will come when they'll put men on the moon, naturally I didn't believe a word he said, but low and behold they're building a rocket now to get there, he was right, in fact my Albert was right about everything," she reminisced, tears running down her cheeks as she went on. "We bought our car in 1960 and we've had many an enjoyable hour travelling in it around the countryside. He'd have been here today but for that mistake I made with the handbrake, he never stood a chance..."

"Handbrake?" queried Llew.

"Yes...you see, Albert was very methodical with his driving, he always put the handbrake on when he parked the car. The trouble was I couldn't tell which was the gear stick or the handbrake, and when Albert was checking to see if the radiator was leaking I reached down to pick up my lipstick and moved what I thought was the gear stick to get it."

The tears started pouring down her cheeks as she continued, "It was then that the car started to move down the hill pushing him over and under the car and… and… he, he was run over."

For at least half a minute she was quiet as Llew put his arm around her, with her sobbing saying, "There, there, don't worry love, don't reproach yourself." he sympathised, "it wasn't your fault!"

THE MACE GOES IN

"Can you see why I want to sell the car? I can't stand to see it anymore…"

They quaffed down their tea thanking Mrs. Stevens for the thought and commenced in the direction of the front door.

"Put the key on Llew and I'll give it a whirl."

Llew turned the ignition and pulled the choke. Bill re-inserted the handle and felt for compression. Re-assuring himself all was ready he put his instep on the handle and kicked down. Immediately the engine sprang into life bringing a smirk to the face of Llew, "Not a bad motor eh Bill?"

"Well it is, and there again Llew it's got a bit of a rattle - p'rhaps it's only the shells gone?" he pretended, knowing full well that in an advanced engine, all the rattles are heard louder.

"Listen to it Llew - there y'are, can yer hear it?" he directed.

"Er, well, p'rhaps there is a bit of a noise, but it's not that bad is it?" he pleaded.

"Maybe I could get away with about £17 for the big end shells and the gaskets for a fiver, yeh, £22 odd should do it," Bill assured him, "anyway Llew 'ow much will yer take for the old 'eap?"

"Oh come on Bill, this is a good little runner mate, yer could give me 20 quid for it couldn't yer?" he said hopefully.

"What about all the cash I've gorra spend on it Llew, I meantersay, it's gonna cost me £42 pound now - I've only got £18 on me, 'ow am I gonna be able ter get the shells?" (Big end bearings)

"Aw heck Bill, I need the money meself, desperate like. 'Ow much can yer give me?"

"Fifteen quid mate, that's the best I can do!"

"Eighteen pound and it's yours," he determined.

"Sixteen," retorted Bill.

"Seventeen an yer've gorra deal."

"Oh alright Llew, but yer keepin' me poor," assured his friend, Bill gave Llew the cash there and then and took the log book from him as Llew went into the house with the ten pounds for the widow.

"Here you are Mrs. Stevens, the money for the car," he said softly and bade the woman, "Tara love." He left the house just as Bill was driving the car out into the street. He banged on the window and asked him for a lift home, Bill dropped him off and then drove his car home.

"Hey Zach, look what I've got fer yer," he cried shaking his friend from his stupor.

"Augh," was all he could get from him which disgruntled Bill who was literally spitting feathers for a drink. He reached down for Zach's rum bottle; but to his dismay found it empty. He feverishly scoured his living room for his whisky Bottle but found that empty besides and to cap it all - by the side of Zach's Sofa, "Drunk as a skunk and on my whisky too!" he groaned. In a frenzy he took hold of his friend and shook him, shook him hard - screaming abuse at him, reprimanding him for the loss of his alcohol.

"Oookay, okay Bill, I'm sorry mate - 'ere, I'll buy yer another bottle," he said fervently.

"I'm not worried about the cost," he emphasised, "it's the principal of the thing that bothers me."

"Principal?" exclaimed Zach incredulously.

"Yeh Zach, there should be some kind of honour among thieves, some kind o' trust between 'em," he explained.

"Oh that," said Zach sheepishly, realising full well to what his friend was alluding.

"Bill, I'm truly sorry mate, the fact is I've been dodgin' the law for so long and not able ter relax, that when I do find a place of shelter, I tend to go a bit overboard and I beg your forgiveness at this time, can we forget it mate?" he pleaded.

"Well Zach, looking at it like that, ah what the heck ...life's too short for worryin' over a silly bit o' scotch innit?" he said forgivingly, "just cast yer 'ead out o' this window, me ole mate," he added.

Zach sat up and spied through the glass, "Where, what?" he asked.

"The Morris, I've just gor it fer yer?" Bill answered proudly.

"Wow, you mean that pink one?" he asked, "that's a cracker. It's the millionth car Bill," he enlightened.

"Millionth?"

"Yes, apparently, Billy Morris has this tradition of painting pink, each millionth car produced, in that lovely colour to enlighten the world on how popular the Minor is selling," he explained.

"Well mate," said Bill, "yer learn somethin' new every day!"

Zach went into the bathroom and put the lather on his face continuing the conversation, "I'll be with you in a couple of minutes Bill." He commenced to drag the stubble from his chin, until finally all that remained were his side burns to trim.

"Where's the nearest car showroom mate, the biggest I mean?" Zach queried.

"Well, we've got Roberts and Henly's and then there's Carltons Cars, that's about it in Newtown I'm afraid Zach, but if yer go along a bit nearer Birkenhead yer'll find Lings of Fawley."

"Lings, you mean that big Southampton firm? I didn't know they'd come all the way down here Bill. That's the one we need to hit mate, the bigger the better," he revealed. "Let's have an egg on toast to soak up the whisky and rum, then we'll go."

"Right y'are Zach," Bill complied.

The two men sat at the table smacking their lips in appreciation, followed by two cups of tea which proved to restore them both.

"Two o'clock Bill, just about the right time, now then let's see, insurance?"

He scanned the certificates to convince himself that he'd brought the right one along. He then started to fill one of them in signing HIS signature at the bottom, "Right," he stated, "what's the registration number Bill?"

"S M A 6 2 7," replied Bill adding, "lOOOcc Nineteen Sixty."

Zach continued to write the details down until finally the document was complete.

"There, we can go now."

"You take the cake Zach, now I've seen everything," he stated aghast, "'ow the 'eck can yer write out yer own insurance?" only half-believing.

"I'm an agent Bill, I sell it for a broker down south, and to top it all, I get commission on it," he added, "imagine getting commission on your own money, ha, ahha," he giggled, causing Bill to guffaw in chorus.

They continued to laugh all the way to the car, "Here's the log-book Zach, yer'll need this won't you."

"Too right I will Bill, thanks."

Bill then did a hurried job on the distributor retarding it back to normal running. Twenty minutes later saw both of them near to 'Lings of Fawley' where Zach, before their arrival, said to Bill, "Listen mate, what I want you to do now is go and have a couple of vodkas in the local, here y'are take this pound, it should buy you enough," he stated, "now then mate, don't have more than you can hold," he stressed.

"Why vodka Zach, I mean it's not my scene really?"

"It doesn't pong on your breath Bill and besides, I need you sober enough to buy the Minor back straight after I've sold it, savvy?"

"Just as you say Zach," he concurred, "but I still don't know why it's so important that you'd want me ter buy it back?" he questioned dubiously.

"Just do as I say Bill, a lot depends on your ability to buy back our car, if you don't, then all is lost," he stressed, "don't pay any more than £30 for it either or we could come unstuck."

"Okay Zach," he agreed, stepping out of the car, "I'll see yer later in the 'Rural Soak,' see - over there?" he pointed.

His friend nodded and they both parted.

Bill walked into the pub brandishing Zach's pound voicing to the barmaid, "Double vodka love," and eyeing her up and down as she left to fill the glass added, "'ave a drink yerself love."

"Thank you," she replied and passed him the drink, I'll have a glass of bitter," she said modestly.

"'Ave a vodka love."

"Oh all right thank you sir," she replied and commenced to re-use the optic, "that'll be 9/10d," she said remitting Bill with 10/2d change.

"You're not from these parts are you?" she said gently.

"Newtown."

"Ah yes, isn't that over by that delightful river?" she said romantically as only women can.

"Oh yeh," agreed Bill, quaffing his drink. He was starting to take more than just a passing interest in this dark-eyed medium sized beauty behind the bar.

He studied her. She was a middle aged woman of fortyish, who had obviously kept her figure well and her beauty, turned the heads of all who came in to the pub. Bill found himself unable to take his lustful eyes from her. She had also become attracted to him, for Bill held himself well. Due to his hardened army drill routine of most of his life. They stared into each others' eyes drawing pleasure from each other's presence…

Meanwhile, Zach had entered into Lings and was carefully examining cars from the driving seats with a purposely stupid smile on his face. He was doing his best to appear as naive as possible. Before actually trying each car for size in the seating, he had scrutinised the labels inside each vehicle which held the buying in price paid in letter code, as well as the selling price on the label of the windscreen. The code used by Lings was simple to apply to which Zach was quite familiar,

No.	1	2	3	4	5	6	7	8	9	0
Let.	B	U	Y	A	T	L	I	N	G	S

He searched through each label for a car which was under priced for e.g. Ling's Ford Thames van was marked NS, which represented £80 part exchange allowance in conjunction with £120 purchase price on the windscreen which would show a profit of 50% for tax purposes.

Compared to the Vauxhall Velox marked at YTS=£350 trade in and selling price of £400, £80 under priced this possibly due to the bad state of paintwork, in need of obvious respray to restore it to former splendour.

"This is the one!" breathed Zach greedily and walked into the showroom office.

"Yes sir?" asked the startled manager, not used to un-announced people entering.

"How much is your Velox?"

"The price is on the car sir, if I'm not mistaken," said the manager adding, "I am Harry, what can I do for you?"

"Well with my family increasing rapidly, my faithful old Moggie Minor, isn't substantial anymore and I need something bigger…" Looking around him he pretended to discover the Vauxhall. "Now this Velox seems to be much roomier and…oh, I don't know if I could afford it? I mean…"

"What car have you got now sir, a minor you say?"

"Yes a Morris minor, but I don't know if I could afford the deposit using my car?" he moped, looking glum.

"Well let's have a look at it sir. Er, is this it?"

Zach nodded, trying to smile.

"What year is it?"

"Er, 1960."

"Oh well, p'raps you're right, it's only worth about twenty pounds – tops, isn't it?"

"But it cost me hundreds, and it's a good runner."

"Well sir, let's face it, the trade in price at the most I could agree to, would be thirty pounds at best."

Zach's face put on an awful frown, as though he were convinced by the manager, of the hopelessness of the situation.

This expression was perceived by the manager to be a typical mug, thinking (there's one born every minute). For the look of disappointment, Zach's frown emitted, caused the man to realize that with this country bumpkin, he could work a scam on.

"Unless sir?" he faltered, allowing Zach's face to change, in the hope of success. "That is unless…we could work out some kind of deal, now you look like an honest man sir, so I feel that perhaps we could reach some agreement, where you could afford to pay over a long term, to make the payments smaller and easier to pay, eh?" Zach's face lit up with an expectant smile as the man continued, "How would you like to be the proud owner of this Vauxhall Velox?"

"Oh, Oh yes, but how?"

The manager continued with his glib approach and said, "Well sir, seeing as your car is not worth very much, perhaps we could change

THE MACE GOES IN

things to work in your favour?"

"But how?"

"Well these perishin' governmental restrictions are of NO use to the working man or even the average man. Upon whom they insist such impossible demands, that a potential buyer, 'has to have at least a cash deposit of one third of the actual going price of the car.' I mean in this day and age, who could actually afford that. It takes a flippin' lifetime to actually save such a figure in the bank, doesn't it sir?"

Zach's head nodded in agreement saying, "I couldn't agree with you more?"

The manager smiled and said, "Well sir, I've been giving this matter some thought," and purposely he faltered to gain Zach's attention. "Of course sir, our selling prices are base upon a car's overall condition and if it's not up to scratch, we naturally lower the price, as in this occasion. Now if there are some breaks in the paintwork, as is this model, an average bloke could quite easily restore it, just like you've done with your Morris?" Zach nodded as the manager continued. "If the Velox were in first class condition, then it would be priced comparatively more at the top end of say, £480 pounds at the highest estimate? Then in order to be in compliance with government restrictions, you would need at least in total, a sum of £160 pounds – yes?"

"Bu, but…"

"Let me finish sir – now remember this transaction is merely on paper – yes?"

"On pa…"

"Yes sir, now judging by your car's scruffy condition – yes?"

Zach said, "I've loved this old girl…"

"Of course you have sir, but if she were in top condition, she would be worth perhaps £160 pounds to trade in, and who's to say it isn't, 'cos it's only on paper when all said and done."

"Oh I see what you mean!" Zach cried in exclamation.

"Yes sir, now like I said, it's only on paper so, if we were to agree that on top of your £30 pounds, we were to say it was traded at the sum of £160 pounds, then instead of £400 pounds, we could charge

£480 pounds at top, this would certainly fluctuate your £30 pounds to now be £160 pounds, leaving £320 pounds to pay. Then it would conform with the chancellor of the ex-checker's restriction. How's that grab you sir?"

"Brilliant, yerse, absolutely…"

"Right sir, so if you would accompany me into the office…"

Zach's head was nodding all the way as he said, "Oh yes, yes, that'll be just lovely, where have I got to sign?"

"Erm, first there'll be a credit check, and if this works out okay, you could drive your Velox – today!"

About an hour later, saw Zach happily driving away his Vauxhall car.

When he'd arrived back in the 'Rural Soak, he gave Bill the 'A Okay', to sometime re-acquire the Minor.

Bill then arose upon his feet and sucked peppermints to kill the aroma of the drinks he'd consumed. He then left the pub and strolled over to the car sales, and walked to the rear outside, where all of the cheaper older cars were stored for cash bargains, which were aimed at the less discerning punter.

He discovered an assortment of cars there, of the Ford collateral further back, but blocked by the Morris Minor which had been parked there within the hour – still warm. He was aware of being observed and so concentrated his attention upon all of the Fords – giving cries of delight, as he exclaimed them merely to give the impression to the sales assistant's glare, that it was Fords he wanted.

He looked up with happy glances to his watcher. That is until he saw him turn around, to report to the manager of the stranger he'd observed.

When quickly Bill reached into the Minor's bonnet catch to release its lock, and familiarly raised its front.

Quickly, he swapped its sequence of leads, then with urgency, brought its bonnet down again, and hurried back amid the Ford cars. But only just in time for the manager suddenly appeared from a different direction, causing Bill to colour up at the terrible thought; 'had his sabotage been observed?'

"Anything I can help you with sir?"

THE MACE GOES IN

Bill looked up and said, "Could I hear the engine of this Ford Eight?"

"The keys are on the label of the dash, Mr....?"

"Bill, will do." he remarked. "And you are?"

"Call me Harry, I'm the manager," he replied, with a welcome smile.

So Bill put on the ignition, and even without choke, it started and sounded well, but Bill said, "Sounds a bit ropey, what's that one on the right sound like?"

"It's fine sir, here, come and listen, where he switched on and the Ford Ten engine sprang into action.

"Hmmm, now this seems better, what about those two at the back, do they run as well as this?"

"But of course sir, you can take my word for it."

"Well, how much do you want for these four Fords then?"

"Right sir, you know of course that these are the bargain basement so's to speak, and there's no comeback."

"Okay, well 'ow much are you askin' then?"

Just then, George the manager's son came to the scene, "Here George, this chap wants to know how much we're asking for the Fords?"

"What all of 'em?"

"Yeh," said Bill staunchly, "all of 'em?"

"Well Dad as you can see, I've got 'em all marked at £25 pounds each, so 'cos we've got a Minor as well, it might be a bit more. Are you a breaker then sir?"

"Am I that obvious? No son, although you've sussed me out, I think we can still do a deal. Are they all M.O.T.'d then?"

"Well not all of 'em, but if you want 'em all, yer'll 'ave to give me a price on the Morris as well."

"But I don't want the Morris, 'cos folk only want Fords these days, and I don't want ter get stuck with an old Morris, which should'a bin scrapped years ago."

"So what's your offer on the five of 'em?" George pushing the sale of five.

"But it's only the Fords I want, and I'm willing ter pay yer, £60 for the four."

"Oh no no, that's no good, I want at least £20 pounds."

"Well, you just said, they haven't all got M.O.T.'s?"

"Well er no, but the Morris has got two months left and a months tax."

"But I don't want a…"

"Hang on you haven't heard it yet, it's sweet as a nut – listen," And George turned the key.

'P'fwat, brat-fwat, it hissed trying desperately to explode the gases, which just past harmlessly away as he continually turned the key.

The look on the manager's face was a picture. "What the hell 'ave you done to it George? yer silly…"

"Doesn't sound very good does it, that's the trouble with Billy Morris cars, they all 'ave this problem with the valves, they can go - just like that. Now when it comes to a Ford, they 'ave special coils, but the Morris's, phew, looks like this one's gone as well?" Bill smirked.

"George, what on earths wrong with it?"

"I can't seem to get it started Dad," he moped.

The manager clutching at straws said, "Oh but it's a lovely example for its year, and was driven here today, so I know it is a runner, here, I'll come out and start it." So he came up and did his utmost to get it to fire, but failed. So he lifted up the bonnet to inspect the plugs, but didn't suss it out. "But I can't understand it, it ran well coming in?"

"Tell you what George," said Bill, "I'll give yer £15 pounds each for the Fords and take 'em off yer 'ands – irrespective of their condition!"

"Oh no sir, you'll have to take the Morris as well!"

"Nay lad, I don't want it, I've only got a buyer for the f…" and quickly stopped speaking.

George sussed him out or so he thought and said, "Oh no, you either take the five or none at all!"

"But George, listen to reason, I've only got a buyer for the engines, I couldn't possibly take the Moggie, I'd never get rid of it?"

THE MACE GOES IN

George's face turned to a frown, until he noticed the new-ish condition of its tyres and so now smiled saying, "You take them all, or none at all!"

"Well okay George, you drive a hard bargain," said Bill, "here I'll give you £15 pound first for the Ford Ten and come back each time with £15 pound for each of the Fords?"

A triumphant George convinced now, that Bill would leave the Morris, now thought, 'I've got him, so said adamantly, "No, it's £15 pound for the Morris you will take first or the deal is off!"

"Oh ay, be'ave yourself George I can't pay yer fer 'em all right now. I've only got a buyer for the Ford an'…"

"You take the Morris away first and pay me for 'em or you don't take any," said George firmly, convinced that Bill wanted the Ford.

Bill thought for a while pretending to weigh up the situation and finally he said, "George, you don't think I'm very honest do you? Now that really gets to me inside and to prove to you that I'm not that sort of person, I'm willing to pay you £15 for the Morris - right now, and take it away and come back for each car so's you'll know I'm on the up and up , 'ow's that grab yer?" he offered with a sombre voice.

"Seems all right to me, hang on, let's see the Colour of your money first?" George asked, still not sure of Bill.

Bill's face assumed a hurt look as he grasped his wallet and yanked out a bundle of fivers, "Happy now George, is this what you mean?"

George smiled saying, "I'm sorry Bill but you know how things are these days.

We get so many coming here trying to con us, I'm sure you understand;" he apologised.

"But of course," he agreed. "It's chaps like that who give our business a bad name."

"Give Bill the log book Harry, he needs it to comply with the breaking regulations, now sir, if you give me the £15 I'll give you a receipt for the money,"

Straight away Bill complied and was handed his receipt.

"Right sir, if you have any trouble removing the car, come back and let Harry know and we'll try and help you out," with that George shook Bill's hand and disappeared with the money. Harry gave him the key along with the documents and beat a hasty retreat back into the office, to avoid getting his hands dirty helping Bill, This suited Bill for he lifted up the bonnet and restored to their rightful plugs the leads he had crossed. He drove the car - which responded obediently - quietly away into the car park of the 'Rural Soak' and rejoined his friend who was sitting at the bar,

"Hiya Bill," exclaimed Zach, "come and take a seat, Mary, give Bill a pint of bitter and a double whisky will you love?"

"Whisky, but he drinks vodka doesn't he?" she questioned frowning.

"Course I do," agreed Bill, "what's this Zach about whisky?" he pretended.

Zach cottoned on right away that Bill was trying to create a good impression on Mary whom he had attempted to proposition in Bill's absence but without success, and realised why - smiling to himself.

"You 'aven't lost your touch eh Bill, still the ladies man I see?" he grinned, "how did you fare at Lings?" he asked, changing the subject.

"Oh here you are Zach, I originally got the car for £17 so there's £8 change from the £25 , now out o' the other £30 you gave me there's £15 change makin' a total of £23," he handed this to his friend.

"Keep the £3 Bill," he gestured generously.

"Oh ta Zach, by the way, what shall I do with the Morris now?" he queried.

"Is it worth twenty quid to you Bill?"

"We-ell."

"Tell you what mate, if all goes well next week, you'll probably get it for nowt - and a bit of cash besides to pay for all your trouble. The important thing now, is that you don't sell it before my deal goes through - understood?"

"All the way Zach, you can count on me," he assured him, "we're in this together," he professed in camaraderie.

Inevitably the towels went up on the pumps, as Bill made his way to Mary proposing dinner at the 'Cotswolds' restaurant in the posh

THE MACE GOES IN

end of Chester. She relented but not to that night, but to Saturday following.

Bill agreed to this and arranged to pick her up in Bromborough where she lived. Then he and Zach left and drove both motors back to his flat respectively.

In the flat Bill told Zach, "I'm going ter get me 'ead down mate till seven, d'yer fancy that game o' poker later?"

"Y'mean Fred's Gym?" he remembered.

"The very same!"

"Loverly."

Bill smiled and went into the bedroom and threw his head down into instant oblivion, as did Zach on the couch. Later upon awakening, they ate a light meal and then proceeded to the 'gym'.

The Bronze Pump

CHAPTER 5

Entering the door above the outside steps to the gym, Bill and Zach noticed that it appeared to be empty.

"Wonder where every one is Bill? It doesn't look like anyone's here?"

They walked to the far end of the room to the source of some grumbling they now heard. Opening the door Fred appeared looking glum. "What's up Fred?" asked Bill.

"Flamin' bailiffs took the lot, all the weights an' rowin' machines. The only reason they left the Buk, was they couldn't fit it through the door. Without me equipment I'm jiggered," he said miserably.

"Aw heck Fred, that's terrible, I didn't know you where in dire straights with yer cash. Yer never said anythin', I mean with all them poker schools yer 'ad, I'd o' thought you'd 'ave been makin' a bomb in this place? So worra yer gonna do now mate?"

"I 'aven't got the faintest…"

"'Ave yer gor anywhere ter stay?"

"Well, I can stay 'ere till next Wednesday that's when the lease runs out."

"I can't believe this - I don't believe it!" Bill exclaimed. "Yer've bin 'ere since I was a lad. I've 'ad a lifetime in the army an' you were still 'ere when I came back. It's not right Fred, it's not Blummin' right," he bleated.

"Well that's business, Bill," said Fred resignedly.

"Come on Fred we'll take yer fer a drink," said Bill.

The 'Bowling Inn' was full of cheers and toasts that very night as Fred, Bill and Zach, sampled the Northern brew of 'real ale'.

"Ha ha ha ah, can yer remember in 1957 when Del nearly got nicked for 'is road tax, for the wagon Bill," asked Fred.

"Let's go somewhere new for a change?" said Bill.

"Where?"

"Oh I dunno, whar about that posh 'free 'ouse' in lamb's 'ead village?"

"'Ouse' in lamb's 'ead village?"

"Aye, ok Bill," said Zach, eager to please. "Are we going in the Morris?"

"Yeh, why not?" Bill enthused. And then replied to Fred's query with: "I wasn't home then Fred, what 'appened anyway?"

"Heh, heh, heh, - yeh, well, I can remember it like it was yesterday. Del parked the wagon outside the Town 'all in Chester, full o' rags an' tats and PC plod come up swingin' is baton, just like Charlie Chaplin. We was both laffin' at 'im an' 'e got uptight about us. 'E come up all serious like lookin' at the wagon, ter see if 'e could find anythin' wrong with it. He spotted the tax was out of date. 'E took out his pad an' pencil askin' all kinds of daft questions. Del told 'im that 'ed sent off fer the tax, but 'e didn't believe 'im," Fred related.

"'Ow did 'e get on with it - did 'e get done?"

"No chance, not Del, heh, heh, 'e's a wide boy alright. 'E goes ter the post office an' buys a 4/6 postal order, makes it out ter Vernons Pools and sends it with the coupon through the post ter the Castle Tax office. Naturally they thinks that 'e'd sent 'em the wrong postal order. 'E then gets a postal order for £29/10/00 an' rips the receipt off it and puts it in 'is wallet. 'E then goes ter the cop shop ter produce 'is documents and 'ands in the E29.10/- receipt with 'is insurance," says Fred.

"Didn't they suss 'im out?" queried Zach.

"No, that's the funny part about it, 'cos by the time the coppers 'ad checked up with the tax office over receivin' the postal order, they made a joke about Del sendin' 'is football coupon by mistake with the Four and a tanner instead o' the £29.10/- so 'e gets away with it. Naturally they never checked ter see if 'e did tax it later 'cos Del scrapped the wagon the followin' week."

"Aaaah, ha ha ha, that's just like Del, 'e 'asn't changed, he's still as hard faced as ever," assured Bill.

"'Oo's round is it?" asked Fred.

"Zach's," said Bill.

"No! - it's yours Bill," Zach corrected.

"Are yer sure?" Bill pleaded.

"Yeh,"

"Okay then, wor are yer 'avin' Fred?"

"I'll 'ave another double," he replied, with a smile.

"'Ow about you Zach?"

"I'll 'ave another treble rum Bill, thanks."

Bill wandered back up to the bar and returned with the drinks.

"Yer very quiet Zach - a penny fer yer thoughts?" invited Bill.

"It'll cost yer more than a penny mate," he stated.

"That bad eh Zach?" sympathising.

"I need a woman Bill," he mumbled.

"Well that's easy Zach we'll pick a couple up in the snug," his friend assured him.

"No, not that kind of a woman Bill - no, I mean a real woman, something like that bird in the Rural Soak but I was too slow there and you pipped me to the post."

"Tell yer what Zach I'll ring up Mary now and see if she'll bring a friend along for yeh, we'll make it a double-okay?"

"Would you do that for me? Thanks Bill, you're a real pal," he sobbed emotionally.

"Yer know mate, I think that it's high time I got meself a wife and settled down, yeh, and forget all this nonsense about conning car dealers," he determined.

Then in retrospect, quite out of the blue Bill thought of Cynthia the barmaid at 'The George'. She was just whom he had in mind for Zach. She'd been through two marriages, both of which had ended in tragedy.

The first had been the love of her life dating back to childhood in school. For whenever danger threatened from bullies, Robert had always been there to protect his true love.

The writing was on the wall for them, everybody expected the pair of them to marry.

Because of her protected lifestyle, and the constant attention of Robert keeping her safe, she was able, through her early years, to promote her artistic talent of drawing and painting and her eventual graduation into a mature position of newspaper advertising.

Her adoration of her hero, Robert, made evident by her portrayal of him dressed in a superman suit in oils, which she hung over her fireplace.

Most of the famous film stars she could depict to catch a true likeness of in her adverts of future films to come.

All this was achieved by her access to grammar school, and subsequently, scholarships to the art academy.

Robert also by which time graduated in his field of expertise, which was drawing and his aptitude for math, had enabled him to secure a post in a drawing office and eventually become a junior architect, which he loved in the Liverpool based firm of his office. From which also he was able to exact a good living salary, and then marry Cynthia. Also, he was able to put down a deposit with a mortgage on an old house in the Wirral, in bad need of repair and thus keep the principal figure low. Their wedding bells were the most celebrated in the land. Hundreds of people attended, for their joint popularity was renown.

Cynthia decided to remain in her job for as long as were possible and would have, had the news of pregnancy not suddenly have appeared. She gave three months notice, and waited for the event to happen.

Robert was overjoyed at his latest promotion to senior architect, and he rang Cynthia to enlighten her of his dinner plans for them both, in the cute little Italian restaurant recently opened in Newtown. He made kisses and was about to ring off when she told about the baby forthcoming…

"…Are you still there Rob………"

"Er, yes love…it just came as a bit of a shock… baby, a baby? – A BABY? I can't believe it, a baby? Well love, perhaps we should get that builder now, whilst we can still afford it. What d'you think?"

"Yerrrr……!"

"A baby, that's absolutely marvellous Cynth, I can't wait to get home. I'll be at the newspaper office at 5.15 pm, to pick you up and we'll have 'T' bones steaks with tomato puree. Angelo makes them so well. Ok then Cynth, gotta go now," kiss, kiss and he was gone.

That was the last time she spoke to him, or heard his voice for Robert was killed instantly in a pile up on the New Chester Road's A41. After the news Cynthia was devastated. She went to pieces, unable to work or even go to work.

THE MACE GOES IN

This is where Bill had first met her where he lived in Undermere, from where he and his pal had embarked on their cold canvas of the area in which to sell insurance. Her house had been the last door on the drive. She answered the door – blown out with her pregnancy with her baby's arrival imminent. It was obvious she had been crying, as the tell tale looks of grief showed even more with the pain, and discomfort she'd received with the baby due.

"Good afternoon madam, my friend and I are conducting a survey at this time, and wondered if you could help us out with answers to some questions? It'll only take three minutes of your time at the most, and would greatly benefit the research of this survey."

Cynthia smiled and said, "What is it you need to know?"

Harry was overjoyed as he held his clip board high and asked, "Is anyone in this household insured at all?"

"Well, we are, that is 'er aghah, ahah," she wept realising that Robert was no longer there, as she choked back a sob, and corrected herself. "Er yes, my late husband was with the 'PRU', I think, before the accident."

Then profusely - a million tears just poured from her, as she sobbed openly on his shoulder.

"There, there now chuck, you just get it all out of your system and don't worry love," Harry sympathised and compassionately put his arm around her enabling Cynthia to cry it all out. "If there's anything we can do, just say the word and we'll be glad to help out?" he assured her.

She seemed to be consoled by this and said, "Would you like to come in, there is something you can probably help me with?"

They followed her into the house where she pointed to the

door at the rear access which was unable to open.

Right away, Harry who had served a joinery apprenticeship took hold of the door and wrenched it open saying, "Oh look Bill, this poor lass has had to put up with horrible door. Well miss 'er?"

"Astbridge," she said adding – just call me Cynthia, Mr. 'er?" she ventured.

"Harry, Harry Lyme - you know like Michael Rennie portrays?" This is Bill Foggit my partner, we work together don't we Bill?"

She Shook Harry's hand as he proffered it and then Bill's saying; "It's nice to meet you both, would you like a cup of tea?"

"Thank you, yes thank you," they both chorused.

Harry once more took the handle of the door saying, "Y'know Cynthia, you could have house insurance to cover you for joiners' maintenance of your home, did you know?" he enlightened.

"Really, how much would it cost?"

"A mere shilling and six pence a week," he encouraged.

"Oh, I don't think I can afford it, you see since my Robert…ahag," more tears came, "since he was killed I haven't been able to work, and my Mum is keeping me and paying the mortgage so's I don't lose the house."

"Don't worry love, I'll take care of the door, I'll come back after work around 6.30pm, and it'll only take a jiffy to do," he assured.

"but, bu, I can't pay you anything?" she stammered.

"Not a problem love, I used to be joiner. All this door needs is planing down - no problem."

"Oh, could you? You're very kind, I'll put the kettle on for about 6:30, would that be ok?"

"Yes love, that's great, we'd better get off now to finish the survey," he motioned and Bill arose with him and they walked toward the door.

"Well, I'll look forward to your return Mr. Lyme," she beamed.

"Yes, 6:30 it is" he answered, "until then."

"How d'you do it Harry, you must have the gift of the gab. You 'ad 'er eating out of yer 'and!"

In a flash, Bill was back in the present and engaged in conversation with Zach.

"You know Zach there's a certain barmaid that works in the bar at 'The George' called Cynthia, good lookin' lass too, single an all…"

Fred had slipped into the realms of sleep whilst they had talked and slumped forward nudging Zach's glass across the table.

"Whoops," voiced Bill, quickly grabbing the rum before it had a chance to roll over.

"That was close," thanks Bill," he remarked gratefully.

'Ting, ting,, ting,' sounded the bell for last orders.

"Want a carry out Zach? I'm gettin' Scotch," Bill determined.

"Right first time me old mate, half a rum."

Bill returned with both bottles saying, "We'll 'ave ter take 'im back ter the gym Zach. Give us an 'and will yer, I'll get me arm under Fred's shoulder if you could do the same?" he asked.

"No sweat," replied Zach and they both quaffed down their glasses and commenced to carry out Fred.

Soon Bill arrived at the gym and a full ten minutes had

elapsed before they were able to ascend the outside steps to deliver Fred to his back room.

Saturday morning saw Bill knocking Del's front door.

"Hiya Del," greeted he, as the door was opened for him.

Del didn't answer, his head was banging from the late night he'd experienced.

He called to Beth to rustle up Bill's breakfast and started to pour some whisky into a cup of tea for 'a hair of the dog.'

Fifteen minutes later both of them entered the Bedford to drive toward the chemical works of Cobden & Allbright. They drove straight in. Starting at the far end of the mill, they were able to secrete a 15 feet long phosphor bronze pump, enclosed in a large cast iron pipe with two 90 degree returns linked to it, onto the wagon, by the means of a winch operated by Eddie Shaw, who had hidden the cache for his friend Del during the early shift he was now on.

"'Ere's a fiver Eddie and ta very much!" cried Del, as he threw a number of drums on the back to cover the new cargo.

Bill gathered as many empty drums as he could find whilst Eddie shuttled to and fro with the portable winch loading up a new cache of heavy scrap for Del's return. After carefully depositing the drums on Mr. Evans' tip they took the bronze pump to Eric's yard for perusal and left it there, informing him of their intention to return soon.

Back into Allbrights they quickly returned but upon their arrival, were dismayed to find that Eddie Shaw had been assigned a different part of the mill. Frantically they sought him out and finally they located him sweeping up the yard. He spotted them looking and hurried over informing them, "It's okay Del, this is only a temporary arrangement while the fitter

THE MACE GOES IN

fixes my crane. Er, it sort of ceased when I lifted that pump," he said, "oh, here he comes now - hey Billy, 'ave yer done it?" he shouted.

Billy drove the mobile toward them and stopped keeping the engine running as though he feared it would stop, "Hop up here and Clog this pedal," he ordered.

Eddie complied and asked, "What's up with it mate, is it okay to use?"

"I've adjusted the diesel pump," Billy enlightened, "it should be okay as Soon as it's warmed up, here I'll leave it with you," he informed him.

Eddie climbed aboard the winch thanking the fitter who walked away. "Follow me Del, I've got it stashed over here," he told him.

Bill brought up the wagon to the area directed and started to load up pieces of cast pipe, broken grids and the like, until a third of the deck of the five ton Bedford was covered. Then he followed the usual procedure of covering the load with chemical drums, to mask its true definition

"Take this to the weighbridge Bill - quick as yer can and we'll take the rest ter Eric's."

"Right Del," he agreed and started the motor…

After weighing the load they sped off in the direction of the tip.

Later in Eric's scrapyard they congratulated him, on his success in locating the bronze amid the cast pipe.

"It was Gerry who broke it," he pointed to his labourer in the yard who was busily swinging the 14lb hammer at the cast piping, which had surrendered under the barrage of his blows, to reveal a beautiful gleam of yellow.

Del looked up the yard and murmured, appreciably, "Looks like gun metal," rubbing his hands together. He approached the man with the hammer saying, "Good man. I'll see yer right for this."

The labourer mounted the crane lying nearby motioning Del to wrap the chain brother's around the bronze's girth which resembled fifty odd 3/4" bronze tubes connected all together parallel and sealed at each end by bronze lids, totalling 15 feet long. After securing the hook on the 'brothers', Del signalled the man pointing his right hand upward. The driver moved the load toward the scale depositing the pump long ways across it. Bill dashed across helping Del remove the chains. Eric came along and moved the cantilever gauge until it registered 15cwt odd, which he carefully tilted back as far as he dare, in order not to pay too much for the load.

Back in the office later, he enlightened the boys of the good news, "Yes Del, you've done very well today mate, here's the receipt for all the gear. Oh by the way Bill, ask Gerry to come out of that crane will yer, Del 'ere wants ter give 'im a drink fer 'is trouble - don't yer Del," he pretended, to get Bill out of the office. As he left, Eric uncovered a second receipt and thrust it into Del's hand saying, "Right mate, this one's for two 'undred weight of bronze at fifteen nicker a go, that makes it thirty quid - okay?"

Del was still chiselling Bill out of his cut. He thanked Eric dropping £5 and as Gerry walked into the office, gave him £2 for his trouble, "Ta mate," said Del, "I won't forget this," he assured Gerry.

Eric waited for Bill to re-enter the office before handing Del the 'bent' receipt.

"Thirteen hundred weight of bronze at £15 a go comes ter £175, then yer've got eighteen 'undred weight of cast at eight bob an 'undred weight comes ter."

"'Ang on Eric," Bill interjects," 13 x 15 doesn't come ter

175, more like 195!" he indicated.

"Er, oh aye, yeh, yer right Bill that 9 does look like a 7, Yeh, yer dead right mate - where's that flippin' typist?" he bleated attempting to excuse himself.

"Gone for her dinner Eric," said Gerry.

"Hell, that stupid little…, I've 'ad enough of her blunderin'. 'Ere Del, I'll adjust this myself," he assured him. Eric took his pen and re-wrote the figures, "Right," he said finally, £195 fer the bronze, and 144 shillin's that's 'er £7 four shillin' which brings it ter the total of £202 – 4 shillin's - fiver's all right Del?"

Del's eyes came out like organ stops as he started to shake with delight, "Ye ye yeh, anythin'll do," he gurgled.

Eric counted out forty fivers and topped it up with two £1 notes and Del wrapped it in a bundle and jammed it in his back pocket,

"Take the motor out Bill," he commanded his partner, as he shook Eric's hand with his thanks.

He entered the vehicle and they were off.

"Listen Bill," he proposed, "how d'you feel about us gerrin' a new motor? 'Cos if you do, I know where we can lay our 'ands on a luverly Ford diesel five ton with a Perkins 45 an' if we 'urry up today and get finished by three o'clock we should be able…"

"Three o'clock?" asked Bill incredulously.

"Yeh, we'll work right through dinner with no ale," he affirmed.

"This must be some motor yer've bin lookin' at?" he mused, "okay mate, I'11 go for it, but it will have to be all legal like with a partnership I mean," Bill stressed.

"Tell yer what mate, I'll 'ave yer name put on me cards with mine," he suggested.

"Thanks, but no Del. If we are goin' ter be legal, we'll 'ave ter call ourselves somethin' original like Foggit an Bovis," he determined.

"No, Bovis an' Foggit sounds better mate," said Del panicking, "anyway, let's get back ter work and..."

"Wait a minute Del," said Bill stopping the motor and applying the handbrake.

"Get going Bill we'll miss Eddie Shaw, 'e goes off 'is shift at two o'clock," he voiced urgently.

"Aren't yer fer gettin' somethin' Del?"

"I don't know what yer mean Bill?"

"D'you think I fell for all that claptrap about a new motor an' a partnership?" asked he.

"I hope yer did believe it Bill - I meant every word."

"If yer meant every word mate, yer'd better cross my palm with £101 right now or the deal's off!"

"But I'm the one that takes the mace Bill," he reasoned.

"There you are Del, that's another thing, first yer say a partnership and now yer say it's YOUR mace. Well mate, make up yer mind now, d'yer want a partnership or not?" he questioned, waiting for the reply.

"Oh all right Bill, here y'er are, 'ere's £100."

"No it's half or nuthin'," determined Bill.

"Yer'll 'ave me in the poor 'ouse Bill," he relented handing him 20 fivers. "What about the petrol and the oil?" he pleaded.

"Yer've got that already Del," he reminded.

"But that'll be gone soon Bill."

"We'll cross that bridge when we come to it mate," he reassured, starting up the motor.

Cobden and Allbrights loomed up ahead and they moved smartly in to the entrance of the factory where Eddie Shaw was working.

THE MACE GOES IN

"Hiya Del, Bill," he welcomed, "I've got some good stuff 'ere. Follow me quick as yer can?"

They complied to this request by re-entering the salvage yard, where Eddie had just steered his winch.

"Catch old o' this lot lads," motioned he, handing them some assorted copper pipes painted and bent, recently removed from the chemical plant. Bill couldn't believe it. The yard was completely covered with old copper piping, leaky boilers and connections which littered the area.

"Where's all this lot from Eddie, there must be a ruddy fortune 'ere," breathed Del.

"It came in while you were out," he related, "Arthur Pearson brought it out of Sector 24. It's been there for two years and that's the limit here for copper due ter the chemical eatin' into it. There'll be a load more soon so we'd better get it all loaded up now before they bring the rest, 'cos this is where all the scrap goes for auction ter the two dealers we've got in here on contract."

"I see Ed, okay mate - hear that Bill, we'll 'ave ter move!"

"Right mate," Bill concurred and threw the bundle onto the wagon, rushing back for more. Within ten minutes the copper pipes and boilers on the wagon, represented about 1/10 of the capacity of those in the yard, with barely enough to mask the load over with drums to conceal the true contents. Bill started up the wagon and they bade Eddie farewell assuring him, that he would be on a good cut of the profits later in 'The George'.

Going over the weighbridge to their delight the load total came to six tons odd which gave them an urgency to return to Eric's yard. Del thought quickly,

"£30 a hundred weight times 4 tons that's 80 hundred weight so that's 80 x 30 is....mmmm" he thought getting flustered, "What's 80 x 30 Bill?"

"2,400 Del."

"T, t, twenty four 'undred?" he spluttered, "D'yer realise just what we've got 'ere Bill? we've gorra flamin' fortune 'ere mate," he exclaimed, "Ferget that small fry Eric's, we'll go through the tunnel ter Cohen's, 'e pays over the odds fer quantity."

Bill turned the motor toward the Mersey Tunnel and clogged the gas travelling at 55 mph.

"Take it easy mate, we don't want them Scuffers ter stop us now," Del advised.

Bill slowed to 45 mph until they reached the tunnel. He stopped applying the handbrake and paid his shilling. Up went the bar and off they drove into the traffic.

At the other end his partner directed, racking his brains to recall the vague route, "Turn left here Bill and when yer come ter the end of Scotland Road yer'll find yer 'ave ter turn right and come back on yerself ter go left for London Road. Right, you've gorrit now, yeh, that's it, now left. Yes mate we're 'ome and dry now mate. Cohen's is just about a quarter of a mile away on the left."

A large notice with the 'Four Hundred Group' suddenly came into view, "We're here mate, turn left now - a quick right." Bill suddenly found himself in a large well organised scrapyard, with various loading bays aligning the edge of the yard and a weighbridge on the approach of the gate.

"Pull in 'ere Bill, I'll go and announce our contents."

Bill turned to the right as Del stepped down and returned soon after,

"Get them drums off Bill, throw 'em over there in that skip mate," he pointed.

After Bill and he had removed them, he drove the Bedford onto the scale,

"Six ton 14 cwt one quarter," informed the weigh-man, "here take your copper up to number seven and see Gus, he'll take it off you."

Bill drove over the yard with Del, where Gus indicated, "Okay throw it here."

Before doing so, Del mentioned to the man that the office had quoted £840 per ton.

The man replied, "Yes, it's risen £40 a ton today so it'll be a good time to sell now." he advised, "is this clean copper then?"

"'Ave a look mate," invited Del, as he dropped the tailboard. Inside the copper lay all nicely cleaned off.

A smile appeared on Gus's face as he commented, "Oy yoy yoy, yes - that will do nicely!"

After they had unloaded the metal, Gus asked them for the weigh ticket which had various gradings printed on it. He signed it in the non-ferrous column number two copper which designated light tubing and brazen boilers.

"Hey yer've put yer monica in the wrong column!" Bill complained.

"Oy vay, were did you find dis fella Del? Take 'im out of my yard," said Gus in despair, waving his arms.

"Come on Bill, take the motor back over the scale - and this time get out of the driver's seat."

"What 'ave I said mate?" pleaded Bill.

"Listen Bill, you can't tell Gus Cohen anything about scrap – 'e was born with the business in 'is blood, 'is family's been at it for centuries."

"But I didn't...."

"Just drive the wagon Bill."

Bill turned the wheel until the motor covered the scale and jumped out of the cab at Del's signal. By this time Gustav had arrived on the scene complimenting Bill on how well he looked as he stood by the scale. Bill smiled and commented about his army life and the correct diet.

"Speaking of diets, do you diet to keep your skinny figure - what do you weigh about 8 stone?" he queried sarcastically.

Bill felt hurt and blurted out, "No chance, I'm 12 stone!" he said proudly, puffing out his chest.

"Twelve stone," repeated Gus," yes I'd say that was about right," he affirmed.

Bill smiled - really he was 10 1/2 stone- but thought it more manly to be heavier.

"Well Horace, add 1 ½ hundred weight on the tare," he said gleefully to the weigh-bridge-man, enjoying the look of dismay on both Del and Bill's faces.

"You stupid nit, what did yer 'ave ter tell 'im you was that 'eavy for. We're gonna lose out now by about £72 fer your braggin'- well it can cum outer your share."

"But Del?"

"And I thought you were a wide boy, ha, ha, har!"

"'E must 'ave known we was tryin' ter pull a stunt Del?" pleaded Bill.

"It's really uncanny Bill," said his partner.

"What is Del?"

"Your grasp of the obvious, ha ha ha, yer've gorra 'ave a laugh though 'aven't yer Bill?" mused Del, who was almost falling over laughing.

"Two ton, 1 1/2 hundred weight," announced the weigh-man.

"Don't forget the driver Horace," Gus prompted.

"Oh yes Mr. Cohen, so really it reads 2 ton 3 cwt. Now let's see that leaves 4 tons 11cwt 1 1/4 Mr. Cohen."

"Thank you Horace. Now Mr. Bovis, and er, Mr. er?"

"Foggit," chirped Bill.

"Yes, Mr. Foggit," repeated Gus, "if you'd both like to follow too, I'll give you what I owe you."

Sheepishly they walked behind him too humiliated to make conversation.

They reached the cash office and waited whilst Gus moved to the drawer to withdraw the money.

"Let's see now; 4 ton at £840 comes to £3,360, plus 11cwt which is £462 and a quarter which is £10.10/- so that little lot comes to a grand total of, mm«m, £3,832 and 10/-."

Del and Bill were shaking uncontrollably more out of fright that they'd been guilty of theft for which they both feared retribution. Gus had his thoughts of the origins of the load but because of the old paint covering it dismissed it from his mind.

"Where did this lot come from Del, I'll bet you paid a fortune for this lot?" he probed.

"Me, bought it? You know better than to ask that Gus - no pal, this was strictly a 'mace'."

"I might have known it," Gus agreed, as he handed Del the cash, "here y'are mate three thousand, eight hundred and thirty two pound, ten shilling. Not bad for a morning's work, eh mate?" he smiled, "do you want this into two parcels?" he asked.

"Yeh," said Bill, before Del could say otherwise.

"Right then friends," he motioned splitting the notes and handing them the parcels complete with two half-crowns each, "one thousand, nine hundred & sixteen pounds and five shillings each!" he said.

Bill snatched up the cash and squashed it in his inside pocket before Del could interfere saying, "Thanks Mr. Cohen, it's been a pleasure doing business with you!"

He left the office with Del in hot pursuit.

"Hey Bill, 'ang on mate - yer can't take all that money 'ome yer might lose it.

Better give me £1500 of it fer safe keepin'?" he questioned anxiously.

"No yer all right Del," he replied, "I'll 'ang on to it for the bank - it'll be safe enough there."

"They'll be shut soon Bill, it's three o'clock."

"Then we'd better get goin' 'adn't we?"

Del went quiet, realising he was outwitted, cursing under his breath as Bill started up the motor.

Scheming on how to relieve Bill of his money Del decided to play on Bill's greed.

"Er Bill, remember that wagon I told yer about, well p'rhaps now is as good a time as any to go and see it?"

"Wagon? Oh yeh, wagon. now I remember, that Perkins 45, yeh, good idea Del. where is it?" he enquired.

'Got him," Del thought, "but how to get 'is dough? I've got it,' he schemed. "When yer get in the tunnel Bill, turn left for the Dock Road and carry on up to the four bridges."

"Okay Del," said his friend excitedly, anxious to see the Perkins diesel. The road loomed up and he turned left toward the docks where Del paid the toll as they arrived at the end of the tunnel.

"Right, now mate - go along here," pointed Del, "until you see the jib of a crane 'angin' over the wall," he indicated.

Bill spotted the jib and slowed down the Bedford until he espied gate.

"Okay mate, this is it," Del enlightened.

Bill cut the motor as Del said, "Just wait 'ere mate, I'll see if Danielle's in.

Del stepped down into the entrance and disappeared. Bill stayed in the wagon switching on his portable radio as he rolled an Old Holbourn and lit it, 'Ah,' he mused, 'just hit the spot,' he inhaled long and deep murmuring appreciably.

Del was talking to Danielle Pitagruber, a buxom blonde filling her in about the Ford diesel he intended to buy and the woman took Del up the yard to hear it running.

Putting in the key of the ford, Danielle turned the starter, 'drum drum, drummmm'. The engine purred quietly.

"And that's without using the heater plugs Del, so it must be in good nick inside eh?"

"Aye yer right Dan," agreed Del, "is it plated this year?"

"I'll show yer the ticket," said Dan, "I've got it 'ere." She handed Del the proof and he murmured agreement.

"'Ow much Dan?" he queried.

"Oh, about fifteen 'undred Del," she replied.

"'Ow much ter me girl, I mean cash in yer 'and?" he encouraged.

"Oh in that case Del, I could let yer 'ave it fer 12."

"Ave yer got Glass's Guide on this Dan"?"

"Hey Del, yer gerrin' a bargain believe me, the book price is 2 grand, here take a look!"

Del flicked the pages over until he came to a picture resembling the Ford, £2150 it read but further on it also read: 'Up to £2,700 depending on condition'.

"Right Dan," he motioned, "'ow would yer like ter make another 'undred?"

"Eh?"

"'Ere's what yer can do fer me…"

"Bill," called Del, "would yer like ter come and see this motor. Dan's gonna start it up for us and I want yer ter 'ear the engine if yer would?"

Bill jumped down from the cab feeling privileged that his skills were needed.

"'Ave yer got the key then Del?"

"The key Dan, 'ave yer gor it?" Del enquired.

Dan winked at Del as she handed him the key saying, "Don't forget the heater plugs or it won't start mate."

Bill took the key from Del as they all walked up the yard.

"What year is it and 'ow much is she askin' Del?" he questioned.

"Three thousand five hundred for a 1967 Ford 45," he said.

"That's a bit dear innit?" he retorted, "I'll soon see if it's worth it, watch this mate, I'll educate yer!" winked Bill.

He entered the cab of the Ford as the two looked on. Pretending to hold the key on the heater plugs, Bill held his hand to one side. After about 60 seconds he gave the starter a whirl thoroughly expecting the engine not to start. It burst into life, causing him almost to jump in the seat. Both Dan and Del enjoyed the scene, by the look of astonishment on Bill's face.

"Start's well doesn't it mate? It's not bad for the price is it?" she pretended.

"It's not worth thirty-five hundred."

"Oh, then how much do you think it's worth?" asked she.

"'As it been plated?"

"Course it has - look," motioned the woman, handing the certificate.

Bill couldn't argue with the Ministry of Transport's stamp.

"Hmm," he pondered, he could see by the look of the truck that it was in a fair condition.

"Well Bill, what d'you think it's worth?" enquired Del.

Bill looked on for quite a while, clutching at straws to fault the motor saying, "I'll be able ter tell yer when I've driven it," he stated.

"Feel free to take it around the yard mate," she invited.

Bill put it in gear and commenced to drive it around the

yard trying all of the gears which seemed A1.

He returned to the spot and turned off the key.

"Well Bill, what d'yer think?" Del asked.

Disgruntled Bill suggested they pay only £3000 for the wagon.

"I dunno, mate let's see what Danielle 'as ter say?" he suggested.

"Danny, are yer there? Bill reckons yer wagon's worth three grand - are yer game?"

Danielle re-appeared from the workshop she had retreated to and smiled as she heard the offer communicating with,

"Did yer know Del, I could have sold that wagon last week for more than you are offering." She strutted up and down in her yellow corduroy cat-suit pretending to be upset by Bill's offer, "Oh come on now Del, you know it's worth more than that!" she pleaded.

"Not a penny more," Bill told her and taunted her with the cash as he pulled it from his pocket.

"I've got nineteen 'undred quid 'ere, eh Del, 'ave yer got your fifteen 'undred fer this motor? We'll go down the middle on it eh?" he prompted.

"Okay mate, sounds well ter me, give me the fifteen 'undred and I'll go inside with Danielle ter draw up a receipt fer both of us."

Bill feverishly separated his share and handed it to Del.

"Be back in a minute," said his friend, "see who's winnin' in the test match Bill will yer?" he requested, in order to ensure no intervention on his scheme.

Danielle was one step ahead, busily making out a receipt of sale to both Del and Bill – 'The Del and Bill Partnership' for £3000.

"Will this do Del ?" she queried adding, "y'know, I

wouldn't do this for anyone but you Del." she determined, nestling her mouth by his in a passionate clinch, as Del pocketed the receipt. He handed her the £1200 they agreed to, plus the £100 for her 'performance' earlier with Bill.

"Listen love," she asked, "are you around tonight, perhaps we could re-live old times again?" with feminine allure.

The thought of a fresh encounter with Danielle caused a deep excitement to well up inside him as he returned the answer she hoped he would speak, "Oh yes Danielle, I'll pick you up at seven o'clock, okay?"

"D'you remember the old times Del?" she jibed, flaunting herself before him.

"How could I forget?" he replied unable to take his eyes from her shapely figure.

He forced himself to move away replying, "Until tonight then luv?"

"Tonight," she echoed.

Del returned to Bill saying, "We've got it mate - thanks to your expert haggling."

He showed Bill the receipt saying, "'Ang on ter this Bill til we get back an' I'll get Beth ter make out a copy on her comptometer."

Del weighed up his latest 'mace' on his new partner Bill and he already had £1700 profit to show for the day not including his share from the copper and cast iron.

"I saw what yer were up to," Bill told him.

Del nearly swallowed his cigarette thinking, "I wonder how much he's heard?" he thought.

"You think yer can kid old Bill do yer? Well let me tell you Vandel, I know a come on when I see one!" he stated.

Del breathed a sigh of relief as Bill continued, "Yer dirty lucky bloke, bet yer off with 'er to the coast ter night in one o' them motor 'otels aren't yer - admit it, come on, d'yer think I've just came down the river on a boat?" he voiced.

"I can't kid you Bill, can I, you're a wide boy and no mistake, yeh, you're right of course, we're goin' out ter night and 'oo knows where we might end up?"

"What about Beth, 'ow can yer kid 'er Del - don't yer luv 'er anymore?"

"You know Bill, I've always loved Beth, but come ter think of it, she maybe going off me."

"Off you?" asked Bill puzzled.

"Yeh, yer know mate, I was there the other night 'avin' a night of passion and somethin' with what she said made me think, she was losin' interest."

"What did she say Del?"

"Well Bill, she looks up in the air and sez, Hey Del, this ceilin' could do with distemperin' ha, ha, ha, ha," he chortled flippantly.

"Aren't you ever serious?"

"Sure Bill, now let's get down to business. I'll drive the new motor back today and I'll see yer at the front of me 'ouse in about an hour, okay?"

Garrison's Gorillas

CHAPTER 6

"That's a good looking motor Del," Beth commented, "was it very expensive?"

"It's a long story Beth and I've 'ad a busy day," he replied trying to avoid her questions.

"Come in and have a cuppa, I've had to take the afternoon off for the dentist's."

Beth worked part-time as a seamstress at a local sweat shop, in order that Del and she could live to pay the rent on their council house. If she had depended on Del's support then they would have been out in the street long ago. She had met Del just after the war, where he had been studying law for his degree. Because of his humble origins he was held in low esteem at the college in Cardiff, which had been part of the cause that Del had gone bent. He had run up a bill at the local pub and not paid, he had bought three suits without even a weekly payment, and he had put the squeeze on every student in the college promising them the earth in their investment in his non-existent cheese factory, but actually paying none of them dividends. Because he had put himself in this unenviable position, he felt the need to stay away from the local pub and do his drinking in town. It was here that Beth had met him and fallen for his glib talk. She had been a struggling opera singer but with no success since her last part almost a year previous, she had resorted to the job of barmaid in order to pay the bills.

Because of the pressure exerted on Del for payment, he had decided to skip town, and convinced Beth to join him. Madly in love with Del, Beth would have followed him to the ends of the earth. They both had enough left for a train journey north and arrived in the recently industrialised Newtown, where they had remained for twenty seven years. Del had got into the habit of running up debt and gambling, conning his way out of every situation and Beth had come to accept this unenviable state of affairs because of her love for him.

Del, as the brilliant con man who - had he worked at it long enough - would have become an even brilliant lawyer, but chose to 'drop out' of society and join the ranks of the low.

Although Beth secretly desired that one day Del would make the big time and find a fortune in something, it sated her needs to be married to him, even if she did have to support him. Thus became her life, being reduced to dependence on the clothing factory's employ.

"What 'ave yer 'ad dun Beth?" he quizzed.

"A filling on this side," she pointed, "by Jove, he didn't half hurt too."

"Yer don't want ter go there again."

"Oh he's not bad really Del, he's about the best there is around here," she insisted.

"Well, whatever turns yer on?" he mused. "Let's 'ave that cuppa Beth and get the Scotch out, I want ter celebrate."

They entered the house and Del sat on the easy chair pouring himself a large Scotch.

"Rat-a-tat, tat," sounded the door knocker.

"If that's Bill, tell 'im ter come in will yer love?"

Bill entered the house, "Hiya Beth," he beamed.

"Go in Bill, Del's in the living room."

"'Ave a drop o' Scotch Bill," his partner offered.

"Don't mind if I do mate," he replied, pouring the golden contents in to a deep cup.

"Mmm, that's a good year Del," he complimented, as they savoured the taste.

"It's Teacher's Bill."

"Thought it was - it's so smooth."

"Shove the telly on Bill will yer?"

"Right," his friend complied.

Beth was just coming through the door with a bowl of hot stew freshly made.

"I'll get you one too Bill."

"Oh ta."

"One thing that Beth is really good at," said Del, "is makin' a pan of tater 'ash."

"Too true," his friend agreed, as Beth brought in Bill's dish. Both the men slurped and smacked their lips appreciably as the tasty fare disappeared down their throats.

Sounds of gunfire from the television suddenly intervened as the announcer stated, "Garrison's Gorillas."

"It's on Bill, turn the sound up."

"Yeh," he answered excitely.

The two men sat with their eyes glued to the set.

"Hey Bill, wake up it's half past seven!" said Beth shaking him.

"'Ugh 'er, wha' what's up? 'As it gone off," he mumbled, "did you say 'alf past seven? I'm suppose to be in Bromborough fer seven to meet…can I use yer bathroom Del, and can I borrer yer tuxedo fer the night? I've gorra birastuff ter take out."

"Oh aye, romance in the air 'eh Bill, and at your age too. Yer should be ashamed of yourself, tut tut tut, an old man of 52 courtin', heh, heh, heh."

Bill's non-verbal communication of having his dignity removed, was immediately noticed by Del who perceived the perplexed look on his face.

"Go on then, yer can borrer it - but take care of it mind! I don't want any dinner dropped on it," he warned.

"It'll be as clean as when I take it," Bill vowed, thanking Del, then excusing himself as he dashed up the stairs.

After Bill had left, Del called Beth into the living room and sat her down on the settee.

"Now it's my turn," he resolved, "you sit here and get your feet up on the pouffe whilst I go and get you a meal."

THE MACE GOES IN

"But really Del, I'm alright, I'll get some egg and chips," she replied lovingly.

"No egg and chips for you," he determined, "tonight's the night for celebration," and with that he changed the channel to number three for 'Coronation Street'.

Beth smiled and leaned back resting her weary shoulders, just as Del donned on his coat and opened the front door.

"Mushroom omelette and chips," he declared, in the Chinese takeaway shop, "with an extra helping of mushrooms, also chicken and chips."

As it was being prepared he excused himself promising return and dashed next door to the off license for a large box of chocolates and an assortment of sweets and candies for his wife. Also in the shop he proceeded to select three various flavours of 'Schloeur' bottled drinks and paid for it all at the till. He returned to collect the meal and went home.

"Here you are Beth," he announced. "Here's your favourite dish. When you've eaten that lot I'll take you out to the local for a nice drink."

Beth smiled and cooed gratefully as she viewed the tray containing the meal.

Her husband brought in a jar with a fork tucked in it saying, "Here y'are, your favourite 'Sawer Krout' to go with it."

"You know how to make a girl happy," she admitted, giving him a hug and kiss. She then sat down beside him tucking into the meal. He in turn made short work of his chicken and chips.

At 8.15pm she had completed her dinner with appreciable 'oohs and ahs' wiping her mouth with the napkin and washing it down with large glasses of 'Schloeur'. Del took the signal and donned on his coat bringing Beth's into the living room to put on.

She took the coat from him but instead of donning it she pulled Del to her, embracing him in a kiss murmuring, "Do we have to go yet, it's really early you know?"

"Well Beth, there's not much on telly, and I thought there's nothing much left to do is there?" he remonstrated, with hands open in gesture.

"Nothing?" she hinted, looking up at the ceiling alluringly, Del felt perplexed thinking, 'Isn't it always the way? When I get a bit lustful Beth's always got a' headache, but when I want to take a drink, she's Always in the mood!"

He decided to take advantage of the situation remembering that it had been quite some time since they had got together and took hold of her hand leading her upstairs. Only to be instantly reminded of this earlier promise, "Oh no, Danielle…I'd forgotten all about her?"

Arriving in Bromborough, Bill took the last turning on the left to come to a halt outside of the house of Mary's address. It was a huge mock Tudor structure, finished externally with wattle and daub, contrasting well with the stones set in its corners. The oaken beams all liberally covered in Rotterdam tar, and its tiny paned windows - set in brilliant white frames. Its Georgian style chimneys, silhouetting against the sky, like huge monoliths, menacing everywhere above the roof. Bill left the car and arrived at the door giving it a hearty rap with his knuckle. He had to knock quite a time before he received an answer.

"Yerrr?" answered the tall slim woman with a thin cigar tucked in the corner of her mouth.

"I'd like to speak to Mary Valesque," he requested smiling.

"I'll see if she's in - who shall I say's calling?"

"Bill – er, Bill Foggit," he said, still smiling.

Although she grated her voice, for her age she was really quite attractive.

"'Ang on there," she commanded and disappeared around the door, "Ma-a-r-ry," sounded the voice like a knife grating on a tin, "Ma-r-ry - where are you?"

He heard Mary answer and then some whispering take place. Eventually the tall woman returned to him saying, "She won't be long, stand inside out of the cold."

He thanked her and closed the door behind him. The house had a large Victorian influence, of which tall ceilings prevailed in the hall and lounge, that he walked into. He was somehow glad to get away from the hall, which was adorned with old dark pictures from the turn of the century. A moose head loomed up in the centre leering at him. Queen Anne chairs sat alongside the walls and tapestries of a bygone age. The wallpaper held dark dust, dust which had never been feathered or cleaned. It was just as if the house had been left since the First World War.

The living room he reached and was invited to sit down, by the large woman who commenced to explain, "I'm so sorry for the way in which I greeted you," she said in a pleasant gentle voice, with a refined accent, "we have so many would-be burglars knocking our door," she assured him, "are you local?"

"No, I live in a flat in Newtown, it's not that far away, about six miles."

"Did you meet Mary at her work?"

"In a way," he retorted, secretly trying to impress.

"Are you an executive?" she asked snobbishly.

"No, I tend to do the work myself, most of these executives do nothing but chalk up loads of expenses - expenses which could easily be avoided. Now in my line of business, the market moves from one way to another without warning and does not leave much of a margin for expenses. Besides, the competition is so strong a firm could go bankrupt in one week or make a killing the next, it's so unpredictable."

"What line of business is it then?" showing greater interest.

"The movement of non-ferrous metal bullion and the shift in markets," he enlightened, trying to be as impressive as possible.

"Hmm," she awed, unable to comment.

"Am I interrupting?" hailed the soft voice behind them.

"Ah Mary," said the woman relieved at the intervention. "I'll go and see what Arthur's doing."

"Hello love," he said, after she'd left them.

"Bill!" she replied, throwing her arms around him, "I'm so glad you could come."

"Sorry I'm a bit late love, business got in the way and - well, you know how it is these days," giving a shrug with his hands open.

"Don't worry about it Bill, you're here now, that's all that matters," she assured, giving him a hug. "Would you like some tea?"

"No love," and with a smile said, "I thought we might go out for a meal and then a drink?"

"Wonderful, where would you like to go?"

"Thought about taking you to St Clairs'"

"St Clair's?" she echoed, "that would be truly marvellous. But are you sure Bill, I mean it IS rather expensive, don't you think?"

"I don't think so, in fact, I thought they were quite reasonable," he lied, trying to make a good impression.

"Then St Clair's it is," she agreed happily.

Bill drove the Morris Minor slowly down toward Wallasey with Mary snuggled up next to him, whispering, "You're a careful driver Bill, I feel safe with you."

"Have you lived in Bromborough all of your life Mary?" he probed.

"No love, we had to come, due to daddy's bankruptcy in 1965."

Bill felt like he shouldn't pursue the conversation for fear of digging up the remains for her, so he changed the subject with, "By the way who was that huge woman at your lodge tonight?"

"Oh yes, you wouldn't believe me if I told you!" she voiced convincingly.

"'Course I would," laughing as he said so.

"Oh I wouldn't want to bore you," she teased.

"No really," he stressed, "I'm interested."

"Very well," she smirked, "you asked for it! D'you remember all that scandal in the papers about nine years ago about a washing machine fiddle?"

"Fiddle?"

"Yes, you know, that chap who made millions out of a cheaper model."

"But of course - but what has this to do with that woman?"

"It was because of her that he lost all of the capital and was later gaoled for fraud. It started when he made his first million and met her on the way up. His first wife had died soon after the baby was born and George had really no-one he could turn to except his secretary, in whom he paid more than just a business interest. He promised her the world and with all those champagne parties that followed, almost fulfilled it. All the profits which should have gone to the shareholders were mis-appropriated for world cruise expenses for both of them, until that dreadful time when the auditors were called in and George was nowhere to be found. A deficit of £14 million was discovered and he was blamed for the lot! Actually there was a lot more but they couldn't trace it at all. If the truth was known, the true figure was more like £30 million, but George was no fool - he salted a large amount of the profits in an investment at an unknown location…"

"An investment - in what?" he probed.

Mary went quiet for a time and glanced about furtively before replying, "I did hear a whisper about bullion!" she said with a more seriously poised face.

Bill's interest unmistakeably showed on his change of expression immediately perceived by Mary who continued:

"He's at present serving five years hard labour at Wormswood Scrubs, fraud they called it," she added lowering her voice, "before he was apprehended he bought this house in Bromborough in my name for Dinny and I," she enlightened.

"Dinny?" he frowned.

"Geraldine," she interpreted, "yes I suppose you've guessed it by now have you?"

"Er? yes love, no really what I was going to say was, where d'you fit in all this, when suddenly, it became all clear to me…you were that baby and George is your father, also he's made you the chief executor of his estate, power of attorney etc, to keep mum in his absence?" he fished.

"You're very quick Bill," she voiced, trying to avoid his query. "Oh I meant to ask you, what kind of business are you involved in?" she queried, attempting to change the subject.

Bill smiled completely taken in by this tactic but wary that he must effect a good impression, put on his best act by replying, "Bullion," bringing a look of shock to her face. Oh no, not the sort that George invested in, not by a long chalk - no, mine is merely non-ferrous metals such as copper and tin, lead and the like," he explained, bringing a look of relief to Mary's face as she smiled, she clasped his hand in re-assurance with a gentle squeeze.

He in turn gripped her fingers and stroked her knuckles.

He arrived with the lights on green and filtered through turning right and then left, cutting into the clearway and then the dual carriageway. All too soon the neon lights came into view of 'St.Clair's Restaurant and Bar', All Night License notice.

"Here we are," he whispered and Mary sat up in her seat.

The restaurant at some point resembled a manor house, lavishly converted to suit the needs of the public. Its approach still retained the original stone slabs, giving way to newly fired road tiles, set all the way from the road to the threshold.

Its proud fort like towers on each corner grasped the sky above, built on huge sandstone slabs supported by even larger pieces of stone, which looked by their size immovable. It exacted a 16th century influence, upon which it was constructed. Mary was enthralled by its inner ground presence, and wondered what next they would encounter.

Bill parked the car in the front of the forecourt and opened the door for Mary.

"There's still chivalry in the world - I'm glad to say," she noted, admirably as they entered the building. It was dimly lit with soft yellow and purple lights set against the walls' huge stones. For anyone who entered its domain of bare walled interior, could be convinced they were going back in time. Even the tables and chairs were typical to the Elizabethan era.

"Table for two sir?" asked the waiter, then proceeded to show them to a table.

Bill thanked the man holding a chair out for Mary. They both sat down and immediately studied the menu cards.

Silence reigned for many minutes until, "The lobster looks good," Bill commented enquiringly.

"So does the crayfish," she replied happily.

"What d'you think of this caviar love?" he asked, trying to

THE MACE GOES IN

impress.

"Depends on how long it's been frozen."

"Fro-zen?" he queried bewildered.

"Yes, and whether it was obtained from a virgin sturgeon," she stressed, knowledgeably tongue in cheek.

"You're kidding aren't you?" he asked naively.

"What d'you think?" she said with a smile

Bill wasn't sure what to make of this dark eyed beauty. Looking back at the events in the Rural Soak, he had first perceived her as a simple barmaid - uneducated to say the least, and yet here he was with someone who was not only educated, but possessed all the etiquette and gourmand's discernment needed for successful ordering and good eating at the best establishments. Bill felt really proud to accompany her that evening. He decided to try to impress her by ordering a bottle of table wine to enhance their appetite before, which he poured liberally in both glasses, that they relished whilst awaiting the crustaceans which arrived with the bottle half gone. Mary's crayfish arrived adorned with parsley and tomato decorations, in contrast to Bill's lobster, which came devoid of any contrasting herbs.

"How can you eat it like that," gasped Mary in disbelief.

"I'll show you in two minutes," he said, inserting the nutcrackers and splitting a 'claw,'crunch, crunch,' sounded Bill with the tools, causing many heads to turn. Mary laughed nervously trying her best to ignore the noise as Bill directed the fork in the area of white meat. He drove in the implement and retrieved a large portion, which he peppered hastily, desperate to sate his hunger. "Mmm," he murmured appreciably. He took up the claw and forced the fork well into the flesh taking another portion, repeating the procedure before stuffing it in his mouth. Finally, after exhausting the claws' source of food, he then commenced to break the main body. Mary had become engrossed in her quest for meat also, but due to the small size of the crayfish, found it quite difficult, and made noises of disgust apparent to Bill who suggested, "Tell you what love, why don't I order you a spot of lobster, you'll enjoy it more than that tiddly thing?"

"What a good idea, how thoughtful you are!"

Bill snapped his fingers for service and instructed the waiter of the fish order who complied immediately, returning with a lobster almost the size of Bill's.

Mary pounced on it and right away started to dissect the animal into pieces which she attacked with her pair of crushers so expertly and almost silently, that it brought great astonishment to Bill and other onlookers. Mary was completely oblivious to anyone and continued her purge to quell her appetite. Suddenly her fork was in the meat and emptying the shells onto the side of the plate.

After the approximation of two minutes, she had all of the contents readily peppered, prepared for consumption which she caused to disappear with that same adeptness. "Yummy, that was very nice, I could just eat another one," she hinted.

"Be my guest," he invited.

"Ah no, I couldn't - they're far too expensive."

"Nonsense," he replied, "money's made round for going around."

"Oh well, as long as you're sure."

Bill put his hand up once more and ordered two more.

"Any more wine sir?" queried the man.

"Yes, why not! Only this time bring me some Vermouth."

"Certainly sir, Vermouth it is."

He arrived back as quickly as he'd gone with the fare, to which they tucked into together savouring every forkful.

Thirty minutes later heralded nine forty-five and the presentation of the bill, 'Five lobsters 1 crayfish, 1 bottle of white wine,1 bottle of Vermouth, that's thirty seven pounds and ten shillings sir."

Bill nearly had a heart attack, but tried to hide his emotions with a smile but his para-language let him down.

Mary perceived just how he felt and suggested, "Here, I'll pay half," taking £20 out of her purse.

"I wouldn't hear of it, if I take a girl out, I don't expect her to go Dutch," he determined, searching through his pockets. He located just £35 asking, "Perhaps the loan of a fiver would be in order?"

She put down the fiver adding, "What a stout hearted fellow you

THE MACE GOES IN

are Bill!"

"You'll get it right back luv."

Bill settled the damages and put on Mary's coat behind her, "Thanks love," she said with a smile.

The drive back to Bromborough was composed of both of them reminiscing about the meal as Mary quipped, "Did you see the face on that posh French waiter, when you started cracking the claws? Ha, ha, I thought he was going to swallow his false teeth. He gave an enormous gulp and backed toward our table trying to quiet the racket," she explained mirthfully.

"What about when you attacked your lobster?" he cried, "that chap with the snooty blonde, his eyes nearly popped out of his glasses. It made the blonde kick him under the table to gain his attention, hee hee hee," Bill remonstrated.

Mary saw the funny side of it too and laughed with him,

"It's good to be able to laugh at one's self isn't it Bill, why, I haven't enjoyed myself quite so much in ten years, yes, those were the good old days," she suddenly went tearful and then quiet. Bill perceived her mood realising that she missed her father and he went quiet too.

After some time he invited, "Want to talk about it?"

"We-ell."

"It doesn't matter love, I quite understand."

"No, no," she answered, "it's not that I don't want to talk about it. It's just well, things used to be a lot better for Dad - George I mean," she corrected. "We used to do so much together until that damned Dinny came on the scene," she wailed.

"That Geraldine?" he scolded, "yes she's got a lot to answer for. By the way, how soon will George be released?" he probed.

Mary didn't answer right away, but when she did, her attitude changed somewhat.

"Are you sure you really want to get involved Bill?" she asked.

"Really love, all I thought about was if I could be of any help?"

"Let me think about it love," she hedged, "I've so much on my mind presently."

Bill changed the subject with, "If I put my clog down we should be able to get a few drinks at that little pub down the road from the 'Rural Soak'."

He drove the Morris alongside a tiny quaint inn with a low roof. As they entered the lounge they both had to duck narrowly missing the wooden lintel above the threshold, bringing a low chuckle to both of them,

"What's your poison love?" he joked.

"A drop of Canadian Dry."

"Canadian Dry single, and double Scotch please?"

He joined Mary with the drinks in the far corner of the room.

"Happy?" he murmured.

"Ecstatically."

They stayed in the inn until it closed where Bill signalled Mary with her coat motioning her through the door. They entered the car and drove towards her home. Thirty minutes later saw Bill giving a goodnight kiss to her and then returning to his home in Newtown.

The drive home to his flat had Bill reminiscing, about the antics of the French waiter earlier that night in a bid to quieten Bill' noisy acquisition of meat from the shells of the lobsters they'd both managed to eat, the look on the waiter's face when Mary ordered 'same again?'. It was still funny, for he'd observed the man's moustache had almost stood on end like 'Hercule Poirot's', the famous detective. Bill chuckled all the way home.

Quite out of the blue, he thought of his ex-wife, Eva's treachery and even before when they had first met in Penang, where he'd rescued her from her attacker - beating her about the head with a leather strap, who upon Bill's encounter, felt the force of Bill's aggression, striking his head on the dirt wall of the inn, causing future attacks of 'Petis Mal' Epilepsy for the rest of his life. "Poor chap," thought Bill, "he probably regrets what he did, as do I. Why couldn't I have left well alone?" Bill had regretted his marriage to Eva, for she proved all of their married life, to be unfaithful and subsequently running off with a tea planter.

He later heard of the tragedy of both, as they had lost their lives when their chalet had succumbed to flames in the monsoon.

After Eva, Bill had vowed never again to get involved personally with any woman, and to play the field of one night stands, upon each successive female he had encountered. This way he'd avoided any commitments with either - until now, where he believed he had actually fallen in love.

In his mind's eye he could still see that beautiful countenance of Mary and her angelic face.

He drove slower and slower savouring his experience of Mary's company. That deep aroma of her perfume which she wore with her alluring smile he just couldn't forget.

His car was bought to a halt outside his block of flats and he stepped out of the car, "Oh heck, Del's tuxedo?" he remembered and panicked. It was far too late to return it now, so he resigned himself to the fact that he'd just have to enter the flat.

He opened his front door and was met by Zach.

1/6d For a Spoon
CHAPTER 7

"Where the heck have you been Bill, I've been frantic here and...oi, what's this, a tuxedo?" asked Zach fingering the material.

"Careful tosh," warned Bill, "Del'll kill me if anythin' gets on it," re-assuming his colloquial tongue.

"You've bin ought wiv a bird, I can smell the scent!" said Zach cynically.

"Right first time, yer get ten out of ten."

"On Monday dinnertime Bill, I think we'll pull our stunt at Lings Motors," his friend enlightened.

"Right Zach, I should be home by then, Sunday termorrer Zach - 'ere I'll lend yer the spare key and if yer wanna stay out late yer'll be able ter let yerself in, won't yer?"

Zach nodded with, "Thanks Bill that's very considerate of you!"

"I'll be in 'The George' all day mate, I've gorra give Del 'is monkey suit back, so if I don't see yer before, I'll be 'ere by 12 on Monday."

Zach and Bill awoke at the same time Sunday morning and went their separate ways. Zach toward Chester and Bill to his local, 'The George'. Bill entered the lounge and ordered himself a pint of bitter, picking up the 'News of the World' and browsing through it. He stopped on page four to read: George Valesque released on Friday, then the Queen Mother's at Ascot, Then. frantically he doubled back to and thought, "Yes it was, George Valesque the one time Mr. Economy Washer....so this was what was going through Mary's mind the night before. No wonder she couldn't make that dinner date on

THE MACE GOES IN

Friday - George's return was the reason." He read on which stated: Valesque checked out of Wormswood Scrubs bound for an unknown destination after serving 5 years hard labour.

"Hard labour," he voiced out a loud, "that means no remission, poor devil," he remarked with empathy, "fancy sitting on all that loot with no remission?" Then a thought struck him, "No wonder Geraldine took so long to answer the door, I'll bet George had arrived there earlier and was making up for his lack of her company.

He pondered the thought of George for many minutes before making a decision.

"Funny how opportunity knocks your door?" he mused, "I'll tell Del about George when he comes in, but then he thought of his feelings for Mary, and felt that he couldn't live with himself if Del decided to 'mace' her father.

"No," he determined, "I'll see to it that George gets a fair deal with his loot."

He racked his brains through the long list of metal buyers whom he knew but couldn't decide just who to choose from, due to their all being somewhat shady in business.

"But who?" he repeated. In a flash he received the revelation he needed, Anthony Johnson, "Hmm, I'm sure I've got his card somewhere, yes, here it is," he said with relief, "Anthony M Johnson, Insurance Recovery, Settlement, Agent. Hmm, I'll give him a ring now." He left his pint on the bar and walked into the foyer which housed the phone.

Just then, in walked Del as he was about to dial.

"Hiya Bill," he remarked, "What are yer drinkin'?"

"Bitter Del, thanks."

"Bitter it is, mate," Del concurred.

"See yer in a minute Del, I've Just gorra phone this birra stuff," he lied.

After Del had gone into the lounge, Bill ran into the bar foyer where the other phone was situated, in order to avoid intervention from his pal.

After contacting Mal, he explained the situation and Mal agreed to come to the 'George' and five minutes later he arrived.

"Yes Mal," he agreed, "that's about it, now if you'll bear with me, we could make a bob or two if we screw on our nuts. Do me a favour and don't mention my connection in this ter anybody or both our gooses are cooked," he warned.

"Cooked?" replied Mal bewildered.

"Yeh, this bullion ties in with that bundle lost in 1965 by National Refineries - remember?"

"Yes," cried Mal, "I recall the police were baffled, £20 million quid's worth. Six, eight leggers disappeared didn't they? The drivers all woke up on a beach in St Tropez, drugged and tied," he affirmed.

"That's the one," Bill agreed, but Mal continued oblivious to his conversation.

"Block tin, copper Bananas, Bronze shot and silver Ingots," he explained, "all gone, and none of the grasses knew where?"

"I don't know fer sure Mal, but this could quite possibly be that very same load?" Bill envisaged. "Listen, can you meet me somewhere and we'll go over all of it, but remember this - not a word to anyone or there's no deal."

"My lips are sealed Bill, tell you what, I'll call by your place tonight to discuss it."

"No," vowed Bill, "I'11 see you at Eastham Woods' car-park at 4.30 on Monday okay?"

His friend had to agree promising not to tell a soul.

"Bye Mal, til Monday then..."

Bill walked back to the lounge to be met by Del with, "Where've yer bin, I've bin everywhere lookin' for yer?"

"Oh, nature call - yer know," he lied.

"Course, I never thought of the gents…, I looked everywhere else," he added.

Bill picked up his pint he'd left and slurped down the remains and proceeded to upend the new pint that Del had bought him.

"Hey Bill, there's a poker game in the back room later, Jimmy Artsorn's lettin' us use 'is part o' the pub at three o'clock fer our 'Buffs Order', and sez we can 'ave it till 6.30 pm. So me an' the lads decided ter 'ave a coupla 'ands of cards - what d'yer think mate?"

"I've got no pokey left Del ter play with," he said, pulling his trouser pockets out emphatically.

"No pokey, no pokey - what 'ave yer been doin - eatin' it?" screamed Del incredulously.

"Er yeh, in a way mate, I took that birra stuff fer a meal and the bill came ter quite a lot."

"What, fer fish an' chips?" quizzed his friend sarcastically.

"No chance Del - yer know I won't eat chips with my bad gut!"

"Then where did yer take 'er, not that rudddy St Clairs?" he further insulted.

"The very same," nodded Bill frankly.

"Strewth, Bill, yer 'ave ter pay 1/6 fer a spoon in there," voiced he insistently, "tell yer what, just so's yer don't go short, I'll lend yer a tenner mate - 'ere yare."

"No Del, what yer really should of said is: "I'll give yer a tenner ter play with!"

"Give yer?" said Del, a worried look appearing on his face.

"Yeh - give me, in fact Del, really what yer should be saying is 'ere y'are Bill, 'ere's the poke I 'maced' yer out of on the wagon deal!" he said with derision.

"Wha', what d'yer mean Bill?" mouthed he with horror.

"Listen Del, I 'ought ter knock yer schemin' 'ead off yer shoulders conning me like that. First yer say we're partners, then yer mace me out of my share." Del coloured up as Bill continued: "Yeh, I looked through Zach's 'Glass's Guide' at 'ome, an' that wagon's price starts at £2150 bottom an' £2700 top bat, an' yer really ad me kidded with that bird, what took me ter the cleaners - Danielle wasn't it?"

"Er,"

"Yeh, an' 'ere's another thing mate, if yer really paid £3000, that means you got ripped of for about 1,000 nicker, an' knowin' you, yer never pay top bat fer anythin' so it's my guess yer only paid a grand at the most..."

"£13 'undred Bill, honest!" confessed Del, who coloured up even more when he'd realised he'd let the cat out of the bag. "I was only kiddin' Bill," he pleaded desperately, trying to avoid a broken jaw.

"£13 'undred?" he gasped in disbelief. He was stopped in his tracks, "this means that..." he started counting on his fingers, "you macer, you conniving get, you've took me fer seven 'undred er, eight 'undred an' fifty quid - yeh, 1050 quid." Bill's face was like thunder. He couldn't believe it. Suddenly something snapped inside him, then all hell broke loose.

He could see Del's head being pounded intermittently on the floor of the lounge. Looking down in disbelief he realised that he - and only he, was responsible for Del's bloodied condition. Horror stricken, he dropped his partner and took a large gulp from the pint of bitter on the table. He looked down at Del who was stirring. A large crowd had gathered, but their knowledge of Bill's temper stopped them from intervening. Most of them had had some experience of Bill's capabilities to fight and none of them even ventured a polite query of 'what happened' as they all stood terrified, wondering who he would start on next? Bill picked up Del, and sat him on the bench seat attached to the wall saying to one of the bystanders, "'Ere Fred, get me two double scotches will yer?" handing the man a ten shilling note.

"Okay Bill," Fred concurred, only too glad to be of service to such a notorious celebrity. The man returned with the double scotches.

"Ta Fred, get yerself a drink," said Bill, handing him back the four shillings change.

"E y'are Del, get this down yer," prompted Bill, pushing the whisky glass near to his friends' mouth.

"Wha' wharappened Bill," asked a bewildered Del.

"Yer fell back when I got hold of yer," he lied.

"Oh, I see, believe me mate - I only took that cash off yer fer a laugh, Beth's gorrit at 'ome and it was 'er who made me come over 'ere ter give it yer back," he pretended, "in fact mate, I said to 'er I'll just take five 'undred fer now 'cos me wallet won't take anymore. 'Ere it is Bill, I'll go back 'ome now ter get yer the rest."

Bill felt sorry for all the mess Del was in and told him that if he didn't say anything to Beth about the scuffle, then he'd run Del home for more money.

Del agreed and they both left for his home and as they arrived

THE MACE GOES IN

Del motioned, "Wait there Bill, .I'll see if Beth's up yet."

He appeared shortly afterward brandishing the crisp new bundles of fivers.

"Here, y'are Bill,' he stressed, 'I 'ave counted it."

But Bill commenced to count it nonetheless, "This is £175 short!"

'Oh I'm sorry mate, I've given yer the wrong bundle," said he, determined to 'con' Bill even to the end.

Bill counted the other bundle which Del had fingered but due to this distraction of Bill's, had panicked him into giving Bill too much. Bill continued to count and to his surprise found £275 all together, "Yeh, this is okay Del." he lied chuckling to himself.

Del feverishly checked his other pockets and then he gave Bill eye to eye contact, "Who's conning who now Bill? Come on mate, give us that £100 back!" he commanded.

"£100?" replied his pal with a feigned look of surprise, "I thought you said that this bundle was right?" he pretended.

"Ey Bill, stop muckin' about," said Del in disgust.

"Ha ha ha," smirked Bill, "yer don't 'alf look mad when yer get upset."

"Upset, I've gorra right ter be - 'aven' I?"

Bill returned the money to Del who murmured, "Well mate, let's see if we can't win some money shall we?"

They started back in the Morris and Bill blurted out, "Listen Del, we'd better get it straight from here on, that I play my own game. There'll be no 'shill' in this game," he determined.

"But Bill, if I don't 'ave a shill's help, how can I hope to win anything?"

"For pete's sake Del, see if yer can play it straight fer once," stressed Bill.

"Well, all right, I'll see what I can do," he agreed reluctantly.

They arrived back at 'The George' and Del, in a bid to keep Bill in a good mood ordered, the pints and took them over to their table.

"Another week at Cobden's should see that Job through Bill, so if we get there at 9.00 am Monday we can do 2 loads a day easily," he assured.

"By the way Del, ave yer 'eard any more about the 'Brass Miller's swarf job?"

"Swarf, Bill?"

"Yeh, yer know - 'Arry Parker the foreman," he reminded.

"Oh drat, I'd forgotten all about 'im!" he exclaimed.

"'E goes in the 'Bowling' on Sundays Del, tell yer what, I'll run yer there before one o'clock. Yer'll be able ter do a job on 'im ready fer us ter take the contract over."

"Okay Bill, sup up an' we'll go."

They arrived at the 'Bowling' just in time to see Harry Parker replenishing his bitter glass after which he walked over to the dart board and instructed the chalk marker, Ray, that they were to play together next game of 301.

"Right 'Arry," nodded Ray, "closest to the bull, you know the score. Oh lend us yer arrows will yer, 'Arry?"

Harry passed the man his darts, who commenced to throw one near the bull returning Harry his darts for his turn. Harry threw his dart almost in the centre smirking, "My first throw."

He put the first dart into double twenty, the second another double twenty and the final dart in the treble twenty.

"That's 140 start," he indicated writing 161 on the board.

The other player looked sick and commenced to throw for a double, missing. He anxiously placed another dart but with no success, finally in desperation he threw higher and luckily landed in double one.

Parker chuckled tossing the darts back into the board. Treble 20, treble 20, and finally treble '9 taking his score down to just 14.

His opponent threw his darts and landed all of them in single 20 reducing his score to 239.

Parker then put one shot in double '7' calling "Game" adding, "I'll 'ave a pint of bitter Peter, thanks."(Each loser forfeits a drink)

"Hiya 'Arry," blurted Del.

Harry spun around as he heard his name mentioned with a smile, which turned to dismay as he recognised Del.

"'Ello Del," he answered, "Ow are yer?" he probed, anxiously trying to discern Del's need.

Del was waving the pawn ticket with the number 467 in his face.

Harry recognised it immediately saying, "Oh thanks mate, I've been looking everywhere for that," reaching out to retrieve it.

"No chance," said Del, pulling it back. "This stays in my wallet for Hans Muller, 'e's comin' to 'The George' tonight ter get 'is property back."

At the mention of Muller's name, Harry paled and started to shake, "What d'you know about 'im?" he quizzed in a commanding voice. "Anyway, yer can't prove anythin'," he determined.

"Oh no? I think you're wrong. I've seen Cohen the pawnbroker and he described you to me when I asked 'im!" he jibed.

Silence reigned for a full minute until finally Parker broke down with, "Ow much Del?"

"Ow much, 'ow much what?" he drooled, enjoying the cat and mouse situation.

"Ow much d'yer want fer that ticket?" he asked.

"Parker, listen 'ere, I want one thing off you!"

"Anythin' Del, you name it?" he pleaded.

"You 'ave a dealer in scrap comes in ter buy yer swarf once a quarter - am I right?"

"Wha', oh no, not that - I can't do it, he'd cut me fingers off if I blew 'im out."

"Not ter worry Harry, Hans'll give me a good price for it - I meantersay it is his stamp after all, an' I know 'e's desperate ter gerit back," he smiled.

"Okay Del, I'll do it, I'll do it, but promise me yer won't grass me to 'im will yer?"

Peter arrived with Harry's pint and Harry forced a smile,

"See yer in a minute Pete," he voiced.

Peter moved away with his drink as Harry repeated, "Del - Del? Listen mate I'll get the ball rollin' for yer, it should be ready in a week: - or so," he assured him, "It'll take that long for the paper work to go through."

"Okay 'Arry, I'll be contacting you on Friday for the griff on it,' promised Del, with a serious tone.

"Sup up Bill, we'll get back ter 'ock country,' (The George) he commanded.

"Right," Bill agreed, lubricating his throat.

Del gargled the remains of his glass and they left.

They re-entered the lounge of 'The George' and Bill said, "Get me a pint Del, I'll ger us an 'ock each. ham or pork?"

"I'll 'ave an 'am one," he replied.

"Two 'am 'ocks Cynthia," he ordered, "and Del's payin' fer the ale..."

After receipt of the hocks, they sat down gorging the meat with lashings of mustard, washing it down with bitter beer. They had gotten through their meal and a few beers, when Del remembered, "Blast it Bill, we were suppose to be back 'ome, Beth, she's cooking us dinner.

Last orders sounded and in a mad panic they ordered four more beers as 'carry out' to take back to Del's.

Beth greeted them at 2.30 pm with, "Where have you two lachicoes been till this time? The dinner's going cold. I've got turkey roast and baked potatoes with sprouts and Yorkshire pud! It was already half an hour ago," she fumed.

"Mmmm," remarked Bill, "that smells good Beth!" This remark calmed Beth down.

They both sat down by the dinner table as Beth served up their meals, with Bill opening the beer bottles he had brought.

Del wolfed his meal down and relished the beer's taste in conjunction with the food.

"Yeh, the simple pleasures in life are the best!" he gurgled drunkenly.

Bill had taken just two mouthfuls of turkey, when he put his hand up to his mouth yawning and feeling already full.

"Tired Bill?" asked Beth.

"Yeh, I 'aven't 'ad much sleep lately," he yawned.

"Go upstairs into the box room and throw your head down on that single bed love," she offered.

THE MACE GOES IN

"I'll do just that, thanks Beth, I should be all right after half an hour."

"Take as long as you like Bill," she assured.

Eight o'clock was registering on the alarm clock by the side of Bill, who awoke feeling completely refreshed.

"Funny," he thought, "how a few scoops in the daytime does yer a power of good,"

He arose from the bed - still fully clothed from the afternoon session and wandered into the bathroom to freshen up.

Del and Beth were already moving around when he came down and Beth motioned him to the table where a pot of tea awaited him.

"Help yourself to biscuits Bill," she invited, "I've also got some turkey sandwiches here," she offered.

Bill pounced on them now with great relish and washed them down with the tea.

"Ready to move Del?" he asked, as his friend put on his jacket.

"I'll foller yer in a minute Bill, I'm bringing Beth out as well," he enlightened.

"Okay mate," Bill replied and commenced to walk to the local where he'd left his car. He arrived there and ordered a double vodka which he downed immediately.

He then left word at the lounge bar, to suggest to Del that he would be back later that night. The barman nodded as Bill gave him a ten shilling note to buy himself a customary drink for the favour.

Bromborough village loomed up as he turned at the lights and drove down the road, which led to the unadopted driveway on the access of Mary's lodge.

Dinny was sitting in the garden at the rear, which he was soon to find out, upon his investigation as to why no-one answered the door. He called her name and 'Geraldine,' swung around,

"Oh hello," she called upon recognition of him, "George, I'd like you to meet Bill, Bill - this is George."

The man stood up, whom Bill immediately recognised as George Valesque, the ex-jailbird from Wormswood.

"Pleased to meet you Bill, come and sit down, Mary will be along in a moment."

Bill parked himself in a wicker-work chair, after shaking George's hand.

Mary appeared soon after, completely at ease wearing a light pink summer dress.

"Hello Bill," she greeted heartily, "so you've come to watch the sun go down too?"

Bill smiled and offered her a cigarette, which he lit for her and she breathed out with enjoyment.

"Where would you like to go luv?" he searched.

"Bill, didn't you say something about the bullion business when you first came around?"

"Yes but - surely you don't want to talk about all that boring business?"

"Well actually, George - I mean Daddy, now that he's come home has been looking toward that area and would like very much to learn the business. Would you consider taking on a partner who has quite a substantial stake to invest in some form of business?"

"Oh, about how much?" he probed.

"Well," George interjected, "I might know just where one might put his hands on some block tin…"

Mary and Dinny discreetly disappeared.

Bill lit a John Player and offered him one also and they spoke for many minutes.

After the preliminaries were over Bill asked, "So you think this friend of yours is trustworthy enough, to have sat on the load for these last five years?" he quizzed. "How d'you know that he hasn't already sold the stuff?"

"Well, I could tell you Bill - but I won't, put it this way, it wouldn't be in his best interests to do so. Now, all you have to do, is either find me a buyer for the stuff or the back door of the insurance settlement officer. I take it you've done this kind of work before?" he probed.

"You can count on it, where can the stuff be inspected, d'you have a sample we could work on?"

"One moment, I'll just make a phone call," he said. After approximately five minutes George returned saying, "By Monday lunchtime I can have you a few ingots of the same if you're really interested, by the way d'you have a number I could ring to contact you when I'm ready?"

Bill thought quickly, "No George, tomorrow I'm rather busy, but if you think you could let me know before three o'clock, I could give you a ring, then perhaps I could make a deal for you, that you couldn't refuse!"

"Couldn't refuse?"

"Yes George, tomorrow if you were to give me the samples of the full list of all your holdings and the 'carte blanche' of the same, I could have a cheque or good old used fivers in cash, to compensate you for your 'time' and trouble - if you get my meaning?"

"You could lay your hands on cash in the eight figure bracket?" said George incredulously.

"Eight figures? Hmm," murmured Bill, "as much as that, well now - that may pose a bit of a problem?'

"Really," jibed George.

George quite enjoyed the charade until Bill delivered his trump card, "This metal you hold, could it possibly include: block tin, copper bananas, bronze shot and silver ingots?" he challenged.

George stood open-mouthed, unable to speak for half a minute. Finally he replied sternly, "Who have you been talking to - Mary?"

"No, no, no, George, please - give me credit for some intelligence, I read the papers don't I? Any fool who'd followed your exploits, could 'ave put two and two together and made five. Listen mate, my insurance company hired me years ago as a middle man to retrieve stuff through the back door - without the criminal being brought to justice. It's cheaper that way and without much loss too," he stressed, "otherwise the insurance companies would probably all go broke wouldn't they?"

"Oh," said George, not quite sure whether or not he'd taken it all in. "Are you still in that very same position?"

"Right now, I'm playing the markets - buying and selling ingots for a quick turnover, and some times I get involved in a deal like yours and work on a commission basis. By the way, what kind of commission could I expect from you for my part in all this?" he quizzed.

"Five percent Bill, how's that?"

"Make it fifteen and you've got a deal!" he vowed.

"Ten percent, and when you marry Mary, I could make you a director,' George offered.

Bill pondered for a bit and subsequently replied, "But I haven't asked Mary yet and I don't even know if she loves me?"

"You want to watch she doesn't ask you!"

"Really," asked Bill, enthralled at the idea.

"Take my word for it."

"Okay, it's a deal," he said, "I'll ring here tomorrow by three o'clock and then you can tell me the worst," he joked.

They both spat on their palms and shook like the dealers they were.

'Mary," called George, "you'd better come down now and take this fellow of yours out for the night!" he commanded with a smile of approval.

"Okay Dad," she answered, taking Bill by the arm and walking him to his car.

Both he and she had to duck, to miss the low threshold, to gain access to the stairs in the old pub at Grouchmere. Bill had brought her there for a chance, to be away from the locals. For at first they both stood at the anciently decorated bar but later retreated to a table near the windows of the snug aptly named, 'The Thrushes Nest'.

For it was here that Bill was spinning his usual 'bullion stories' to entertain Mary, who then whispered as to whether or not, he had agreed to clinch a deal with her father.

He assured her that 'all was well' and the wheels were turning in the process to ensure George was well catered for.

Mary squeezed his hand at this revelation, as Bill got onto the subject of his 'case book' in prior insurance assignments.

"It happened that one day in 1963, I had gone through the

process of arranging a 'back door' retrieval of copper 'bananas' when no sooner had Everton Refineries received them back and re-assigned them to the Royal Mint, but they were re-hijacked in transit and gone again. The Refineries were really sickened by it all and came onto my firm for compensation. My superior exerted pressure on me for a fast return, but what could I do? I was dumbfounded, none of the narks knew who'd done the job and we were all at a loss of how we would stay in business. Then suddenly, word came through that a scrap dealer had 'blown the gaff on some southerners who had done the job, but had gypped him on the weight."

"How d'you gyp a dealer, I mean they're the ones who weigh it, aren't they?" she reasoned.

"Oh, ha ha, you haven't heard about 'bent' weighbridge men have you?" he explained, "anyway," he continued, "The police were able to retrieve most all of the loot, but it was then that they made the mistake of the century."

"Mistake?" she echoed.

"Yes, it appeared that Arthur Lucas' finger prints were all over the ingots and he was subsequently arrested in view of the evidence."

"And?" she searched.

"Yes,' he agreed, "and Arthur couldn't have been involved, because he had just finished a two month sentence in Strangeways for common assault. He wouldn't tell the police though, oh no - not Arthur. He merely went through the whole thing protesting his innocence. They put him on remand without bail and eventually his case came up at Chester Assizes. It was here that he made complete fools of the police. They had even contrived the appearance of two separate witnesses, who had actually 'seen' him enter the premises on the alleged night. His barrister actually questioned the police witnesses who swore that without a shadow of a doubt, they had both witnessed Arthur's entry into the Refineries' compound. Then came the bombshell. Arthur's barrister George Brown called upon his client to take the stand which he did. He then asked Arthur to tell the jury just exactly where he was situated, at the alleged time of the robbery.

Arthur refused on the grounds that it may influence the jury to be biased toward him. The judge explained to Arthur that he must answer truthfully, irrespective of the cost.

The jury listened intently as Arthur replied, "I was serving a two month sentence for common assault, against which I am still appealing for wrongful arrest and..."

The judge interjected at this stage with, "Never mind that, it is irrelevant to this case - were you, or were you not held on Her Majesty's pleasure at the time of the crime? Answer the question or I'll hold you in contempt!" Arthur's mouth was agape, he's a real good actor when he tries!

"er,er,er er, y y yes sir, I had two weeks left to serve, when the crime apparently was committed," he stammered.

"Twenty fourth of April was the time of the crime, was it not Mr. Kelvin?" the judge asks the prosecuting barrister.

"That is correct sir," says the lawyer.

"Mr. Lucas, at what date was your release from prison?"

Brown his barrister, interrupted with, "If m'lord would kindly read this release note?" handing him a slip of paper with 'Her Majesty's Prison Strangeways', date stamp and chief officer's signature written upon it.

The judge's eyes narrowed as he called the prosecutor,

"Mr. Kelvin would you attest to this being a legal document?"

Kelvin scrutinised the note and his face turned pale.

"Well man, is it authentic or is it not?" demanded the judge.

"Er yes sir - it is," affirmed the barrister.

"Then I suggest Mr. Kelvin, in view of the circumstances, you should withdraw your charges of grand theft from Mr. Lucas and enlighten him of his rights at this time, for wrongful arrest and compensation for undue suffering!" moved the judge adding, "No doubt some heads will roll for the perjuring of witnesses. I suggest you open an enquiry on behalf of the Crown, for suspected corruption of the police force!"

"Yes, yes, your lordship," replied Kelvin in a subservient manner.

The judge continued, "And furthermore..."

The courtroom was in an uproar as the judge released the jury from further duty with a word of thanks as the chief inspector collared the DI in charge of the case, whose face had turned a brilliant red."

"Gosh Bill, with those sort of experiences you'd be able to write a book," she voiced proudly.

Bill put his hand into his wallet saying, "Oh whilst I think on, this is yours."

He handed a fiver to Mary who looked puzzled.

"The meal, remember?"

"Oh but of course, oh really Bill - you shouldn't have," she remarked cordially.

"No girlfriend of mine is going to pay for her meal ever," he vowed adding, "although I admire your spirit for offering, thank you," he said with a smile.

"Oh you are old fashioned Bill," she mused, "but I think, that's what I like about you best," she voiced in admiration. "Isn't it funny how we met - I mean your being an authority on bullion and Daddy with that problem of his, that's no longer a problem - thanks to you," she said gratefully.

"Let's forget about business now and enjoy the night."

"Yes," she agreed, snuggling up to him and squeezing his hand, "you know Bill, it's nice being out here with you, I feel I can trust you, you know," she pledged.

"I feel that way about you too," he lied, unsure of his feelings.

Funny, he thought, women - you can't trust them. Turn your back on them and that's when they turn on you - no, I think I'll play this by ear and not be committed, he determined, although deep down inside of him, was the hope of finding in Mary a potential partner for life. He weighed up the situation as he felt her hand squeeze harder. Here I am, hopelessly in love with the first dark eyed beauty I meet. What's happening to me - could she really be the one?

"Penny for your thoughts Bill?" she whispered.

"I was just thinking how lucky I was to find you," he replied with mixed feelings smiling, trying to hide his suspicions. But she had noticed his non-verbal communications.

"Come on!" she demanded, "out with it, what's the problem? You can't kid me Bill Foggit, I know when men have problems. My experience as a barmaid serving men has taught me that," she assured him. She sat awaiting his reply.

"Well," he replied finally, "although Mary, I suppose you've guessed by now the way I feel about you?"

"I know," she joked, "you've fallen madly in love with me."

"Yes," he admitted pausing, "and it's because of this that I can't express myself in the way I'd like to due to my feelings of emotion, but none-the-less, I feel that I must enlighten you of my fears - even at the risk of losing you."

"Yes love," she assured him, "ask me anything you like?" she invited amiably.

"There you are again, you're making this very difficult," he moped dejectedly.

"Ah," she sympathised, putting her arm around him. He ignored her arm around him and asked her if she'd come outside, where he could speak without fear of an audience.

She agreed and he helped her on with her coat. They arrived at the entrance as he decided to make his move.

"Now then Mary, I feel a lot of love for you, but my instincts tell me - call it discernment if you like, that you are not being entirely truthful with me, what do you say?" Determined to pin down this femme fatale.

"I don't know what you mean Bill?" she asked innocently, but for a fleeting moment Bill noticed the expression on her face which she was quick to remove but Bill's 'schema' had already recorded it and affirmed his innermost fears.

"You're withholding something from me," he accused, looking her straight in the eyes.

She was unable to face his gaze and almost broke down there and then.

"I, I, it was Dinny's idea," she sobbed, "she and George concocted the scheme to involve you in the marketing of the bullion and my part was to seduce you into thinking, that I cared for you - enough to clinch the deal and then give you the heave - ho...but then I found myself really falling in love with you and I couldn't go through with it," she sobbed even more.

THE MACE GOES IN

"Just my luck," he cursed, "I knew there was something that didn't ring true," he determined angrily.

Mary had started to run away from him, and at first he was so upset that he didn't notice but then he realised just what she had said, and ran after her. He caught up with her almost breathless and put his hand on her shoulder, she looked up at him, her eyes all puffed up from crying. He was full of pity for her as she sobbed.

"I know that you won't have anything to do with me after tonight Bill, and I don't blame you. But I want you to know you're the most sincere person I have ever met and probably the only man I've ever loved. I just had to be honest with you, do you understand?"

"I understand all right, and I'm glad to say that you are the only woman I've ever loved too," he confessed, "and if we give it a chance, then maybe something will blossom out of our relationship," he assured, "but I can't do it if you're running away from me can I?" he reasoned, "shall we give it a try Mary?"

She looked up at him full of love for this man and took him in her arms with an embrace and hugged, then hugged him again.

He in turn returned the embrace, tenderly kissing her lips and face. He was overjoyed and she was crying tears of joy, as they made their way back to the car.

"I'll take you to the 'Oatsheaf' he told her, "you'll like it," he added.

Within minutes of driving along the country lanes, a quaint thatch roofed inn appeared through the windscreen. He stopped and parked the Morris and they entered inside.

"Rye and dry and a double scotch please?" he asked and the barmaid conformed. He gave her a pound and told her to have one herself. After picking up his change, both he and Mary occupied the chairs near the fire which was glowing with heat from its oaken logs and pieces of coal, Mary sipped her drink and Bill did the same.

"Happy?" he asked caringly.

"Oh yes, I am now."

The night drew on and 10.30 came suddenly with the shout of last orders.

Bill took and paid for a bottle of Scotch which he put under his arm as they were leaving. He drove her back to the private driveway, which led to the entrance of her lodge.

"Don't tell George or Dinny that you've blown the gaff love, it might be better if they were not to know, that way, things will remain the same won't they?"

"But of course, I can see the sense in that."

He kissed her goodnight adding," I'll see you late Monday afternoon love - that is if I don't get my daily business done before then. Don't forget to remind George that I'm giving him a ring before three on Monday, to accommodate his offer of samples."

She smiled and waved goodbye as he drove off.

As Mary climbed up the stairs to her room, she was aware of some conversation between her Father and Dinny: "What if he doesn't take the bait?" she queried.

"I know My Mary, and what she's capable of," he mouthed knowledgeably adding, "how d'you think we managed to sell all the washing machines? She was the one who swung it, sold every last one even during the bankruptcy, no don't worry about Mary, she's a Valesque!"

Mary entered Dinny's bedroom.

"Oh hello love," said George, I was just telling Dinny about your capabilities."

"I can't go through with it Dad" she choked.

"Of Course you can, just keep reeling him in. Promising him everything and he'll swing the deal for the ingots - and we'll all be on easy street," he mouthed convincingly or so he thought.

"It's too late for that, I've told him about the whole dastardly plot," she sobbed.

"Oh your idiot," screamed Dinny, "you've blown the gaff."

George was aghast, "You haven't - have you love?" he bleated, but the sad serious look on Mary's face spelt it out for him.

"Mary, what have you done…?"

He thought for a while and voiced "I suppose you realize that we'll all come unstuck about the bullion - he knows you know?"

"But how could he know George?" queried Dinny "you didn't tell him did you?"

"Oh do me a favour and give the man some credit for brains. He guessed it, he used to be an insurance assessor for back door recoveries - minus the police."

"He always struck me as a lovesick fool George," she smirked, winking, so Mary couldn't see.

"I love him Dad, and I want to spend the rest of my life with him."

"And so you shall," he smiled, putting his arms around her reassuringly, as only Dad's can.

Thank you Mary for being so generous with your truthfulness – yes, I do believe that we are actually going to pull it off.

Mary said, "Goodnight," and left them.

After Dinny had ensured she'd really gone George said, "Right Dinny, after the contact has been made, here's what you need to do…"

Just as he'd finished speaking, there came a knock on the door. It was Mary.

"Just to remind you Dad, Bill wants to ring you on Monday before three o'clock to get him the samples.

"Okie-dokie love, thank you, and goodnight, God Bless," he voiced, to signal her leaving.

It's Because I Love Him

CHAPTER 8

Zach answered the door of his flat just as Bill entered the key, "Oh thanks mate, did yer get yer business sorted out in Chester?" Bill asked in colloquial speech.

"Oh aye yeh, things are startin' ter look up. I'll tell yer what though Bill, I need a few more bangers buyin' ter do my deal, 'ow are yer fixed?" he queried.

"Can't you buy 'em - oh no, I remember now, yer said yer couldn't be involved in the sale. Aye okay Zach, I'll see what I can do," he promised.

"Twelve thirty still okay by you Bill, fer termorrer I mean?"

"Certainly Zach I'll be in 'The George' by that time ter pick yer up."

"No mate," said his friend, "it would be better if Lings don't see the Morris again!"

"Just as yer like Zach, I take it we'll go in your Bedford then?"

"I can see that you're on the ball Bill," complimented his friend.

"Ere Zach 'ave a drop o' Scotch."

"Don't mind if I do," mused Zach, picking up a pair of glasses.

"Say when Zach," asked Bill as he filled up the glass.

"Er…, when," said he as the liquid reached the top.

Bill awoke as the alarm sounded 6.00 am Monday morning. He crept round the flat to avoid waking Zach. Leaving a note which read: See you in 'The George' at twelve thirty Zach, don't worry if I'm a bit late, Bill.

THE MACE GOES IN

Beth opened the door to admit Bill and he entered.

"Have you eaten yet Bill?" she queried.

"Not yet."

"Then go into the kitchen, you can have Del's, I don't think he's hungry this morning, I'll see if he's awake yet," and she ascended the stairs.

Bill mouthed the bacon and eggs and chomped on the fried bread with great relish, washing the meal down with two cups of tea. Finally rolling a cigarette, lighting up, then taking long large drags to round it off.

Del came into the lounge with an ice-pack on his head, and seeing his condition, Bill decided he needed cheering up.

"Hiya Del," he greeted, "heard a joke last night, d'yer wanna 'ear it?"

Del looked green but tried to hide his true feelings with, "Go ahead Bill, let's 'ear it?"

Bill commences with: "Two fellas shipwrecked on a desert island, for no-one knows 'ow long, anyway their beards are eight inches long and they're both back to back leaning against the only tree, when one of 'em sez ter the other,

"What day is it Frank?"

The other replies with, "Monday Pete!"

Then Pete comments, "Strewth, 'ow I 'ates Mondays!"

"Ha har, get it? 'Ow I ates Mondays , heh hehe heh," laughs Bill.

Del was not amused. He just scowled at Bill replying, "If that's the best yer can do, yer'd be better shuttin' up!"

Del reached for the whisky bottle and added the last drains to a cup of tea, for a hair of the dog.

"Ah," he murmured at last, "that's better," glugging the contents down and adding, "come on Bill we'll 'ave ter get goin' if we're gonna do two trips."

Beth looked at the dirty dishes they'd both left with disgust, "Men, that's all they think about, filling their stomachs with a good meal with a cuppa, and a smoke to follow - damn that Billy, he leaves his ash everywhere, on the floor, in the sugar and even flicks it on my washing."

She took the dishes to the sink and turned on the hot water. Thinking aloud about their recent night of passion "That Del, he can be –so loving. He gives me so much pleasure, and I do love him dearly, oh why - why did he have to give up his law studies? He could have been a brilliant barrister with his brain."

What is it about all these good looking blokes, who always seem to take the easy way out? Mind you Beth (says me) I've got a lovely fellow in Del and he'll always be faithful to me?

She commenced singing in a part from 'Madam Butterfly,' and also some excerpts from 'Tosca' in her operatic singing voice, half believing she was back in Cardiff where she'd lived all those years ago, and allowed her tears to gush out at the end of each rendering.

She finished the dishes and left them to drain off, going upstairs to get into her working apparel for the 'Sweat Shop,' where she worked. She changed her blouse and skirt and put back on her comfortable old shoes, which she favoured for work.

Then after descending the stairs, prepared for herself, some lunch to eat there, putting them into her shoulder bag and saying aloud, "Oh what's it all for?" She almost sat down again, but then shouted, "It's because I love him," and off she went walking to work.

As they drove into Allbrights, the gateman handed Del a note to read as he feverishly picked up his office phone and spoke into it, "Yes Mr. Evans," he enlightened, "they're here now."

"Is that the chief engineer?" asked Del.

The man ignored him as he listened to his superior answering submissively, "Yes sir, he's to come in minus the wagon?"

Del looked perturbed and asked, "Why doesn't he want the wagon?"

"All I know is sir, that he'd like you to go to his office, alone, for a talk - ah, here comes the staff car now sir," he signalled, as the large Austin car pulled up from the direction of the factory.

Del looked as Bill and said in a quiet voice, "Not sure what's goin' on 'ere Bill, keep the wagon tickin' over."

Bill just nodded.

THE MACE GOES IN

"Would you get in please Mr. Bovis," called its driver.

Del broke into a cold sweat as he entered. The driver didn't state any more but started to move his vehicle in the direction of the chemical plant.

"Here we are sir," he motioned, as they drew up to Evans' office. The driver opened his door adding, "Glynne's waiting for you upstairs,"

Del's thoughts were full of falsehoods he could dream up as he climbed the steps. He reached the door, knocked and Evans called, "Come in Mr. Bovis."

Del entered and sat down, after greeting the man, "Good morning sir," but the man was silent.

After approximately one minute Evans put down his pen and spoke, "I've just been filling out a complaint to the police on behalf of yourself and your driver, along with Edward Shaw who incidentally won't be starting his afternoon shift today," he affirmed.

"But I don't understand?" bleated Del perplexed.

"Oh come now Mr. Bovis, I gave you credit for more intelligence!"

Del was quick with his explanation, "Has my driver not been going over the weighbridge?" he ployed, "I've told him a thousand times sir, but he thinks that if he's got twenty-eight drums on today then they'd weigh the same tomorrow. I'll get onto him right away and…"

"That's not the problem - and you know damned well!" screamed Evans petulantly. "D'you think I'm an absolute fool? How d'you think I got where I am today if I were to be taken in by every 'Diddy ky' who came into the plant? D'you realise, I've got two other scrap dealers in here working day and night - and paying good prices too for the metal they take out, £30 a ton not £2 that you offered."

"But what about the drums sir, I need them to complete my contract with Mr. Sayosot, at the docks?" he bleated.

"You conned your way into this plant - admit it Bovis! You're not taking drums at all."

With the change in Evans' attitude to resort to surnames, Del realised that the jig was up and the man meant business.

"Okay sir, you're dead right, I confess, I was under so much pressure from the Japanese dealers, that I had to resort to these underhand tactics, tell you what sir, I'll make restitution for everything that I've taken out. How much did you say they're paying you per ton, £30 is it? Well sir, I'm quite willing to almost double that offer for any heavy stuff you care to offer me," he pledged, in a bid to contrive another deal. "Yes sir, I can safely offer you £48 a ton and still make a profit," he promised, "how does that sound sir?" said Del generously.

Evans was still perturbed and Del perceived his un-surety and so added a tempting carrot.

"And I'll pay that very same price on all of the stuff which I've taken from you up to the present," saying, "Now I can't be fairer than that can I?" he remonstrated, raising his palms in a protesting fashion.

Evans was still perturbed. He arose from the desk looking defeated. It had been his plan to scare the living daylights out of this 'wolf in sheep's clothing' but instead of that, he somehow felt that this 'snake in the grass' was again taking him to the cleaners. He had to admit that the offer seemed genuine enough, and perhaps the man really did want to make restitution with his offer, but he still felt uneasy about the whole thing. After all he reasoned, no money had changed hands as yet and so clutching at straws he announced,

"What about payment, NOW, Mr. Bovis?"

"Now?" echoed Del, "Oh you mean right at this very minute, hmm, let me see…" he acted, "I wonder if my driver has my cheque book in his dashboard. D'you have a line to your weighbridge sir?" he asked.

"Of course," replied the man, only willing to help, "Here I'll get it for you."

He commenced to ring a number and make some orders to bring Bill to the phone and handed it to Del.

"Bill?" asked Del, "bring the blue coloured cheque book out of the cab Will you?"

"Right Del," he agreed and dashed off to the motor returning with the article, "I've got it Del, but I think the last cheque was paid out yesterday for these 900 x 20's for the wagon."

"What?" screamed Del in disgust, "and you didn't tell me, you crazy idiot, what am I going to do now? Oh, I've had it with you - you and that flamin' shell shock, you can't remember anything any more. That's it – you're sacked! Get your things out of my wagon and get out of my flippin' sight," he demanded.

"What's happening Mr. Bovis?"

Del became a lot happier at Evans, new attitude of calling him 'mister' as he turned to the man trying to gain sympathy,

"That fool of a man - he's let my cheque book run out of cheques…I'll kill him!"

"Don't worry Mr. Bovis, please don't sack him, I'm sure that he has your best interests at heart?"

"But what about payment sir?" pleaded Del.

"Oh I'm sure we can come to some agreement Mr. Bovis,' he assured pleasantly.

"Oh all right." Still holding the telephone Del spoke to the weighbridgeman, "Hello, yes will you put my driver back on please?" Del waited whilst Bill returned until, "Hello, yes, is that you Bill?

"Yes, it's me Del."

"Listen mate, I'm sorry I blew up like that. Put your stuff back in the motor, you're on the payroll again and wait there for further orders, alright mate?

"Yes," Bill replied,

"Good, well, I'll contact you soon, cheerio."

Del reached into his back pocket and pulled out his wallet. Opening it, he pulled out a wad of dirty oncers (pound notes) and counted out fifty of them handing it to the chief engineer whose eyes nearly popped out of his head.

"This is for you Mr. Evans, no, not payment for the scrap, but for your patience with me and to compensate you for all the trouble I've caused you in the past, now if you'll let me continue delivering to and from my boat via your weighbridge, I will get a cheque to you on a weekly basis in due course."

"Happy to do business with you Mr. Bovis," he relented," bye for now, see you soon."

Del smiled adding, "Until later then, goodbye sir."

"You owe me fifty quid Bill," Del told him, "I've just had blummin' murder in that' office. I had to leave 'im an' 'undred pound to pacify 'im. 'E was in an 'ell of a mood. We're lucky ter be still 'ere," he lied.

"Oh come on Del," laughed Bill.

"If yer don't believe me Bill, ask Eddie Shaw 'e's bin rumbled. Evans sacked 'im on the spot. I don't know 'ow we're goin' ter make it up to 'im, got any ideas?'

Bill reluctantly handed over the ten fivers he had in his pocket still unsure whether or not that he was being conned but nonetheless taken in by Del's sophism. Del took the money from him consoling him saying, "Yes Bill, now that we're partners we share everything - even the debts."

"Hey Del, is it okay to bring the wagon in now?"

"Yer, take it up to that copper compound Bill, we'll load up all the copper and cover it with drums," he directed.

Bill complied immediately and climbed into the cab as Del walked briskly away in the direction of the factory when he neared S62 marked 'corrosive,' he made a mental note of the whereabouts of all the empty drums and the quantity, then doubled back to the compound where Bill was busily loading up with painted copper tubing.

"Here mate, I'll give yer an 'and," he offered grabbing the piping and thrusting it onto the carrier. When the load was approximately two feet from the top Del signalled Bill to load no more, but to reverse the wagon to S62. Before Bill reached the area Del chose five drums and pulled them to the access road. Bill pulled up and jumped to the ground and followed suit with Del who by now was in the process of topping up the load with the blue chemical drums. He climbed onto the back shouting, "You chuck 'em ter me Bill, an' I'll stack 'em up uniform like."

His friend did so, and between them they had 'doctored' the load to make it appear as if it were merely a wagon load of drums. They then pulled up the tailboard and commenced to drive in the direction

THE MACE GOES IN

of the weighbridge. Bill left the drive seat: They then drove out, through the tunnel to Liverpool, to Cohen's yard.

'Seven ton 4 cwt' it read even without the presence of the driver. Del cornered Gus at the far end of the yard asking for a tonnage quote, after which Gus quipped,

"If I remember rightly Del, this motor weighs 2 ton 3 cwt, am, right?"

"No Gus, I've 'ad some alterations to it since then, 'ere Bill, chuck that metal off into number 2 copper and then drive back up 'ere," he commanded.

Bill complied and upon his return the tare weight read: 2 ton 3 cwt.

"Hmm, that makes it 3 ton 3 cwt of number 2 copper," Del affirmed, adding, "I notice the market's moved upward this morning Gus?" Del lied, hoping it would be so.

"How d'you know that Del, I mean I only received word about an hour ago. You must be pretty well informed!" accused he, "as a matter of fact, it's risen to £780 per ton, which makes your little load today worth mmmm..er 27 hundred plus 135, yes Del that comes to a total of £2835. Would a cheque be all right Del? I've a lot of payouts today and a figure like this takes away my small change, he explained.

"Gus, as much as we'd like to oblige, we'd rather not, we've got that many expenses ter pay out terday, we need the cash ter do it and yer know what it s like in our caper – it's cash or nothin'!" he stressed.

"I could always give you nothing," Gus joked, but seeing Del's face seething added, "Only kidding Del."

He went into the office and returned with crisp new £5 and £20 bundles,

"Here we are Del, all correct if you'd care to count it?" he offered.

Del took the money stating to Bill to count it, as he rolled two cigarettes.

After a quick check Bill assured him all was correct and they divided up the cash there and then.

"One more hit, and we'll call it a day Bill," Del told him handing a him a rolled cigarette.

They headed back to Cobden's with Bill stuffing his wallet with fivers and twenties.

Soon the all too familiar sign of 'Cobden and Allbright' appeared on the horizon and Bill steered the truck into the left lane. Taring off on the weighbridge, Bill made sure that they both stayed in the vehicle that tared off at 2 ton 3 cwt ¼ of which comprised Bill and Del's body weight also.

"Right Bill, I've had the okay from the weighman, get up to the compound - quick as yer can!" he directed.

Bill turned into the compound lane and finally into the scrap copper area, as Del jumped from the cab to organise the drum topping camouflage. Bill set about dropping the tailboard and struggled to organise the straighter pieces of tubing, less obtrusive, to facilitate a compact load.

"Where's that flippin' 'Lachicoe' gone?" he cursed, "'E's always missin' when there's work to do!"

Del was surprised to find Eddie Shaw at the factory 'hand balling' drums to the scrap area.

"What happened Ed, why aren't yer on yer winch, I thought yer 'ad a job fer life there?"

Eddie looked at him with contempt,

"Nearly lost me job through you - yeh, and I got threatened with a court job an' all."

Del completely oblivious to his pleas asked, "Can yer borrer the winch, there's some old copper flanges in the yard that're a bit 'eavy an…"

"Get lost yer scutching fool, if I listen ter you I'll end up in the nick," he Accused. Walking briskly away from this hard-faced fraudster, adding: "I'll kill 'im, I'll kill 'im!" he swore as he re-entered the factory.

"Some people," muttered Del bewildered, "I thought 'e wanted ter make a few bob?"

He hurried in the direction of where Eddie had deposited the drums and started to arrange them to enable a fast removal. He then rejoined Bill who was struggling to fill the wagon.

"Hiya Bill, listen, over in the far corner are some copper flanges what's come off them 9" copper pipes, now if yer like, I'll stack 'em all up," he offered helpfully.

"You do that Del, yeh, you do that small thing!" he voiced contemptuously.

"What's up Bill?" asked Del innocently.

"What's up - what's up?" he echoed, "What the 'ell d'yer think I've bin doin' while you've bin walkin' around with yer 'ands in yer pockets?"

"Now 'ang on a minute Bill…"

"No you 'ang on Del, partners aren't we, that means we share everythin' - right?"

"That's right mate."

"Then let's 'ave a vote of confidence in our partnership, an' you get yer flaming finger out when we come in ter this establishment."

"Look Bill," Del whispered, "someone's gorra sort them drums out ter top the load up. I meantersay, if that engineer knew we was nickin' 'is copper, there'd be 'ell to pay - now be REASONABLE?"

"Listen Del, all them drums are already stacked up, all we 'ave ter do is just pick 'em up - Eddie fixes it all, yer can't kid me," he challenged.

"Eddie? Evans nearly sacked 'im on the spot on Saturday, 'cos o' what 'e loaded with the winch didn't 'e?" Del indicated.

"Oh sugar, yer right, so 'e did, I'd fergotten about that, sorry mate, I jumped the gun a bit there."

"I should think so an' all," Del remarked, a hurt look across his face.

"Ave a fag Del, 'e y'are," he offered handing him his tin.

"Okay Bill thanks," thinking, you're so naive Bill.

"I'll go an' get these flanges Del while yer rollin' one," he determined, trying to appease the situation. He hurriedly turned the wagon around and backed it up to the far corner of the yard. He then dropped the tailboard and started to fling the heavy flanges into the hollows of the cache. Approximately 40 or so, he continued to load until the pile grew in height and he decided that there was just enough room remaining to camouflage the load, to appear as mere chemically filled drums.

"Got the lot mate!" he exclaimed, as he returned to Del, who was just stubbing his roll up.

"Let's get off then Bill," he suggested.

They started off down the access road, just falling short of the exit for a few drums, which Bill jammed upwards in plain sight to mock up the load and convince the weigh-man of its contents. Then driving over the scale both left the wagon to inform the man to weigh the gross.

"Eight ton four hundred weight, here's the ticket Mr. Bovis," he directed.

"Thanks a lot," said Del and they left.

As they put a mile or so behind them, it was then that Del dropped the bombshell.

"That's the last time we're goin' in there Bill."

"But, but, but…"

"Listen Bill, what d'yer think is goin' ter 'appen, when Evans finds out about the copper goin'?"

"Oh, I see what yer mean," said Bill ruefully.

"Ey Bill, guess what? We've got more on terday than we've 'ad at any time!" he estimated.

"'Ow much Del?' he asked hopefully.

"Well Bill, yer know our wagon is 2 ton 1 cwt?"

"Yeh?"

"Well mate, if yer subtract that from 8 ton 4 then yer get 6 ton 3," he enlightened gleefully.

"Wor about the tins then Del?"

"Do me a favour Bill, 'ow much do a few silly tins weigh? I'll bet we've gor at least 6 ton o' copper?" he speculated.

"Oh aye, yeh," Bill agreed with visions of a bankroll on his hip.

"Gor any change Bill?" he asked, "I used all mine last night gerrin' that carry-out."

Bill let go of the wheel with his left hand and fiddled about in his jacket but to no avail. Then he replaced his left and used his right to frisk his trousers and jacket, "Gorrit," he exclaimed, "ere y'are Del, 'eres a shilling."

They neared the approach to the Mersey Tunnel and Del lowered the window and paid the toll.

They entered the tunnel's traffic, which suddenly ground to a halt. "Oh sugar," cursed Bill, as he went down the gears, "what the 'ell's up now?" he voiced exasperated.

Sounds of cries and shouts filled the air and there appeared a knock on the nearside door. Del opened it, looked down and saw a frightened girl whimpering.

"What's up queen?" he asked.

"It's 'im," she pointed toward the direction of Liverpool, "E's tryin' ter kill me!" she sobbed.

"Ere girl, gerrin the motor, I'll look after yer - won't we Bill?" assured Del, as he took her arm pulling her into the cab.

She was about twenty years old and well dressed but very nervous.

"Yer askin' fer a load o' trouble Del," Bill exhorted.

Just then two men came running up from the Tunnel.

"Get yer 'ead down luv, I don't like the look o' these two" Del warned.

She complied and the men neared with one of them shouting breathlessly, "Seen a dark haired bird running past mate?"

"No I ain't," lied Bill.

The man ran on with his friend close behind. The traffic jam had started to move and Bill pulled away. Ahead a policeman was directing the inside lane to join the middle traffic, to avoid collision with the single-decker bus which had turned over on its side.

"Phew," breathed Bill, "never thought we'd get out o' that jam. Who are yer girl, an' why did dem fellers want yer so badly?"

"It's a long story but I'll try to tell it to yer," she replied. "I've just come into a fortune in property, an' have 'eard the will made out, makin' me sole beneficiary. Those two fellers have been made my guardians, and because they are related to me, upon my death could stand ter gain all of the inheritance what my Grandad's just left me," she cried convincingly.

"Don't worry luv, I'll look after yer, listen we've just gorra weigh this lot in, an' then we'll see yer all right - won't we Bill?" he assured, looking at his driver who was completely oblivious to Del's comments.

"Oh, thank you - you're so masterful and kind," she cooed appreciably, snuggling up to Del filling him with joy. He was still on cloud nine when the '400 Group' of companies loomed up ahead.

"Ere we are Del, 'ad she berra jump out before we go in? Yer, know what Gus is like about the weight!" he stressed.

"Oh aye yeh, listen luv, wait till we get ter the road scale then Jump out. I'll say yer name's Bovis - that's me, yer can say I'm yer dad, gorrit?" he directed. "Okay Del," she agreed and complied as they approached the scale.

"8 ton 2 cwt," voiced the weighbridgeman.

"Eh, are yer sure?" pleaded Del, "I've just bin weighed at more than 2 cwt over that."

"Well Mr. Bovis, 'ave a look fer yerself." offered the man.

"Vot's der problem here Cecil?" boomed Gus's voice.

"No problem boss, Mr. Bovis is just takin' 'is load in aren't yer Del?" winked he.

"Er, yeh, hiya Gus, cast yer beady eyes on this lot!" Del beamed with pride. Gus climbed up over the wagon side replying:

"Oy yoy yoy, Del vot a load is zis? I haven't seen copper flanges for years. I'll bet zis is a 'mace'?" he predicted.

"Ha ha ha ha, yer know Bill, yer can't kid old Gus," he mused, "by the way Gus, what are yer payin' fer copper terday?"

Gus's face dropped, 'Hmm...you'll not like it Del," he warned with a serious look.

"Well, 'ow much?" Del repeated worriedly.

"You remember on Saturday how it went up ter £700 per ton, well since then the dockers have halted their strike, and they came back in," he said sadly.

"Yes?" voiced Del expectantly.

"Well mate, then a miracle happened."

"A miracle?" piped Del.

"Yeh a miracle," Gus affirmed," some silly beggar of a docker decided to lift the overtime ban in Ellesmere port and it's caused the Liverpool men who were sacked at the start of the strike - who stopped unloading - were the original cause, and they want them re-

THE MACE GOES IN

instated before anything else."

"Well where does that leave us Gus?" queried Del worriedly.

"Well Del, flippin' well 'ome and dry!" he exclaimed, "because Everton Refineries could get supplies, the copper had dropped to an all time low until last night after the strike but now the strike's back on, and it doesn't look like the National Dock and Labour Board are going to give in. Consequently the bullion buyers have shoved the market sky high and it's now out-priced itself." he confirmed.

"Ow much – 'ow much Gus?" egged Del impatiently. "Eleven hundred I can pay per ton mate," he replied.

"Elev, elev, eleven 'undred did yer say?" Del's blood pressure went up and up. Bill's eyes nearly popped out of his head.

"Yes, that's right mate, eleven hundred a ton," Gus repeated. "Now then," he commanded, "take the drums over to the number 6 container and return back here to re-weigh the load."

Bill drove the wagon toward the skip and complied with the order. After removing the drums he drove back to the scale.

"Eight ton one half hundred weight," shouted the weighbridgeman.

"Right mate," said Bill turning to Gus who was working on some paper sheets, "where to?"

"Oh, I'll come with you Bill," he instructed, climbing alongside Del who had just re-entered the cab.

"Turn over to the left," pointed Gus, "now, pull alongside this container 4 and start throwing the flanges off. Put the lighter copper in this other one," he indicated.

Del and Bill hurriedly did his bidding and soon were down to the copper pipes' removal and had finally unloaded. The whole operation lasting only twenty minutes or so.

"Now back to the scale Bill," Gus pointed.

Bill drove the wagon back to be met with, 'Two ton even Bill," from the weighman.

"That gives you 6 tons 1 half a hundred weight - it's getting better all the time,"

"Let's see now 6 x 11 hundred, hmm, £6,600 to the good mate," he enthused.

"Not fergettin' the 'alf an 'undred weight eh mate?"

Gus's face dropped in false pretence, "Oh aye yeh, I'd forgotten about that mate, Er, I'll give it you now," he assured him.

Del was so excited at the prospect of the fortune in cash he was to receive; his legs went like jelly as he attempted to walk to the office.

Bill perceived his condition and jumped down from the cab girthing Del's shoulders with his hands, "Are yer all right mate?" he queried.

"'Er, yeh Bill, I think I've had a funny turn," holding his forehead.

"I've got yer mate, lean on me and walk slowly. No sense in doin' yerself an injury. We've got all day mate," he encouraged.

They went into the office as Gus drew the cash from the safe.

"Here we are Del, would you sign your monica on the dotted line mate?"

Del scrawled his name and dropped the pen.

"£6,655 pound, ten shilling, it's all there if you'd care to check it. Here Bill, give Del a hand," he called to him at the door and pointed to the cash.

"Right," he agreed and commenced to lick his index finger and check the £20 notes.

"Three thousand here Del, what 'ave you got?" he asked.

"I've got the same Bill, what's that load of loose stuff?"

Bill pounced on the fivers and tenners and started to count the total,

"Six 'undred and er, fifty 5,6,7. Yeh, six 'undred and fifty five quid 'ere."

"Hm, that makes it a total of six thousand six 'undred and fifty five quid.

That's three thousand, three 'undred and twenty seven pounds and ten shillin' each.

Not bad for a mornin's work eh Gus?" he mused, handing Del his share before he could argue.

Bill stuffed the money in all of his trouser pockets and with a pleasant gesture took Gus's hand shaking it saying, "A pleasure to do business with you - well, we've gorra go. Are yer ready Del, I've gorra get ter the tailors for a fitting," he lied.

"Wish I had the money to go and buy a suit - just like that," Gus pleaded.

"Ha ha ha ha, yer breakin' me 'eart mate," Bill remonstrated adding, "We've got the cash and you've got the metal. I wish I was fifty grand behind yer!"

Del was still in a daze, when suddenly he realised just what a partnership meant, as he pondered...

Here was Bill with an equal share of the spoils and I haven't even had the chance ter mace 'im out of 'is share yet, he regretted, as he climbed back into the cab. His money, he put safely away into the cash box in the dash board and put his hand into his pocket for his wallet, to discover how much he could put there to deceive Beth. It wasn't there. "Funny," he thought, "could have sworn I put it there."

Bill started the engine and drove to the outer gate commenting, "Where's that Judy gone Del?"

"What judy - oh her," he replied with recollection.

"She's not 'ere Del," stated Bill.

"She's not 'ere, and neither is my flamin' wallet," fumed he.

Bill didn't say anything, he looked the other way giving a silent chuckle.

"Connivin' birds yer can't trust 'em. After me takin' 'er in away from them blokes an' all," he said angrily, "you said I'd 'ave a load o' trouble, why didn't I listen to yer?"

"Don't worry Del, yer can get another wallet, and yer can get a duplicate license an' all."

"No no Bill, I 'ad a load o' money in there," he moaned.

"But I thought yer told me yer'ad nuthin' this mornin'?" he quizzed.

"Er, it was the rates I had ter pay Bill," he reasoned, his face colouring up.

"Never mind mate, it could o' bin worse, I meantersay if she was still 'ere, she might o' took yer three grand." he jibed.

"Perish the flippin' thought Bill, yer right, if ever I get my 'ead turned by another pretty face mate, give me a good kick will yer? I reckon I was lucky ter ger away so lightly," he breathed with relief. Bill drove the wagon out and Del said, "Put the radio on mate see 'ow the test is progressing."

"Now for the news, England cricket has taken a turn for the worst, two out for a duck and …"

"Two out for a duck?" squealed Bill.

"Shurrup, I can't 'ear a word 'e's sayin'?"

"The escape of the twelve women prisoners from Southport Prison still goes on, they've been at large for an hour at present and the police expect to locate them soon. Here's a spokesman for Lancashire Constabulary," voiced the newscaster.

A roving reporter held the mike to the spokesman who was speaking, "And since the tunnel incident we have located eleven up to now and expect to find Jane Ashton before the day's through. She can't get far, she has no money…"

"No money, no money?" screamed Del, silly idiots those coppers - they'll never catch 'er now, not since she's got my 'undred and forty two quid. No chance of that, she's probably 'alfway to China by now."

"And that concludes the news for the mid-day," stated the announcer.

"Turn the bloomin' thing off Bill."

Soon they were moving through the tunnel and then paying the toll at the other side.

They arrived back at 'The George' and Bill parked the motor facing the building to hide the excise license. Although it was not out of date, he'd decided that if people saw the wagon always parked in that position then they wouldn't probe further to inspect it's tax disc.

"I'll see yer termorrer then Del," Bill told him, "cheerio Del."

"Tarah Bill," said he - making a bee line for Peter Strate's whose running commentary relay of Cheltenham could be heard from the wagon.

Bill headed back to Del's house and retrieved his car and then left in time to catch Zach who was just leaving his council flat as he arrived home.

21 Day Clause

CHAPTER 9

"I'd given yer up fer lost Bill," Zach criticised, "I've bin waitin' 'ere fer an 'our and an 'alf."

"I'm sorry mate, I couldn't get away, the tunnel was choc-a-bloc, anyway I'm 'ere now an' ready ter go," he assured him.

"Right then, let's get started, you follow me down in my work bus whilst I take the 'Velox' back to Lings." he directed.

"Okay Zach, are these the keys?" he asked, picking up the key-ring. His friend nodded and they both left the flat.

Zach turned into Lings and Bill drove into the 'Rural Soak' car-park that ran alongside it. Quickly he locked the Bedford and joined his pal, who was still sitting in the Velox in the forecourt of Lings. Bill opened the passenger side and Zach proceeded to drive the car to the entrance.

"Now, whatever I do or say Bill, I want you to back me up-okay?" he posed.

"Right yer ar Zach" he agreed.

Zach stepped out of the Vauxhall, and Bill followed him into the sales office.

"I want you to come outside, you need to hear this," he assured the manager who looked puzzled, but complied with his request. Bill looked the other way in case the manager recognised him.

Zach followed the manager who after five minutes or so came back into the building.

"No, I'm sorry Mr. Bleen it's just not possible, I mean, you've only had the car what - three days and the big ends are all rattling? Well, I can tell you sir, that the car was perfectly all right when you took it from here, why? I even had one of our boys in the garage check it out that very day you bought it. No, I'm sorry sir, but you surely can't hold us responsible for that particular damage sir."

"But it's rattling terribly - I mean you can hear it from here, listen?" pleaded Zach.

Sure enough, Harry could hear that tell tale banging, even from the saleroom.

Meanwhile, Bill just stood looking out of the window saying nothing, trying not to be recognised.

"No sir!" the Harry was adamant, "I'm not being held accountable for that," he determined adding, "p'rhaps you've run it without oil sir?"

"It's full of oil, have your fellas check it," challenged Zach.

The manager by now was really perplexed and called out a loud, "Artie, go and check his dip-stick will you?" and the mechanic agreed.

Because the engine was running this took longer than they first thought, which gave Zach his opportunity to pile it on.

"Disgraceful, that's what it is," he pleaded, "you go and buy a car in good faith and the next thing you know is you're being taken to the cleaners…There ought to be a law about things like that," voiced he, "I meantersay, blah Blah…"

The mechanic returned with a worried look on his face.

"Well?" demanded his boss.

It a very quiet voice the mechanic explained, "It's absolutely full of what looks like Castrol XL chief, I mean I can't honestly understand why it's banging, I mean it's not even advanced on the ignition?" he stressed. "It's a complete mystery to me?"

"What's happening?" Zach demanded, unsure of what they were whispering about.

"Mr. Bleen could you come into the office please?" requested the man.

"Not until you give me something definite about fulfilling your responsibility in all of this," he threatened.

Zach looked over for support from Bill, but Bill just put his hand up to the side of his faced and shrugged his shoulders and turned away to carry on looking out of the window.

"My responsibility, now look here, you can't even think that the condition of your car is our fault?"

"Be that as the case may be," stressed Zach, "It's all a matter of what you're going to do, to resolve it!"

"But it's not our responsibility," he reasoned.

"Isn't there a clause in any H.P. agreement which states that the purchaser - provided he returns the unsatisfactory article within 21 days - if it's not up to standard - then he can demand his money back?" Zach quizzed.

"Oh no sir, we couldn't stay in business implementing something like that," he indicated.

"Even so, I think that I'm right," said Zach insistently. "Look at our HP agreement - the small print, I think you'll find I'm right?"

"But you haven't received your agreement yet, the HP people couldn't have dealt with you that quickly?" he probed.

"I was referring to the copy you gave me last week," said Zach, "the twenty one day clause? Don't let's beat about the bush whether or not I've received my forms, what are you going to do about putting the car right?"

"We can't, I mean it's not - I mean, it would cost a small fortune to fix it sir - be reasonable? I'll tell you what, you pay for the cost of the parts, and we'll fix them on free of charge. I can't be any fairer than that can I?"

"I haven't got any money for this, I told you my circumstances last week if you remember. No, this is just not good enough, I demand that you nullify our agreement as of today!"

"But but btt…"

"And give me my old Morris back, strikes me that I wouldn't have had any trouble if I'd stuck to the old girl, she'd start - no problem, and never had any rattles at all," he argued.

By now, Zach had given up on Bill's lack of support and thought, "I'll give him what for after all this is done."

The manager looked sick, his face was the colour of a boiled army blanket. He quickly took stock of himself with: "Well sir, I'm sorry we can't possibly do that due to your 'Morris' being sold for scrap, however, it was really only worth about £5 wasn't it?" he taunted, peeling off a five pound note from his wallet.

"Oh no - that's not what the agreement states!" Zach said firmly.

"You couldn't hold me to that sir, it was only on paper wasn't it? I'll tell you what, I'll give you fifteen pounds for your trouble," he offered concluding, "it wasn't even worth that, but I feel in a generous mood today."

"Then if that's the case, add another £145 pounds to your offer and I'll be satisfied. It's either that or you get me my Morris back."

The manager's mouth was agape. For a while he just stood there open mouthed and then taking control he angrily peeled off the additional fivers until they totalled £160.

"I need a signature on a receipt," he demanded.

"Listen mate," Zach threatened, taking the money from him, "I didn't ask you for one, because you've got my blummin' car, which you've obviously sold for much more than you paid me, so we'll call it quits on this. Now think yourself lucky that you've still got all of your teeth, while I'm still in a good mood!"

The manager offered a slight smile to hide his embarrassment saying, "I'm truly sorry sir. Accidents can happen can't they?" And after plucking up courage asked in a meek voice, "Could you give me the log-book please sir? I need it for the file."

Zach reached into his inside pocket giving the documents to the frightened man.

"Thank your sir, well, I'll bid you farewell," he voiced graciously, quickening his pace away from Zach.

Bill came out into the forecourt hot on Zach's heels and he entered the Bedford in the pub car park, opening the passenger door for Zach who got in.

"Thanks for all yer support Bill, I thought I was goin' ter lose out there," he voiced with contempt.

"Now 'ang on Zach," he reasoned, "what could I possibly do - the feller knew me, I was the one who bought the Morris - remember?"

"Oh aye yeh, I'd forgotten about that, sheesh, imagine me slippin'

THE MACE GOES IN

up like that - I could've blown the whole deal couldn't I?" he agreed. "Anyway mate, what did yer think o' me performance?" he asked with pride.

"It wasn't bad mate," Bill complimented, "especially when you pulled that stroke about the twenty one days clause, well, that was pure genius, is this 'ow yer make yer livin' then - just connin' garages?"

"The very same."

"But why Zach, you've got brains to take you places - to do things, you could do much better than this, I mean it's so risky isn't it?" Bill argued.

"Don't knock it mate, where would I get such a challenge to my professional ability? I get a free car ter run around in ter go places and I get a test of nerves in the bargain. Bill, I thrive on the excitement of all this – don't you see? Now, I'll bet that you don't do a great deal of honest toil - do you?" he fished, "why, because there's no future in it is there? I mean how many jobs have you had since Nicosia, that have paid a good livin'?" he reasoned.

"I see what yer mean Zach, I've gorra agree with yer there, although, I sometimes yearn ter be in a regular job, with everythin' that goes with it - yer know, a mortgage, a small car, kids ter come 'ome to an' the love of a good w..."

"Oh perish the thought Bill, yer'll 'ave me cryin' soon, ha ha har," he retorted. "Yer've gorra admit Bill, that this little fiddle is a good 'un and it's legal too," he favoured, "anyway mate, consider the Morris yours an' 'ere's a tenner fer yer trouble, I think I'll be goin' now ter the next county, but we'll go back ter yer flat first ter collect me things," he directed.

An hour later saw Bill waving to Zach who promised to keep in touch somehow, irrespective of his circumstances.

After a change of clothes Bill was just in time to catch the bank in Riverton before it closed to deposit his three thousand pounds worth of twenties which was entered into his account by the teller whose eyes popped almost out at the sum, as Bill pulled it from every pocket.

"Won the pools 'ave we sir?"

"Naw, me week's takings from the market," lied Bill, who was puffing a Churchill cigar.

George Leadbetter the manager arrived on the scene and called Bill in through the side door,

"Could you follow me sir?" asked the man.

Bill complied; colouring up wondering what was amiss.

"Sit down sir, you may be wondering what all this is about, well p'rhaps I'd be better saying to you, have you ever considered a credit account?"

"No, not really," Bill replied, "I don't really get that much on the markets these days," he stressed realising the furore he had caused with the large sum he'd brought in. "Today's example was merely a killing on the shifting prices. I happened to be in the know about pepper prices, when all that trouble in India started. I bought everything I could from anyone who was vaguely connected to the trade and was able to secure two whole tons of the stuff and being in the right place at the appropriate time, I was able to sell it at a right old profit too. Yes, being in the know can be the difference in riches or bankruptcy," he lied, tongue in cheek.

"Amazing," breathed the manager in awe, "Do you see a shift in any other markets Mr. Foggit?" he asked meekly, completely taken in.

"Yes, there is one!"

"Would you care to share it with me?"

"Hmm, you're a fair man, yes, if I were you, I'd invest in copper bullion shares as soon as you can - but," he warned, "keep your eye on the docks' strike, 'cos if there's any break in the deadlock then it could send prices plummeting," he assured him.

"But of course, thank you very much Mr. Foggit," he replied, "Cigar?" he offered with the open box, "help yourself to the brandy," leaving Bill with the bottle as he almost ran to the outer phone. Feverishly he barked orders into the mouth piece as he was connected, "Yes, that's right, I want 55 shares in Everton Refineries until further notice." he waited a while, until he could hear the recipient reply "£16,500 er, yes, do it, right away. Thank you, speak to you tomorrow, goodbye,"

He rushed back into his office where Bill was silently drinking his health.

"Mr. Foggit, would you like to invest yourself or have you made prior arrangements, oh no, how silly of me, you'd have already been in touch with your broker in the city wouldn't you?" he probed.

"Actually no, I haven't contacted him yet."

"Oh then, there's still time for you to phone in, the stockbrokers don't close until five, would you like me to advise him for you?"

"Thanks, but not at this time, I need all the cash flow I can get to pay for my stock. I'm cleaned right out! Well Mr. Leadbetter thanks for the cognac and cigar, most enjoyable," he smiled.

"Thank you sir for that hot tip you gave me," drooled the manager appreciably. "Feel free to drop in any time."

Bill left the bank with, "Well cheerio Mr. Leadbetter," and hurried to his car. He glanced at his watch, 4.00 pm, "Hmmm, I'll be just in time," he thought. He drove the car toward the A41 leaving Riverton far behind and soon he approached Eastham Woods at the rear of the day college.

Anthony Johnson was pacing impatiently up and down the car park, when suddenly he spotted Bill's approach.

"Ah Bill," he voiced in recognition.

"Hiya Mal," he replied, "'ow are yeh - all right?"

"Let's sit in my car mate? And you can clue me in on this lot."

"No mate, I'd rather you hear it from me, as we walk across the Heath," he indicated. Bill complimented himself for this approach, although he'd known Mal for many years, he had his reasons for not trusting him too much and the possibility of a taped conversation was always a danger in an unfamiliar car.

"Now look Bill, I didn't come here for a walk through the woods…"

"D'you want in on this Mal - or aren't yer bothered?" challenged Bill.

"No no, it's not that Bill, yer've got the wrong end of the stick, we're… I'm interested, really I am!" he pleaded.

"I'm disappointed in you Mal, who've yer bin talkin' to on this?"

"What, who, nobody, I swear it Bill. I 'aven't told a soul!" he emphasised, waving his arms about frantically.

Bill picked him up by the Scruff of his neck and repeated, "Who've yer told MAL?" loudly enough to instil fear into the man.

"You're choking me – cough, cough," he spluttered.

Bill took Mal's collar and replied as he exerted pressure around his neck, "Blimmin' sell out, that's what it is, isn't it, isn't it?"

"Bill, Bill! I had to tell my boss...to get the authority for a cash transfer - that's all mate, honestly," he pleaded.

"How much does he know about me then?"

"Nothing, nothing at all, I swear. Let me tell you what's transpired since Saturday," he cried when Bill relaxed his hold. As Mal related, so Bill released him.

"....And that's about the strength of it Bill."

"So, you need a sample of each ingot to verify its existence eh?" Bill queried.

"Yes Bill, if you could contact Valesque as soon as possible to provide the samples, we can do business!" he affirmed.

"But a wait a minute Mal all of this just doesn't ring true," he challenged.

"In what way Bill?"

"Well, what fool of an insurance company is goin' ter hand over millions of pounds for just mere samples?" he quizzed.

"Oh that's nothing to worry about Bill," he assured, "Ranson has given me authority to inspect and assess the worth of the main cache."

"Oh, I see," said Bill, feeling pretty foolish for his naivety, "Mind you Mal, you'll have to work through me in all of the dealings you know."

"That is expected Bill, I wouldn't want it any other way. Hmm, five o'clock already, by the way, when are you contacting your friend - or have you already done that?" he probed.

"Flamin' hell, that's torn it - I promised to ring at three to..."

"Three o'clock?" Mal repeated.

"Got to go Mal, listen, those terms are fine, I'll get back to you on this. I'll call you at 'ome sometime," he promised, and with that he turned on his heel and was gone.

THE MACE GOES IN

Mary's home appeared on the landscape and he stopped the Morris a few houses away at the phone box. Feverishly he selected the numbers and heard the dialling tone.

"Hello, 46290 here," sounded Mary's voice.

"Mary? It's Bill here."

"Oh hello love, how are you?" she asked lovingly.

"Mary is George there?" he requested.

"Yes, daddy's right here love - did you want to speak to him?"

"Put him on love," he added. George lifted the receiver,

"That you Bill, I thought you were ringing at three?" he accused.

"Terribly sorry George, I was unavoidably detained. Listen can I come around and talk things over?" he pleaded.

"Where are you now Bill?"

"I'm only around the corner, but I thought it best to ring first and apologise for being late."

"I'll get Dinny to put the kettle on Bill if you'd like to come up," he invited.

"Right George, I'll be right over," he assured him.

He walked around the rear of the house, where George greeted him with, "One lump or two Bill?" handing him a cup of tea.

"Two please George."

George complied and dropped them in. Bill sat at the outside cast iron table and George joined him.

"Right mate, now this is the plan. I need a sample of each ingot, that is; a copper banana, a bronze shot, a tin ingot and finally a silver ingot and I need them all as soon as possible," he determined.

"Who's the settlement officer, and is it him that I deal with?" he queried.

Bill felt threatened by this latest ploy by George.

"No, you work through me as a mediator and I'll ensure that you get a square deal," he determined, "this is the situation; firstly you get hold of the ingots - by the way, how long d'you think this would take you?"

"Er, about six hours tomorrow. Hang on - no, I mean," he whispered to himself, locked in reasoning things out - "Yes Bill, if I go tonight, I could get them for tomorrow morning," he affirmed.

"Tuesday, are you sure?"

"No, don't worry, Bill, I'll deliver the goods on the nose! Now then, what time d'you think you can be here to collect?"

"Can I use your blower George, I'll let you know right now?" And he rang Malcolm Johnson who picked up his phone.

"That you Mal?"

"Yes it's me mate."

"Listen, can you?"

"Okay George it's all set, I'll be around tomorrow at a place of your choosing, - now then, in the cause of security, don't tell me where, until you're actually ready to hand the stuff over, this way nobody gets to know anything about your whereabouts, to slap an injunction on you should the case arise. You know what these Special Branch boys are like, once they get their hooks into you," he warned.

"Too 'flippin' true Bill, I've had too many of 'em visiting me at the nick, not to know what you're on about."

"Righto then George, I'll leave it with you then till some time tomorrow. By the way, please try to make it after one o'clock, that way it won't, get in the way of normal business procedure."

"Okay Bill, you're the boss," he affirmed and left him outside, just as Mary was leaving the back door.

"Have you two finished yet? - Oh you have," she mused, "about time too. Right Bill, where are we off to tonight?"

"Can I use your bathroom to freshen up Mary?" he gave a great yawn as he asked.

"Of course you can, you can have a lie down in the spare bedroom too - you poor dear, you look worn out," she invited.

"You're very kind luv, are you sure I'm not putting you to a load of trouble?" he asked caringly.

"Not at all, come on I'll show you where it is," leading him by the hand up the stairs.

They arrived at the head of the second set of stairs and she led him into a medium sized bedroom and immediately began adorning the mattress of the double bed with sheets and blankets.

"There we are," she said finally, "now if you'll give me your clothes, I'll hang them in the wardrobe." Detecting his embarrassment she added, "Oh don't worry Bill, you won't offend me, I used to be a nurse in the WRAC."

Bill became re-assured by her revelation commenting, "I'll bet all your patients fancied you?"

She smiled as he commenced to disrobe and handed her his suit and shirt. Reduced to his -Y-fronts, he climbed into the sheets and lay down as Mary put his apparel on hangers. She then came and lay alongside him and began to run her fingers through his hair, but it was too late; Bill was already in the land of nod.

She found Bill hard to awaken where he had slept until 8.30 pm.

Bill had never experienced sleeping so well. He finally did reach consciousness as she offered him a cup of coffee, which he sat up and drank.

"Eat those sandwiches Bill, Dinny made them especially for you - she thought you may be hungry after such a hectic day."

"What time is it?" he asked between bites.

"Oh gosh - look, it's nearly ten to nine Bill, we'll have to move if we're going out!"

Bill flew out of bed whispering, "Which way to the bathroom luv?"

"Directly opposite Bill," she said smiling.

He grabbed his clothes from the hangers and bolted into the small bathroom. After giving himself a thorough wash he located a safety razor, which he commenced to use after first lathering his face. Finally, he smelt fresh and clean once more and donned his clothes. His throat was being cut by his shirt collar, so he slackened the top button noticing it was not his shirt. At first he felt quite honoured that Mary could think of his welfare, but later felt threatened, that perhaps he was being manipulated somewhat?

He heard the front door go and out of curiosity re-entered the bedroom to catch a glimpse of who was leaving. His innermost suspicion was proved right. It was George who eyed the area furtively, glancing back to see if he was being observed. Bill instinctively drew away from the window although he was three stories up without even the remotest chance of being discovered, he didn't want to 'queer his pitch.'

"Are you ready then Bill?" sounded her voice.

"Be right with you love," removing his comb to groom his hair. "Right," he said finally, "off we go then."

He took her hand as they descended the two flights of stairs and passed through the front door.

"Where to love?" he quizzed.

"I'm not sure Bill, how about you? Not St Clairs?" she mouthed hinting excitedly.

"The very same," he concurred, "and I suggest we partake of a couple of lobsters for starters...."

Later that night saw Bill and Mary sharing the same house in Bromborough, upon where they had slept soundly into the early hours of the morning.

On Tuesday morning they both awoke at the same time and she immediately planted a kiss on his cheek whispering, "Good morning love, isn't it a glorious day?"

"Hell, look at the time, it's 10-30 am!" he fumed, "I'll have to dash Mary," he spoke, leaving the bed and heading for the bathroom.

Between his shower and brushing his teeth he continued his conversation and enlightened Mary of the latest happenings.

"So - that's where Daddy went?" she assumed knowingly, adding, "I knew he was up to something yesterday after he left you, by the way he was acting so suspiciously."

Finally Bill was satisfied with his appearance and left the bathroom accompanying her along the landing saying,

"Look love, I've really got to go now - listen I'll call you later and you can let me know if George is back with the samples? Well," he kissed her lips, "see you then, bye." He descended the stairs and left.

Glisten Like Gold

CHAPTER 10

"Where the 'ell 'ave yer bin? I've bin 'ere since seven!" Del demanded aggressively.

"Sorry mate, couldn't ger away - these women, yer can't leave 'em without tears," he explained, adopting his colloquial tongue.

"Yer won't get 'itched - that's your problem, p'rhaps then yer'd be able ter gerrup earlier? Anyway Bill we've gorra be at 'Swinburns' the brass millers before twelve o'clock, so we'd berra be goin' mate. I'll get the Austin A60 out of the garage," he said urgently

"The car Del, what's wrong wi' the wagon?" Bill said looking puzzled.

"Ave yer got no sense Bill, we've gorra negotiate the deal first 'aven't we?"

"O' aye yeh," Bill agreed, cursing himself for his stupidity. "Let's go then mate."

"You foller in the wagon Bill," he indicated.

"But, I don't get yer?" queried Bill, "I mean..."

"Listen Bill, just do as yer told will yer, I'll explain it when we get there."

With haste, they arrived in New Ferry and were soon outside 'Swinburns'. Del signalled Bill to stop and left his car to elucidate.

"....So you see Bill, that's what I need...," he added finally.

"Okay mate," Bill concurred, locking up the cab and entering Del's car, as his friend turned the key and drove into the factory yard.

Del gave the office door a gentle rap and waited for the reply, which came from an office girl, whose face appeared at the side window with, "Can I help you sir?"

"Mr. Parker's expecting me."

"I'll get him for you sir." She ventured into the factory returning with the foreman.

"It's me 'Arry, yer remember, I told yer I was comin' terday?" Del said smiling.

"Er, I 'aven't add a chance ter, 'ang on… you can go now Collette," he instructed the girl, who was listening to the conversation.

"Right Del," he resumed, happy at the girl's departure, "if yer can foller me, I'll show yer where the stuff is."

"But I thought you said…"

"Oh that was for Collette's benefit, now then if yer'll foller me out ter the skip Del?"

Del and Bill followed him across the factory floor, when Parker stopped suddenly, then spoke to a well dressed man saying: "Mr. Swinburn sir, this is that new dealer I told you about to replace Frankie Baines."

"Baines?" queried the young man.

"Yes sir - you know, the one who was cheating us on the weight!" he stressed.

"Oh that fellow," he retorted, "not that nice chap who used to leave the cigars?" he asked.

"That's him," said Parker adding, "no wonder he could afford the cigars sir."

"Yes, no wonder," agreed his boss, "I'll have to tell Pater about the change. Better leave me your name my man."

Del gave him a card headed; Vandel Bovis & Partner, Machine Dismantlers.

"So this is you Mr. Bovis?" he queried, pointing to the name.

"Yes sir, I've been in the industry since the end of the war."

"Right then, go with Mr. Parker, he will show you just where the scrap is located."

Del nodded and followed the foreman with Bill trailing along. An opening at the end of the plant revealed a large rusty skip containing mounds of brass swarf, which to Del's eyes glistened like gold.

"Oh I see 'Arry - this is it eh?" pointing at the ship.

"Is there any more besides this?" asked Bill.

"Around the corner we have another skip but it's got a mixture of both in it, if you'd care to take a look Bill - you too Del," he indicated.

They all proceeded around the building to encounter an even larger skip, which was over flowing with both brass and stainless steel turnoffs which were a tangled mess.

"'Baines' refused to take this away because it was mixed. Can you make me an offer on it Del?" he pleaded, "Mr. Swinburn junior's kicking up holy hell, because the skip's on hire an' costin' a fortune."

"I'll give yer a price mate, don't worry, 'course it will only be for 'stainless' y'know, I'd 'aver ter employ a couple o' fellas ter sort it out."

"That'd be fine Del, 'is nibs'll be made up with that," he breathed, relieved at the thought.

"About shiftin' it, when d'yer wan' us ter come an' gerrit?" Bill piped.

"Now's as good a time as any mate, 'ave, yer got yer wagon 'andy…no, that's a stupid question isn't it? If I remember rightly, Del comes in ter negotiate in 'is suit and Bill follers through with the wagon outside, am I right?"

"That's it 'Arry, yer've gor us taped mate," Bill laughed. Then they all laughed together.

"You'll never change Del, ha, ha."

"I'll get the motor Del."

"We'll 'ang on fer yeh then mate," Del assured.

"Okay," he replied and headed off in the direction of the Ford.

"Listen Del, I don't want ter get screwed up on this deal, so before Bill comes back yer'd better tell me exactly 'ow much yer payin' an' just what my cut will be?" he said impatiently.

"The goin' rate fer brass is £12 an 'undred weight but that's what we get, course it's gorra be clean an' not light stuff like this is, then of course it's gorra be loaded an' unloaded, an' then there's the runnin' of the wagon an' diesel etc., which brings the price down ter £5 an' 'undred weight- if yer catch me drift?"

"Oh aye yeh, I can understand that Del it's only 'natural' yer've gorra make a profit. Well 'ow much can yer quote us fer the mixed?"

"Stainless mixed? Well - I'll be honest with yer 'Arry, stainless fetches about forty quid a ton an' then I've gorra separate it as well with a couple of fellers that's er...an' then there's er...mm...Probably I could give yer five pound a ton, but even then I'm not sure thar I'd make a lot out of it- But - go on, I'll take a chance an' give yer a fiver!"

"That's fair enough Del," Harry voiced, blowing his cheeks out with relief, "Now then Del, when yer've loaded up, I'll direct yer ter the weighbridge where yer can weigh off. Right now, Bill's taring off the wagon first. It's a practice we encourage on all incoming vehicles loaded or empty - security yer know," he enlightened, (indicating to Del that he wouldn't be ripped off).

"Okay mate, I get the point," he stressed.

"Now then Del, what's my cut?" he asked with a serious look.

"Well 'Arry if yer can bring the weight down a bit on the weighbridge, I'll drop yer a 2/6d for every 'undred weight yer knock off - that is if yer weighman's 'bent' that way?"

"Leave it ter me mate, I reckon I should be in for a score terday at least out o' the first load!" the foreman speculated.

Just then Bill arrived back with the lorry and Del signalled him to draw alongside the skip.

"Start throwin' the brass on first Bill, we'll come back fer the stainless later," Del urged.

Bill jumped from the cab donning his gloves and proceeded to drop one of the wagon; sides down. He then commenced to throw bodily large armfuls of swarf into the wagon. Within ten minutes both Del and he had fully loaded almost 3/4 of the turnoffs onto the rear.

"Ger a couple o' tins Del," Bill shouted.

Del reached over to the side of the factory where a number of corrugated sheets lay. He carried them back one by one and passed them to Bill, who at once slid each one down the sides of the wagon trapping it between the swarf and the frame, thus enabling them to load even more of the swarf. This little ruse proved positive for all of the turnoffs were then collected.

THE MACE GOES IN

"Must be a couple o' ton 'ere Bill," envisaged Del, rubbing his hands with expectancy.

"Yeh, I'll go an' weigh it off Del."

Del followed Bill with his car as the wagon drew across the scales.

"Gerout o' the motor Bill!" he ordered, as Bill realised that he'd be weighed also.

He left the cab and they both went into the weighbridge with Harry.

"Leave it ter me Del," breathed Harry, "I'll sort Peter out," he motioned, taking a 2/6d from his pocket

"The usual Harry?" asked the man.

"Yeh Pete, and 'ere's a little something."

The man hastily grabbed the 2/6d and commenced to weigh the load, "2 ton 11 cwt 1 quarter - let's see, so that's er 10 cwt dead Harry," he lied.

"Right Pete, 2 ton tare subtracted and 1/2 ton blind, let's see, that's 1/2 ton Del?" he shouted as he came out, and then as Del approached he whispered, "£2/10 yer owe me mate."

"Right er, well I'll er, ey, Bill lend me £3 pound ter pay 'Arry will yer? I'll give it yer back when I've bin ter the bank."

Bill gave a disgusted look but on second thoughts changed the scowl for a smile saying, "Certainly Del here yer are," as he reached into his pocket. Bill was no fool; he carried two wallets, one with small notes and the other with large ones.

£3 totalled in the one he handed Del as Del was soon to find,

"There's only £2 'ere Bill!" he joked to see the look on Bill's face.

Bill's expression was livid. He couldn't state that the wallet held £3 because that would have given the game away and Del knew this also, but to keep up the deception Bill had to agree commenting, "Is there mate, surely not, I thought I had £3? Oh, I remember now, I had to pay the rates yesterday of thirty nicker. Right blummin' con that is. I meantersay, what d'they ever do for yeh, for the money?"

Harry was looking impatiently on just as Del perceived his mood and added: "Ave this £2 'Arry, an' I'll get back ter yeh!"

Harry begrudgingly received the notes with Del attempting to appropriate the 'missing' £1 note into his back pocket, but intercepted by Bill who whispered, "You forget I grew up with yer Del!"

"Start the motor Bill, I'll see yer at Cohens," he indicated embarrassed.

"What about the tunnel?" asked Bill, holding out his hand for the toll money.

"That's right mate, go through the tunnel," he stated, employing a clever ruse to avoid giving Bill the payment, saying this he closed the door of his A60 and drove off.

"That 'flippin' macin' conm...I'll kill 'im,' cursed Bill, "I'll banjo 'im."

Bill was met by Del outside Cohens and hailed to drive straight in - He didn't.

Del came up alongside the cab screaming, "Drive in Bill, Gus is waitin' for yeh. I've gorra good price out of 'im fer the stuff."

But Bill pulled the wagon up alongside the brick wall and took the key out.

"What the 'ell are yer doin' Bill, an' where the 'ell 'ave yer bin, I've bin waitin' an hour 'ere for yeh?"

"Rif kits," came the simple reply.

"Rif kits - Rif kits, what the flamin' 'ell 'ave yer bin there for, yer 'aven't weighed it in 'ave yer?" Del jumped up onto the wagon's rear wheel and inspected the none-existent load.

"You rotter, you've pinched the load. Gus'll do 'is nut. I'll never be able ter come 'ere again."

"'Ang on Del," said Bill, stepping down from the cab, "if yeh look at this I'm sure you'll find it satisfactory," he offered, as he pulled a receipt from his jacket, "2 ton 13 cwt."

Del read as he scanned the paper, "But I was goin' ter sell it ter Gus mate," Del pleaded with open arms gesture. "What am I goin' ter tell 'im now? What I can't understand Bill is, why yer took it there in the first place. We were to get good price 'ere off Gus?"

"I'll tell yer now Del it's because by my goin' ter Rif Kits - we don't get maced out of our shares," he said stone faced.

"Maced, but how?" asked Del colouring up.

"D'you think I've just come down the river on a boat mate?

THE MACE GOES IN

You've bin macin' me on all of the deals an' I've never said anythin' 'cos you were the boss then, but now that we're legal partners, I feel I've gorra stake in it, so in future there'll be only one receipt - just like this one terday. Now then mate, yer notice that I've got 'top bat' for the stuff, £16 an 'undred weight comin' to a total of £848. Furthermore, I got Rif kits ter make out two bundles of £424. You'll notice that your bundle is minus £3-10 which is the equivalent of alf the £7 I 'ad ter lay out this mornin' to 'Arry," he announced boldly.

"Stone me," mouthed Del exasperated, "So yer've finally sussed me out eh Bill? Well mate, I take me 'at off ter yeh," he demonstrated, removing his cap with one hand , spitting on the other hand and clenching hands with Bill in typical 'Diddie Kye fashion'.

"Y'know what I like about you Bill? Yer straight ter the core, real honest – an' I trust yer!" he admitted.

Bill's face coloured up almost too red to hear this commendation from Del. He felt rather guilty, and even ashamed of his immediate behaviour. Yes the mace had finally got to him: He had withheld eleven hundredweights of brass, for where 'Rif kits' had given him a receipt for 2 tons 13 cwt, they had also furnished him one for 11 cwt making a total of 3 tons 4 cwt.

He was now on the same level as Del in honesty and he hated himself for it.

A hundred and seventy six pounds had robbed him of his integrity. All of this passed through his mind in a split second. Del's words were boring a hole into his head but he decided to brazen it out.

"Well thanks Del," he mused asking, "are we going back ter Swinburn's terday?"

"Naar, let's get back ter 'ock' country," he suggested, licking his lips.

"'Ock country' was interpreted as being the 'George' hotel with its bacon hocks, served hot and Bill licked his lips also in anticipation, "Shall I see yer back at the "George then Del?"

"I'll be along a little bit later Bill."

"Later?" echoed Bill puzzled.

"Danielle Pitgruber, I've got ter take 'er out," he clarified.

"Say no more," winked Bill smiling, "see yer tonight then - I'll put the wagon away."

"Right thanks Bill, see yer later mate!"

Bill drove the wagon back to Del's home and retrieved his car whilst Del travelled along the Dock Road in Birkenhead to reach Wallasey. He arrived at Danielle's place and entered the yard seeking her out.

"Oo's a naughty boy then? Two days late and 'e still turns up for our date," she complains, "okay, out with it, what's the excuse this time?" she accused. Del took a long time to pacify Danielle but his production of a necklace from his wallet soon had her eating out of his hands. Followed by his invitation to wine and dine her - clinched the deal.

He immediately poured out a large scotch in her office which he savoured whilst Danielle had a wash and brush up, leaving her manager in charge. Both she and he then left to take lunch in the 'Waverley' Restaurant at Leasoe, where Del lavished her with her choice of the best of food and drink. After which she stressed her desire to go home, where Del gladly took her relieved to have sated her enormous appetite.

They entered his car and Del drove quickly to her home in Higher Bebington.

He stopped the car only to find she had succumbed to sleep, "Poor lass," he thought with sympathy.

Gently he shook her until she awoke, "What are we home already Del?" she gently asked.

"Yes luv, here we are," he smiled.

"Come on in Del, Mum's probably still here. She comes in to clean up for me."

As they approached the semi-detached house, a seventy year old woman greeted them both with a smile as she opened the front door. They both, stepped in and Danielle led him into the living room,

"Take a seat Del I'll get you a cuppa."

"I'll go home now Danny," said her Mum, "seeing as you're early, I'll be able to do some shopping before I get home," she kissed her

THE MACE GOES IN

daughter goodbye and left.

"Alone at last!" cooed Danielle, as she appeared with the tray of tea and biscuits. She switched on the gas-fire which greatly enhanced their comfort. She then poured the tea.

"Y'know Danielle," Del murmured appreciably, "there's nothing nicer than a good cuppa by a warm fire ter give yer comfort. I can remember when I was a lad, that my parents couldn't afford a penny for the gas light when it was goin' dark, so we all used ter sit around the fire with a cup o' tea in our 'ands and watch the light of the sun go down. 'Ere, I'll show yer 'ow nice it is."

He pulled the curtains across blocking out the sun and allowing the flames of the gas fire to light the room.

"Mmm, yes," she mused, "I see what you mean." she snuggled up to him on the sofa as they sipped their tea.

Del put his cup down and suddenly rose up and said, "Danielle, I'm sorry love, I can't go through with this," he determined solemnly.

"With what love?" she queried with a puzzled look.

"I'm not the same feller you used to know love," he said convincingly. "I know that at onetime among my pals, I was know as the Casanova of the north, but now I'm not, I finished all that malarkey years ago.

"You don't mean…?"

"Yes love, and I've got to say it I…"

"Say what Del?" she probed.

"I, I I'm married now Danny and I have been for…"

"Oh, is that all, hah? Well most of us are in that category but it doesn't stop us from…"

"I'm sorry, it does for me, you see I still love my Beth and I couldn't dream of… even just thinking about being unfaithful - let alone do it.

Danielle went quiet and thought for a while with tears dropping and eventually said, "Well Del, I have only one regret."

"Regret?" he repeated.

"Yes love, if only 20 years ago we'd tied the knot when we first met - before you'd ever known Beth, I know that we'd be happily married now and you'd be ever faithful, tonight I made the mistake that you'd come courting…and now ahah, ahah…I find you're married," she burst into tears.

Del didn't know how to deal with this situation so he crept out of the house stealthily.

At seven o'clock Bill arrived back at the George, but still he couldn't find Del anywhere. Beth, whom he had brought with him to the local was going out of her mind with worry and voiced sadly, "Oh Bill, I do hope that nothing has happened to him?"

"'E'll be 'ere before yer know it Beth, in fact, I'll bet 'e's 'ere before quarter past seven," he speculated. Bill knew the significance of this time. It was Harry Parker's practice to visit at that time and sure enough the foreman suddenly arrived through the swing door with Del behind him, shooting him with 'all kinds of bull' and Harry replying, "Yes Del, but I need the rest of the cash before you come again."

"Del? Oh Del, I was so worried, but Bill said you'd be all right," Beth murmured with joy at the sight of her husband. She approached him and gave him a hug not even noticing the perfume upon him from his earlier encounter. She took his arm and walked to the bar asking, "Have you got a Hock left Eric? Del hasn't eaten yet!"

Eric the barman replied, "I'll just check if Charlie has left any under the cover?"

Jean the barmaid arrived and asked, "Bitter Del?"

"Yes luv, and get Beth a Babycham would yer? While yer at it, ask Eric where 'e's gone for that 'ock?'" he inquired sarcastically.

She smiled and pulled the pint handing it to him which he commenced to drink, as she poured out Beth!s Babycham. Eric re-appeared saying: "Sorry I took so long Del, Charlie had left this one in the oven to keep warm and it was too 'ot ter get out. Anyway, I don't think it's over done in any way - see what you think eh?" he motioned. "Er, three shillin' ter you."

Del paid him saying, "'Ere y'are Eric, get yerself a drink!"

"Oh ta Del, I'll 'ave a glass," he replied.

The trio then moved to a table leaving Harry Parker at the bar.

In a quiet voice Del said, "'E needs £24 before we go back ter

THE MACE GOES IN

Swinburn's Bill an' I think we'd berrer pay 'im hadn't we mate?"

"Oh sh - sugar Del, 'ave we gorra pay 'im, or couldn't we threaten 'im again?"

"It's 'is job on the line Bill, 'e could get the push if the weighbridge feller blew 'im up." he warned.

"I see what yer mean Del," but Bill was not convinced, so in a bid to put things right he decided to test Del.

"Have you got change of a twenty mate?" pretending he needed change.

"Er twenty, yeh, I've just gor it 'ere," he returned.

"Good, 'ang on a minute, 'ey 'Arry!" he shouted. The foreman looked over as Bill said, "Could I see yer a minute?"

Harry motioned nearer and upon acquisition of their table was met with, "Del and I owe you twelve pound each don't we, well 'ere's mine and Del's got 'is 'ere - 'aven't you Del?" Del's face was brilliantly purple. He was furious but had to put his hand in his pocket to pay the man. Bill had tricked him into revealing his pocket contents. He pulled out £12 with a false smile saying, "It's a pleasure doing business with you 'Arry."

Bill renewed Del's drink along with Beth's at the bar and bade them farewell. He then used the foyer phone to contact George Valesque, who informed him of his access to the samples. He then rang Mal Johnson's number who appeared delighted at the news and arranged for the inspection later that night in New Ferry.

Bill drove to Bromborough met by Mary who opened the front door and drew him to her with a welcome kiss.

"Come in Bill, what's that - you want to see Daddy, Right Dad? - Bill's here to see you," she called.

"Right, I'll be there in a moment," he answered and gathered the ingots back into the suitcase, which he deposited under the table.

"Hiya Bill, come into the lounge, I've got something to show you," he invited.

Bill followed him in and George motioned him to sit down. He withdrew the suitcase from under the table, opening it saying, "Cast your eyes upon this lot."

Bill attempted to pick up the case but hefted the weight and decided against it.

He looked under the brown paper to reveal the ingots which were green and corroded.

"Are these out of that original cache?" he mouthed excitedly.

"The very same," he said with an honest look.

"Well, that settles it mate, I'll get Mal on the phone and arrange to show them to him. To be on the safe side George, I'd like you to hide the ingots in a suitable place and bring the suitcase with house bricks in it - just in case Mal decides to turn bandit at the last minute," he warned.

"We don't have to go through with this Bill, I could leave it y'know."

"What! and miss all that commission? Not blumin' likely George, I'm in this all the way mate," he affirmed.

"Right then, if you go now and take them somewhere safe - bury 'em if you have to okay?"

"Right Bill, whilst I'm away will you arrange the meeting?"

"But of course George, so that when you return we can go out and confront him," he confided.

George put the ingots in separate bags, removed the spade from the shed and bundled all the items into the boot of his car making sure that the suitcase with the bricks was put on the back seat of Bill's car, then left.

Mary came into the living room, after seeing George go enquiring, "All the business taken care of Bill?"

"I'm afraid not luv, this is just the beginning," he said sadly.

"Not to worry Bill, p'rhaps we could go out afterward?"

"Perhaps," he concurred, but somehow he knew that the negotiations would probably take most of the night. He then lifted the phone receiver and contacted Mal to meet him at the junction of Bebington Rd, thirteen shops down on the left. Mal agreed to be there at nine o'clock and Bill replaced the receiver. George arrived back at 8.30 pm and he was quickly enlightened by Bill of the arrangement.

"If Mal turns bandit on me and has me followed by the CID, make sure that you stay well away."

THE MACE GOES IN

"But how will I know if you're being followed Bill?"

"I'll flash my left indicator six times and take the first left. If this happens, you get the hell away from me with your car. Right now Mal thinks I'll be on my own and so the scuffers will not be on the look-out for you."

"Got you Bill," he said gratefully.

"Right, now then George, give me the suitcase for my car and if things go okay then I'll flash my lights three times for you to follow. When I slow down, you drive past and I will follow you to where you've hidden the ingots. They're buried in Eastham Woods - I suppose?" Bill probed.

"How did you know?" he answered shocked.

"Just the place I'd put 'em too! Everything clear now?"

George nodded signalling Bill to kiss Mary assuring her he'd be home soon.

Both cars approached New Ferry toll bar where Bebington Rd intersected. Bill drove down and parked his car beyond the 13th shop into the car park at the rear as did George, then after signalling George to stay put, he approached the shop.

Mal wasn't there so he paced up and down. Finally Mal showed his face and Bill waved to him to cross the road.

"Come to my car Mal," he instructed, "I've got the suitcase there."

Mal walked along with him to the car and got into the back seat with the case which was locked. As Bill turned around Mal lifted the case and felt the weight.

"Got the key mate?" he asked.

"I'll open it when I get to your place mate," he assured him. He started the car up to drive away and noticed in the rear mirror two other cars follow him also.

He started to chuckle and drove off. Both cars followed him as he turned first right, then he flowed down to locate George who was just turning behind the two cars. Bill put his left blinker on and noticed that they did also. He allowed it to flash six times before he attempted to turn to signal George who had interpreted the message and who had overtaken them all on his way in the direction of

Bromborough.

Bill drove into the turning and stopped awaiting the inevitable.

"Why are we stopping Bill? I live in Newtown you know." he reminded him.

"I thought this place would be as good as any Mal, 'ere's the key."

As Mal opened the suitcase to uncover the contents, Bill looked in the mirror in time to see the occupants of the cars at his rear approach them.

"Cops," he screamed.

"Don't be daft Bill," Mal said, reaching into the case.

"Leave that now Mal," he said, pulling it from him as the men opened the rear door.

"It's Bill Foggit isn't it?" asked one of the men.

"Oo the 'ell are you?" queried Bill in feigned surprise.

"D.I. Hampstead at your service," quipped the man proudly displaying his ID adding, "Going away are we?" pointing to the suitcase.

"No, that's my sample case, I'm a brick salesman."

"Ha ha haa, he's all laughs isn't he lads? Sergeant, help Mr. Johnson out with the case would you?"

The man complied, struggling to remove it. At last he got it out. The top came open as soon as he turned the key put there by Mal. The bricks came tumbling out much to their shocked looks.

"Oi, mind my samples - oh look you stupid great oaf, you've chipped 'em, my boss'll do 'is nut. That's the second set of samples I've had broken this week! Why don't you do something useful like directing the traffic- instead of upsetting honest folk trying to make a living, what do you say Mal?" he turned to his friend. Mal was dumbfounded, he didn't know what to say. He didn't know what had gone wrong, in fact he didn't know anything right now.

The sergeant made an effort along with the plain clothes constables who had arrived on the scene to replace the bricks back in the suitcase.

The DI spoke, "I'm so sorry sir, there's been some mistake," he stammered, shooting daggers fiercely at Mal who was leaving the car.

Bill drove away turning around with his head out of the window as he did saying, "I intend to complain to the Chief Constable about this through my solicitor," with that he sped off leaving the detectives arguing strongly.

"But how did you know the police were on to you?" quizzed George, after meeting up later at his home.

"Perhaps I'm psychic mate?" he suggested, "some things that Mal said, just didn't ring true George."

"I suppose that's the end of the deal now, we'll never get a buyer now will we Bill?" he rued.

"Course we will mate, we'll use Mal still."

"But, but you said he was bent?" he insisted.

"He is," Bill agreed, "but how long d'you think 'is credibility will last, if word of this episode leaks out?"

"I don't follow."

"Then I'll try and explain, Mal makes a living liaising between the criminal and the insurance company - right?"

"Right" George concurred.

"Then it's that which I intend to blackmail him with. I think that Mal had made a deal with the police to clear their files of the bullion robbery - obviously due to their threatening him in some way of court action against him, probably due to his success of locating past robbery hoards which the police do not condone, in fact it tends to make them appear rather silly doesn't it and more than anything it doesn't contribute the teeniest bit toward their making an arrest - wouldn't you say? Consequently they inherit a back log of unsolved crimes. But they're not as daft as we give them credit for. Somehow, through past trials and error they have sussed out Mal, and are now using him as their go-between to locate the crooks. Pretty smart eh?"

"But how can you blackmail him now - I mean if he's working with the Old Bill, then he's got nothing to fear has he?" George argued.

"Not from the police, I agree, but how about the underworld?" Bill reasoned.

"Oh ha ha haaa, you're a clever one mate, I can see the point, his life wouldn't be worth nine pence if you ever blew him up, yes, but who'd ever of thought of us using him still. Certainly not the 'Old Bill' who right now, are worrying about future suits in court action from you, over their recent 'mistake'. They've probably washed their hands off him now for fear of his being sussed out by the villains.

By the way Bill, when d'you intend to re-contact him?" he asked confidently.

"That George, I intend to do tomorrow, after Mal's had a chance to sweat it out. I suggest that we all get a couple of bottles in tonight and celebrate our coming venture."

"Good idea Bill, exactly my thoughts too."

Never Mind That Now Bill

CHAPTER 11

Bill awoke from his stupor, he still held the whisky glass from the previous night's party. He hopefully upended the glass, but it proved empty. He removed the blanket which Mary had placed over him and re-adjusted the one on George who also occupied the same sofa, as he arose for the stairs leading to the bathroom.

He dried his face and hands and commenced to descend the stairs. He arrived back in the living room and wrote a hurried note to Mary placing it on the sideboard:

'Mary, I'll see you tonight, love Bill'.

The note for George read: 'George I'll set it up again with Mal - hopefully for tonight, see you soon, with regards, Bill'.

He then left and drove to Del's.

"Well, you're early today Bill, had a bad night?"

"No, I've 'ad a good drink Del, and I feel on top o' the world today. Listen mate, 'ave yer gor a pair of jeans yer can lend me? I don't wanna get my suit dirty y'know," he pleaded.

"Aye okay Bill, there's a pair on the clothes-maid over there. See if they're dry?"

Bill ran his fingers along the denim which proved to be suitable, so he slipped off his trousers there and then and donned them on.

"Can I hang me suit up somewhere Del, I need it fer tonight," he stressed.

Del passed him a hanger saying, "Go and get your breakfast Bill, it's getting late."

Bill got the message and hung the suit on the picture rail of the living room.

Beth gave him his bacon and eggs and disappeared. Re-entering with Del's old jacket

"Here y'are Bill, Del thought you might need this," she tendered.

Bill put it on thanking her and arose from the table saying in a loud voice, "Are we ready to go Del?"

"By the way Bill, thinking about what you said - about pullin' my weight and the way my gout keeps actin' up, I decided to take on a couple o' lads fer terday so's ter speak."

"You decided, an' oo's gonna pay'em then - you? Yer'll 'ave nowt left?" Bill scolded with sarcasm.

"Oh come on Bill, only a fiver, a flim each, be fair mate, we wouldn't miss it just fer one day, an' we'll be gerrin all the 'eavy collar taken care of?" he remonstrated, with open hands in gesture.

"Who are they Del?"

"Cecil and Roy McTee."

"Not those two flamin' lachicoes, they'd pinch yer eyeballs and come back fer the sockets. Honestly Del, you can't 'alf pick em? I'm exasperated at yer choice."

"Yer I know that Bill, but we'll be with 'em all the time an' yer know 'ow 'ard it is ter get good 'elp these days.

"Yer breakin' me 'eart Del," he mouthed (pretending to play the violin). "OK then, well ok, we'll take em, where are they right now?"

"I gave em the key ter the new Ford wagon"

"Check they 'avent nicked the radio," he warned, as they walked towards the door.

"Right mate, well tarah Beth, yes, I've got my lunch," he concurred to her queries. They entered the wagon which contained two of Del's cronies who had transformed the cab into what resembled an opium den with their roll-ups puffing away.

"Right Roy, you go with Bill in the Bedford, and I'll stay with Cecil in the Ford," Del ordered.

Bill left the cab and approached the shed where the Bedford sat. Turning around he blurted to Del saying, "Don't go until you're sure that we've got it started!" Bill entered the driving seat carefully setting the choke before inserting the key. 'Rrr Rrr Rrr Rrf - umph,' the engine sprang into life.

"Okay Roy, get in and we'll go," ordered Bill. He drew the wagon alongside Del shouting, "Lead the way mate," and off they went.

Fifteen minutes later they arrived at New Ferry and Bill reiterated the instructions he had given Roy.

"So you want me to put all the brass swarf into bags on the Bedford, yeh, and shovel all the remaining stainless turnoffs onto the Ford? Yes Bill I've got that," he agreed.

They followed the Ford into the yard and pulled up, as Del drove over the weighbridge. Soon they were able to take their own tare and subsequently arrive at the mixed metal skip. Roy jumped down, and immediately started to fill the hessian sacks he took from the wagon. Cecil joined them and under Del's direction he commenced to remove the stainless and throw it out on the ground.

Harry Parker appeared on the scene and drew Del to one side and whispering asked, "I've got some 'eavy bronze 'ere Del, what's it worth to yer?"

"Just move out of earshot o' the lads 'Arry - no sense in lettin' 'em know everythin', warned he.

"Follow me Del, I'll show yer what sort of stuff it is."

Del shuffled along behind him until they arrived at another skip but this one with lids on it. Harry lifted one of the covers and put his hand into the container to reveal a large bronze seven inch diameter valve to which Del took from him to scrutinize.

"It's got stainless steel inside Harry, nah, it's not much good ter me mate, I meantersay, it'd take an 'alf an hour ter strip it. Better you try an' strip this yerself," he emphasised.

"But there's about forty of these Del, and I can't take 'em back now," he pleaded.

"Why not?" he questioned disbelievingly.

"Well Del, our Boss told me to chuck 'em in the rubbish last month, cos he'd ordered 'em by mistake and 'e didn't want 'is superiors findin' out," he said, with an urgency in his voice.

"But these must of cost £100 each," he reasoned, "Ow could 'e justify that mount of debt?"

"Exactly Del, so you can see why they've gorra go. Take 'em with yer anyway, yer can always pass 'em off as stainless steel over the weighbridge, no – one will ever know will they?" he said clutching at straws.

"Oh all right Harry, I'll take 'em, mind you, I don't know who'll buy 'em the way they are, but I'll take a chance on 'em. Now listen, don't mention any of this ter the lads, leave it ter me - okay Harry?"

"My lips are sealed Del, I can't afford to tell anyone about it except you. Anyway Del, will yer come and take 'em away so's I can use this skip for the canteen rubbish?"

Del nodded and hurried back to Bill who was sweating profusely.

"I sometimes wonder Del, just what you are a partner of?" Bill fumed.

"Eh?" expressed Del, Confused.

"You're always flamin' well wanderin' off when there's graft ter be done - 'ere cop 'old of this mate, he motioned, offering Del the shovel.

"Never mind that now Bill ..."

"Never mind that now Bill, never mind that now Bill, never…," he mimicked. "Come on Del this 'ad better be good - out with it!" he demanded.

"'Ow much cash 'ave yer gor on yer Bill?"

Bill's face turned red, he was furious, but before he had a chance to blow up Del said, "I've just made a deal with the chief engineer," he lied, "'e's gor a big bundle of gun metal valves that's come in by mistake, an 'e wants ter get rid of 'em before anybody discovers the cock up, therefore, 'e's offered 'em ter me fer two quid each -'ow's that sound?"

"'Ow many as 'e got?' asked Bill showing interest.

"Forty at least, we could ger 'em all for four score mate, what d'yer think?"

"Let's 'ave a look at 'em first Del, where are they?"

"Bill, can yer 'ang fire with that, I 'ave seen 'em but the man's had ter doss 'em for the time bein' 'cos 'e doesn't want 'em seen. Tell yer what, give me forty an' if I don't get 'em after all, yer can take the money out of the weigh in ok?"

"Fair enough," said Bill, completely taken in as he handed over his forty pounds.

"Just give me a quarter of an hour Bill and I'll be right back."

Bill nodded in agreement as Del moved toward the works canteen. He arrived there and ordered a cup of tea and a bun and sat down, after which he rolled himself a cigarette and smoked it to the end. He then returned to Bill instructing him where the valves lay- swearing him to secrecy of their existence.

After Bill had inspected them he noted the stainless steel centre commenting,

"We won't get a lot for these Del they're full o' rubbish!"

"Take the Ford off Cecil after he finishes fillin' it an' chuck the valves on the top, this way we can take 'em off at my place first, before Cecil and Me weighs the stainless in at Newtown. Meanwhile, you and Roy can go through to Gus's with the brass an' I'll meet yer back at the George okay?"

"So yer 'er? Oh right yer are then Del," he agreed and off he went.

"Heh heh heh, thanks Bill for that forty quid - you're so gullible!" he chuckled when his friend was out of earshot.

Bill was instructing Cecil to load the valves into the Ford as Del was assisting Roy un-mix the swarf. Finally, all of the brass was loaded leaving a small amount of stainless to be added. Cecil drew back with the Ford just as Bill was moving out. Del shovelled the remains onto the Ford and they drove away for the weighbridge

Bill waved as he left and Cecil moved onto the scales.

Arriving back at Del's, Cecil threw all of the valves down outside the house and Del quickly carried them through the back gate into the coal house.

"Go now to Spenner's, I'll show yer 'ow ter get there. If yer take this road 'ere…

Five minutes later Cecil drove the Ford down toward the docks and Del called Billy Spenner out of his office to inspect the load.

Billy looked over the tailboard from his perch on the back tyre and commented: "It's rubbish Del, number six light iron mate!"

"Naw Billy, it's stainless - 'ave a closer look?"

Billy took a piece and studied it … "Oh aye yeh, yer right Del, but even so, it's only worth about £60 a ton at number one - this is number six." he said disgusted.

"Make me an offer Billy." Del invited

"Oh er, well that is, er, fifteen pound a ton Del, that's all I can offer," he said without interest.

"Make it £25 and you've gora deal," said he hopefully.

"I'd be cuttin' to the bone at eighteen Del." he stated.

"Tell yer what Billy, 'cos you're a pal, I'll give it yer at a score per ton," he ventured.

"Now I'll tell you what I'll do Del, I'LL give you eighteen pound ten per ton, take it or leave it," as he jumped down from the wheel.

"I'll take it, I'll take it," piped Del excitedly and signalled Cecil to drive over the scale.

Bill met Del back in the 'George' with the receipt of £340 for 1 ton dead weight and he handed him his bundle of £170, secreting the other £340. (Maced)

"Ow come you get £17 an 'undred weight Bill? Gus was only payin' me £16," he said pretending.

"Well Del, p'rhaps 'e found 'e was dealin' with an 'onest man for a change," giggled he.

"That's not funny mate," said his pal - a hurt look appearing on his face.

"Anyway Del, we need ter talk about 'ow much we're payin' Cec and Roy don't we?"

"Give 'em a fiver each Bill 'ere y'are, take this fiver fer Cecil an' you can pay Roy out of yours," he offered.

Bill couldn't believe it, here was Del giving him money - without even an argument.

He became very suspicious of Del's apparent generosity which was unlike his true character, and decided there and then to keep a closer eye on his partner.

He paid off both the men thanking them for their efforts and even bought each of them a drink, ensuring them, should anything else come up, then they would be the first to hear about it.

He then re-joined Del in the lounge of the 'George' leaving the two men in the bar.

Upon entering the room Bill was met by Del, with a hock and a pint of bitter.

"Welcome back mate. Y'know Bill, I've been thinkin', we make a pretty good team don't we? Not many fellers could be trusted in the way that they're honest in business. Yeh, your a real credit ter me," he admitted amicably. "I've bin thinkin' Bill, it's high time we took an 'oliday each - I mean we're not gerrin any younger are we, what d'yer think mate, d'yer reckon we'd survive a week's rest each? Beth wants me ter take 'er back down south ter see 'er family again an' I thought the old A60 would ger us there. 'Ow about you, d'you 'ave anywhere special yer'd like ter visit?"

"Funny you should say that Del, I've bin wantin' a break for a long time," he stressed, "I've been tryin' ter get a poker hand for some time now, an' I think a trip ter Manchester ter 'Fatso Jones' place might do the trick."

"Fatso's? 'E's bin done fer ringing' cars, 'e's inside doin' 'a carpet'," Del explained.

"Not Jimmy Jones - it can't be. 'E's the best poker fixer in the north, oh sugar, why does everythin' 'ave ter 'appen ter me?" Bill rued.

"Course, there's always Freddie the Fly in Knutsford Bill."

"That old codger - is 'e still alive? 'e must be all of seventy-five years now. Naw Del, I shan't bother, I'll spend a week with me Judy instead."

"So it's as serious as all that 'eh Bill. I knew there was somethin' different about you," Del implied, as he upended his bitter. Looking at his empty glass he said, "Are we, er, goin' tee total then?" he hinted, after Bill had downed his beer.

"Oh sorry mate, I was lost in thought - right, a bitter is it mate?" he asked. Del nodded as Bill arose toward the bar. He returned with his bitter and a double scotch also.

After downing their drinks Bill said, "Ave a good 'oliday Del, I'll see yer in a week's time," he indicated adding: "Yeh, do us both good, takin' a week off," he turned on his heel and left.

Bill almost ran into the foyer of the bar on the other side of the George, to make his phone call to Malcolm, but he was met by Cynthia who bumped into him and exclaimed, "Bill, I've met a wonderful man, a friend of yours, it appears? I'm going out with him tonight - we're having a meal at the Italian restaurant, why don't you come?" she invited. "You could bring that posh girlfriend of yours along too," she encouraged.

"Who is this bloke Cynth?"

"Big Zach who else?" she smirked.

"'Ach 'er Zach - oh you don't mean Zachary Bleen?"

"But of course Bill, he told me all about your escapades in Nicosia," she murmured excitedly.

"He told you all that?" he mused.

"Anyway Bill, here he comes now…"

In a flash, Zach was there in the foyer where they both stood. When he saw them both together Zach's face fell, but Bill realised that Zach was worrying about losing her to Bill, so he sidled up to Zach and in a quiet voice whispered, "You crafty old sod Zach, I thought you'd gone, but here you are preying on a poor defenceless lass like Cynthia?" he scolded.

"It wasn't like that Bill," stepped in Cynthia who overheard the whispering, "it was me who asked Zach to take me out?" she chuckled.

Bill guffawed with laughter "I'm only windin' him up Cynth," ha, ha, laughing in unison.

"Well Zach me old Pal, it's great ter see yer again, but really I had intended to introduce you to Cynthia myself, but it looks like you've already taken up the incentive?"

"We're just off now Bill, to shop around for some clothes so we'll see you soon - ok?" she voiced taking Zach's eager hand.

"Tarah then chuck, see yer later Zach," he bade them and they were gone.

He then rang Malcolm, terrifying him with the threatened blackmail and arranged to meet him, in the pub opposite his insurance office.

Malcolm arrived and sat down in the spot directed to him by Bill, in the phone conversation earlier. A short time later Bill arrived, he spotted Mal and walked over to him.

"Well hey Mal, fancy meetin' you 'ere?" As he sat down on the opposite side of the table.

You Treacherous Basket

CHAPTER 12

"Yes Mal I think you owe me something don't you?" he his," he pointed to the door of the 'Lordship'.

Bill followed him out of the lounge of the pub into the foyer, where his friend whispered: "Keep your voice down Bill, here, let's go to your car?" he suggested.

They both made a bee-line for Bill's Morris and sat in the front seats.

"Now listen Bill, before you start accusing me about anything, first let me tell you how it was."

Bill just sat listening without commenting as Mal continued, two minutes later he was still explaining:

"...and to top it all, Inspector Jeffries not only threatened me with a court action, but also said he'd charge me with receiving stolen property, I had no choice Bill, he had me over a barrel," he pleaded.

"When did all this happen Mal, was it before the Eastham Woods meeting or after?"

"Er, it was before we met at the woods."

So Bill's assumption of the situation was correct, it had been a set up from the start. He complimented himself for perceiving the action and told him so…just as Mal interjected

"But how did you KNOW?"

"Don't ask me Mal, I don't know exactly - maybe it's an in built form of self preservation, anyway, where does this leave you I ask myself, you've lost all credibility with the police now 'aven't yer, and if word of this ever leaks out ter the underworld, yer life won't be worth tuppence, will it?"

THE MACE GOES IN

"You wouldn't tell anybody about this would you Bill, you know damn well I was forced into a corner and had to go through with it, don't you?" he pleaded.

"Yeh Mal and what would've 'appened if there had been ingots in that case, yer'd 'ave gone through with it wouldn't yer? I ought ter knock your scutchin' head off yer shoulders and nobody'd blame me for it, since after yer tried ter blow me up ter the law, would they?" he threatened, "but I'm a big softie Mal, no I couldn't do that, grass on anybody, even though you grassed on me!"

Mal breathed a sigh of relief, but it was short lived as Bill continued, "I seem ter remember the 'Stoi twins' gettin' done by the law last year. Appears they were caught red 'anded with the loot. Funny thing that, and they being connected ter the old Tong Brigade," he commented, "yer'd think that an organisation like the Tong wouldn't allow its operators ter get involved like that, and wasn't it Ashbrook Insurance involved in the case if I remember rightly," he drooled, "that's the same outfit you work for isn't it Mal?"

Mal's face was a picture, it had changed to the colour of a boiled army blanket.

"What are you getting at Bill?" he screamed.

"SHH, someone may hear you Mal," Bill mocked.

"Surely you don't think... I had anything to do with it do you? I wasn't assigned to that lot, it was Perry, yeh, he was the party involved who put the finger on..." he suddenly realised what he'd said.

"You treacherous basket, that settles it, I am gonna blow yer up ter the villains, you and your Ashbrook wallers - they'll all go," he determined.

Mal's face paled, "You can't Bill, you'll be writing my death warrant, don't do it mate, we could make a deal - anything, I'll give you anything?"

"Hmm," Bill pondered letting him squirm a little. "Would yer like ter gerroff the 'ook Mal, for good?" Bill inquired.

"Yes Bill, you know I would," he bleated.

"Well mate, I think I can put something your way for the last time and after this, I want yer ter give up the insurance racket fer good, agreed?"

"Yes Bill, I agree, I'll go into accounting, I'll do anything, just tell me what I have to do and I'll do it," he pledged solemnly.

"Well, shake on it Mal," said Bill, offering his hand after spitting on it.

"Mal clenched hands and pleaded, "What is it, what's the deal Bill?"

"Right Mal, tell me just one thing, was your boss in on any of the blow ups?" he probed.

"Ranson? No chance, he's as thick as two short planks - no mate, he's strictly an honest man. The coppers can't touch him. All the back door negotiations were done by Perry and me. If it was left to Ranson, the firm would have gone for a 'Burton' long ago," he assured.

"Then why does the firm keep 'im on?" asked a puzzled Bill.

"He's a wizard accountant with figures Bill, he can work faster than a computer, so the firm puts up with his other shortcomings," he explained, "why d'you ask anyway?"

"Well, as far as Ranson is concerned, he's still waiting to catch a glimpse of the missing National Refineries haul, right?" Bill searched.

"Yes, but...."

"Then we'll still go through with it Mal?"

"But of course Bill, that's flamin' brilliant, the law would never in a million years think that we were still going through with it - not after that cock-up in New Ferry , right then, when could you fix up the inspection?" he queried.

Tonight Mal, I can get the ingots to you. I'll tell yer what, you go back in there and I'll arrange for the samples to be seen okay?"

"The deal's on George, he bought it," he spoke into the receiver in the 'Lordship' foyer.

"Jolly good show Bill, I'd better give you the location of the samples' whereabouts."

Bill drove home, first to collect some tools and fifteen minutes after, found him entering Eastham Woods. He located the samples

THE MACE GOES IN

by the use of the directions received from George. The spade hit something metallic and he viewed the landscape to ensure no intervention. He removed the silver ingot first, then the block tin, the copper banana and finally the bronze shot. He struggled with the 'banana' to mask its presence by the hessian sack. He covered the others with broken ferns as he raunged it into the boot of his car, "Whew," he puffed, "must be a hundred weight at least."

He then returned and retrieved the remaining metal blocks which he also carried to the car rear. He replaced the spade and drove back to the 'Lordship1. Mal was just about to leave upon Bill's arrival and his friend beckoned him.

"Where the hell have you been? I'd given you up for lost."

Bill motioned to his friend to join him and when he arrived on the scene his eyes popped out with disbelief at the discovery of Bill's boot contents.

"Bring your car up Mal and y'can take 'em!" he suggested.

Mal quickly drew up alongside him and hastily transferred the metal to his rear seats covering them with his overcoat.

"I'll get these to Mr. Ranson right away Bill, you ring me about 5.30 pm and I can tell you more about the agreement," he promised.

"Right," said Bill, feeling proud of himself. He drove the Morris home and curled up on the sofa to catch some well earned sleep. But within an hour he was rudely awoken:

"Knock, knock, knock, knock, knock, knock, knock, knock, knock, knock, knock…"

"All right - all right I'm coming," he shouted.

He opened the door still bleary eyed to be confronted by Mal who commenced excitedly to tell him the news.

"Ranson says National Refineries have identified the ingots and are willing to take them back at the going rate of £37 million. We're 'ome and dry Bill, listen, when can you lay your hands on the rest?" he enthused.

"Give me a minute to make phone call, Mal, and we'll see," Bill assured him. "Tell yer what, you 'ang on 'ere, I'll use the downstairs phone and I can let yer know right away."

Bill had contacted George and arranged for the inspection just as Mal had started to walk down the stairs in an attempt to gain earshot.

"Right mate, I'll see to it right away, thanks a lot, bye!"

"Was that Valesque, Bill?"

"No," he lied adding, "it was his associate."

"His associate?" he raged, "I thought you told me it was just him and you?"

"Well, not exactly Mal - you see he had to have an agent on the outside these last five years didn't he?" he reasoned, eager to protect Mary's connection in the dealings. "I'll let you know more tomorrow Mal, about where and when we can do the deal, but until then, I'm afraid you'll just 'ave ter trust me," he added, enjoying his newly found power.

Bill spruced himself up and glanced at his watch which showed 7:30 pm, "Hell," he chuckled, "no wonder Mal was so impatient when he turned up here - I promised to ring him two hours ago."

George was eating a meal served to him by Dinny when Bill arrived and motioned him to join him.

Bill took up the offer but merely requested a sandwich and a cup of coffee.

"I really came here George, to discover the whereabouts of the Mother Lode," he joked.

"Do you really need it now Bill or will it wait until tomorrow?"

"Naw George, there's no real hurry…actually, yes there is mate. Y'see I've dallied a bit at my end and the intermediary's getting a bit impatient. You understand what I mean don't you?"

George nodded knowingly as Bill continued, "Now then, if I could just offer sight of the ball in our court, it would encourage his side of the net."

"Right Bill, tell me, how long does it stay light for?" he asked.
"Oh, up to about 8:30 pm I should imagine."

"And how long can you stay with us this time without going back to Newtown - I mean would you be missed by your business associates if you were to remain in our company for the next few days?" he inquired, forcibly pinning him down.

"My time's my own George, I'm my own man."

"Then that settles it Bill, you'll stay the night then. Nobody followed you here I hope?"

"Not a soul George, this address I hold sacred. No mate, I always come in a different route each time to avoid that possibility," he assured.

"Good, good man, now then Bill I'd like to insist that you stay here tonight in order to preserve the security measure of tomorrow."

"Tomorrow?" queried Bill, still in the dark.

"Tomorrow Bill, we go to arrange for the transfer of the main cache - how does that grab you?' voiced he, triumphantly adding, "let's crack open a bottle of 'Scotch' and have a game of bridge, then tomorrow we start work - okay?"

"Suits me George, but what about…"

"Oh yes, I almost forgot Bill, ring up your go-between and enlighten him that we move on Friday. It should take that long to organise the 'eight leggers' at our end. Tell him that we can arrange to have the metals delivered to a pick-up point and they can take it from there."

"How on earth are you going to obtain six 'eight legger's in such a short time?" asked Bill incredulously.

George tapped his nostril with his right forefinger, "Leave it with me Bill, all is in hand."

"Well all right - but as long as you're sure?" he conceded.

At this point Bill had to admit to himself that George really did have associates in the deal and that perhaps he had better play it by ear from then onwards, for somehow he felt that he had let himself in for something much bigger than he could handle.

He contacted Mal there and then allowing George to hear the conversation on the dining room phone.

"Yes Mal, it's just like I said, we can get the metals delivered upon receipt of the United Refineries cheque," he instructed.

"Do you require the usual arrangement with the Swiss account number?" asked Mal.

"You said it!" Bill replied, "Deliver the number to my address Mal, by Thursday, and we can then do business. You'll arrange for

'United' to collect the metals will you, then I'll inform you of the location on the Friday okay?"

Mal agreed and Bill replaced the phone. He then explained the situation to George instructing him to have someone at the 'Banque De Palomino' in Guttstart Parade, Zurich, to confirm the arrival of the Thirty-seven million.

"Mary, this is where you come in," said George, "I want you to fly out to Zurich tomorrow and wait there until Friday, at mid-day, at this address to establish the arrival of this figure in a numbered account. You'll need a CARTE BLANCHE for the same. I'll give you a letter of introduction," he promised.

"Now Dinny, could you contact our transport agents - you remember, the ones we used originally?" She nodded as he continued, "And see to the 'other' side of the business," he instructed using his eyes from the right to the left, to indicate Bill to her.

She nodded knowingly but Bill had not observed this action. He had eyes only for Mary who was keeping his attention.

"Scotch Bill?" asked George, who had commenced to pour.

"A large one George," feeling relaxed.

Mary left the room and returned soon after with the decks of cards. They all played a number of games well into the night and Bill retired to bed completely inebriated.

By this time, Zach and Cynthia were engaged in the process of twirling spaghetti on their forks, succumbing to the delights of Italian food.

"You know Cynth, I've only known you a few days but I feel I've known you all my life?" he murmured appreciably.

"Funny Zach, I 'er(slurp slurp) I was only thinking on the same lines myself and … oh drat, I've dropped it again," they both laughed at each other, for Zach was experiencing the same problem. He ended up just shovelling it into his mouth forcibly, but even then it refused to remain there, and lot of it just fell back onto the plate.

"Ho ha ho hah," she gurgled and he laughed too. His eyes met hers and she looked at him in adoration.

She really enjoyed his company, for he had such a lot of humour.

THE MACE GOES IN

This is the part she loved. His dark eyes and hair also filled her with so much love for him. Yes Zach was not unlike Harry her second husband, who also had been blessed with the same temperament. But Harry was gone and now thankfully, here was Zach whom she had loved immediately after they'd met. She reached across to him and tenderly embraced him kissing his forehead.

He in turn found her lips and returned the kiss.

Throughout the meal he commented on her beauty, and she returned each compliment with her appreciation of his good looks.

They finished the wine and Zach settled the bill, to then drive her home where her old mum had fallen asleep with Cynthia's young daughter Sarah, curled up with her head on granny's lap.

Cynthia took her away gently, so's not to disturb her mother, but old Mrs. Maitland awoke immediately.

"Wha' 'er 'er, oh it's you Cynth, did you have a good time? Sarah fell asleep early and I didn't want to wake her so…'er it looks like I have too?" Sarah was stirring. "Oh hello, you must be Zachary, I'm pleased to meet you. I'm Geraldine Maitland, Cynthia's mother," she proffered holding out her hand.

"I'm glad to meet you too," he said "but I thought Cynthia was a Lyme?"

"Oh yes but that was her married name before she was widowed," she explained just as Cynthia rose up the stairs to put Sarah to bed.

"Would you like a cup of tea?" the old woman asked. But Zach refused politely for he could see Cynthia's feet descending the stairs.

The old woman perceived the situation and put on a (yawn) "Oh Cynthia I'd better get off love, I've got to get Dad up at 5.00 am for pigeon flights to Paris."

"Ok Mum, I'll get your coat," smiled Cynthia, winking at her Mum. Finally the old woman left and drove away with a wave from Cynthia.

Zach looked over to Cynthia, "you've still got your coat on love - here let me," and he pulled it from her and hung it up in the hall.

"Let me take yours off Zach, although I suppose you'll be off soon won't you?"

"Not for a while yet love, come tell me about yourself?" he motioned as he gave her his coat.

They both walked back into lounge where Cynthia turned up the gas fire for more warmth, then they sat on the sofa together.

Zach just gazed at her beauty where they sat, gleaning as much pleasure from her looks as was possible.

"What?" she smiled.

"I'm just admiring your pretty face," he smirked. She looked back at him with admiration and with frivolous things made conversation - just for the sake of communication, but then the topics became more sensible and their talk hit a serious note as he said; "Just hold that look Cynthia," but she just laughed until he said, "No love I'm serious… you have the sort of features which could invoke love in any man?"

She looked into his eyes and found all the innocence she had ever believed possible in any man. Zach had been sincere in everything he'd said.

Although she knew that Zach associated with low life like Bill and Del, because Zach had been completely honest about all of his life, she held this in high esteem, for you'd go a long way to find a truthful man, of this she knew.

Somehow she couldn't see herself with any other man, and in the twinkling of an eye, she took him into her arms and kissed him tenderly at first, but after he responded, she held him tighter and impressed upon him her whole body passionately.

She couldn't understand just why, but all she could feel was a great love for this wonderful man? Who'd made her laugh and enjoy herself without embarrassment, from any experience she'd ever had. She couldn't remember finding this kind of achievement at any time before meeting Zach.

He also had been affected by her latent embrace. It filled him with such loving feelings toward her, as his heart beat became faster than he had ever experienced before. All he could compare it with was the way his first partner Doreen had made him feel, but that was now nothing, compared to Cynthia's sincere gestures, which now invoked a love within him-he'd never before experienced.

Cynthia now uncoupled from his mouth, just held him in a loving embrace, didn't want to let go.

She held him for many minutes, before relaxing her grip and when she finally did, he discovered her to be in tears, running unashamedly from her.

"Why the tears love?"

She looked up "I've never been happier in my life"

"So why are you crying then."

She didn't answer but just held him tighter.

He thought for a while, "I'll never understand women as long as I live…?"

Eventually she explained, "Sniff, Sniff, it's just that you've made me feel so happy, and I want this feeling to go on forever, I don't want to lose you?"

Zach smiled, wondering just what he'd said to affect such a response in Cynthia? Perhaps it was his honesty, or maybe she hadn't been taken out for sometime and this new contact was affecting her. Zach just couldn't believe his good fortune. For the girl of his dreams, to have the same feelings of love for him, he had for her, then he spoke, "But you won't lose me love-ever! D'you know Cynthia since last week on our first encounter, I fell in love with you there and then but thought that with your good looks, that you would be married at least? But when I found out you were on your own, I was overjoyed. I prayed for inspiration and when I came back to the bar for another drink, and you accidentally spilt that pint over me - as I took it from you, I couldn't believe my good luck, for it gave me a chance to communicate with you, it was so fortunate for me - perhaps fate made it happen?"

This proved only to bring more tears from her, for she knew that she herself had engineered the whole episode of their meeting, as the spilt drink was not an accident-but planned, with the motive of getting to know him better. The tears became stronger prompting Zach to take her in his arms to say; "Look love, can you believe this when I tell you that there's someone for everyone on this earth, and sometimes we meet our soul mates and other times we don't, but I honestly believe from what you've just told me, that we've found each other at last, and we were to meet and be together forever. Now I realize why the prompting to come up north and visit Bill Foggit, inadvertently, something was pointing me to you and I'm so glad I did, he gestured as his lips found hers and they kissed tenderly, and then he kissed her neck and held her tight to him.

"Ohh h h h," she wept

"What is it love?"

"But it won't last, it can't, both of my husbands were killed in road crashes and the same will happen to you, Ahugh Ahugh."

"No it won't, I've faced machine guns fire, rifle snipers targets and blown up by grenades, but I'm still here and can I tell you that I'm not meant to go until I'm a very old man. Old soldiers never die. I'd like to take this opportunity - knowing that you love me the same way I love you, to ask you to marry me Cynthia.

I want to make you Mrs. Bleen, and also adopt your adorable little daughter Sarah as my own, and make her into a Bleen also. How do you feel about this love?" he implored.

"Oh Zach, I'm so choked up by what you've said."

He bent down to her and again took her in his arms saying, "Come on Cynth you've suffered enough I feel that providence has sent me here to Newtown, no not to just visit Bill to reminisce old times, but more importantly to meet you and to claim you as my eternal partner. Will you marry me; before you answer I can tell you that I'll settle down and change from my insurance brokerage to get myself a proper job to provide for you and Sarah. I was apprenticed as a stonemason all those years ago and I'm a dab hand at bricklaying and…"

"Oh yes, yes, I will my love, I love you forever." She smothered him with kisses and then hugged him tightly.

Tears then came from him, bringing such happiness to his innermost feelings, and he returned his embrace and they just appreciated each other's presence far into the night.

Silver Bullion

CHAPTER 13

Mary awoke Bill supporting the breakfast tray of ham and eggs with hot buttered toast and coffee to follow, which put him right back to normal once more. He walked across to the bathroom and noticed a clean shirt there and trousers, linen and jeans.

"Are these mine Mary?" he queried pleasantly.

"Oh I forgot to tell you Bill, we're going to do a spot of work today, that's the reason for the jeans," she enlightened.

"Are you coming too?"

"No love, I'm afraid not, I've got to go to Switzerland to tie up the other end but I should be back by Saturday afternoon."

"Saturday, you mean I won't see you till then? C'm'ere you, I'll give you something to remember me by." He pulled her to him as she walked into the bathroom and took her in a passionate clinch which lasted for many minutes.

Five minutes later heard Dinny's voice, "Come on you two, we'll be late!"

"Bill we'll have to go love," she prompted.

He reluctantly changed to jeans and followed her downstairs where George had suddenly appeared, "Aren't you two out yet, I thought you were both in the Land Rover with its trailer?" he urged.

The drive to Ledsham was made minus Mary who dropped off at Bromborough Cross with a small valise. They all bade her goodbye as she kissed Bill saying, "Till Saturday love," and she was gone.

They arrived at an old beaten track which converged into a large loose stoned area with a huge windmill, minus the blades positioned in the middle,

"Right, Dinny you get the tools out. Billy, you follow me into the mill," George commanded.

Bill trailed behind him wondering what was forthcoming as George was met by Dinny who gave him a long pointed iron spike. He took it from her and after alighting the stairs immediately started to aim its end at the inner walls, whose plaster fell away to reveal gleaming yellow and green Ingots of metal, which had been laid as bricks against the existing plastered walls.

"We have all day to remove these Bill," he indicated. "When we get down to floor level, we'll resume downstairs to dismantle the other half."

Bill was aghast, no wonder the police had been baffled, these ingots had become the actual structure of the mill. He took the other spike from Dinny and commenced to ape George's actions. As the ingots and bananas fell to the floor, he found he was in danger of getting engulfed by them. George also noticed the situation and suggested they throw the ingots out of the window for safety, Bill agreed, but worried about their being spotted by others, until George assured him that no-one ever came around.

Two hours later saw the last of the upstairs ingots piled up outside and both men descended the stairs to inspect the lower wall which proved to be a double layer and much hardier a task to perform.

"You continue here Bill, and I'll start to stack those outside," suggested George.

Bill continued, but was showing signs of fatigue. Dinny came in with two flasks of soup and bread and poured out the contents.

"Try this Bill," she offered, and he thanked her and sat down.

George also who was tired out, appeared and sat down beside him.

"I must have softened up inside the nick," he laughed.

Bill chuckled, "Yeh, it has that effect on most."

"This soup is good Dinny, I can tell it's none of that vegetarian rubbish is it?" he remarked.

"That's exactly what it is, it's spun soya protein," she answered

THE MACE GOES IN

tongue in cheek.

"Well it's damn good."

Bill lit a full strength and drank his coffee. After ten minutes had lapsed, he put out his cigarette and commented, "Well, I must carry on George, by the way I haven't come across any silver yet, is it enclosed in this lot?"

"Er, yes I suppose it must be," he replied undecidedly.

Bill picked up the bar and walked over to the other side of the mill so as not to disturb them. He jammed it into the wall and used the leverage expertly, to force each ingot out of its position. He had learned a long time ago, the value of a lever and as he progressed, he found himself to have become quite adept, as he succeeded to jib out each member against the iron.

He found also that the secret of success was to use the bar, only where it could prove to move the metals. This was discovered by its insertion upon the very end of each banana, whose individual removal, tended to loosen its neighbours around it. Within 15 minutes Bill had attacked and dropped down half of the ingots on his side of the building, much to George's surprise who commented on his tour de force,

"Well done Bill, you shifted that lot like a good 'un."

"I think I'll have a fag," said Bill, as he sat down.

"You have a blow Bill. Dinny, shove that lot out of the window will you, while I carry on?"

She complied joined by Bill who puffed and panted to help.

George, revitalised by the meal, had also found a certain knack of removal and carried on shifting the blocks.

Upon completion of the movement of the ingots, Bill sat down to finish his weed and upon putting it out, told George to take a break as he continued to arrest the remaining wall.

Dinny had disappeared and upon the completion of the removal of the final blocks, Bill and George walked outside to re-stack the booty.

"I still haven't found any silver George?" he puzzled.

George didn't answer right away but went to the L.W.B. (long wheel based) Land Rover to collect some blankets, with which he returned and covered up the stacks.

"Give me a hand Bill will you? You'll find more blankets in the rear of the motor."

Bill did his will without question and when all of the blocks were finally covered, did George reply to his query.

"Didn't plant the silver here for fear of losing everything Bill," he murmured, "Jump in the motor mate and I'll explain."

Bill entered the vehicle as George started the engine and proceeded to drive away. He stopped to unlock the farm gate and re-secure it with the key.

"Not far from here," he motioned, will only take five minutes to get there… Ah here we are, I had this old property put in Dinny's name for safe keeping."

An old cottage appeared in the lane with a large brick double garage alongside, into which George drove the Land Rover after unlocking the doors. He closed the doors behind them saying, "Drop that switch down will you Bill?"

Bill flipped it down and three fluorescent lamps flickered and filled the area with brilliant light.

George then withdrew the pine boards from the centres of the two concrete floors, to reveal the gleam of a whitish greeny metal.

"Still all here," he beamed, "good old Dinny I knew she wouldn't let me down."

Bill was flabbergasted. Here it was, the whole ton and a half of it, merely sitting inside the inspection pits of a double garage.

"How could anybody be so cheeky to get away without detection?" he complimented. "I'll bet the police were doing their blinking nuts over this lot?"

"Well Bill, all you need is a bit of cheek, it's surprising what it'll bring in dividends. Right, now give me a hand to load this lot into the motor and I'll see that Dinny runs you home to collect the account number, which I can then telegraph to Mary's hotel in the Prague."

Bill complied with this request just as Dinny arrived in an Austin Mini to take him home. They continued to load up the Land Rover and trailer until the last silver ingot was on Board.

"Ready Bill?" called Dinny from the Mini. He nodded and

THE MACE GOES IN

climbed into her car.

The thought occurred to him as they sped away, just how Dinny knew about George's plan to take him home exactly when. This idea disturbed him as they travelled along to Newtown.

"What kind of work do you do Geraldine?" he whispered, treading carefully.

"I do mostly secretarial work Bill why?"

"Oh I don't know," he mused, "I'd have thought you'd be capable of much more responsibility than that."

"Well, originally I was an SRN, but when George arrived in hospital many years ago, he made me a proposition I couldn't refuse." she reminisced.

"I knew it, I knew you were a responsible person, you struck me as someone with more nous than a secretary."

She smiled as he directed her driving, "Turn left just down here, now a right yes, the road just follows to my flat down here."

She continued along the road until they reached the block of his abode, until he suddenly cried - "Stop here, I nearly forgot to tell you, oh we've just past it.

Never mind we can walk back it's only about twenty yards."

"We'll drive backwards," she voiced, "why walk when you can ride?"

As she selected reverse and drove back, her hand bag dropped by Bill's leg and something rolled out on the floor. Un-noticed by her but seen by Bill, who tried to tell her as she reached for her bag, but she had already started to leave the car.

He put the object in his pocket meaning to give it to her but got side-tracked by, "Is this where you live Bill?" she asked.

"Just above the ground floor," he answered, "come on, I'll show you."

They alighted the steps which led to his door he turned the key and they entered.

On the floor was a brown envelope with his name on it. He picked it up and its contents proved positive.

"The number?" she quizzed.

"Yep," he nodded, "I'll have to phone Mal to arrange the

collection, but first I need to ring George to learn the location and time."

"I can do that if you like Bill, d'you have a phone handy?" she probed.

"One just below," he told her, "down the steps and it's on the left. Whilst you're doing that, I'll get a shower."

"Okay," she replied and off she went.

Bill walked into the bathroom and as he dis-robed out of mild curiosity, he removed the object from his pocket and put it on the shelf, deliberating whether he should open it. "Oh what the hell," he thought, as he pulled off the metallic top.

"I don't believe it!" he breathed aghast as he gaped at the hypodermic in the case, "She's a flamin' hop-head," he voiced, "who'd have thought it?"

He put it back into place, and then his curiosity he could control no longer. He removed the instrument once more and squinted a short burst onto the palm of his hand. He tasted it and immediately it dulled his tongue. "Flamin' hell, this is powerful stuff." He at once squirted all of the contents into the sink which he swilled down the drain. He then quickly filled a cup with water into which he inserted the needle washing out the hypodermic and with a freshly poured cup, he replenished its content.

"Ha ha." he chuckled, "will she be in for a shock when she uses this?" He then dried the hypodermic of water and replaced it into the case, putting it back in his pocket. He pondered on how to replace it without her knowledge, and then remembered that Dinny hadn't locked the Mini. He hurriedly re-dressed and ran along the gangway of the flats to descend on the opposite stairway. He reached the car, opened the driver side and just dropped the object onto the floor of the nearside. He then returned up the stairs the way he had came. Only just in time to see Dinny with a worried look on her face arrive at the car. She was smiling when she left it and Bill noticed she held the object. He flew back to the flat threw off all his clothes and entered the shower. Dinny arrived once more and shouted. "I'm back Bill, George wants you to tell Mal to come to the flat as soon as possible, for us to arrange the deal," she informed him.

THE MACE GOES IN

"But he hasn't told me how?"

"Don't worry Bill, George wrote it all down here for you to read," she put the note down on the edge of the sink bowl.

"But why didn't he tell me before now?" he called, "that's a bit unfair."

"Oh it's the way George has of doing things, we all receive our instructions on pieces of paper, that way we don't forget do we. You'll soon get used to it, you're becoming a ten per cent partner I believe?"

"And a board director," he added proudly.

"Well there you are Bill. I'll soon have to start calling you sir," she smirked.

Bill thought a while and finally reached for the towel covering his body, before stepping out and re-dressing.

"I'll ring Mal when I've read the note," he told her. He scrutinised the contents and when he was conversant with the plan, he descended below to the phone.

After a lengthy phone message and minus a bundle of sixpences he concluded with, "…right now Mal, come round Carver's Lane, turn left and then right. My pad's just off Brunswick - got that? …Okay then, I'll see you in ten minutes, right." He returned upstairs to find Dinny in the shower and so he called to her, "Do you like tea Dinny?"

"Yes with two lumps Bill," she replied.

"Coming right up," he said and soon had set out his living room table with three cups for her, Mal and himself.

The door bell sounded and he let in his friend taking his coat.

"Go right in Mal, I'll introduce you to Dinny," he motioned.

Mal sat down and Bill began to pour. He opened a biscuit packet and filled the plates.

Going into the bathroom, he shouted through the door, "Dinny, you'd better get dressed, Mal's here."

She cursed slightly and returned to her clothes which she quickly donned.

She appeared back to join them in the living room. She drank her tea almost in one gulp and motioned Bill for more. He replenished her cup and commenced to show Mal the location and time of the collection.

After which Bill asked, "Any questions Mal?"

"Yes mate, how will your contact in Zurich know just when the deal has gone through?" he queried worriedly, "I mean suppose there's a slip up?"

"We've thought of that eventuality, don't worry, our contact will remain on the line at the precise point that the deal is clinched and you in turn will contact Ranson, who will authorise the transfer of cash from Lloyds to the Banque De Palomino at Guttstarte Parade."

"How d'you know we'll up our end of the deal?" he further probed.

Bill took a note from his pocket. Upon it contained the movements of both Hanson's children and Mal's offspring during the course of the day, which horrified Mal who asked, "How did you find out all this lot?"

"Oh we didn't, it was noticed by one of our 'soldiers' who looks after that side of things," said Bill threateningly.

"You wouldn't hurt our Tanya would you Bill?" She's worth more than money to me."

"Then see that nothing goes wrong - eh Mal?"

"Nothing will Bill - I assure you!"

"I notice that you didn't mention Ranson's daughter Jean," he mouthed sarcastically, "doesn't she matter?"

"But of course Bill!"

"Then you might mention that to him when you deliver this plan now that you're going."

"But I'm not..."

"I advise you to start now Mal, time is of the essence; we don't want any slip ups at this stage of the game - do we?" Bill urged.

"Perhaps you're right mate, I'll have to outline this plan to the boss and that's going to take time. Let's see, it's 4.30 pm now. We're just got time to contact Everton Refineries to make out a cheque," he proposed.

"Oh no Mal," Dinny interjected, "we don't want any connection with them. No, it's Ashbrooke's money we want - you'd better get that clear!" she warned.

"Oh yes, but of course," he concurred, "I don't know what I could be thinking of?"

"Don't forget Tanya Mal," Bill reminded.

"I won't forget Bill - you can trust me," he pleaded, and with that he left.

Thoughts Of Instant Riches

CHAPTER 14

"Ha ha haaa," Bill guffawed, "did you see that look on his face when we mentioned his kid?"

"Never mind that now Bill, have you any gin handy?"

He opened his drink cabinet to find only scotch, "Plenty of whisky but no gin I'm afraid."

"I suppose that will do," she said disapprovingly.

"Say when," he offered but she allowed him to fill the whisky glass to the brim.

"That's what I like to see," he complimented, "a girl who can hold her liquor."

He poured a large one for himself also and joined her on the sofa.

"What kind of man are you Bill Foggit?" she challenged.

"Nothing out of the ordinary Dinny - by the way why do they call you that? Why not Gerry, I would have thought that was more apt?" he reasoned, as he quaffed his scotch.

"Yes Bill you're right," she agreed adding, "you're so understanding Bill."

She put her right arm around his waist and gave him a hug. He didn't object for she, was attractive to him in a weird sort of way. He took her right hand and squeezed her fingers. She in turn tickled his palm indicating an encounter. He responded by delicately kissing her cheek. She in turn kissed his lips.

"What AM I doing?" he thought, almost aloud (Dinny will probably be my future Mother in Law). He reached back down for his scotch and downed it and refilled it once more, the more they talked the more they drank, for she was a much more hardier drinker than he and when she was aware he was almost unconscious, she arose complimenting him on his effort to keep pace with her drinking.

"That was absolutely perfect Bill," she breathed, "let's try it again. Bill - Bill," but Bill was in the realms of sleep.

He almost didn't feel the pain of the needle, as she emptied its contents into his rump, but although it was expertly administered, it was enough to awaken him. As his eyes fluttered he realised that she had punctured his skin with the doctored needle and he pretended to become dazed and slurred his words "wha' how I, is - wha'," he then carried the act to the end and closed his eyes.

Dinny apparently was most distressed with what she had done, "I'm really sorry to have put you to sleep Bill, you're the best I have ever known. That damned George, he always gets others to do his dirty work. There's enough heroin in you now, to keep you asleep for two days. Anyway Bill, one good thing about all of this, you won't be hurt by that damned Mary, who just used you for all you were worth and you fell for it, hook line and sinker - you poor sap…"

After she had gone, Bill hurriedly put on his clothes and ran down to the public phone, but stepped back in horror. Dinny was using it speaking to George,

"All right love," she said, "I'll come back now. What are you doing with Bill's car did you say - oh that's right you're bringing it down here aren't you, well love, I'll wait for you outside, bye for now."

Bill flew upstairs just as Dinny retreated to the hall for the entrance door. She walked out of the building and entered her Mini.

Soon after, George arrived with Bill's Morris Minor and opened the bonnet to detach the 'hot wires'. He then clambered into Dinny's Mini and they were gone.

Bill observed all of this and entered the phone kiosk in the hall. He inserted four sixpences into the slot and commenced to dial a number, it was the Flying Squad in Manchester.

"Is that Chief Superintendent Holly's office? …Well could I speak to the Super…What's my name? Certainly, Sergeant Foggit," he replied.

The line was quiet for some time until, "Still trying to locate him sir, would you like to leave a message?" the voice asked.

"Tell Freddie it's about the United Bullion robbery of 1965," he informed him.

"Billy, is that you Billy Foggit?" hailed an older voice.

"That's never Freddie Holly is it? I'd know that shout anywhere," he voiced in recognition, "How are you Fred, this is Bill, Bill Foggitt - you remember Cyprus in 1962?" he enlightened.

"Oh yes of course Sergeant Foggit, my old pal...how are you Bill?" he queried in genuine interest.

"I'm fine Fred that is now that I've located you. Listen mate, I'd like to do you a favour."

"Is this to do with the bullion robbery of 1965 Bill?" he queried urgently.

"That's the ticket," he agreed.

"Are you serious Bill?" he asked.

"I most certainly am, I've never been more serious in my life mate, tell me how long would it take you and a couple of car loads of your men to get to Newton on Mersey?" Bill queried.

"Are you quite sober Bill, I mean - well you know?" he humoured chuckling.

"Listen Freddie, I'm trying to do an old pal a favour - how sober do I have to be? P'rhaps you'd like me ter pass it on ter the local Plod?" he reasoned. "I meantersay, what d'you think the headline would look like if the County coppers made the pinch?"

"But Bill, I can't just move seven of my men from Manchester just on the strength of a phone call, can I now? Be reasonable."

"Still the same sceptic you were in Nicosia eh, Fred. Look chum, d'you want to recover the 84 tons or not. Only this morning I inspected some of this load. No doubt by now the rest of it will be unearthed and loaded up well on the way to the back doors of Everton Refineries."

With this piece of information Fred's attitude changed completely as he speculated on various proposed stratagems, but met with derision by Bill who replied: "What's to stop you doing a 'Sweeney' on the four loaders? Well, I'll tell you Fred - yes, granted you would probably nab a few minor crooks on such a swoop, but would you get the real culprits of the original job? I doubt it!" he stressed.

"You never got the 'stealers' before, what makes you think you'll get 'em now?"

"Without my evidence you'll never get a charge to stick. Now then, working with me and the information I've got I could arrange for you to converge on the spot where the wagons are being loaded. Anyway Fred, if you need further proof of all this, I suggest you contact the Birkenhead Police about their little fiasco of Tuesday night in New Ferry. I'm ringing off now, before one of your trusted sergeants gets a trace on this phone - I'll be in touch...."

"But, but," Freddie cursed as the line went dead.

"Did you get a direction Henry?"

The shaking of the sergeant's head caused Freddie to blow up. "Damnation, and to think I let him go. Listen Henry get me Birkenhead on the line - get 'em right now!" he fumed, instructing his assistant.

"That flippin' Bill Foggit, he hasn't changed," he raged. His inspector handed him the mouthpiece commenting:

"Birkenhead here for you Fred."

After 20 minutes with the CID his face paled as he asked, "He did, he was, you were? Hmm… so you had to let him go? - I see, I see. Okay then, thank you for your time Inspector Hampstead," he voiced, "What's that? Oh no, I couldn't possibly reveal my source at this present time. However, if anything else comes up, I'll be in touch. Goodbye and thank you again!"

"Inspector, keep your ear to that phone, if it rings and it's him - put the call through to my office."

Just then the phone rang,

"It's him sir, I'll put him through."

Freddie scampered to his desk and lifted the phone, "Yes Bill, it is me, listen where can we meet?"

"At the white horse in Helsby Fred, but come alone."

"But Bill…?"

"No buts, I need to talk to you only Fred. Be there at eight o'clock and the phone went dead.

Coming in from the Manchester Road, Freddie slowed down, for situated further up on the left he spotted the White Horse sign and turned into its driveway. The tall 'London Brick' building in olive, contrasted with its blue engineering brick adorning its corners. The wattle and daub-halfway up the front to the eaves, gleamed in its white stone paint, reflecting a warm light, invoking a welcome to all who ventured to visit. Also the bright Spanish tiled roof gave a European influence of holidays. Together with a garden which seemed to contain every conceivable type of rose in existence. Each in variant modes of opening and colour, but as he stepped out of the car, he became aware of that unmistakable musk like aroma, emanating from them all. Other fragrances contrasted these from the centre borders but were too weak to compete, for the roses took prominence.

Somehow it put him in touch with his child hood of the place - then felt in a safer age of a lad growing up, amid the blooms of his Father's bushes and standards. In his minds eye he recalled, which had been the envy of the Trafford Park coppers, of which his Dad was Sergeant.

At Mariot Green where they lived, his favourite pastime was to de-head the dead blooms, and the weeding of the borders, giving him licence to record of each the special aroma emitting from the various strains.

There was something special and subtle about the smell of roses, and his first introduction to them stemming from his Dad's need of his son's help in the large garden, leaving the sergeant to catch the crooks prevailing.

Freddie's Mum would inspect his weekly weeding of the borders by the promise of three pence each, from his Mum and Dad. At first encouraging him giving incentive, but after which he thoroughly enjoyed and even spent some of it on plants for the borders. His special contribution.

Even long after they'd buried his Father from the bullet wounds received in the line of duty, his Mother Elsie Holly used the same dedication for the borders she had tended, when he was alive.

She pampered each of the legacy of reddish pink tea blooms left by Freddie Senior, as though she expected him to return.

It was this memory impressed on Freddie's mind, as he left the garden to make his way back to the car, it was getting close to the time he'd planned with Bill earlier.

Exactly at eight o'clock Freddie Holly was in the car park when the phone rang in the bar, "Yes, White Horse here - who? Freddie Holly, no I don't think we have anyone with that name here sir, …oh the car park, well I don't know sir. You say Mr. Holly will give me a pound note for my trouble - oh very well sir, I'll tell him."

Freddie came to the phone growling, "What the hell's this Billy, it's just cost me a pound to talk to you?"

"Don't worry about mere pounds Fred, how much reward money was offered for the return of the bullion?" he queried.

"Er £500,000 why?"

"Well mate, think now, what restrictions were made on the reward?" he further questioned.

"That the thieves be brought to justice etc.," Fred explained.

"Tell me Fred, how much pension are you expecting this year?"

"Point taken Bill, if we share the reward, that's what you're suggesting isn't it?" he connived, "Now listen Bill, I'm very interested, but I need to talk with you - not to you, where are you now?"

Bill enlightened him and Freddie turned around to confront him on the foyer phone which was visible through the door.

"I don't believe it!" he said, as he replaced the receiver and joined Bill in the bar.

"Let's go and sit in the snug Fred, I've got two pints of bitter waiting there."

Fred followed him to the table and lifted one of the glasses, "First one tonight," he voiced.

They both sat down and Freddie asked, "Let's have it Bill from the beginning."

It was nine o'clock by the time that Bill had explained all of the details and by so doing, had involved himself also, but he had decided to make a clean breast of it all.

"You realise of course that you could be charged with being an accessory after the fact, don't you Bill?" he warned.

"Listen Fred, I don't expect any favours , but the only way I can see anybody claiming that reward, is for me to do it on behalf of us both. You remember Korea, and the pact we both made to lookout for each other's welfare?" he reminded him.

"Only too well, yes Bill, you're quite right of course. The only reward I'll get is a pat on the back saying, "Well done Fred" and a £40 a week pension. I sometimes wonder just why I even went back to being a copper at all?" he rued. "So you think that if I keep your name out of it and only mention you as an informant, then you could claim the prize? Yes, I must say, it does have its possibilities Bill. Of course you know that they wouldn't pay the cash if the thieves weren't brought to book - I mean, all of them. How could you ensure that we get them all Bill?"

"Don't worry Fred, if you follow my instructions, tomorrow night, to the letter, I can guarantee success and all the rats caught in the same trap."

"You know Bill, isn't it funny how things turn out? You saved my life in that Korean village by using your bayonet on that enemy soldier. Most men wouldn't have kept their bottle like you did and used their rifles, which would have got us all dead if their main company had awoken. How did you do it mate - come on, what's your secret? I'll bet you weren't even afraid at any time?" he complimented.

"I was flamin' terrified Fred, but somehow I psyched myself up through that yoga I learned earlier, when I took that bullet in my shoulder. The hospital doctor taught me how to do it through meditation."

"Well hell Bill, so that's how you managed it? All the boys in the brigade thought you were an 'ard knock - so did I!" he stated, "I still think you're a blumin' 'ard knock to be able to bounce back after all this and turn this lot in. It takes a lot of courage to do what you're doing. Anyway Bill I daren't delay things any longer. I have to enlighten my subordinates of the plan of attack. Now listen take hold of this, sign it and give it me back."

Bill put his signature down on the blank sheet and upon redeeming it was handed a small bundle of fivers. "What's this for Fred?"

"Your Expenses Bill, I don't want you to go back to Newton until Saturday, by which time all of this will have blown over, 'cos if you do - knowing how desperate this crowd is, you may be in danger of losing your life," he warned.

"Yes and if they spotted me it might queer the pitch, yes Fred I get the picture. Don't worry mate, I shan't be going anywhere near Newtown until Saturday night," he voiced agreeably.

"Right then mate, I'll keep in touch, I've got your address here." He held out his hand and Bill shook it saying jokingly, "Keep your head down Fred!" They both laughed aloud - this saying had followed them from Korea's battlefront.

As soon as Fred arrived in 'The Swinging Gate' at Frodsham, he called all of his men together by a pre-arranged signal. They unitedly followed him into the back room he had booked earlier, where he made the announcement: "Okay boys, this is about it, if you'll all gather round."

The Chief Super grouped all of his inspectors about him as he explained the situation to them. After five minutes or so, they in turn all instructed the sergeants, who sped off in the direction of Manchester to gather more support.

Two of the inspectors accompanied him to the main Chester Constabulary, and after an hour of Instruction in the main precinct, they departed for the Birkenhead dept and later Liverpool at Hope Street. Finally, Fred was satisfied that all the routes were covered for Friday and he was able to take his evening meal. His first in command, Superintendent Graham Baxter, he left in charge. He himself was accompanied by Inspector James Edwards at the dinner table.

He outlined the plan with him in the canteen; checking and re-checking, ensuring him of the need for an alternative plan should things go wrong.

"Yes sir, each of the teams will be armed with Smith and Wesson hand guns. The snipers will have the usual long range with Parker Hale telescopes and we have four SMG operators should the occasion arise sir."

"Plan A at 06:00 hours, we move in and surround all four areas of bullion bays. On the eventuality of their fighting back, tear gas will be directed at them, and our men to attempt a breach in their ranks. Eventually our back-up boys will reinforce our position by attacking the other side of the operation. If they use gunfire, then we follow, but only if they commence. We will instruct them by loud hailers to surrender to a time limit. Failure to observe this arrangement by them, will result in our utilisation of firearms, upon which we will shoot to kill. Yes sir, I'd say we've got that point clear. Plan B requires us to further investigate, upon our first point of contact with the robbers' failure to acknowledge our communication in the first place. Tear gas will be directed at them and our boys will follow up with the hand guns. Snipers at both operations will be instructed only to fire, as will all personnel upon receipt of the order directly from their inspectors," explained he.

"Well done Jim, you've got it all off pat. Now then, I have a picture of George Valesque and Geraldine something or other, I can't pronounce her name- apparently his mistress. These people must not be killed at any costs. The Home Office would have our guts for garters, if we were left with no-one to take the blame. Make sure that all of the inspectors are aware of my orders, circulate the two pictures to all offices and inform them that they are to keep close radio contact with me, throughout the entire operation's progress. Now then Jim, I'll get onto Graham Baxter, but remember, if I am not available, all directions must be obtained from him - and him only," he emphasised.

"Right sir, you can depend on us sir, we'll see it through just as you ordered," he affirmed.

Jim Smiled looking Fred in the eye and said, "All we really need now Sir, is for your man Bill to go back to Newtown to queer the pitch, I mean…"

THE MACE GOES IN

"No way Jimmy, he's not that daft, he's a very shrewd businessman, no son, with only ONE exception, 'e's gorraneye for the fillies, has Bill."

Bill fingered the small bundle of fivers he'd been given and counted them up, for that he'd originally been given he thought, now proved to be quite a substantial sum totalling nineteen fivers, all crispy new, without any obvious numbers but totalling ninety five pounds. "Oh 'eck, this can't be right, oh 'eck Fred's probably given me the wrong bundle 'cos these must be his wages?"

Then his thoughts turned to Del, whom he thought was probably living it up on the proceeds of this last mace. Lucky blighter, 'avin' a life of leisure with me stuck here, 'avin' to stay away from all the women. Isn't this like it always is, Del livin' clover, idle to the bone, whereas ME 'avin' all that 'ard collar, yeh and 'avin' ter plan out all the maces to keep our business goin'? But then he thought, just in time that he'd better stay well away from business, whilst the Valesque's were bent on silencing him? Of late to protect themselves from police intervention. So now he reached for his liquor, but as he did, a card was posted through his letter box. Seeing it appear made him reach down to pick it up. For seeing the words, 'Wish You Were here' caused him so much gloom, sickening him. So he unstopped his whiskey bottle and drank from it until he had reach oblivion.

Upon awakening, late in the morning, he had a wash and then entered his car thinking, Why shouldn't I take a vacation, so pointed his car northward, visiting all the bars he could remember until finally ending up in Blackpool, by knocking the door of an old girlfriend, of whom he discovered, from the person now living there, had upped and got married to settle in Blackburn. He got in his car and arrived in Blackburn, where he found himself a bar to prop up, on a drinking holiday.

Del To Ve

CHAPTER 15

"Enough, enough love, heck you'll 'ave me bevied. 'Ave one yerself," he offered.

"'Ere's the cash, get yer mam and dad one an' all."

Beth ordered a Pimm's Number one, a Gin and its, and a pint of light which Del helped her carry back to the table of the snug of the Bean and Billet Inn.

"It's wonderful seeing both of you again," her mother Eve expressed with a tear and a sigh. Her father Alfred also nodded in agreement saying:

"You've only been home two days and it seems loik you've never left the place.

What kind of business did you say you were in Del, solicitors office?"

"No Dad," Beth interjected, "Del's in salvage."

"Sandwich?" he echoed.

"Put your hearing aid in Alf," said his wife. "Honestly Beth, he's so vain, doesn't want anyone to know he's gone deaf, silly old beggar."

"I heard that," Alf accused, as he turned up the reception. "Now what's this sandwich business you're in Del?"

Del fell into guffaws of laughter and replied, "No Dad, remember when we were down 'ere before - well it was then that I decided to go into the scrap business. There's loads o' poke in it, and it pays the rent, also it keeps me in clover with the bookie and landlord. What more could a fella' want?"

"I see your point Del, p'rhaps me an' Mum could move out of

Cornwall and come and join you - what d'you say Mum, shall we go up North with Del and Beth?"

"Cornwall born and Cornwall bred, strong in the arm and weak in the head - that is you Alfred. Don't be daft love, who'd look after the chickens and the pigs?" she reasoned.

"Yeh, you're right love, you're always right," he relented tearfully.

"'Never mind Dad," Beth sympathised, "perhaps you could come for a week if our Valerie would come to stay here to feed your livestock."

"Good idea," said Alf, "now THAT, we could manage. When are you going back love, not till Tuesday I hope?"

"That's correct Dad, Tuesday midday we're returning to get back by nine o'clock, but let's not talk of Newtown, let's discuss PERRANPORTH. Does old Mrs. Axtel still live in that ancient mansion, mum?"

"Yes Beth," said Eve, "she's still going strong."

"How about Campbell, does he still have that bunch of old mackeral skiffs at St. Ives?"

There was a deathly quiet between Alf and Eve as they both dropped their eyes downward.

"He hasn't.... he isn't... is he?" asked Beth tearfully.

"I'm afraid so love. It happened so quickly through that bad squall last year and before we knew it, both he and his brother had gone down together with each of their boats. Two others were lost with them also. Only bits of wreckage were ever found, damn shame, the Campbells have done so much for Cornwall..."

Eve, her mother then said, "Not to worry love, but your old pal, Delvene, still lives in Perranporth, only a stones throw away love. So why don't you go and visit her?"

"Mm, Praps we could invite her..?"

Bring…Bring…Ring.., pealed the alarm and a well manicured hand instinctively came down on its bell at the top of the clock to quell its noise, "Shurrup!" she screamed, knocking the contraption to the floor, and in doing so arose to be met with the 'Big Daddy' of all hangovers "Ohhhh oooo moi par 'ead, I'll 'ave ter stop drinkin' those babychams." To make matter worse the hammer of the alarm continued to strike to the bitter end. "Oh no… it's Sar'turday."

Delvene lay there still once more cradling her forehead in her right hand feverishly reaching blindly for the glass of water strategically placed last night to deal with her dehydration expected - which was now.

Slowly she arose holding back her head in poise to enable her inner ear to cope. She located the glass and also the multivitamins lying along side the small container, of which flew open scattering its contents all over the dresser.

Eyes half shut she managed to grasp one and thus swallow it down with the water, which to her sour mouth tasted sweet. She quaffed it down to the end, and lay back once more savouring the pleas Melvyn had made last night to make an honest woman of her and her reply of maybe? It had caused almost a tantrum within him, to keep him dangling for so long on a string. Quite frankly she didn't know why he liked her so much, the feeling wasn't really mutual, but still he persisted.

She arose from the bed with the intention of getting a shower, until she discovered it was only 5.00 am but somehow she was by now - not really tired at all and got to her feet to reflect in the mirror and examine her complexion. It wasn't quite as bad as she thought. Some fresh mascara, a little eye shadow with some lip gloss would just put her right thanks to the cream she'd remembered to apply the night previously.

The tall full sized mirror returned her image of a woman in her mid thirties, with features and figure resembling the Italian movie star 'Gina Lollabridgida,' complete with black flashing eyes like coals on fire contrasted with white. A petite woman with a copy cat figure with trim waist, giving way to her shapely hips, which she interpreted to being too full, without realizing that her figure was her greatest asset, but like all women before her, she desired not to be so full and rounded.

She secretly admired the Audrey Hepburn waif like look most women preferred.

At most mornings she would prance up and down by the mirror, clothed only in her night negligee imitating the moves familiar to cat walk models, with the cute occasional head turn and alluring smile she'd used in front of Melvyn and his friends in the club last night, after which Melvyn made an utter fool of himself on one knee, when in front of all concerned had 'popped the question,' but her 'maybe' caused him to lose face and he was furious.

Perhaps marriage with Melvyn didn't really appeal, but she patched things up anyway building up is ego.

Although getting married did have its returns, she felt that she hadn't yet made her mark on the world. Granted she was an almost famous model in big demand, deep down inside she felt that she still hadn't given her best to modelling.

"If only I could get the respect for my effort,s instead of just my looks?" she yearned, thinking of herself as a great stateswoman or barrister - instead of flaunting herself before male buyers in her role of model, with her famous smile known in most of Cornwall, London and Paris. Her smile being her most prized asset. Through this alluring look, she'd prove to charm all of the buyers to order the dress designs she'd worn and thus she was in great demand.

But of late, she stood at a signpost in her life, not knowing quite what to do next.

Melvyn's offer of marriage to ensure her future's best economy and she must admit, it did sound tempting, but somehow she felt, that because she was seen as a mere woman, she must stand up for all the females in the world dominated by the male gender.

Even the thought of Melvyn's job and the prospect of simulating his occupation, had crossed her mind of late and she hinted to Melvyn about this prospect.

He was the main agent for the St. Ives based McVeldan Company of builders and civil engineers, a similar job with them she now envisaged.

She remembered how Melvyn had related about the proposed demolition of the ancient electric presses, with their consolidated machines, which had provided most of Britain's air raid shelter corrugated sheets for the 2nd world war, but now too antiquated to compete in world markets and had to be cleared, to make way for modern housing in big demand.

Melvyn had hinted about the hundreds of buzzbars, set in the abundance of machines installed there to make contact. Melvyn was no fool, but sometimes his tongue ran away with him, in his conversation with Delvene.

"Yes Del, if only we could find a contractor to dismantle these machines. He'd make a small fortune with all the salvage returns."

Delvene's ears pricked up and thoughts of instant riches, immediately filled her mind. By acquisition of a said contract she could hire a load of 'doalies' on a daily basis and through the contact of Melvyn, could insure that she became that contractor. Her mind and her dreams of affluence with the prospect of vacating her dank dark Victorian flat, she suddenly relished and at once decided to change her address, to somewhere more suited. She knew that a mere word in Melvyn's ear would ensure that her 'company' would be the only considered prospective demolition contractor, so she contacted him to put forward her aim.

"Good for you love, I'll help you register your company" he offered, but these arrangements were made last night in the club and she hoped that Melvyn would remember. Nonetheless she decided there and then to change her flat for something dryer.

Yesterday's paper lay still in the hall where it had been delivered. She picked it up and browsed through the flats to let. Eagerly she thumbed over the various modes of rooms, until she realized they were too expensive for her budget. Their terribly inflated prices put her off completely. Then she saw it: Des. Res. In rural area to let: £350 per annum. Feverishly she checked the area and found it to appear off the beaten track off Pen Perrin. She at once rang 'Fitzsimmons and Carter' to arrange a viewing and to her surprise discovered that today she could actually see it, and a time was set on the hour.

A very mature male voice had intercepted her enquiry, assuring her that the property had just entered the market on their books and was a snip to anyone who had wheels, but preferred privacy. Armed with this knowledge she thanked him and rushed to the shower.

It was quite an old shower powered by the tap pressures but its cascade was nine inches in diameter and proved to respond at anytime of the day. So refreshing was the shower - for it caused the hangover to recede, but also she felt the tumbler of water and multivitamins were also responsible for flushing out her kidneys.

She then exclaimed, "Oh no, I've been in here for twenty minutes," realizing that her appointment with Mr. Carter was in less than 15 minutes.

Gingerly she stepped through the shower curtains and out of the bath and feverishly dried herself, missing some parts in her haste.

Almost running to her wardrobe, she snatched at her almost transparent designer clothes, but chose a dress which was more modest, but even this barely covered her thighs.

"Can't be helped, I'll wear my jacket to cover it," and this proved to be the answer. Only on an afterthought for the sake of decency, did she don on the black sheer tights which worked well for her, to look decent and also professional, her high heels she entered, but changed them to her pink ones to match her frock as she reached for her lipstick with not too much. A movement from her mouth distributed the off pink daub to her lips area. A quick glance in the mirror satisfied her of her smart appearance. She ran out of the flat to the works van outside, devoid of any dresses left there by Henry, to allow her access to attend the fashion show.

She entered her key into the large van's ignition and it roared into life, with the gears responding so well and sped off in the direction of the town,

Upon locating the estate agent's office she pulled in and stopped outside. She peered out of the van and could see through the large shop front window that it was busy with activity - prospective customers all with designs on obtaining property, thumbing their way through various properties and commenting to their spouses for approval.

She stepped out of the van and with urgency she entered the premises making a beeline for the solitary male behind the desk, dressed in a partly creased suit of green fleck with matching tie and black lace up Gibsons. He was very tall and handsome. Delvene fell in love with his face the first time seeing it and pledged herself to get to know him.

"Mr. Carter?" she queried, rolling her head in provocative slant she'd experienced on the cat walk which would always get men's attention. She stared right into his eyes and smiled, showing her white teeth.

He in turn looked her up and down, starting from the front of her dress, which by now showed through the undone buttons of her coat. He then feasted his eyes on her face.

By his non verbal communications; she could tell he liked what he saw.

He smiled back at her and again looked her down and up.

His dilating pupils unmistakably gave Delvene the edge. She assessed him to be fortyish and probably married with kids so she didn't push the boat out but said, "I rang earlier this morning."

"Oh y, y, you mean the flat?" he stammered, losing his normal control.

"Yes do you still have it?"

The effect she was having on him was hilarious. She tried not to laugh, but he was motionless, enthralled by this beautiful feminine creature that now stood before him.

Words just wouldn't come for his senses were inflamed by her beauty. She was everything he had ever dreamed of or could be possible in a woman. Her well balanced face in symmetry, her raven hair, her dark Spanish like eyes set within dark brows, her well balanced nose, supported by a full inviting mouth with pouting lips now, really took his breath away, his heart beat increased. Finally, words did come and he affirmed availability of the flat in question.

In a lower sensuous voice she murmured, "Could we, (and then paused), could we go and take a look?"

The girl sitting behind Delvene was about to interject, when Mr. Carter said, "Erm don't worry Jean, I'll look after this one today."

Jean sat down again with knowing smile saying, "It's no trouble really Jack, I could just run her…"

"No Jean, I'll take it from here," he pressed, thinking, "that Jean, always trying to keep me in the office, I'm sure she fancies me?" He glanced over at Jean, of her slim petite figure so pleasing on the eye, but no comparison to Delvene's beauty, which he found difficult to remove his eyes from.

"It's, it's Miss Wakely isn't it?"

"Call me Del, everybody else does," adding "although it's really Delvene.

"Ok then Del, I'm very pleased to meet you," he offered, as he put out his hand. She shook it and it was warm so she hung on to it, for as long as she dare to.

Embarrassingly, he broke the grip for his heart was now thumping, which frightened him and he felt disorientated to say the least. He fought for control but her eyes were upon him, penetrating his innermost feelings.

He was in love with this beauty and his face flushed, over which he had no control. His condition, Del was made aware of, for she herself was now experiencing similar sensations, as she studied his physique, of which he reflected a gym fanatic with muscular arms set in his creased jacket, rippling through the material his broad shoulders, suggested a rugby player or an athlete. His face square and evenly set like the men she'd seen depicted in American action comics, who all had features of Greek gods. This man with his brown eyes and well balanced nose, sensuous lips supported by a well set chin, she fancied immediately and envisaged them out together romantically, in some setting by the sea…

"I'm Jonathon Carter, but most folk call me Jack."

"Right Jack, I'll remember that, is the flat very far from here and do you have access for us to view it?"

"Yes of course Del, I'll go and get the keys now."

He had to fight off the urge to actually run up the stairs but when out of view, bolted up them two at a time. Coming back down saying, "I've brought a picture of the cottage with me."

"But I thought you said it was a flat?" she fished.

"Originally it was, but old Mrs. Epsom decided at the last minute to vacate the premises, to join her son locally and has now left the entire house to let. Would this not suit you?"

"Oh it's better than I'd hoped for Jack, I'd have more privacy on my own. Oh yes, let's go and have a look. Oh by the way, would it be the same price?"

"But of course, we'll go in my car if you like?"

"Yes Jack let's do that, shall we?"

He made some comment to Jean, observing him from behind her desk, assuring her he'd be back as soon as was possible and motioned Del to follow him.

Outside sat an old 1952 'sit up and beg' Ford Prefect with two wide black doors showing a red interior. He approached and opened the nearside for Delvene and after she'd entered, closed the door, he then entered the driver's side.

The old Ford responded to Jack's pulling of the choke and the engine sprang into life.

"Are you comfortable Del?" he asked, turning his eyes to hers.

Quite blatantly she said, "Ooh it's nice sitting here,"- it wasn't in fact, some of the springs poked through the rexine to annoy her posterior but she didn't mind, sitting here close to the man of her dreams was enough, to cause her heartbeat to increase.

"That's good, I'll take the short cut and we'll soon be there," he assured and drove forward.

The scene changed, and the hum drum of the town surrendered to the warm inviting greenery of trees and bushes in blossom, alongside the fields of grazing grass flying by, as they approached. Del looked over at the hedgerows which were covered with honeysuckle, its yellow pungent blooms' influence on the air in proximity of it. She wound down the window, filling the car with its deep aroma. Giving way also to the musk smell of wild roses, which now permeated the air and released their delightful scent, she gulped down pleasantly mingled with freshly cut hay.

She leaned her head outward imbibing of its desirable fragrance for some time; that was until the pungent smell of cow manure invaded her nostrils, responding with a quick winding up of the window.

Jack chuckled to himself with her latest action, as they ventured deeper into the rural domain.

He didn't speak, for he was affected by her actual countenance, for her mere presence sated his desires. Every so often he'd pretend to make a show of slowing down to a cross junction, but viewed Delvene's face more than he checked the road for safety. Of all the beauties he'd ever seen this one took the cake. It gave him so much pleasure to look and meet her eyes with the smile she gave him back, as he almost careered from the road over the grass. He fought for control of the ancient car, which bounced under the protest at his careless driving, as he negotiated the twists and bends in the narrow road.

"Oh, here we are," he breathed in a sigh of relief, and turned up an even narrower road, un-adopted and made obvious by its sparse tarmac and muddy pathway. "It's only a short way up here," he encouraged and slowed down to stop the car, until they could see the small cottage loom up.

Delvene couldn't believe how attractive looked the small house, with its long approach of front garden standing on the right of the car, the house set back in a mass of colourful plants of yellows, blues and greenery surrounding, and upon further glancing, she saw the rose bushes in pink and white, with the flashes of deep purple rhododendrons contrasting amid its evergreen leaves. She looked now to Jack, met his eyes still dilating and said, "Oh let's get out and take a peep?"

He complied and said, "I'll just pull into the drive so's not to encumber the tractors."

She left the car before he did and walked to the front gate. She edged through it, where she perceived of the sunken Spanish garden obscured by the hedge row with a sundial, occupying its centre. It was made of green slate surrounded by Yorkshire stone crazy paving.

Which emphasised the garden's need for different colours contrast, to exhibit its splendour giving-way to its borders, which were a blur of almost every conceivable plant's colour she had ever seen, but loved absolutely. It took her breath away, but best of all stood the standard roses, most of which sported huge blooms, lending the air with their rich pungent aroma, which filled her nasal imbibe with excited perception.

Butterflies inhabited the flowers and bees in their industry of pollen gathering, flew in and out successively.

The plants, all of which seemed to represent, the spectrum of rainbow colours, quite took her breath away, but installed a great urge to stay there and make it her home base.

As she approached the front door, she saw a frame built like a tall bridge over the face of the stone, that protruded outward to carry a flowered hanging vine of pretty colours, which grew up and over its span, and dangled in the breeze like a pennant blown.

As she viewed the cottage, it appeared to be built with random stone to the front, in pieces of all shapes and sizes, like a giant jigsaw puzzle, finally tied together with uniform corner stones giving it the balance it needed.

The more she saw, the more desperate she became to secure this little dream house. She just stood there taking it all in and almost going into a daze, dreaming of her hopeful residence there in the near future…

Jack by now had locked his car and walked to the door with the key in his hand saying, "Ok Del, let's take a look?" But really he had eyes, only for her exquisite beauty.

The door opened easily in response to his Yale key and he gestured for her to enter, which she did.

The hallway of ample width, allowed good access to the steep stairs to the left and the downstairs room to the right. Parked by the front door, upon a half round wall table, sat a ceramic polished pot containing an 'eau de cologne plant, of which had out grown its situation, causing any visitor's clothes to brush against it. Delvene discovered as she had tried to navigate passed it, but struggled as it was vary large, thus it released its aroma to permeate the hall, filling her nostrils with its delightful scent.

The ceilings were in fact quite a bit lower than she'd been used to in her Victorian flat. But the mere construction of each wall of wattle and daub breathed 18th century, and its quaint 'latch gate' like doors so attractive to the touch, to the sound of its small latch, which was quite different to anything she'd ever seen.

As she entered through its inner area, she was aware of the existence of two further rooms, one a living room with a kitchen to its rear. The kitchen, of which contained walls of the same construction as the previous rooms, with the exception of the rear wall which had bare stone showing, with a thick ceramic sink, supported by pillars of ancient bricks and a large access under its outlet pipe, to cope with any possible blockages. Alongside this stood a galvanised corrugated tub, with its 'dollie' of two handles on a long stem, based on short legs to agitate the washing of clothes. She smiled as she tried to envisage some old woman turning and plunging her clothes dollie, just as she remembered seeing her Gran do the same in the pre-washing machine age.

"I'll keep this dollie and tub as a feature," she decided, but vowed to have plumbed in her large washer.

The rear Georgian windows' minute six inch panes, were contained in ancient cast iron frames and although smallish, reflected quite some light which made the kitchen bright. Also reflected by its daub walls in lime colour of distemper. The oaken beams contrasted by low ceilings which served likewise.

She progressed into the sitting room with its small cottage furniture and was impressed by the simplex oven cum-fireplace, containing paper and sticks in readiness with coal. Also a large cast iron kettle sat on a swing-to alongside the fire, all ready to be boiled for tea and in her mind's eye she could see it bubbling in future times and imagined herself with not Melvyn but Jack, lying down enjoying the fire radiating its heat. "Strange," she thought and dismissed it from her mind as she now concentrated on the room.

"Nice isn't it Del, it quite reminds me of my old granny's home," he reminisced.

"Yes, it does have that effect, doesn't it? Yes you'd rather expect some old dear to be putting on and off that old kettle for tea? I just love the kitchen, it's so 'oldie worldy' and the panels in the front room here, look Elizabethan don't they, I wonder just how old really this place is?" she asked.

"If I'm not mistaken Del, it was first erected by the original farm workers themselves in 1637. Apparently in those days, a law was decreed whereby if anyone wanted to occupy King's land with an abode, that at the end of their work shift at the farm of employ, they would then rush to the site of erection and have the need to complete the work with the roof intact before dawn. This is probably why cottages are so small. The windows are of a later edition, obviously because of avoiding the window tax, until it was abolished. Yes even the stair case with its upper floor would have been later editions."

"But what about the houses, did they stay up?"

"Probably a lot fell down, oh and I forgot to mention, that before dawn, a fire was needed in its fire place, in order to qualify for occupancy."

"Must have been awfully hard days to live? I mean after slogging all day in the fields, to have to then go and build a house in less than 12 hours must have been a miracle?" she determined.

"This is probably why they are so small?"

"Well Jack you've got it all up there," she commended.

"Yes," (completely oblivious to her reply) spoke aloud his thoughts, "I wanted my old Mum to sell it, but she had this idea to rent it as a flat."

"You mean it belongs to YOUR MUM then Jack?"

"Yes Del, that old dear I spoke of, lives now with me yonder in that oldish farmhouse."

"Yonder?" she laughed.

"Opposite." He coloured up adding with emotion, "She's forever bumping into things, falling down knocking herself out. I moved her last week."

"Oh good for you Jack, it was an admirable thing to do!"

"Mum loved her garden, she'd planted all the roses and my Dad set the Spanish garden before he died. We haven't seen the bedroom yet Del, go on take a look," he proffered, to change the subject.

She nodded and moved back into the hall, and again, her sleeve brushed past the scented green and purple leaves, filling the area with lovely scent.

At the top of the stairs she discovered one large room, accompanied by another room and obviously some additional later construction within it, housed a door, which she opened to be pleasantly surprised, for it contained a shower.

The larger room was equipped with a medium sized double bed,

THE MACE GOES IN

high above the floor on cast iron runners, popular at the turn of the century.

A dressing table in oak Victorian with a tallboy to match, graced its floor equipped with a full sized mirror in the door, placed centrally which caught her glance, and naturally she began with poses fit for the cat walk.

Jack pretended not to notice, but his eyes were on her beautiful figure most of the time. He couldn't help himself. He only knew one thing, since meeting Del - her mere presence made him happy and he wanted to savour the sensation it gave him, yes he had to admit, he was really smitten with this girl.

Del tried the bed, springing on the mattress and with satisfaction arose and then clutching the heavy brass bed knobs upon its end.

"It's well sprung Jack!"

"You like it Del?"

"Oh, yes," she envisaged future evenings relaxed tucked up at the end of the day. Not wanting Jack to see how eager she was, she pretended disinterested and left the room.

Jack had noticed her change of expression and thinking the worst of the loss of a customer said, "You haven't seen the rear garden, come and look through this window."

Pretending she was bored (a ruse to reduce the asking price of annual rent) she took a quick glance at the garden and was pleasantly surprised, because of the recent sweltering heat they had all experienced, almost all of the fruit in the orchard at the rear had ripened and abundantly displayed on all the trees and bushes, prompting her to walk outside for a nearer view.

"P'raps I will take a closer look?" she relented and moved out of the room, went downstairs and out through the back door leading into the rear garden, after sliding back its ancient squarish bolt.

Spotting a ripe Victorian plum, took it off and sampled it. For it reflected such sweetness to her taste-buds, that she picked another - just as Jack appeared.

"Try these plums Jack, they're out of this world."

He reached for one, but upon tasting it proved to be sour. He smiled, (lying) "Oh yes, they're sweet, as he moved the briars, which threatened to engulf Del. He threw away the offending fruit "Hmm, that was nice," he lied again. He smiled through his grimace and remarked, "I've never known Mum's plums taste so sweet."

Del smiled and reached for yet another.

"Well Del how d'you like it?" Jack enquired.

"How much did you say – three hundred per annum, Jack?"

"Well 'er Mum did want seven pounds per week to enable her to live. She only has her old age pension you know?"

"Oh Jack, I was so looking forward to seeing more of you, but alas I'm only a model and us catwalk girls as you know don't earn a fortune."

He looked on sympathetically thoroughly enjoying her eye contact, as he did, she flashed her eyes and pouted her mouth disappointedly. Looking at her appealing face before he spoke, as if working out something, "I'll see if I can get the old girl to come down a bit," he stammered, especially since she'd mentioned - see more of him.

"By the way, how much can you afford love?"

"About six pounds a week, this is what I pay now," she lied adding, "if only I could afford to take out a good looking Beau like you, but I suppose you're married with kids? The handsome ones are snapped up early."

Jack looked so pleased and spoke up confidently, "No Del, I've never tied the knot with anyone, in fact I'm looking for 'Miss Right' to enter my life.

His senses were all of a meither, as he started to breathe louder and his heart pumped faster, as he viewed her concentration upon him. Trying desperately to stay in control of the situation, he tried to avert his eyes from her, but her well developed figure took precedence over his thoughts, then he found himself saying it, "By the way Del are you doing anything special tonight?"

She flashed those radiant pools of black dipped in pure white and he looked at her alluring mouth as she replied, "No, not a lot really, I was going to wash my hair and then watch television, why? What do you have in mind…?

THE MACE GOES IN

After securing the cottage lease from Jack, on her terms, Delvene did date him that night where he behaved in a most gentle fashion of prim and proper - namely because he didn't want to lose her, and rescheduled for a time later in the week for an encounter, where he planned to take her to the movies.

Delvene contacted Melvyn on the pretence of getting to know the ins and outs of the construction industry, as she drank her gin and its, the next night, with him at the Wheatsheaf. She listened intently whilst Melvyn droned on about what a good job he was doing for McVeldan's and how fortunate they were to have him on the payroll, on and on it went with Del nodding in agreement, smiling to keep him sweet.

"I'm making a lot of money for McVeldan's but speaking of which, anybody with any sense could make himself a right load o'cash dismantling those presses at Catchpoles, merely by the scrap value of the copper buzzbars located in them, not to mention all the platinum points."

She smiled bored out of her wits until he mentioned, 'a right load o'cash' which seemed to waken her senses.

"Oh surely a load of old iron won't fetch that much will it love?"

"I don't just mean old iron, there are at least two or three tons of old fashioned buzzbars, and platinum points situated there.

"Oh Mel, I've seen the points put in cars' distributors and they're tiny."

"Not these love, these are the size of half crowns," he assured.

"How much does scrap fetch these days?"

"What you mean copper?"

"Yes."

"Well local dealers offer £300 pounds a ton."

And the platinum, what's that worth?"

"Well it's hard to say but to be on the safe side it's normally fetching £60 an ounce."

Delvene's eyes nearly popped out of her head, but pretended not to be really interested just as Melvyn droned on.

"Yes Del, if I could find a contractor willing to demolish the machines, between us we'd make a bomb."

She thought for a moment, her mind drifting back to a telephone conversation she'd heard a few days earlier of Mrs. Dickens who informed her that her daughter Mary, Del's old school chum was due to arrive at the weekend for a fortnight perhaps, which meant that she'd be there now in Perranparth, but more to the point, her husband Mr. Bovis was accompanying her. If she remembered rightly, somehow he was connected to scrap metal. "I wonder if…?"

It was now on the spot she decided to put her plan in action. She knew that with Melvyn he would agree to any of her whims and fancies and decided there and then, to investigate this lucrative scrap game once and for all.

"A penny for 'em?" fished Melvyn.

"Eh, oh well p'raps I'm being ambitious Mel, but I think I can probably help you in your job and we could help each other."

"Ey, how could YOU possibly help me?"

"If I was to tell you I know of a demolition man, who could be the answer to the removal of those machines, how would that sound?"

"Delvene, you never cease to amaze me, here you are amid the centre of the rag trade with fair knowledge of an available demolition contractor's whereabouts. How d'you do it love?" he quizzed exasperated. "Now if I thought you were really serious…?"

"Melvyn have I ever been not serious?" she raged.

He looked perturbed - sorry he'd even criticised her but answered, "If you could get me a good demo man, I'd buy you that MG Midget you've always wanted."

"Really Melvyn," she cooed and took him into her arms, giving him a passionate kiss.

"Steady on love, people will think we're serious?" he laughed. He was aware of the chuckles of patrons in the snug where they sat, and it made him feel good.

The following day Delvene called upon the Dicken's home, telling old Evelyn that she hadn't seen Beth since operatic college entry. Also what a great help Beth had been in school, to protect her from older girl bullies, and she loved her for it.

THE MACE GOES IN

The Dickens home was a modern council house, Alfred had qualified for, after his tractor accident, which denied him of his tied cottage to Raven's Head estate. He was a keen gardener and the array of colour in his front garden attested of this. Also he enjoyed the beauty of home grown vegetables in his large rear patch, which complimented his disability pension.

He was just then in the process of sprout collection for the dinner table, carrying in his spoils which included King Edward potatoes, when Beth's old school chum appeared.

"Oh, it's young Delvene isn't it," he exclaimed, "Oi never fergits a pretty face."

Del smiled enjoying the compliment.

"Vandel and Beth'll be comin' back soon." Eve exclaimed. "Here they are Delvene, they nipped into town for groceries."

The door opened and in walked Beth.

"Lisbeth, guess oo's given us a visart?"

At first Beth didn't recognise her, but suddenly she did, "My little Delvene, let's give you a love. What are you doing now? Did you become that English teacher Del? Oh it's so good to see my friends again."

"No Beth," Evelyn interjected, "Delvene 'ad that anorexia nerve or zomthin', and it put 'er roight back. After that, she de-soided to do modelin', an she's done very well now."

"But you had such good grades - cleverest lass in the school, didn't you go on to grammar school?"

"Yes Beth, but that's where the illness started and grades just went downhill."

"Oh I am sorry love, but looking on the bright side now, I'll bet you're glad you didn't, with all this modern schooling, teachers haven't got as much authority now and the kids run riot."

"Yes Beth you're probably right."

By this time, in walked Vandel with arms full of shopping bags.

"Oh by the way Delvene, this is my Butler," she laughed.

"I feel like one, an all, isn't anybody gonna give me an 'and?" he puffed.

"Oh sorry Del, let me," and she eased his load.

Beth looked Delvene up and down, just as she noticed Vandel eyeing her also, "You wouldn't think she'd suffered anorexia - would you Del?"

"Er, never, I mean look at 'er, she's gorra lovely figure, 'aint she?"

"Luckily for me, a specialist had developed a new technique and by his use of hypno-therapy, he helped me out of the illness, and assigned me a dietician to advise me onto eating healthy foods," she explained authoritatively. "Digestion starts here," pointing at her mouth. "Did you know that if you eat slowly, it sates your appetite and you don't eat half as much?"

"That's what's wrong with Del 'e always bolts 'is food, then wonders why 'es always 'ungry."

"Aye Beth yer Dad's a bit loik thart, aren't yer 'Alfred."

"What's that Eve?"

"Bolt's yer food" she repeated.

"Oi doesn't arv no bolts either," he assured.

"Put yer earin' aid in Alfred? Honestly Beth, 'e gets worz."

"Where I work now I sort of drifted into, but it wasn't really my best choice, I'm popular enough and…

"Yes, we saw your name on the telly in some London fashion show but we must have missed you, mind you, you have changed love - quite a lot since I saw you last. That wee slip of a girl doesn't exist now does she. You've got a lovely figure now, pr'aps this is why we couldn't see you, I was lookin' for a Twiggy not a Gina, isn't that right Del?" she shouted, to stop him ogling Delvene.

"I couldn't agree with you more love," he laughed.

"You have 'aven't 'eard a word I've said 'ave you Del?"

Delvene looked up, "Did you say Del? I'm Del."

"No Love, I'm the Del," he confuted "'ain't that right Beth?"

"Yes love, you're the Del," rolling her eyes.

"But that's what I'm called, short for Delvene."

"Then while yer 'ere I'll 'ave to call yer 'er,r,r,r 'Ve' yeh that'll do Ve it is," he decided.

"Ok," she agreed, "Ve it is!"

"What other options for work are you thinking about Del 'er Ve I mean?"

THE MACE GOES IN

Delvene thought for a moment and then turning to Del asked, "What kind of work do you Del?"

"As little as possible," he laughed.

She took hold of his hands and inspected them - they were really clean.

"Oh don't tease 'er Del, tell 'er about the two wagons you own," Beth urged.

"What's up with my 'ands then, I'm a scrap man?"

"They're so clean for a bawlie."

"I'm Norra Bawlie, I 'ave blokes ter do all that for me. I supervise 'em, cos I'm the boss. I'm a salvage man really, an' I make a lorra dough."

"No scrap?" she asked.

"Well sometimes I do, here's my card."

"It says; machine dismantler, here, are you in demolition?"

"All the time!"

"Then I think I can offer you a good deal."

Eve then suggested that they all go and sit on the comfy chairs in the other room, so they all moved to the sitting room.

"How d'you fancy a working holiday…?"

"I take it you don't mean 'op pickin?"

She was perturbed and angry, ("can't any men be serious?") she thought. "No Del, I'm talking about a worthwhile operation involving thousands.

"Well Delv…" he said.

"Call me Ve," she admonished, "this way we'll be able to agree."

"Ok then Ve I'm game but there's got to be a lorra cash in it, ter give up my 'oliday for? And there's Beth to consider as well?"

But then his wife stated, "Oh don't worry about me Del, if Ve needs you to help her, where's the harm in that? No love you go ahead."

Feeling manipulated, Del made a snap decision after some quick reasoning – thinking, No flippin Judy is going ter boss me around…but there again, wor' if she 'as got brass, yeh I think I'll go along with 'er, cos she's only a Judy and what do females know about our business? "Yeh well ok Ve, d'yer want ter come out in the back garden ter fill me in on the details?" he said aloud.

After about twenty minutes he had gathered most of what she said, but mentioned labour.

"Oh don't worry about that, we can get some doalies signing on, they'd be glad to take something on for a few days, you've only got to visit the employment exchange to get 'em," and he had to admit it but she was right.

"Yeh sometimes the obvious isn't always obvious is it love?" he admitted. "The dole queue's are full 'o blokes on the fiddle workin' on the Q.T..." They then ventured back in doors to rejoin the others.

"I'll contact Melvyn now Del. Eve is it ok if I give him a ring from your phone and set it up."

"Yes love," said Evelyn in reply to Ve's quest, "I don't think Alfred would mind."

"Thanks Mrs. Dickens," she rang and smiled at Evelyn who then went to give her privacy.

"What, already, I am impressed Del, you have excelled yourself today, yes send him round now."

Thirty minutes later saw Del and Ve in Melvyn's office striking up a deal.

Melvin finalising the details said, "...Depending upon Del's agreement to use Ve as an equal partner."

So there it was and they all shook hands to secure the deal. Del and Ve then took a trip to the dole queue and selected twelve men with instruction to supply their own tools consisting of a lump hammer and a chisel.

Ve Suspects

CHAPTER 16

The day following, out of the twelve recruited, only six turned up for work at 8:00 am at the factory gate to be identified by Del and Ve who vouched for their credibility with the gate guard and they then drove them all in Ve's Van to their place of work, minus the usual fashion clothes she changed earlier. She now wore jeans and boots.

Del instructed the men how to chisel off the bolts holding the copper buzzbars, after which he took Ve with him to show her the ropes.

"A small shifter is all you need love."

"Me, but I thought we were partners 'er the bosses," she pleaded.

"And so we are, but we don't want those blokes gerrin' their grubby little 'ands on the platinum, do we? In fact I don't want them to even suss out that it's here." he whispered.

"Oh yes Del, I see your point. If two of us have a go, then we'll get the precious metal out before they know."

"Exactly Ve, Y'know you're showin' a lotta promise."

She just smiled thinking, "Perhaps this is the affluent career move I need?"

He described the easy way to conduct the task by removing the shackles containing the actual points which could be removed by him at Alfred's house later. The shackles just fell into his hands as he demonstrated with a pair of long handled steel fixer's pincers, on how to lift off the platinum from the striker plate.

"Approximately two of these are equivalent to an ounce," he enlightened.

"And how much does an ounce fetch Del?"

"About sixty quid."

"Wow that much, then each of these 'excuses for a shilling', is worth about fifty quid for just one?"

"You're very quick Ve, you'll go far, right then I'll leave it with you and this canvas R.A.F. bag ter carry the shackles in?"

She nodded as he explained that he'd attack the machines on the next aisle, immediately in front of each pair for security reasons. Then he left her.

The first the job went like a dream and with visions of affluence in her head, each successive shackle removal she became faster even more, but then her hands grew sore and painful as her skin protested with the continual pressing and friction, drying out her skin causing more pain. She had to stop, and then she remembered the gloves in the cab compartment. Carefully she carried out the contents on the drive side floor, which she then pushed under the seat out of sight afterwards.

Her white cotton gloves she'd bought, would help a lot for future acquisitions. Later though, they proved to develop holes, but determined, she merely removed the gloves, turned them over and then used them on opposite hands. This proved to suit the task.

Before long Ve estimated there to be forty of the points stripped out, not even counting Del's effort, but where was he?"

The shackles were all poking out from under the seat, so she decided to remove them, to deposit them at the Dickens' home. When she knocked the door Del opened it. "What are you doing here," she demanded.

"Don't yer mean what're YOU doin' 'ere. D'yer realise that yer've left the job wide open?" he reasoned, trying to avoid her onslaught.

"I came back with my forty points, to keep them secure. Hang on, how many have you stripped?" she demanded.

"Er none," he looked down.

"None…NONE? So this is how you keep your hands so smooth, look at mine they're bleeding. Come on let's get back to work, or the deals off!" she warned and Del didn't reply but just followed behind.

She was absolutely furious with him and going back to the job they didn't speak.

THE MACE GOES IN

She gave him her spanner saying, "I'm now going to see the blokes output," and she stormed off.

Hurriedly he scrambled through the job rushing and not even having a smoke, but kept up a mad purge, in which to compete with her out goings.

Ve was at present encouraging the men to deposit each successive buzz bar removal, to place them into the van neatly, in order to accommodate the large load, which they now proved to dislodge. Most if not all buzz bars had been placed against their places of origin and so Ve decided to collect them with the men.

Because of their large sizes, they were awkward to carry, but with a struggle between two of the men, they managed to load the van, until the springs went right down.

Suddenly Del appeared and offered to drive the van to the metal dealers, this she agreed to and off he went.

Firstly he made a detour back to the Dickens house and upon arrival removed the shackles from under the seat, the amounts of which had grown enormously. He removed them and transferred them to a sack.

Enlisting the help of Alfred to help carry in the load, which they did and deposited their 'treasure' to the safest part of the shed.

Alfred who was very willing, agreed to contain in his bench vice each shackle, and deftly remove the points after a demonstration by Del was instructed. Del promised him a 'share' in the proceeds to thus guarantee a good conversion of output.

Borrowing another Hessian sack from him, he then said cheerio, and made his way to 'Archers' of the 400 group where he called at the office to negotiate a price, for the buzzbars.

"£300 pound a ton, sound ok Mr. Bovis?" and he nodded in approval and returned to the cab, where they instructed him to drive over the weigh bridge. Finally after taking off he discovered that the net load had been exactly one ton and the prospect on £300 to the good.

Deviously, he instructed the metal dealer to withhold four of the hundred weights on a separate receipt, making the main one 16 CWT of a total of £240 pounds. Armed with the £60 bonus, he instructed the dealer to use the same procedure with any of Del's future weigh ins.

Upon his return to the old press shop, he couldn't wait to surprise Ve with their new found 'wealth'.

"Come to the van Ve, I've got something for you."

He then endowed her with the bank roll of £120 pounds. She became so excited, that showed in her face, that she kissed Del on his cheek.

"Now then Ve, due to the paying of the men, this meant that out of our shares daily, we need to allow £30 pound minus from the total which in all fairness as partners we need to pay."

Her face fell for £15 less was a lot of money, in fact it represented to her a full week of her usual meagre salary for modelling.

Seeing her sadness Del came to the rescue saying: "So for today, make this my special gift to you, today, I'll pay all the men, but tomorrow, we'll take out their wages firstly, 'ows that grab yer?"

She threw her arms around this crusty old man, "Oh thank you," she beamed, thinking only the best of his intentions.

Both of them now agreed to inspect just what was left of the day's production. As they did this, they told the men to break off for lunch to discuss future business.

Upon the commencement of which, both were pleasantly surprised, for true to form they had followed Del's instruction and placed each four buzz bars against the machine of their origin. As they counted them up, they totalled 52 in all "Wow, this means we've got nearly another ton," he lied. "Don't you see Ve, another century for the hip?"

Her eyes lit up and she said "Hey Del, let's get these all loaded up whilst the blokes are eating, we could do it."

"It'll be a bir'of a struggle Ve, I don't know?"

"Oh come on Del - here," and she upended a lump of the copper pushing the end of it to him.

("This Judy? But I've got to hand it to her, she's gorra lot of spirit!") He smiled, as together with her he hefted the bar. Strangely enough, having to actually work, hadn't been as bad as he'd imagined, for as they both struggled to load the flat bars 48 inches long. He

THE MACE GOES IN

counted 26 CWT, which meant he could now cheat Ve out of more money and this prospect kept him going for as long as was needed.

As Ve sidled the vehicle along to each machine, off came Del's coat, for a great sweat had formed upon his work shy body and he sweated buckets. He put in the cab his coat, careful firstly to remove the £60 pound receipt, to which he secretly set fire to as he lit his cigarette.

"They'll kill you those things Del," she laughed.

"Just gerrin' me second wind love, 'poowhgh,' he breathed, 'ang on a minute an I'll be right with yer!" the full strength was heaven, its toasted tobacco's taste really sated his palate, as that wonderful strong gust of tobacco smoke fed his eager awaiting lungs and with each succeeding puff - finally filled his addiction.

He felt a lot better, "Ok love, I'm alright now."

They continued to struggle with Del now wearing his cigarette in his mouth, which he savoured right down to its bitter end, finally spitting out the stump which he ground down with the sole of his shoe.

As they progressed he asked if she had eaten.

And she replied, "No Del, I don't stick to a set meal time and I only eat when I am hungry."

"Aren't you hungry now?"

"Not really, I could go a long time yet."

"But where does all this energy come from?"

"Oh it's easy Del, us models have to psyche ourselves up, to thinking of other things more than food, anyway," she reasoned, "just look what the incentive of this job has done for you?"

"Eh?"

"Exactly, you haven't even thought of drinking have you?"

"Well 'er, (he had to admit to himself, that this girl was right) "I suppose yer could say…"

"Of course, you know I'm right - don't you?" she smiled and looked him in the eye.

Although she was exceptionally good looking, Ve also could be very firm in securing a point. Perhaps this is what Del respected in her?

Finally after a lot of struggle and strain by them both, the 18CWT van was loaded down, passed its springs' safety margin and Del wondered if it would make it to the weigh yard, without some terrible catastrophe.

"Don't drive too fast Ve," he warned. But due to the over laden weight, this was not possible anyway, for it took a lot more clogging of the pedal to even initiate movement.

Del realised they'd got too much on board, but greed had got the better of him and he crossed his fingers all the way to Archers which finally loomed up on the landscape. Del breathing a sigh of relief, showed her the scale to drive on which she did, and stopped the now very hot engine.

Del left the cab and entered the office to instruct the manager, that anything over a ton must be accounted for on a separate sheet. This was agreed and when Ve went to tare off, Del whispered to her to get out of the vehicle.

A puzzlement on her face came but she did his bidding anyway. After the tare, Del whispered to her get back in and drive the van to the approach entrance and wait for him there. Upon his access back in the office, he was presented with his receipt, one for £300 and the other for £90 of which he transferred the lesser receipt into his wallet together with the money, the £300 pound remaining, he then brandished in a bundle wrapped inside the main receipt.

Upon reaching the approach, he beckoned Ve as he neared the vehicle and entered the cab.

"Look what I've got Ve, £300 quid to share, first let's take care of the blokes' money?"

"But I thought you'd already allowed for that?"

"Oh aye, yer right Ve, I'd forgotten about that."

"So Del this means that it's £150 quid each."

"Yeh that's right an' that's a good sum isn't it? Now totalled with yer £120 pound, that makes it 270 nicker, not bad for a days work."

Ve smiled thinking, ("Now I've got almost enough for the lease of the cottage of 300 pounds she'd finally bargained Jack to allow. I wonder what he's doing now?")

"You're very quiet Ve, earlier on yer gave me a big sloppy kiss

THE MACE GOES IN

when I 'anded yer 120, now this one's bigger, yer've stopped with the kisses?"

"Oh sorry Del," and she kissed his mouth but very lightly.

"That feels better, now if..."

"Hey Del there's something I don't understand?"

"What's that then Ve?"

"Well, why did I have to leave the cab to tare off?"

"Hah hah har, I thought you knew."

"But…"

"Ow d'you keep that luverly robust figure Ve?"

"But whats that got to do with…"

"At a scientific wild assumption, guess I'd say you were about 8 stone am I right?"

"But how do…"

"Well that's not important now Ve, but what is –that Archers have paid for your weight by £15 pounds sterling – 'ows that sound?"

"Oh you don't mean…you do don't…you, you rotten devil, we'll have to go back and pay them their money back, come on," and she motioned to leave the cab.

"Now 'ang on love, I'm not really cheatin' anyone am I? Cos when these weighbridges register they always go to the nearest quarter an' this means every time we get weighed by 'em we're losin' out," he reasoned.

"Yes Del, be that as it may, but I've always played it straight with everybody, this way I can live with myself! So in the future, I'll stay in the cab," she determined.

"Ok, ok, anything for a quiet life."

They returned to the job but Delvene slowed down before reaching the press shop.

"What's up Ve?" he queried not wanting another lecture today so soon after the other. But his fears were unfounded for she elucidated.

"Seeing as all you scrapmen are such fiddlers, I thought that I might be able to protect our interests to observe, if we are being cheated at source?"

"Oh yer mean the perks o' the job?" he chuckled

"It's still stealing Del, lets hope I'm wrong and they've stayed straight, but when the cat's away…"

"Yer right chuck, I'll cover this aisle first, you pick another, and they both searched high and low for hidden caches and found many, which had been carefully placed, in various hideaways along the factory. Del counted all of the bars and they totalled thirty-eight. He was furious and said: "Flamin' thieves all of 'em, I'll sack 'em all!"

"Hoh hoh hoh, no Del, let them continue to hide 'em, 'cos we'll just come up each night to remove 'em," she reasoned.

"But they're flippin' thieves?"

"Yes Del, but they're good grafters too. No mate, let's keep 'em on the payroll, 'cos they're makin' us both a good living aren't they?" she remonstrated.

And he had to admit she was right again, and remembered something his petty officer had said on the HMS Kelly, 'forewarned is forearmed' and how true it was.

Silently, they both sidled out of the press shop and upon their return played the radio with pop music, to let everyone know they'd arrived.

"By the way Del, how much of this do we need to pay Melvyn?"

"Pay Melvyn? We don't pay HIM - he pays US with the demolition fee we negotiated."

"But I thought, 'er I mean he said…"

"'Es kiddin yer love, yeh, an' tryin to get one over on yer?" he reasoned.

"So that's it, we get ALL the profit? Then, strikes me this scrap business is the best business to be in."

For the rest of the afternoon, she continued to strip the shackles, accompanied by Del on his side of the aisle yonder.

By 4:30 they had both removed a hundred weight each of the shackles and Del with a now renewed interest, in actually working.

They at Del's signal ceased in their labour and Del carried his sack depositing it in front of the passenger seat. He now hefted Ve's sack jointly with her, and then went to pay each man £5 to which they all thanked him graciously.

After which he tied Ve's sack by the neck, before secreting it

THE MACE GOES IN

behind his seat in the back.

"Can I give you boys a lift to town?" Asked Ve but most of them requested, 'The Pig and Whistle' local.

Saying their goodbyes and "see you at 8:30 am at the factory gates," they turned around the van and sped back to the hidden copper caches made by Reggie and Fred.

"All in all it took them almost an hour to load up the van with the bars, but it was just too late for the 400 group and so Del decided to drop it off at the back of Alfred's Garden. He requisitioned Alfred's help to unloading - promising him re-imbursement for the loss of his onions getting crushed.

"Oh what's a few plarnts Del, 'oim 'arpy ter be makin' a wage from yer," Alf assured.

"How much d'you reckon is here Del? Ve asked.

"Oh about 15 'undred weight at least?" he replied keeping up the pretence.

"As much as that 'eh, cor that's at least 220 quid," she reasoned and to think we would have been gypped of that, had I not had that premonition?"

And again Del had to admit she was right.

After unloading, Ve climbed back in the Van saying; "I'll be here back to pick you up Del at 7:45am." And she drove away.

"At last, I'm home," and she was starving. She stepped from the motor and was that tired she couldn't face cooking but completely out of respect for her figure, she bought chicken and chips at the chip shop opposite and upon her return home she just bolted the food hungrily, with no thoughts of her usual 'digestion begins here' rule. After which she went to the shower and really enjoyed the pleasant feel of the warm water, as it covered her aching joints. "I'm definitely a shower addict," she mused as the shower worked its magic.

She thought of Melvyn, but then Jack's image appeared and she savoured her memory of his face. "I wonder which movie he's taking me to, Friday?" she stood under the shower head turning this way and that, with special thoughts of Jack as her aches started to fade, but she remained there still and turned up the heat, enjoying its luxury. Eventually she decided she had had enough and retired to bed. She took a light novel with her, but was asleep before even turning the pages for the ancient cast iron wall heater had ensured a warm clime.

Del quite out of character was a changed man after eating his dinner, he motioned Alfred back into the shed to re-continue with him the chiselling off of the points.

"Oive never seen points this soize' Del, oi mean they're as big as florin pieces are these, an twoice as thark," he emphasised.

Yer right there mate, an' the sooner we ger 'em separated, the quicker we can get drunk."

This was music to old Alf's ears and at once, he commenced to secure his vice with a shackle and deftly remove the points and when he stopped for his tea, Del continued. 8:30 pm saw them both completing the task and the men stood amid an approximation of six pounds (lbs) of platinum, thoughts of a fortune suddenly entered Alf's head - never again having to get up to go to work and the idea enthralled him, as he made plans to buy his own house, "Ger 'em locked up quick Alfred," Del directed.

Later, the acquisition of the bottle of scotch with eight pint bottles of Newcastle Brown, ensured their both inebriation, with their wives having to cover them with blankets before their own retirement to bedrooms.

Jack had just made a sale on an old Victorian house, three storey high and was particularly pleased with himself and felt he was the cat's whiskers today, for the old house had been on their books for months and here it was sold.

The parties had exchanged contracts and everything was going through, "And to cap it all, Delvene moves in on Saturday," he said aloud. "Oh 'eck I forgot to book the cinema seats?" Right away he did so, for 'Cleopatra' was at its peak showing, with Richard Burton and Elizabeth Taylor.

Satisfied, he now locked up the office and went home to his

Mum, who enthused with him of how she approved of his choice of Delvene, as she served up his dinner. Jack was very happy, and so much looked forward to Friday for Delvene's encounter.

Ve awoke from her sleep early at 6:30am and shot straight into the shower, but this time with the job's urgency on her mind and so remained only as long as was necessary. As she prepared her sandwiches, she heard a knock on the door, it was the clothes show driver Henry, who requested she gave him the van key for Mrs. Penthurst the show's director.

"Lynda Penthurst wanted to know where you were yesterday an' I 'ad to lie an' say you'd caught a chill, anyway Del, I've got to 'ave the van for the dresses today and…"

"But you can't take it, I need it?" she pleaded.

"Tell you what, why don't you take my van, it's big though - thirty hundred-weight, oh I forgot you'll never drive it, it is probably way too big for you?"

Ve breathed a sigh of relief, "Course it's not, I used to drive it through London full of our models last year, is there any petrol in her?"

"Full to the top last night in Euston, so she should still be 'alf full at least? He assured.

"Ok then, I'll do a straight swap," and she changed over hers keys for his.

Later she climbed in the motor and between them they replaced from her flat, all the dresses she'd removed, to make way for the copper.

"'Ave you got a broom Del, it's awfully dusty, in this van and what's all these funny lookin' contraptions 'ere?" he quizzed.

"Oh that garage, I put it in for them to service it, and I think that they must have left tools in it. I'll give them back," she lied convincingly taking the three shackles from him.

As she went to get the larger van Henry sat in the other, to ensure he was able to get the 30 CWT started and just as he was about to go she drove past him shouting, Tell Lynda I'll be in on Friday to cover the main show ok? Thanks for everything Henry, see you Friday."

Checking the petrol gauge she decided to fill up the tank and drove to the Esso Garage just opening. She paid six pounds to top up the gauge, and then drove to pick up Del, but suddenly remembered her packed lunch. She raced back to the flat and was just about to leave when her phone rang, it was Melvyn.

"Everything all right love, how's the business world of scrap metal?"

"Oh not bad – in fact it's quite good Mel."

He droned on; "Only I didn't see you yesterday did I, and seeing no progress on the dismantling of the machines, I was getting a bit worried, you do have a workforce don't you?"

"Yes we do but, oh of course you wouldn't be aware we were dismantling from the inside first?" she lied.

"But why?"

"So's that we could locate the holding shackles which contain the securing of the machines at the top, this way they can be disengaged section by section and keep most of the mechanism intact," she lied further, not wanting Mel to discover the loss of buzzbars.

"Oh, I see love, well, I'd better let you get back to it, bye for now," and he rang off.

As she went to leave, she remembered the money and so she deposited her two weigh-ins return, in the furthermost part of the fridges freezer compartment, and then came and entered the 30 CWT motor, which sprang into life.

Del was shocked to see the larger van pull up outside his father-in-law's and was just about to tell the driver to move further away, when he saw it was Ve. He went out to inspect, "Wow, just what we need Ve, 'ow did yer wangle this'n?" She related the antecedents and he gave her a big hug. "Well done love, come an' 'ave a cuppa?"

"Can't Del, it's getting late and we need to start now!" she urged.

"She's flippin' worse than Bill for urgency? He thought. "I'll have to educate her about avoiding stress and soon?"

He said goodbye to Beth and shut the front door behind him.

Ve then quickly she backed up the motor; to get closer to the onion patch, where Del had placed yesterday's collection.

Hurriedly he grabbed wildly at the load and thrust each bar into the larger area of her van. Because of its spacious capacity, he was able to just pitch in the bars without having to stack them as was their previous practise. They loaded up the motor which held the load well, without even bending the springs and as luck would have it with the very last bar Del chucked it into the back awkwardly, and as if with vengeance, it suddenly pitched out, right onto Del's gouty foot. He went white and suddenly screamed, "Eauch, oh shu, sugar, why does this 'ave ter 'appen now?"

There was something out of a comic opera that tickled Ve, as she witnessed Del's action and in order to hide her smirk she sucked in both cheeks to stop herself laughing.

"Oh Del," she sympathised falsely, for the only reason for speaking, was to put a clamp on the laughter she knew was to come. "Here, let me help you, sit on the bench seat, I'll get your shoe off."

Alfred was in his shed and heard the commotion and seeing Ve giving aid to Del, ran over to help.

Del struggled between her and Alfred to reach the seat, where Alfred took charge and undid the lace then pulled off the shoe with Del protesting still "Ow, go easy Alf, ouch, ow, don't, oh it's off?"

He breathed out in relief. Upon Alf's removal of his sock, Del shouted out again, "Oh do go easy Alfred."

The tell tale bruise was made evident and Del said, "It'll be all right I'll get me shoe back on."

But after he replaced his sock, came the awful truth. His foot had swelled so much, he couldn't get it back on.

Just then Beth arrived on the scene and Alf related the what had happened where upon Beth decided, "It's bed for you my lad."

Del's face fell, "I'll be all right," he stammered.

"All right, you can't even get your shoe on? No I'm sorry Delvene, today you'll have to be the Boss!" and encouraged Del to lean on her as she put her arm under his to support him and reluctantly, Del hobbled into the house.

Ve took off in the motor and soon she was back at the factory gate, the men were already in the factory - mainly she thought because she was late.

She decided that she would take the motor to the side of the plant, for somehow she felt something was amiss, and true enough she had been right because of the shouts of enmity rising above. "You lachicoe, you've been 'ere larst noight an' taken all the swag?"

"No Fred, you've gorrit wrong."

"Well 'ow d'yer account fer it not bein' 'ere then Reggie, yer always were a thief, 'bash, bash,' he gave Reggie the old 'one, two.'

Reggie fell to the ground and Ve who was witnessing, wondered why the rest of the crew didn't intervene.

Worrying not about their welfare particularly, but more of their production being affected, she suddenly appeared, "Job going all right boys?"

Reggie got up at once and picked up his hammer and chisel saying, "Yes miss, we're ok, aren't we boys?" and they all nodded in approval.

"What on earth happened to your face Reggie?"

"'E fell over miss," Fred intervened..

"Oh come on now, were you arguing about who stole your fiddle?"

Abashed, they all looked at the floor as she continued saying, "Look, if you feel you're not getting paid enough, say so please? We expected you to want the perks of the job, but remember this - my boss Mr. Bovis is very keen on honesty and insists on this aspect, to be able to rely on his men in his absence. He would actually call the police and press charges for theft, if he thought he was being rooked. He would've done last night when we found the missing plates had I not told him you were working under my direction, so think yourselves lucky that I was there to defend you? Are there any among you who think you're not getting enough?"

"Oh no missus," they all chorused.

"Good," she commended, "oh by the way, there are two men missing today, where are they?"

"Oh that's Pinky an Perky the town drunks they are, you only 'arve ter give 'em a bob or two an' their 'appy as pigs in muck till the carsh runs out."

THE MACE GOES IN

"Oh, I see," she said with a serious look.

"I'll tell you what boys, how would you like to earn THEIR wages on top of your own?"

All of them looked up with pleasant surprise as she continued. "Here's how you do it, strip out the same amount of bars today, as you would if the other two were here and I'll pay you all an extra £2 pounds 10 shillings each - Happy?"

"Yeh, yeh, oh oi miss, ar ar," they all chorused.

"Right well, don't mention a word of this to Mr. Bovis and if I don't tell him he'll never know?" she proved.

By giving them more work to do and the prospect of more money, she had taken away their desire to steal and also this extra work on the copper, would ensure of their not discovering the whereabouts of the platinum, they'd be too busy.

She commended herself for quick thinking saying under her breath, "thank you Pinky and Perky."

She then continued in her quest for more point shackles and with the sack she'd taken from the other motor, she was able to dismantle quite a large amount, for hefting the bag's weight regularly, she transferred the contents under the seats on both passenger and driver.

Her capacity to strip the shackles had improved also and with each successive attempt, she was able to provide an efficient return for her labour, and her ability and haste attributed more peripatetic.

Again she replenished the under seating capacity, until she realised the van front was full and needed somehow, to off load the shackles.

She looked around the job and perceived more bars had appeared. Quickly she commandeered Reggie and Fred to load up the van on top of the part load collected from Del, which they did.

"Mr. Bovis is somewhere in the press shop but I can't seem to discover just where? This way by hiding, he keeps me on my toes, but all in all, he's not a bad employer is he, I mean - where else could you get 12/6d an hour?" she reasoned.

"Ooh arrr, Mum, yer quoite roite!" Fred exclaimed.

"Oil drink to thart misses," said Reggie agreeing.

"Now then boys, how many have you put on today?" she queried.

"Ten from today's effort, and we're nearly ready with four more."

"Never mind that, remember to get a break at ten o'clock for quarter of an hour ok?"

"Yes Mum, d'yer need anyone with yer?"

"No, Reg I'll be back shortly. Tell Mr. Bovis where I've gone will you?" she said carrying on the subterfuge and they agreed.

She drove off to the 400 group and was met by the girl who beckoned her, to 'examine the quality of her cargo. She motioned Delvene to drive on the scales explaining how the boss was busy down the yard. She observed the load via the rear doors and said, "£300 per ton ok?"

Delvene nodded as the girl pointed to the shed of eagerly awaiting strong men to unload the van.

After it was empty she tared off her vehicle and was pleasantly surprised to find a cash bundle of £300 pounds awaiting along with two receipts one of which contained an extra £60 pounds to which the girl gave reference to, "Erm, here's the other cheque and receipt Miss Wakely, will you give this to Mr. Bovis also?"

"Other receipt?" she puzzled, but then not tipping off the girl, she said, "Oh but of course - the expenses."

Delvene said goodbye and looking at both receipts she realised that Del had rooked her, for it gave a separate weight of 4 CWT, which meant the additional weight with £60 return was the apparent 'arrangement,' Vandel had concocted to cheat her out of her hard earned cash.

"Two can play at this?" She determined.

It was at this point she decided to cheat him also, and steered the van for her flat, in which to secrete the huge amount of shackles she'd accumulated, into the corner of her bedroom.

Feeling quite accomplished at her achievement, she then returned to the plant, where she pulled up outside the gleam of fresh bars she saw.

At 12:30 pm she ate her sandwiches very slowly sitting in the cab, allowing each tender morsel the proper digestion it needed, in order that the two double rounds sated her appetite for the day.

THE MACE GOES IN

After which she drank of the water to quench her thirst, allowing fifteen minutes for it all to settle, before resuming work on the shackles.

She then left the instructions with the men to load the van with each successive set of bars from each machine. In this way as she'd counted back each machine's output, was she able to keep track of the outlets.

She then worked quicker with her spanner removing the 9/16 (nine sixteenth's inch), times by two and a half inch and a half long bolts allowing them all to fall in the machines works, as she scrabbled to facilitate their removal, and before very long, her sack was filled yet again and only just being able to carry it to the van, where she transferred its contents to the under seating.

The van was starting to go lower and a look of pure joy appeared on her face, as she witnessed the scene. The men, true to their word had worked harder than she'd ever thought possible, for as she looked a feeling of greed took precedence, and she didn't like what she'd turned into. She vowed not to let it take her over, thinking about her earlier antics dossing the shackles in her flat, but she rationalised this action, to protect her interests with Del. She then locked the front doors and commended the crew on the fine job they were doing.

Now with a vengeance, she worked quickly and just threw each shackle into the awaiting bag, making a lot of clatter as she did for Reggie, who was working close by also, had wondered just what Ve was working on?

"Can oi 'elp yer missus?" he asked and she froze.

She hadn't been aware of his presence at all and wondered just how much he'd observed.

She was thankful that each striker point cover was bolted on also, which shielded any knowledge of what lay within. Also that they hadn't any spanners with them - or had they?"

"No Reggie, you just carry on with the bars loading and... has Mr. Bovis seen you yet?" she implied falsely, to take his mind off her occupative stance.

"No mum 'e asn't."

"Oh don't worry - he will!" and she left him to walk to the next machine's ladder to locate the facing point's cover, but deep down in her mind she'd been alerted of this man's inquisition? Quicker than ever now she worked filling up another bag, and when there were enough contents for her to just manage, she took it to the cab to put under the other seats. Looking down the press shop she soon discovered that out of those numerous machines, she had almost exhausted all of their points, but still there were a number remaining, but thought that another day would suffice to clear it.

The lads continued to load up the back, which by now was getting close to be full and at this point she called them all down, "If you continue to load this motor to its brim by three o'clock, I'll pay you all £7 and 10 shillings each after the weigh in, which means leaving some room for two in the back and fit two more in the front, then take you all to the pub to buy you a drink, how d'you feel about that?"

They all nodded in agreement, and suddenly there was a rush to various hiding places of copper bars they all quickly appeared with, and hastily loaded up the rear ensuring room to travel within.

Ve's expression was aghast for it was only barely 1:30 pm and the van was full.

"All get in then boys and we'll get off to the scrap merchants," she invited and two got in the front , as the remaining two nestled in the back alongside the load. They were all happy as they would be finishing early today, with extra pay.

"Could you droive slowly misses?" came a voice from the rear, "only it's gerrin' dangerous in the barck an' we don't wanna ter get trapped in the load?"

"Ok boys I'll keep it to thirty," she agreed.

Due to the size of the load, 30mph was really the only speed she could muster, for its engine was protesting at the revs it took to even move. But then it did and together with the men she managed to reach the 400 group.

She drove over the scale after first releasing the pair from the rear, who tumbled out happily to stretch their legs.

Her van was weighed and from an after thought, she said to the office girl, "Hang on we'll have to re-weigh it?"

"But why?" said the girl.

"Because my crew are still inside that's why?"

"By gosh, you can tell you're not a gypsy, cos they try all the time to weigh their family in with the load. Miss Wakely could you tell me your first name please?"

"Why?"

"Well I'll tell you, you're the only 'honest' scrap merchant I've ever met, and I want my Dad to meet you."

"By the way, I'm Rachel Jacobs, what's yours?"

"Del, er Delvene Wakely."

"Honestly? Well, don't you remember me Del - it's Racca."

"Racca, I don't know any –oh no, not Racca the lunch pacca, her with the tasty sandwiches?"

"Then you DO remember," she smiled, "Our Simon was very fond of you - you know?

"Simon, oh yes I seem to recall…"

"Yes, broke his heart it did when you got ill that time…anyway Del, you go and re-weigh the load, and I'll go for my Dad to come over and say hi, ok?"

Delvene nodded and told the lads to leave the vehicle, whilst she parked on the scale, and then achieved the correct weight which Rachel recorded.

The crew she instructed to unload the vehicle, which she subsequently drove to the store shed.

She then tared off and reported to the office, where she was endowed with 2 receipts, one for a ton at £300 pound and the other for 18 CWT for £270 pounds.

It was out of this last bundle she kept, in which to pay the men secreting the £300 in her trouser pocket.

"That's a lot of pokey to make in a day?" Said Mr. Jacobs, who had now entered the office.

"What?" she replied.

"Yeh That's a lot of pokey for a woman," he laughed. "Rachel told me who you were, we don't get many honest folk in here love," he commended, "I'm really pleased to meet you again."

"Again?"

"Yeh I knew you're Dad well, we used to play bowls together. 'E was a dab 'and at it. I used to bounce you on my knee years ago, when you were a tot."

Ve's face coloured as Rachel said, "Oh don't tease her Dad, she was my best friend in school."

Suddenly she was back in the war years where she'd been the only child of her Mum Jenny and her Father Sam Wakely, and had attended the council school and met Rachel, who always had interesting things on her butties, such as lamb chops, chicken, beef and gribben (crispy chicken skin) rendered for its fat content.

Then Rachel's father spoke, "How's your Dad these days Delvene?

"You can just call me Del, Mr. Jacobs… and she lowered her head.

There was a short silence… Then Mr Jacobs, looked at Rachel, who just shrugged her shoulders, spoke again, "He was the best crane driver I've ever known?"

"…He's dead I'm afraid and so is Mum," she moped.

"Oh I am sorry love…Well, I can see where you get your honesty from, love, you had good parents and I'm sorry to hear that they've gone. Putting his arm around her he continued, "Anyway love, you'll always be welcome 'ere, I've got to go now, but we will see you soon."

Rachel nodded with agreeance restating, "Yes Del, you are always welcome.

Delvene thanked them for their kindness and said, "Well I better get moving, I got a workforce out there to take care of." She gave Rachel a hug, said her goodbyes and then rejoined the lad's outside.

"Ok boys here we are, seven pounds and ten for each of you," she gestured, holding out the money. "Now the important thing is - not to mention any of this to Mr. Bovis - he doesn't believe in bonuses and he'd have my guts for garters if he ever found out, ok?"

"Oh oi Marm, darn't worry we'll say naught, will we lards?" and they all murmured agreement.

THE MACE GOES IN

Upon acquisition of the Dickens home, she knocked gently but Beth was there already, "Oh Beth, how's Del, is he any better?"

"Better? I'll say, 'e's been drivin' me up the wall since 'es bin off, 'ow d'yer put up with 'im Ve?"

Ve just laughed, "Tell Del, this is his share of the weigh in today. It's £150, minus three wages making £135 pound clear profit."

"A hund...a hundred and thirty-five pound, oh I think I'm 'avin a heart attack - that much?"

By Beth's reaction, it was obvious that Del had not taken her into his confidence about the affluence.

"Wait till I see 'im, I'll give 'im what for, keeping me short of money all the time..."

"Also I'd better leave these shackles and ..."

"'Ello Ve , nice ter see yer," said Del as he appeared.

"How are you Del?"

"Fit and ready to go, let's weigh some in Ve?"

"'Er I've already done today's quota Del."

"Oh, well that's good, 'ow much did yer get?"

"Erm I gave it to Beth, it's £135 pound that's £15 paid for the men. By the way Del, I've got a lot of shackles here, where can we get rid of 'em?"

"Oh they've gorra be stripped yet, Alfred's doin' it in the shed right now."

"Oh?"

"Yes love, I'm payin' 'im good money ter ger 'em clean."

"Good man Del, so you're ready to go tomorrow?"

"Yes I should be fine fer tomorrow; my swelling has gone right down."

Delvene carried the shackles over to the shed for Alfred, said goodbye and she was gone.

A mixed grill of aubergines, tomatoes and green peppers laced with avocado pears, filled her nostril with its sweet aroma causing much salivation. She couldn't wait to get it on a plate with some Hovis brown with butter.

"Oh that's heavenly, she moaned with pleasure, trying desperately to get off the temptation to bolt the food, to quell her appetite, but now that she had the workforce under control, it gave her the will power to chew the food slowly, and she did for it gave her so much pleasure, that before swallowing she savoured every morsel, to elongate the perfect taste.

"Mmm, this is good," she spoke out aloud

Later she partook of the fruit salad and really enjoyed it, thinking, "I've never enjoyed anything as good as this?" Allowing her thoughts to rest on the dedication she had to a balanced diet, and strict observance to this rule, had enabled her to avoid overweight and keep her hourglass figure.

She switched on the TV and watched a real weepy film, 'black and white' about a woman who lost her husband at the end. The tears which ensued, strangely made her feel better about her life until finally, she succumbed to a hot invigorating shower, where she stayed for a full twenty minutes. After which she read a good book till she became sleepy and thought it better to retire for the day. As soon as her head hit the feather she was away with her dreams of that remarkable Jack, whose presence predominated them.

In the dream; He was so romantic and caring also, the complete opposite to Melvyn who just took her for granted as his property.

She and Jack were sitting at the rear of the cottage she'd just leased in complete harmony, when someone was shouting and knocking the door of the cottage to convey the tragedy, which had just happened, of a tractor looming out of control and engulfing Jack's mother killing her instantly.

The wheels had careered off the road thro' Jack's fence, and into the middle of the garden.

Jack was devastated, "If only I'd left Mum in the cottage, this would never have happened," he wailed, blaming his stupidity.

The dream was a long one, for at the funeral, Jack was still not in control of himself, and Delvene stood at his side squeezing his hand.

The dream faded and she awoke. Looking at the alarm which read 5:30am, the finality of the dream had awoken her to a wide awake, almost in a cold sweat.

She prepared some muesli and ate it slowly. Tears began to

THE MACE GOES IN

emerge and she wondered why? Then she remembered that awful dream and the tragedy, but how could she tell Jack about it?

Then she reasoned that really his mother was quite safe, and it had been her desire to enjoy Jack - without his mother's influence, to have him all to herself. Her powers of logic had enabled her to work it out.

Finally, to cheer herself up, she opted for a nice cool shower, in which to cool her body down. She turned down its hottest gauge to medium and, later managed it to tepid. Soon the therapeutic streams of wet caress, succeeded in their efforts to cool her down. Then back to hot to finish, causing her to feel better than she'd felt in a long time.

She left the shower and stimulated her whole being with the towel, and now she looked forward to the prospect of forewoman over so many men.

A packed lunch of avocado sandwiches she now created but an after thought, suggested tomatoes also.

Satisfied now and raring to go, noticed that her working clothes were getting soiled, so she decided to get another outfit.

She couldn't make up her mind about which dress would be most comfortable, as they all looked nice and cool. Finally she took the miniature silk version of the Dior copy designed by Lynda, and pulled it on. It was beautifully thin and not likely to get hot. She adored this pink version, and was just about to pull on the stocking when, "What am I doing? I must be losing my marbles, I'm working on dirty machinery," somehow she had slipped into her model mode, and quickly realised she needed the factory persona. "I know I've got another pair of bib 'an' brace, or have I? No, well never mind, I can take these old jeans and this old T' shirt and yes, that thin jumper, yes this'll do I'll put the cowboy boots on. Viewing herself in the large mirror, she tilted her head this way and that with expressions reserved for cat walk display, she tried on the ten gallon hat, but realising it would only cause her embarrassment, settled for the schoolboy cap she'd worn yesterday.

The clock now registered 7:45am, so she decided to make an early start and walked outside to the van which she entered, which responded to the key as though it were impatient to travel. It surged forward as she clogged the pedal, the engine sounded well and before long she'd reached a steady 45mph, until a familiar part of Penperrin appeared looming up on the landscape, and finally the home of the Dickens.

Stopping the engine, she stepped out and walked up to the front door, but before she could knock it Beth opened it saying, "Come in love and take the weight off your feet.

The inviting smell of freshly ground coffee permeated her nostrils, "Come into the breakfast room love." She did so and sat down.

"Del, pour out the coffee for Ve will you love?" she asked. "Oh how many sugars love - two?"

Delvene nodded appreciably, eager to test this 'real' coffee. Then adding the cream she stirred it and then with eyes closed, pressed the cup to her lips.

Slowly she allowed the fresh liquid to enter her eager mouth and tried to pretend she was back on her Spanish holiday the year previously, where she'd met Francois - also on holiday and that glorious afternoon they'd sipped cappuccino on the front of the café - Gonzalez Byaz.

He had proposed and she'd almost accepted, but for the heavenly mouthfuls of coffee she imbibed.

It tasted gloriously then, and it was glorious now. Because now, she only sipped of that deep brown mixture to savour the proposal.

"You look different today Ve?" Del boomed, bringing her back to reality. "D'yer need more sugar?"

"She's sweet enough Del," Beth scolded. "You know models, they daren't eat anything?"

"Oh aye, I forgot, 'ere give us another cup will yer Beth, I'm spittin' feathers 'ere," he urged.

Ve was still in her dream world, and begrudgingly she came back to earth instantly alert.

"By the way Del, how's your gout? You don't seem to be limping at all?"

Del got up from the chair and almost did a tap dance.

THE MACE GOES IN

"Like a miracle Ve, Beth dosed me up with celery drinks all yesterday and now I'm a new man, look at me - I'm rarin' to go!"

"Well Beth, you'll have to give me the recipe?" she enthused.

Beth told her how she'd put the celery through her Mum's mincer, causing it to liquidise and dissolve into a thick creamy gue. How she'd coaxed Del into drinking it all down - much to his almost refusal, but on second thoughts had held his breath and glugged it down before retiring to bed. This concoction had been one of her Mum's cures for gout dating way back to wartime.

Del's condition now attested Beth's 'cure,' to which he was most grateful.

"Del," Ve said abruptly, I'm so grateful for Beth's curing you today, for we need to go in early to stop the pilferin' of the job?"

"What, when, how, who?" he fumed.

Quickly she revealed about her ruse of yesterday, where she'd discovered the men pilfering the copper and hiding it in the stillages around. How she'd sent them on a tea break in order to observe its hiding places and whilst they drank their tea, she had retrieved it and then loaded up the van.

"Well you're some operator Ve, I take me hat off to yer," he said, demonstrating the gesture.

She smiled in his appreciation of her with the commendation.

"Thanks for that lovely coffee Del, it was so nice, it put me in touch with a working holiday I spent in Spain. Oh by the way we need to be there before 8:30am," arising from her chair, just as Del followed her example.

"You're right love, let's get goin?"

They arrived at the plant and parked the motor just behind the gate, but on second thoughts she re-started it, to drop off Del in the work area, before retreating back to the gate entrance to await the workforce.

Del was enjoying a full strength cigarette, when he heard the commotion. It was two of the workers Reggie and Freddie doing battle with blood spurting from both of each faces, as they punched each other wildly without aim.

Finally Reggie dropped to the floor, and Freddie gave him a

murderous kick in the stomach.

"Ugh," groaned he, in agony and passed out.

Del didn't let Freddie know he was there, and as Freddie reached down to pick him up, Freddie said, "P'raps thar'll teach yer not ter cross Freddie Calvert?"

Reggie stirred and looked up, "Honestly Fred, I never touched nuffin' I 'aven't been near this place since we left?"

"Oi reckons someone 'as been 'ere arn took it?" he pleaded, wiping the blood from his nose.

Freddie felt sorry for the pain he had caused - unaware of Ve's latent interpose ploy to retrieve the loot, and thought "there's a lot of dishonest folk around 'ere?"

He looked down at his old friend with compassion, contrite for all his suffering and dusted Reggie down offering him a 'Cheroot' and lit it for him.

They both puffed at their miniature cigars, and engaged in conversation and before long were laughing together, just as Ve arrived with the rest of the work force. She left the caps and spotted the two men and remarked, "Wow Reggie what on earth happened to your face?"

"'E fell over miss!" retorted Fred, who appeared from behind the machine.

"D'you need to go home Reggie, don't worry love, I'll still pay you, how d'you feel?"

"Oil be alroight misses oi've 'ad worse barngs than this."

"Well take it easy today and don't take any chances, you have to watch your safety y'know? If it's too heavy, get someone to help you ok?" and the man nodded.

Del joined Ve and hurriedly whispered about the earlier event, bringing a chuckle to her as she said, "I was right Del, wasn't I? Oh by the way Del, you and I need to talk."

And the serious way she stressed it, made him colour up for at once he realised, that concerning the 'two receipts' the jig was up.

Pretending not to know just what was up, he decided to brazen it out right to the bitter end and be inspired - to think of something in defence.

THE MACE GOES IN

"Yes love," he edged, "what was that?"

"Lets go into the cab Del, for privacy?" she moved and he nodded in agreement as they both got in.

"Yes?" He invited.

"I don't know quite how to put this Del, I've known Beth for a good many years since I was a kid, and really love her for all she'd done for me, but yesterday when I went to weigh in the copper, the men in the yard unloaded it for me and I went to tare off. The resulting difference in weight came when I got the money. It was £330 pounds for which I thought they'd made a mistake, for I got it to £390 pounds. Then the bombshell...the girl followed me out telling me about the separate receipt of £60 pounds? I just took it from her without realising that it was really part of the main load and some kind of fiddle was going on..."

She waited for him to speak, and eventually he did.

"Well Ve, you've discovered my little secret have you? He brazened it out as far as he dare. "I wondered whether you would, but I thought that you might? Yes, you're right of course, I'm guilty of course, it goes without saying," he confessed.

"But why? You're such a good businessman, Mrs. Dickens told me about your acumen for deals bringin' in lots of cash, why d'you do it?"

"Why Ve, why - why not girl? When you reach my age, your success in business relies mainly on your ability to survive. In most of my dealings, each of my successive partners I've had - to get them to subscribe to fuel for the motor, has been met with NO, not at any price! Always thinkin' of 'em selves, and so I devised this little plot to counteract the problem. I only did it through sheer force of habit and really, I shouldn't have done it at all, for it was you who made sure we 'ad enough petrol - even in both vans didn't you? Good lass, I don't deserve yer!"

She listened intently while he had his say, about that she was a good learner, the best he'd trained, in fact he felt - she had taken to the business like a duck to water.

"So you see Ve, it's really only force of 'abit?"

She nodded with sympathy for him, and finally commenting said,

"Well Del, now I've got all that off my chest, I feel a lot better, but you won't need to do that again will you?"

"Perish the flippin' thought Ve, I honestly couldn't do that to you - ever? He determined. "Let's get back to work shall we? 'Ave yer got the spanners in the bag love?"

"Course I have Del, here they are!"

"Well then lass, we can get started. Look, there are only 14 machines left with buzz bars and about 16 with platinum so I suggest that since today's Wednesday, we concentrate on the removal of all the copper remaining and platinum, before we think of 'iring a 7 tonner for the steel on Friday cos…" he droned on.

"Oh," she thought, "Friday and Lynda Penthurst"

Furious with herself of forgetting about the promise she'd made Lynda via Henry, for it was the special national exhibition of dresses which took place annually at Penthursts.

"Yes Del, so we'd better get on then hadn't we?"

He looked up lighting a cigarette and nodded his agreement.

With utmost urgency, both of them scrambled at their share of shackles until they had reached the last ones.

"Well Ve, it looks like we've finally got all the plat, and by the look of the lads, they've almost won too?"

The 'Lads' were now all winding down and taking out their luncheons, when Del approached them all.

"Look fellas, I know it's lunch time but we're a little bit pushed for time. What if I was to say to you to forgo your lunch break today, until we've disconnected all the buzz bars and when they're loaded up, you can all go 'ome with a fiver burnin' an 'ole in yer pocket long before two o'clock? He offered.

"Yeh, yeh, okay, wow, course, come on," they all chorused and literally ran to continue stripping.

Somehow, Ve didn't think that Del would miss her on Friday in fact, his urgency to tie up all the non-ferrous before two o'clock, gave the game away and so it made her feel better about modelling in London. She dismissed it from her mind, for now and concentrated on scouring the hiding places for any copper bars hidden, and after a thorough search discovered only 14, for try as she may - this was all

THE MACE GOES IN

that had been stashed.

Quickly she contacted Del, who dropped his fag and almost ran to assist, where upon between the pair of them, succeeded in loading all of the missing bars, just before the lads commenced to now load up theirs.

Suddenly all the work was finished and with the 30 CWT almost full to the brim, there was barely room for the lads to sit, so Del paid them all off in the press shop, and they had to walk home. As it was, Del had to share the two passenger seats with bags of shackles piled up.

They arrived at the 400 group, and weighed the wagon for Ve drove on the scale.

Del had a look of fury in his face when he realised that today, one receipt would suffice, but thinking of 'cest le vie' consoled himself he was making a good living and even though he'd had his eye wiped by a woman, he'd enjoyed her company. Of the 36 cwt which was left, his share of half of £540 netted him £270 pounds which wasn't bad for a day's work, but the worst was yet to come? Ve told him that she wanted her share of the platinum now!

"But we can't Ve, it's not yet stripped off?"

"Yes Del, but Alfred (after I'd asked him yesterday) told me there were actually six pounds of it stripped by him, and that's got to be worth a lot of cash."

"But Ve, we can't weigh it in till we've hired the 7 tonner termorrer love, be reasonable?"

"You and I both know you've no intention of goin' back to that job for mere pig iron, don't we Del?"

"But bu bu…"

"No buts Del, you know I'm right 'arnt I? Admit it."

He immediately started a nervous laugh, "Yer a flippin' witch, 'ow could you, a Judy suss all that out?"

"No Del, it's just that I'm not a mug," she affirmed saying, "I just imagined - me calling for you tomorrow, and you not being there, with no coming wagon, and me left holding the baby - do me a favour Del, I'm Cornish not crazy, we're all gypsy origin here? No,

I'm going to the Dickens's home now, to pick up all the platinum," she determined.

"But, it's not just yours Ve, it's mine too," he pleaded.

"Yes Del you're right, so the sooner we get it sorted out, the best it'll be for all concerned."

She counted her share, from the buzzbars, given her by Del saying, "I'm 20 quid short Del?"

"Just testing yer love, an' as usual you're on the ball. I'd not expected yer to find out so soon - don't you trust anyone?" he assured.

"Hah, look who's talking."

Quickly he tore off two tenners and gave them to her brandishing them high.

"You're nothing but a flippin' con artist Del."

"Me, a con artist, what about you with £60 pounds cheque? With bent receipt" I saw you takin' it earlier, an' I know it's somethin' you an' that Judy Rachel concocted, ter jib me outta me share - come on £30 quid if you don't mind?"

"What?" she frowned.

"£30 quid - my share, it's only fair." He laughed.

"An what about Monday, did yer share the £60 quid an all?" she reasoned adding, "and how many more have you gypped me on?"

"Touche," he laughed, tipping his hat in salute.

"You know Del, had you not been so lazy throwing that copper bar into the van and it coming back to hit you, I would probably never have found out that you can't be trusted in anything," she proved.

"Yes, I would probably have thought of you as a great guy - that is until you did a bunk with the platinum? Aren't I lucky? Anyway Del, are you coming back with me?"

"To where - for what?"

"To your place to get the platinum off Alfred."

"But, there's Alf's wages as well."

"How much is that then?"

"Oh, £25 that's: £5 per day for 5 days."

"Liar."

"Eh."

"Can't you even be straight now? Alfred told me you're giving him £2 pound a day." She said accusingly, adding, "if I ever come near you again Del, when all this platinum's gone, it'll be to shoot you."

"Oh don't be like that?"

"Anyway, today we'll weigh in the platinum, and any that's not stripped, we'll share out equally and take care of it ourselves."

"Okay, I'll go along with that," he conceded and they drove to the Dickens' home.

Upon arrival, Ve collared Alfred to show her the platinum, but Alfred looked to Del for sanction and he nodded, "It's 'er contract Alf, show 'er what yer've got?" and Alfred complied.

Ve picked up the silvery metal hefting the bags, which felt a lot heavier than 6lbs. At a rough estimate she judged it to be more like 20lbs with no shackles remaining - except the ones locked in the cab, Ve felt confident that they would make a killing.

She rang up Mr. Jacobs at Archers, and asked for the platinum going rate and was asked if Mr. Bovis was her partner and she said, "Yes, but why d'you ask?"

"Oh nothing really, but yes, I can offer you £60 per ounce."

Suddenly she feared that something was amiss and asked why?

Mr. Jacobs was very evasive on the phone, but then said, "Does Mr. Bovis want the same arrangement?"

"Oh, your not going to tell me he's already arranged a deal are you?" she fumed, "I thought that platinum was fetching more than £60?"

"Well it is, but Mr. Bovis says…"

"Oh don't say it, you've been got at too? Is there no honesty left in the world? Mr. Jacobs."

"I've only ever seen one honest person in this business and she came in yesterday but I haven't seen her since?" he affirmed.

"I was that person Hymie - remember the weighbridge, I'm Delvene."

"Oh, yes you are, aren't you, so you must be Del's partner, right, miss Wakely eh? Right Delvene, let's teach that Del a lesson?"

"A lesson, how d'you mean?"

"Well, Del told me that if his partner came in to do a deal, I was told to give you £60 pound an ounce and give him the £30 per ounce on his additional appearance here."

"Well, what stopped you Hymie, why aren't you doing it?"

"Well, it's because you're honest and it's such a refreshing change to meet someone in this day and age with true ethics."

"So, how can we teach Del the lesson?" she queried.

"Well Delvene, when you bring in the metal, I'll hold back some of it and not weigh it, but to go ahead and pay him the 2 receipts, but to get our Rachel to weigh a quarter of the principal weight, and separate it for you and then I'll give you another receipt for your share," he offered.

"Del will think what is left is the true weight, and he'll ask you to pick up the receipt which you will, but I'll give Del the extra receipt, besides allowing him to think he's maced you out of you're true share he'll then split with you, what he thinks is the main cache but in reality you will get the same share as him."

"It's absolutely perfect Hymie, thank you for being so honest with me," she complimented.

"Well girl, you can safely say that your gesture at the weighbridge yesterday, qualifies you to be the only honest dealer I've ever met, and I've been in the business thirty years. Yes it's nice to meet honesty; really refreshing."

Ve returned to the shed where Del and Alfred had been busy adding to the already large pile of the metal, and were now busily bagging it with Del saying, "Must be at least 6lbs now."

"Oh come on Del, there's at least 20lbs here. Right that'll do, we can go now to get our money," she reasoned.

But we 'aven't stripped ir all?"

"We don't need to today, we can just take in what we've got and weigh the rest on Thursday, after we've had time to strip it Del."

"This Judy's quick, bur I'll 'ave to agree or she'll cause trouble for me," he thought.

"Mmm, it sounds ok Ve, so shall I take it in?"

THE MACE GOES IN

"Er no Del, I don't want to get maced, so I'll take it in, but do come with me won't you?"

"You can count on it love, but first let's sort out the bags 'cos after this I'll need a drink.

They brought in the additional bags and left them with Alfred to clean off.

Ve scurried back and asked Alfred to put the stripped clean points on the passenger side floor which he did. She then entered the motor and Del joined her asking, "How much did the 400 group quote you Ve?"

"£60 pounds per Troy ounce - or whatever that is?"

A chuckle was heard from Del, "Wow that's great Ve, there's no flies on you. I really trust you love, and I want you to know I admire your honesty."

"Don't give me your blarney Del, save it for the blokes - they'll believe it. At least IF I weigh it in nobody get... rooked."

"Huh, huh, huh," he chuckled under his breath as they travelled along.

Finally they reached the 400 Group, and Ve stepped down from the cab. She entered the office as Del sat in the cab guarding the bag.

Ve contacted Mr. Jacobs telling him about how much she thought was there and he came outside to inspect the metal.

"It's all nice and clean Mr. Jacobs - see," said Del, who took out a handful of metal to show him.

"'Erm yes it's not bad Del, but I'll have to get our Rachel to make the final check. Bring it in Mr. Bovis and we'll see if it's worth the £60 pound per ounce? Rachel, take this off Mr. Bovis and tip it into the brass shovel will you love?"

Rachel reached for the bag and hefted it into the cylindrical shovel, which constituted half of the scale lying on the floor, tipping what appeared to be all the contents of the bag and commenced to sort out the metal. She dropped the bag on the floor with approximately one fifth of its original volume still left in, which Ve then picked up to put back in the cab leaving Del to guard the metal which he did. She was then able to transfer the fifth under the seat, and then drop the empty bag on the passenger seat.

She returned and rejoined Del in the office.

"Well Del. It's worth £60 pound oh but what the heck, it's not everyday you get 320 ounces of platinum is it? So my friends how much richer does this make you?"

"Er Er nineteen thousand two hundred pound," said Ve.

"No, no, it can't be that much?" said Hymie, "No Rachel - put it through the calculator will you?" he panicked.

"I already 'ave done Dad and Delvene's roight," she affirmed.

"But that's too much, no, it can't be?"

"It's 320 x 60 Mr. Jacobs and mental arithmetic is what I'm good at," said Ve.

"She's right Hymie she's right!" Del proved, "pay up with a smile?"

"But I haven't got that amount of money."

"Course you 'ave you're the 400 Group and they're the richest in the country," Del guffawed.

Hymie scowled, but then turned it to a smile with, "Ha, ha, har," he chortled, "you should have seen your face Del, you really believed me, when I said I hadn't got it, I wish I'd had a camera? Go and get the dosh Rachel. Do you want all cash Del, it's a bit risky you know, you could get robbed, 'eh?"

Suddenly Del realised the danger and said, "Yerse yer right I'd berra 'ave a cheque please?"

"How about you Ve, do you want a cheque also?" She nodded, she was dumbstruck and just stood there staring blankly.

After they'd received each of their shares of £9,600 pounds each, Del went back for his 2nd receipt of £4,800 to which Hymie made out for both of them, but didn't tell Del of the other transaction, but winked at Delvene saying quietly, "Come back later to weigh your cache in, I'll keep the receipt for you and your other cheque."

Not unobserved by Del, "What was all that about, I 'ope yer not trying ter mace me?"

"Me, mace you Del, how the heck could I do that?"

"Well Ve I dunno, 'cos yer so tricky?"

"Well Del, it was mostly about his daughter Rachel," she lied.

"Rachel?"

"Yes, we were at school together locally."

"You, girls, yer really take the biscuit? Anyway Ve, drop me off at the 'Kestrel' love, I need a drink," he voiced adding, "'ere I'll buy yer one."

"No thanks it's a bit early for me."

"Oh come on?"

"No, I'm saving up to get married."

"I'll marry yer!"

"But you're already married?"

"I'll get a divorce."

"But I don't love you, anyway you're too old."

"That's killed my pig, all my life I've been lookin' for the perfect woman, an' when I finds 'er, I still can't 'ave 'er – 'cos she's lookin' for the perfect man? Hmm, Del thought, wonder what she really wants all this cash for…?"

Ve laughed saying, "I'll see you about twelve o'clock, Ok Del?" and she drove a little way off.

She waited for him to enter the pub, and two minutes later she sped off for a return to Archer's yard.

Upon getting there, she grappled under the seat scooping up the large amount of platinum points, pushing them into the Hessian bag and entered the office.

"Hello Delvene, has Mr. Bovis gone?" asked Hymie.

"I left him at the 'Kestrel' just now!"

"Right love, let's see what you've got?"

Ve tipped up the sack on the large counter and was joined by Rachel who hurriedly inspected the collection and when she was happy it was clean she returned to Hymie with the news.

"100 ounces, that's great - hey Ve, you've surpassed yourself 'cos you've exceeded the amount on the cheque we expected."

"By how much?"

"Quite a difference, so now you need a cheque for £9,000 pound," he smiled. Destroy that other one Rachel and make the receipt out to 100, ounces at £90 pound a Troy," he instructed, and she did.

"Tell me Mr. Jacobs, what d'you mean by 'Troy'?"

"Oh well Ve, now you're asking…?"

"Well my dear, I'm sure you know about pounds and ounces?"

"Yes."

"Well forget all about avoirdupois weight, which is 16 ounces to a pound, and think about how the Troy ounce first came into being. Firstly, in the old England, a penny was not copper, but silver where 12 of these penny's actual weight, constituted a shilling. 20 of which represented a pound of silver. So the ancient pound sterling meant that the four crowns it was, five shillings each, weighed a pound of silver - got it?"

"Er well?"

"Right, to make it easier, 20 ounces represented by 20 shillings each a twentieth of a pound because a shilling has 12 pennies, this means that 240 penny weights there are to a pound, or twenty ounces as the world would put it, get it? To simplify it, twelve pence, multiplied by 20 equals, a Troy pound, gorrit?"

"Er I think so?" she pretended, it was doing her head in, so she changed the subject.

"Mr. Jacobs, there is more platinum to come, and I want you to know, that I don't want any more of this jiggery poke between you and Del - ok?"

"Delvene love - I've seen the light, if ever he even suggests two receipts in any future dealings, I'll just show him the door," he promised solemnly.

Her cheque for £9,960, she received and said goodbye travelling straight to her bank.

Upon her arrival she asked for a statement and the cashier chap gave her the note which read 15/6d.

"Is this all there is?" she asked.

"Yes madam," he smirked.

"I'd like to put a cheque in please, oh how long will it take to clear?"

"Usually three days miss."

"Ok then here it is," and she handed it in, really enjoying the shocked look on his face, for earlier she had attempted to get a small loan from the bank through this particular clerk, who had smugly refused her application. But after he saw the cheque for £9,960, he nearly swallowed his chewing gum.

To make matters worse, Ve also said - "Oh I almost forgot, here's my last year's salary also to go in of £9,000 pound to book."

"You're salary, but I thought you were a model?"

"I am but I'm also an equal partner in a metal salvage business I formed earlier, is there a problem, you do want the money - don't you?" she teased, enjoying the perplexity her presentation of cheques has caused.

He processed them handing back to her the receipt. He was furious.

Laughing almost aloud, she left the bank and drove home, thinking, "So you thought you were going to cheat, did you Del?" she smirked. "I wonder what you'd think if you knew the truth?"

Going Straight

CHAPTER 17

She couldn't wait to get home to the shower and arriving back inside - entered the shower which she switched on to its top heat.

"I wonder if others are in love with their showers more so, I wonder if you could call this an addiction because I'm certainly a shower addict," she spoke out loud.

All of her tensions just washed away, and she thought of Melvyn. "Wonder if men feel the same way as us women about their showers. Oh no they don't, they only use them to wash.

They only take showers to get clean? She thought. "I wonder if men felt like us women, there wouldn't be so many smelly blokes?" she prophesied.

After the shower she reluctantly climbed out of the bath, and laid out her apparel ready for Friday, then hung it to air in the room.

A mixed grill or a roast she debated, and finally the mixed grill won, consisting, green peppers, tomatoes, apples, avocados, mushrooms and olives which she then dished up, as Jack's image came into her mind. She was filled with feelings of love for this man and yearned for Friday, her night at the movies.

She relished her vegan meal with enjoyment and after dispatching it all downward, with a cup of coffee, decided on an early night thinking about Jack and the Friday at the picture house.

She awoke at 5:30 am and arose, renewing her love affair with the shower and afterwards ate her muesli, bringing the time up to 7.00 am.

As an afterthought, she felt she'd call on the Dickens's, to negotiate with Alfred (a renown early riser) about future cleansing of the points and also to discover how many of the existing ones were completely cleansed.

She pulled on her shoes and tied the laces, but they snapped and so she retied them. She got another pair of shoes out, they snapped also, causing her to rue this idea of arising so early.

She couldn't find any to replace them except for a 'cheapo' pair issued by the cat-walk for 'one offs, which she now put on, which resembled ballet shoes - flatties which now served to suffice, but rued the action immediately, due to their malfunction of slipping off her feet.

She kicked them back on, by pushing against the wall as they slipped on, but as she drove to the Dickens's home, and upon arrival at the address she was astonished to find Del putting his suitcase into the boot with Beth's help, who said, "Oh hi Delvene, we're just off back to Cheshire after Del's weighed in the metal."

Ve was taken aback, Del was at it again? And if she wasn't mistaken, he was about to abscond with all the loot.

"We're going to have a picnic after, why don't you come along?" she invited, as Del looked on, embarrassed at being rumbled, in his bid to distribute the small sacks of cleaned platinum.

Ve walked over to the front nearside where Beth sat and unconsciously tapped her foot against the tyre rim cursing, "These ballet shoes," causing a frown to appear on her face.

"Oh Ve, so this is what they teach you on the cat-walk -swearing already?

Ve just laughed and said, "Oh no Beth, ballet, not bally shoes, it's a cheapo insignificant pair. On the modelling day they issue the girls with these, they are designed not to detract from the dress in question. Usually we chuck 'em out on that day, but somehow these survived.

With a barrage of blows, Ve continued to kick the tyre, until she perceived some kind of distinct click presumably in the shoe? Where it suddenly reached new openings, allowing her toes ample room.

Short lived perhaps, for as she attempted to enter the rear of the cab, the tip of her shoe appeared to be somehow impaled between the side of the tyre and its rim, "I've 'ad enough of these horrible shoes to last me a life time," and was almost tempted to reach down to eject them there and then.

Noted by Beth she countered with, "Hang onto 'em Ve, till they get you home."

"Hey Del, wouldn't you know it, Ve's got terribly uncomfortable shoes and …"

He was ready to explode, he'd been rumbled about his 'early dart' to sell off the platinum, delayed by two females and now expected to be humorous – to say the least.

At last he spoke, "Beth, the racin' starts in ten minutes an' it's gerrin' very late love, so unless we get robbed or punctured on the way to Archers, then we've got a good chance of makin' it, but it 'as ter be now!" he raged, trying to hold back his exasperation.

Unbeknown to him right now, but never 'words of prophecy' were not truer spoken? (Attributed to Ve's kicking)

"About the picnic Beth, yes I'd love to come," as Beth smiled, Ve entered the rear of the car.

Del was furious, for when he'd put in the last suitcase, he got in the car and after waving goodbye to Eve and Alf, they drove away.

Ve had mixed feelings about the journey to reach the 400 Group and racked her brains on what to do, but she had no grounds to fear, for it was as if fate stepped in to cause the front nearside tyre to suddenly go flat, which tipped the balance.

"Sh sugar…" fumed Del, "why does this afta 'appen now?"

Resolutely, he got out and he went to the rear for the spare. Beth and Ve disembarked also, "Can I help Del?" asked Beth.

"Ok, give us the spider?" and Beth reached into the boot and handed it to him. Ve fumbled also with the spare, and retrieved it, leaving it with Del leaning on the car, going back to the boot, with the specific intention of removing one of the platinum bags which (after a quick scan up front) she clutched it and literally threw with panic stricken strength, the weight compact booty (which she felt would balance the 'Mace' earmarked by Del) into the ditch alongside the road. She then rejoined Beth and said falsely; "I've got a terrible nature call love, are there any toilets around here?"

"'Fraid not love, couldn't you go behind the bushes?" said Beth,

THE MACE GOES IN

eyeing up the landscape.

"D', d'yer think it'll be alright?" she stammered.

"Course it will," Boomed Del, go be'ind that lot," pointing to the trees by the car's rear.

This was Ve's cue for she shot away convincing them she was desperate. She located the bag furtively and removed it to a safer place where she covered it with thicket and leaves.

Satisfied with its condition, she headed back to the motor.

Del had succeeded in replacing the tyre scolding Beth for not blowing up the tyres more regularly saying, "Look, this isn't punctured, it's just gone flat due to lack of maintenance?"

"Now Del - you're the driver?" she scolded.

"Can y'believe this Ve, he's trying to blame me?"

Ve laughed aloud, and as they all got back in, Ve thought about the effect her kicking had caused, breaking the tyres seal from its rim.

Archer's appeared on the landscape and in went Del and re-appeared with the receipt for 70 ounces at £4,200, which he split grudgingly with Ve, who thanked him saying, "Isn't it better when you play it straight Del," knowing full well that he'd got another cash settlement of £2,000 pounds on a second receipt to collect.

"Yeh, yer right Ve, I feel cleaner, now I know I've done it straight," he smiled (if only you knew?). They went to the picnic area and suddenly realising his petrol was low, Del decided to fill up and made his excuses to the girls. Ve smiled for she'd already sussed the action so she said to Del, "Oh Del, the bank is right alongside the petrol station, could you drop me off there so's I can bank my share of the plat?"

Del nodded as Ve invited Beth to stay at the picnic area, to sample a special ice cream sold by one of the vendors.

Beth agreed, but just as Ve thought everything was going to plan, Beth came up and whispered, "Be easy on him Ve?" she pleaded.

"Eh?"

"I know what's coming love, it happens every time Del starts a job - he screws it up."

"But..."

"Go easy on him love, for my sake - for old times sake," she cried openly, and Ve gave her a loving hug.

Beth knew - but how could she know?

Ve reassured her and said, "I'll write Beth to let you know the outcome," and they both broke down and wept unashamedly, then Ve broke free saying, "I'll see you again my dear."

She followed Del to his car and he drove off. She sat next to him and waited a mile or so, before she asked him to stop.

He was not quite aware of just why, but did so and put on the handbrake.

"I suppose this is where we part company?" she ventured.

"Oh no Ve, I'll see you Monday at 7:30am."

"Oh come on Del, we both know that now the buzz bars and plat have gone, there's nothing but old iron left to exploit is there?"

"But there's those lovely phosphor bronze castings to dismantle, as well as the bits of 'ally to strip," he reasoned.

"Oh come on Del, now you've got all this cash burning a hole in your pocket and judging by the look of your lily white hands you've never had, or ever will subject yourself to honest toil. In fact if not for my interception early this morning, you would have been long absconded with the lot!"

"You're one smart cookie Ve, I take my 'at off to yer!"

"So long as we understand each other Del, in my bag here, I've got your option to dissolve our partnership and if you sign on the dotted line indicated - here, you'll get off Scot free to be able to return to Cheshire to spend your ill gotten gains and be able…"

He started to laugh uncontrollably.

"A bir-of-a kid tellin' Del Bovis about dealin' in scrap - pull the other one! But anyway, how did you suss it out in the first place, I mean how did you…?"

"Oh that's easy, Melvyn the main contractor, never leaves anything to chance and if you examine clause '27' at the agreement you'll see about fraud possibility, which in your case has been grossly over exploited and thanks to my retaining the appropriate receipts, I have enough proof to put you away for life."

"Oh come on Ve, you couldn't…you wouldn't, would you?"

"You'll have to sign on the dotted line in order to escape criminal investigation," she indicated soberly.

"But what about my share of the partnership? Anyway Ve, you're only talking about a few little Maces which anyone can expect…"

"So you prefer the courts?"

"I didn't say that Ve, …er no, having weighed the pros and cons, I've reached the conclusion - you're probably right and signing is the best way out." He did forthwith.

Satisfied she was now the sole owner of 'Demo-Incorp', she said, "Well Del, it's been quite an experience working with you. A male partner, but I must say it leaves a bitter taste in my mouth."

He smiled, making it obvious, that he was entertained by all of this as she continued: "You know Del, up to our partnership, I used to have such a good opinion of men, but meeting and working with YOU, has greatly disillusioned me on all of this. Now I realise of course, that you must be the worst example of chauvinism I have ever been cursed with, but I've had the opportunity to discover more of the opposite gender's nature perhaps by the way they think, and it is this, that I wanted to speak to you about?"

"Oh?"

"Yes Del, you know through my job I've been quite well travelled?"

"And?"

"Most of my work is in France, where they weigh up life and accept it just as easy."

"What are you leading up to Ve?"

"Quite philosophical really."

"What is?"

"The injustices of life."

"Oh not that reformation garbage?"

Ve felt quite hurt. "Let me finish?" she fumed. "Right, now then, what I was about to say was, 'cest la vie."

"So what? He teased. "D'you think you're the only one to realise what life is about? The French give it a name because they are romanticists, but really they don't know all the answers either?"

"Del, do you know all the answers then?"

"It depends on who makes the statement, 'cos in my case it does imply."

"I don't know does it? She queried.

"Well Ve, we worked together as partners, made a fortune, and now we are both suitably affluent to reward our joint efforts, yes this is how it applies to us," he reasoned.

"But Del, it doesn't apply to us jointly, least of all us?" she hinted

"You're not makin' any sense Ve, I'm just merely makin' a statement that we've both benefited, due to a good deal, been suitably rewarded - capitalism."

"Hold it right there Del, don't try to blame capitalism for dishonesty," she remonstrated. "By the way Del, are you a Christian?"

"Course I am - you know I am?"

"Then in that case prove it?" she challenged. "In none of the recent deals, have you been a Christian."

"That's not very fair Ve, I've shared everything right down the middle – 'aven't I?"

"No Del, you haven't, in fact if you hadn't had your 'gouty' foot accident, I don't think anything would have ever come to light would it?"

"Oh, you mean the 'mace', well, everybody does this at some point Ve - you've got a lot to learn, so you can expect this everywhere."

"No Del - not double dealing you can't, I think that's what tipped me off to your dishonesty, was your insistence to come to 'Archers' with no shoe, but for Beth's reasoning about 'discretion being the better part of valour', prevented you from rooking me good-style, and getting back to the French, they realise that good fortune is imparted upon both the evil as well as the good, but I feel that the English interpretation of 'cest le vie' is more to the point, 'you only reap what you sow'! Now look at you for instance, if you hadn't been given this option to dissolve our partnership, the boot would be on the other foot, and you would have lost everything including your good name and Beth's too. But now instead you've come out smelling of roses, with enough money to retire on, to live off the interest of for the rest of your born natural."

"I see Ve, so you let me off the hook in order to protect my name…"

"Not for you - never for you," she raged.

"Oh so you did it for Beth and her family's name to protect?" Del's eyes glistened as he felt so touched by Ve's gesture saying, "This is so very noble and chivalrous of you to do this for me."

"Never for you!" She screamed almost vehemently.

It was at this point that the faint spark of decency within him, almost told her about the latest 'double deal' but then, reason stopped him, 2,000 in fact, at Hymie's yard, but he really was touched by her gesture - even to have to suffer this lecture she was giving, on how to improve his character.

He felt like it was getting late, and so interjected with; "Ve, hold it right there, from now on in. I'm a changed man, and just being able to work straight with you, over these last few days, has purged my soul of all the iniquity which it contained and I promise you that with this future, I'm going to support Beth in the best possible way - all the days of my life - for the rest of our lives," he pledged.

"That's great Del, oh by the way, I've given Beth a copy of all your incomings up to date and she is making an application form for a joint account - in your names.

He looked sick, but the smile on his face would have convinced an angel, "Thank you for that Ve, Beth an' me share everythin'," he lied.

"Yes Del, remember; now you've got the chance to go straight, 'you only reap what you sow!"

"Reap what you sow, yes love, thank you, oh thank you, and he took Ve in his arms and gave her cheek a sloppy kiss, and held her in a long loving hug.

He dropped Ve at the bank, where she commandeered the very snobby bank teller and enjoyed saying, "I have my week's takings here."

After getting back in the car out of earshot of the bank, Del chortled with glee.

"I'll reap what I sow all right, when I get the other cheque, har,

har, harrr!"

After he'd reached Archers, Rachel burst out in laughter when she saw Del, and as Hymie brought forward the other receipt and cash, he also burst out with laughter.

"What's so funny then?" he demanded.

"Oh tell 'im Dad - please do?"

Hymie looked at Del and said, "You've been 'ad old son, and immediately told Del of yesterday's subterfuge. Del was furious, "I've been conned - by a Judy!"

"No Del, nobody's conned you, Delvene had you sussed from the start - she's Cornish through and through. I'll tell you what mate, women are clever creatures. I meantersay look at me, I've got two of 'em workin' for me in the yard, they make less mistakes than blokes, an' yer've only gorra' be nice to 'em, an' you've gorrem eating' out of your 'and?"

"But they're not blokes are they?" Del refuted.

"Now 'ang on Del, they're good at everything they do."

"But they'll never take a man's place, Hymie?"

"Oh, yes, yes, they could, in fact they did, just look at the war, they drove all the buses, manned all the factories and 'ack, 'ack, guns to keep 'Gerry' at bay, in fact they did everythin' that fellas couldn't do, because they were all fightin'."

"Oh Hymie how could yer give in ter that flamin' female, just 'cos she flashed 'er eyes at yer, anyway, I've maced 'er today 'avent I?" he said triumphantly.

Hymie pealed with laughter, "Are you sure Del, are you sure...?"

"Of course, nobody could mace me today?" but his face fell when he thought about Ve's pit stop for a toilet.

"Gar, that Judy, she's done it again, I was sure I'd got more bags than this?" he was furious. "I've 'eard enough Hymie, and I thought I could trust yer, but yer lerra twist yer around her little finger, just 'cos she flashed her eyes at yer, there's no flippin' justice anymore, why did yer do it Hymie?"

"You wouldn't understand? He said in platitude.

Hymie's attitude really got up his nose, so he said, "Oh come on Hymie, what d'yer mean?"

But the man was silent which really irritated him, so he said, "Come on now mate, man to man, what d'yer mean?"

Hymie thought for a while before replying, but when he did, Del wished he hadn't, for he came out with, "Now Del, don't take this the wrong way?"

Del was all ears as the man continued. "How d'you think it sounds to a woman, when you rant off all this chauvinistic and the like?"

"But I don't mate, all I said was…"

"Yeh, all you DID say, was enough!"

"But, but…?"

"'Ang on, let me finish Del, you came out with it in front of my daughter, Rachel the manager, and Yetta, who runs the scrapyard for me. Yeh, you said how women can't take the place of men, didn't you?" He reminded. "But let me tell you old son, that my yard is run by women, and very well run, might I add. Now take a good look around it, can you honestly see ANY men employed here?"

Del looked around in time to see the crane driver, step from her Ruston Bucurus, as she removed her cap to reveal long blonde hair drop down. For even the indoor tat sorter was female, where he realized he was on slippy ground.

But the worst was yet to come, for Hymie to say, "Now take your partner, whom you call Ve, well I call her Delvene, 'cos that's her name. Well didn't you know Del, that this woman is VERY educated?" Del frowned as Hymie continued, "Yes Del, she has such perception too. But the part about her that really impresses me, is her integrity. Yes, she's very honest in all her dealings, with whomever she meets. Yes, I can trust her old son."

"Well can't you trust me Hymie?"

"D'you really want the truth, Del?"

But Del went quiet.

Hymie continued, "Now then Del, because you tried to cheat Delvene out of her share, fate played you a bad card, 'cos the accident with your gouty foot, stopped you going any further, then when she had to do the weigh in, she discovered about the additional receipt and kept the proceeds for herself."

"Bu, But, I need it for my running costs, for the wagon's petrol and oil, and wear and tear!"

"You mean delvene's wagon don't you?"

"Er yeh well, er…" but he had no argument except by saying, "but she stole £2100 quid's worth of the plat., she took from my car boot, how can you say this, THIS is honest? I've been rooked, yeh by a Judy," he fumed.

"No you're wrong Del."

"Oh come on Hymie, she's hit me even tit-for-tat?"

"No Del she hasn't."

"But Hymie, you know she committed this larceny, under the guise of her nature call. 'Cos she took the heaviest bag, yeh, I've been maced good style, by a flaming' common Judy at that," he screamed.

Hymie broke into raucous laughter, "Ha, ha, aha, ho, ho, ho…, hoh ho hoh, ha, hoh, there's nuthin' common about Delvene, 'cos this action proves it."

By this time Del was exasperated, as Hymie again spoke, "No Del, you haven't been hit."

"But you just said…"

"Del, have you ever heard of a Cornish pasty?"

"Yeh, what's that got to do with it?"

"Well you've been pasted all right, so how do you think this pasty got its name?"

"I 'aven't gorra clue?"

"Well Del as you've now discovered, that you just can't hit anyone Cornish, without getting pasted, but in your case, you prefer to call it maced!"

"I've been robbed," he reasoned.

"No Del, you've bin pasted. 'Cos the dictionary definition states; paste: to give somebody a severe beating or defeat someone heavily. So a Cornish pasty is the exclamation of this action."

"No Hymie, you're wrong, I've just bin maced, that's all."

Hymie then came out with it saying, "Now listen Del, the correct

THE MACE GOES IN

term we should use here is: you've been bludgeoned by a feminist Cornish, er, mace'nry, hah, hah, aha, har, har, har."

Del just couldn't take it in. For here it was, that someone had changed, in the twinkling of an eye, his beloved brainchild, MACED, a verb into a noun of – mace'nry, of which this new concept, had never occurred to him. But here he was getting his eye wiped, but educated in the bargain, and vowed there and then, that he'd seen the last of Cornwall. So now with such sorrow he thought..."Mace'nry"

In retrospect, he looked back with tearful remorse, but it was such a stab to his ego, to be hit by his own mace'nry, where he'd come such a long way as Cornwall, to receive such a blow, and to make matters worse – from a Judy too...

"I'll never live it down, never, never..."

He decided there and then, never to reveal to Bill, how he'd been taken to the cleaners – particularly by a Judy, and to make matters worse, it had been by his own mace.

"These Judies," he rued. "Yer can't live without 'em and you can't live with 'em!"

Then as an afterthought he realized just what a gem Bill was, as a partner, yes he could trust him – not like Ve!"

"I should never 'ave taken 'er in as a partner, the next thing yer know they'll be in the city, showin' us what to do?" Suddenly he quoted: "Women', they're schemin', 'orrible, wily, sly, contemptuous, graspin', dishonest, connin', connivin' - beautiful things," he had to admit.

With mixed feelings he drove away from Archer's that day, but the re-assuring crispness of the bundle of 'blueys' on the seat, gave him a very nice feeling of security as a future punter of the turf and in his mind's eye the thrill of handing over the twenty pound notes, in order to place his imaginary bet on the second favourite of the day, with the positive returns of the 'winner' at even odds, gave him enthrallment, as if he were actually there on the course. Somehow, the happy face of Ve appeared on the scene and she was actually smiling at him (in his minds eye).

Hefting the thousands of pounds in his left hand, Del drove along back to rejoin Beth at the picnic area.

At the picnic area his anguish was eminent, as he cast his mind back to the day's events, with utter regret.

"Oh damn, why do I have to be so greedy? I didn't know a good partnership when I saw it. I actually had an honest partner and the opportunity to go straight and change my ways.

Instead of that I chose any type of subterfuge to exploit the situation, to enable me to cheat that good honest lass, out of her true share, whose company I didn't deserve. Why oh why, am I so greedy?" he repeated.

"I have all this cash but perhaps I've lost the only true and honest friend in all the world, and to make matters worse-have corrupted her ethics. Even when I got the prompting to 'come clean' earlier, my greed got in the way?"

Remorseful tears, were streaming down his face, as his thoughts reminisced of how together, they'd defeated the pilfering on the job, and also Ve's exasperation of his not wanting to get his hands dirty, when all the time her own poor fingers were blistered and torn.

By now his eyes gushed forth with emotion, which poured out over the money causing dirty wet patches to stain the notes, as his eyes just poured with tears of shame and self pity.

The bundles of twenty just fell on the floor and he blew his nose and wiped his face with his hankie.

He was oblivious to the fortune, which lay over the foot controls, as he with his feet tore into the £20 bundles to negotiate the clutch, after entering the key and driving toward the picnic area, which now loomed up, and that loving familiar countenance of Beth, who dashed over to the car to open the door, with the money all tumbling out. Quickly she spotted it and scrabbled it, into her bag.

Now looking up and giving him a loving hug, she noticed the wet tears.

"Del my love, what happened? I knew we shouldn't' have come to Cornwall? Del my dear, have you been crying..?"

He was full of remorseful regret. More tears…just gushed out from him, as Beth entered the car allowing him to nestle his head on

THE MACE GOES IN

her shoulder and sob out all of his emotion as she said, " There, there Del, has that Ve upset you, put it all behind you now. Working with women partners has never been easy love - they're too honest and expect everybody to be the same…"

But this caused him even more upset, for it put him in touch with all his early aspirations he'd had as a law student, of how he thought he'd change the world, but now due to basic greed, the 'world' had changed him.

It was this which caused all his anguish now and the more he thought of his loss of Ve, as a true and honest friend, the more dejected he felt, but with a difference, he was now more determined to change his life, for the better.

After Del had recovered, he vowed that on his life, he would never again be a partner to a woman in business - with exception of Beth his wife and lifelong partner. For by his own efforts and greed, he realised that he'd had the escape of his life, hoist - almost with his own petard.

Delvene modelled the very next day and everyone remarked on her new slimmer figure, as she posed for Lynda's creations, but the icing on the cake came, when she presented Lynda with £10,000 thousand pounds for shares in the business, telling her boss, she was sticking to what she does best – modelling. Lynda made her an equal partner.

A day after their arrival home, a letter appeared on the mat from Cornwall.

Del passed it on to Beth, who had just put on her specs for the Liverpool Echo's arrival.

"Dear Beth."

"Who's it from love?" he asked.

"It's from Dad."

"Yeh?"

"He says, to thank you Del for the lovely money you gave him for stripping the Plat, and that he's planted a new bed of onions."

He laughed, "Good old Alfred, he's a keen gardener."

She continued, "He says Ve came around to offer him a job of foreman, over the men at 'Demo-Incorp' at £35 per week and he's taken it, and decided to try to get a mortgage to buy his council house in the mean time," quoted Beth.

"Well Dad well done, it's about time you got an even break in life?" she smiled looking up at Del whose eyes had glistened over, and his tears of remorse flowed out in recall of his memory.

She pretended not to notice for she knew just how this news had affected him.

"Oh I've just remembered, I haven't had the 2nd spare back yet with the new tyre," he said and excused himself.

Beth smiled saying, "Ok Del, see you later," for she knew that any mention of Ve's name would cause tears, particularly now that Alfred her father, had taken place of Del.

What she didn't mention to him was, that Ve had already advanced the mortgage deposit for Alfred's home – thus guaranteeing a dedicated worker, who wouldn't let her down.

"Thank you Delvene," said Beth, "Thank you my dear."

Canal Metals

CHAPTER 18

Delvene, on Friday, had established with Beth's father Alfred, the position of foremanship of demo/incorp, where upon his appearance at the factory's press-shop, had brought forth an added bonus for her profit. For he had uncovered lots of ancient copper feed-pipes all connected to pure bronze valves, which he was able to secure and store ready, for pickup by Delvene. She decided to finish modelling at 2:30 pm and go to finalise the deal with the scrap. She arrived at the press shop, met by Alfred, of whom she'd allowed the use of the 30 CWT lorry, to load up the non-ferrous metal to take to Archers. After dealing with the weigh-in, Delvene travelled back in to town, saying her goodbye to Alfred, who then made his way back home.

Being a partner in Lynda Penthurst Creations had its perks, it felt less restrictive and she was able to leave her modelling early, in order to go and buy another wagon for her new foreman, Alfred, with the proceeds of the scrap. She chose a 30 CWT Ford small lorry with drop down sides, which she then delivered to his home, much to his surprise and delight. She had arrived there just minutes before and while there, she was able to arrange with Alfred, to later collect from her home, the hoard of platinum shackles she had maced from Del. It was getting late in the day so she arranged with Alfred for Saturday to pick them up.

Delvene waved goodbye to Alfred shouting, "I'll see you tomorrow…"

Now driving back she glanced at her watch, "Arrrh," she thought, "never enough time."

She only just made it home, got in the house, made some fast food that she could eat quickly, like earlier in the day, when she had to make some sandwiches, which were loaded with calories, but were so nice, just enjoyed every mouthful. She ate her food and then tried to get ready in record time before Jack would arrived. She had a quick shower, which was never her custom and then without much time to choose what to wear, she'd just grabbed one of the creations of Lynda's, of which proved to be on the lines of similar to the Mary Quant's original Mini-skirt, but with plunging neckline of which she had to cover, in order to meet Jack's prim and proper outlook. So she donned a thin blue jumper of which emphasised her shape and looking in the mirror, turning from side to side, thought, "Yes, this will do nicely."

Outside Jack arrived; he was all spruced up clothed in his tuxedo and black dicky-bow. He walked up to the front door and gave it a loud knock.

Delvene ran down the stairs and opened it

Jack was met with the aroma of her costliest Chanel perfume, his favourite, which they both called desire.

"Oh hi Jack, good to see you, come in love," she mouthed, pouting her lips and smiling.

Jack tried to speak, but his perception of her natural beauty, just took his breath away. Her blue eye shadow, complimenting her eye liners with her naturally long eye lashes and her pale red lip gloss, were almost too much for Jack, who just stood there looking speechless. She was so stunning as she stood before him, naturally flashing her dark eyes habitually, without actually realizing what an effect if had upon him, as she moved her head from one side to the other, as she did normally on the cat walk.

He manage to gain some composure, "I, I, I've really missed you Delvene, it's so wonderful to see you again."

She put out her hands and pulled him to her, her dark eyes flashing, as she gave him a kiss of welcome. He held her now – taking advantage of their embrace and gave her a rendering kiss, for she stirred within him such feelings, which had lain dormant for so long, as she closed the door.

THE MACE GOES IN

She pulled free of their clinch saying, "Here Jack, let me get you a drink love, wine or spirits?"

"Fruit juice for me love, 'cos I'm driving my new M.G."

Wow she thought, appreciating his concern and so replied, "Will you try the elderflower, Jack, it's so tasty?"

"Oh yes, I'd love to Delvene."

They both sat together on the divan, enjoying this non-alcoholic delicious drink, where they gazed, each on the other, completely drawn into each other's eye for a full half minute. His brown eyes and tanned face, she'd experienced earlier that week with his brown curly hair, which really turned her on. With her nubil eyes looking back at him, invoking great thoughts of love, for this adorable creature. Who so much resembled the Hollywood star Gini Lollobridgida, that she could have been her double. But with just a slight difference, yet, it being this difference, which made her so attractive.

He, just as she, could perceive each others pheromones, as they were locked in each others appreciation for such a long time, that they found themselves just embracing, nestling and kissing so frequently and were completely satisfied with each others' countenance, until she said, "Oh Jack what time does Cleopatra start?"

"He checked his wrist watch, "Wow, Delvene, we're really late love, it started twenty minutes ago?"

"Never mind love, we'll get in after the first interval, 'cos it's three and a half hours long, in total," she smiled, adding , "so we've got a bit of time left…"

"Wonder what Bill's up to in Manchester?" Del thought.

Manchester was farmost from Bill's mind as he relished the 'T' bone steak in the Chinese restaurant in Blackburn. He washed it down with a good wine and requested the bill. The petite blonde he had acquired the accompaniment of during his later patrol of the town, he drove home to Feniscowles, where upon arriving at 9.00 pm, she assumed the role of barmaid in her father's pub, The Beehive. Bill sat at the bar of the lounge as she steeped him with scotch.

"Can I book one of your rooms for tonight Cathy?" he whispered.

"But of course Bill, I'll get you the visitors book," she said and shortly re-appeared pointing to the line handing him the pen which he signed and paid the fiver. Later he helped her collect the glasses and wash them in the double sink before retiring for the night.

"Funny, you know Cathy, the sequence of events of the last few days were, the difference of my being able to cast off my daily work yoke and join the ruling classes, until yesterday when fate dealt me a bad card and I realised that I'd been taken for a ride - you'd think that someone my age would know better?" he remonstrated.

"I know just what you mean Bill, in this business you get all kinds of proposals, some fellows proposition you, others promise you the earth and some- yes some even offer you shares in business. It strikes me, that they all want you for what they can get. You don't get 'owt for nowt' anywhere and the next fellow that promises me something for nothing - I'll just ignore completely," she determined.

This brought laughter from Bill who replied, "I'd better not try it on with you then Cath," he rued.

She didn't quite know how to answer his plea but replied anyway.

"Take you for instance, how old are you - about 50 years I'd say. That's about 20 years my senior. I rather fancy you Bill, but what turns me off men more than anything, is the way which they try to lure you to bed. I mean they don't give us girls' credit for any intelligence at all. Why don't they just ask us straight out if we would? I'm sure that most girls will if you are honest with your intentions, that's my thought. How many men d'you know - are that honest?" she inquired.

"Exactly my thoughts entirely Cath," he chuckled. Then after waiting a few seconds he added: "Would you like me to take you to bed luv?"

"What d'you think you are, God's gift to women?" she smirked, "old enough to be my dad, and trying to Seduce me for the price of a few Gin and it's?"

Bill was quite taken aback by this latest ridicule and stood with

THE MACE GOES IN

mouth agape. When he was in control he returned with vengeance, "It's girls like you that make the world go round. No, I don't think I'm God's gift to women," he added, "In fact, I'm not God's gift to anyone - least of all you - no I'll change that, certainly not you. No Cathy, you obviously don't fit the category of the woman of my dreams, no, you're only fit for a one night's stand and I'm not sure that I'm even interested at that," he determined as he walked out of the lounge and up the stairs that led to his room.

Cathy by now was reduced to tears by this callous onslaught and felt quite sorry for herself, "How could he speak to me like that?" she wept and the tears ran down her mascara causing dark stains to appear on her cheeks, "Still, I suppose I was a bit harsh with him. Mmm, perhaps I really upset him?"

Right at this time she decided to apologise to Bill and commenced to lock all of the doors after which she turned off the lights and ascended the stairs.

She entered, his room which was slightly lit up by the sink lamp that Bill was using. The rest of the bedroom reflected the light so Cathy switched on at the wall.

Bill spun around to investigate the intruder, but upon his discovery ignored her presence and continued to wash his neck with his hands.

"I don't blame you for not speaking Bill, you have every right to be angry with me. I had no rights to ridicule you in that way and I'd like to say sorry, to put things right between us." she pleaded, adding, "I just couldn't go to sleep tonight knowing I'd upset someone without good reason."

Bill had started to soften up and replied: "It's a bit daft holding a grudge isn't it. Thanks for apologising, I'm sorry too love," he gestured, as he moved closer to her and gave her a quick hug, then released her. He picked up the small towel, hanging form the sink to dry himself off with.

As he turned around, he was met by her embrace, "Friends?" she asked taking his hand, "Are we…"

"Friends? - Of course!" he interjected, as she happily threw her arms around him and smothered him with kisses. They remained locked in their embrace by a lingering kiss.

"D'you think I'd pass your test of approval for a one night stand Bill?" she said tongue in cheek.

"You cheeky little monkey…," he replied, as he pulled her close in a soft embrace

Bill lived at the 'Beehive' until Saturday morning in his persona of bachelor and was glad to leave Cathy or face marrying her?

He decided to leave.

He reached the M6 road, feeling exhilarated at the prospect of returning to Newtown and wondered what changes had taken place since his absence.

Suddenly all the horror returned to his mind, as he drove along causing him to almost lose control of the Morris, giving other road users an excuse to beep their horns. Bill dropped down into the slow lane and thought of Freddie Holly. He took the next branch off, down the slip road, which led to Leyland where he situated himself in the Pig and Whistle and occupied the telephone Kiosk. He rang the number and asked, "Freddie Holly please."

There was a short pause on the line then the recipient answered, "Here he is now sir."

"Freddie?" he asked fearfully.

"Oh hello Bill, I'm glad you've called. First let me thank you for all the information you supplied us with," he said gratefully.

"Everything okay Fred?"

"'Thanks to you Bill, we caught the bloomin' 'ole tribe of 'em - even the original pinchers. George Valesque's coughed up everything - even the whereabouts of his daughter in Switzerland awaiting delivery, but unfortunately, we've been unable to locate her… Anyway, we're not worried about her - she's only a little fish, George

Valesque's our big catch. Even turning Queen's evidence he's bound to get a handful at least. And as an added bonus, "we were able to nab the 'Big H'," he drooled.

"Big H - not 'Arry Mortimer the Mafia Boss?" Bill echoed only half believing.

"The very same. It appears, that both he and Valesque planned the whole coupe from start to finish, just prior to George going bankrupt. They'd have got away with it too, had you not given us the tip. Listen Bill, about what you spoke of concerning the reward, I'll come up to your place later tonight to discuss that end of the business, alright mate?" he asked searchingly.

"Yeh mate okay, that's fine, by the way, what about Malcolm Johnson?" he enquired.

"Oh yes, I'd forgotten about him, yes Bill thanks a lot, we're doing him for withholding evidence after the fact - yerse, I reckon he'll get about twelve months if he's lucky, provided that is of course that he TIC's all of the other deals he's contrived through the 'back door', otherwise on a conspiracy to avoid justice charge, he could stand to get seven years," he assured him.

"Seven years - that much?" Bill queried, shocked.

"Yes well you see, it's a crime against the crown isn't it?" Freddie reasoned.

"I suppose you're right Fred, anyway mate, I'm glad that you're able to retire with a feather in your cap," he commented, "I'll see you later then Fred, thanks for the gen."

"Bye Bill, have a nice day!"

Bill replaced the speaker and quaffed his drink when he returned to the bar. He then made a beeline for his car, in which he drove off elated. He re-entered the M6 road and drove quite quickly through the rest of the journey, having a low chuckle as he envisaged Malcolm Johnson being caught. He pictured also Dinny and George getting their come uppance, which filled him with sweet avenged feelings.

Finally, he arrived home and ascended the steps to his flat. He lit the gas fire and cracked open a bottle of strong export scotch, where he lay relaxed on the sofa to drink it. After a few mouthfuls, he felt his eyes fluttering and put down the bottle and curled up on the sofa in front of the fire and nodded off to sleep.

The loud knocking noise awoke him and he walked to the door.
"You Fred, but I thought you weren't coming till tonight?" he reasoned.
"Seen the time lately?" Fred directed.
Bill looked at his watch, "Stone the flippin' crows it's 8:00pm - bur I've only just put me 'ead down?"
"Oh these idle rich, or should I say in your case, 'the idle poor? Anyway p'rhaps all that'll change when you hear what I have to say." Fred assured.
"Oh aye?" Bill queried, "I hope it's something good?"
"Right then Bill, this is how the land lies at this time, George Valesque and all of his cronies come up in front of the beak tomorrow. They will probably be remanded to Risley until trial where they will be…"
"Is that wise Fred, I mean Risley is an open nick isn't it?"
"No Bill, you're thinking of Whitchurch."
"No Fred, I mean that Risley is so easy to get out of - isn't it, I'd have thought you'd have put them all in Walton or Strangeways for safekeeping?"
"P'rhaps you're right Bill. My grasp of the obvious is not so good. Must be the ageing process. Anyway, after the hearing, to which we will oppose all bail, we intend to utilise your evidence of the recovered ingots together with the use of the eight leggers etc., to corroborate our case for the crown," he mused.
"You won't be expecting me to appear in court will you Fred?" he chuckled.
"Oh Bill, you're our imperare, without you, we'd have to concoct all kinds of explanations, as to why we broke into private property, with no time to gain a warrant?

As it happened we struck pay dirt, but without your personal appearance, we could stand to lose the case on that mere technicality," he pleaded. "Don't get cold feet now mate, we need you!" he emphasised, grabbing Bill's shoulders.
"I'm not getting cold feet Fred, I want to go to court, I want to

give my evidence, I want to see that treacherous Dinny's face when she finds out it wasn't heroin she pumped into my rump. Yes Fred, I want to see George Valesque's face when the judge finds 'im guilty and gives 'im 'is 'andful. The only problem I can see mate, is that if I'm completely truthful about this whole affair in court, then I'm going to come out of this doing 'Bird lime' don't yer think?"

"Not necessarily mate."

"But how could I possibly wheedle my way out of this one?" he quizzed.

"I'll tell you what to say Bill, Valesque proposed to use you as a go-between. You decided to play along with him, but enlightened me of the proposal and kept me in touch with the proceedings on a day to day basis. I in turn, promised you a reward for their capture and return of the ingots and you attempted to achieve this by your personal involvement of it, which judging by the amount of heroin Dinny thought she was injecting you with, you may have died from. No Bill, you don't need to wheedle your way out of anything - why, I can see you getting the 'Duke of Edinburgh's Medal' for this."

"Really Fred? That's great."

"Anyway Bill, if all goes well tomorrow, then we'll go ahead with our case for Chester Crown Court at the Castle in six weeks time," he envisaged.

"Isn't that a bit far away, I mean can't you get it over with before then?" he pleaded.

"Not protocol Bill, we just don't do things that quickly. How d'you think the villains are going to sweat or have time for second thoughts, if we allow 'em such quick justice. If they get away with it due to some smart lawyer, they'll think that they can just break the law and get away with it any time, so long as they have the lolly for a smart brief to spiel for 'em. No Bill - believe me, it's better this way, anyway six weeks is fairly quick, we normally send them to those places two or three times, just as more evidence appears against them. Provided we can convince the magistrates that the villains, are a danger to the well being of others," he explained. "Don't worry Bill, no-one knows except Special Branch of your connection to this, and they have special orders to reimburse you - reward wise should anything happen to me."

"Nothing's going to happen to you Fred, you've got a long time to go yet mate - at least twenty-five years."

"Let's hope so," said Fred pessimistically.

"Let me buy you a drink Fred, I've got quite a selection here, what's your poison?"

"Got any Gin Bill?"

"Er...yeh mate I've got an 'alf a bottle somewhere," he searched. "Ah here it is."

He produced the bottle of 'Gordons' for his friend with a glass and Fred smiled as he took it. He then sank down on the easy chair and began to pour a large glass of the liquid.

"A lot of water has gone under the bridge since Korea Bill, d'you ever think back to that time we spent in that bag shanty and you thought that girlie tart had short changed you?"

"No mate I haven't," Bill replied. "D'you know, the only time I remembered about Korea was when I rang you at your plod shop earlier this week," he admitted. "But come ter think of it, I was very lucky wasn't I, especially when that mad axe-man, decided that I had too many fingers," he reminisced.

"Yeh, ha ha ha ha," chuckled Fred, as Bill Joined with laughter, "ha ha ha."

"Hee hee hee," mouthed Fred changing key, "yeh, he came at you with that axe like a mad man and suddenly the next minute he's crumpled down on the pavement twenty feet below shaking hands with his maker. You crafty so and so, you must have sidestepped to cause him to fall?" Fred probed.

"Exactly, that's just how it was," Bill admitted, "anyway Fred," chuckled Bill, "let's carry on drinking, I'm so thirsty I could even drink water."

"Yeugh, perish the thought Bill, that's enough to make a fellow go on the wagon."

They both drank into the early hours of Sunday morning, with Fred managing to drink half a bottle of scotch besides.

When Bill awoke he found a note hastily scribbled which read: 'I'll contact you when we're ready Bill - see you then, your comrade at

THE MACE GOES IN

arms, Fred.'

Bill staggered into the bathroom and bent down into the sink to wash up, "Oo'egh," he voiced with disgust. His head nearly came off. The pain was unbearable - a real hangover. He slowly raised himself upward, so as not to make any sudden movement and dabbed his face with a damp flannel applying soap, he then freshened up and followed with a shave. After which he poured himself a large glass of milk and topped it up with four fingers of scotch, which he then quaffed down quickly and steered himself to the sofa. He opened his tobacco tin and rolled a liberal sized cigarette.

"Ah that's better," he spoke with approval, as the inhaled smoke penetrated the back of his throat.

Still in the clothes he wore the day before, he commenced to disrobe and change his smalls and socks.

Having completed this he changed his shoes also and glanced at his watch which showed 11.30 am, "Just nice," he commented, "the George will just be pulling the soda off the pumps!"

He arrived at his local and immediately ordered a Ham hock complete with mustard from behind the bar. A pint of bitter to wash it down; brought a feeling of contentment from his grumbling stomach. After which he replenished his glass and went over to sit with his friend Sam.

"How are yer Bill? I 'aven't seen yer for a couple o' months. Where've yer bin, hidin?"

"Oh round an' about Sam, come ter think of it, it's you what 'asn't bin 'ere, 'ave yer bin on 'oliday ?" queried Bill colloquially.

"The lucky bag detail," his friend explained, "six weeks the magistrate give me fer me cheek," he rued. (debtors Prison)

"Not that gold digger what took yer ter the cleaners after seven weeks of marriage?" Bill quizzed.

"That's 'er mate, an' I'll tell yer somethin' else…that baby what she 'ad after we got married, I couldn't possibly 'ave sired -'cos she dropped it in the July an' we never got spliced before February. I only met 'er in the January, so it couldn't 'ave bin mine. I tell yer Bill, there's no flippin' justice any more. 'Ere I am, after two lots of brown uniform in Walton nick faced with the prospect of payin' maintenance ter that digger an' that little kid whose father I don't think (even she knows)?" he rued.

"Sam, 'ow many times did I tell yer - before yer got wed never ter trust 'em, but what did you do, yer went right ahead feet first an' got yerself lumbered didn't yer?"

"But Bill, 'ow was I ter know she'd turn bandit on me?"

"'Ave I ever lied ter yer Sam?"

"No Bill."

"Well mate, would yer like ter stop payin' maintenance?"

"Cor, you name it - I'll do it, what is it, what is it?"

"What we 'ave to ascertain- so's ter speak, is just exactly when yer first met Rosy Metcalfe mate," he determined.

"It was January Bill, I know that's right, 'cos it was on me birthday, when I was 'avin a few Scoops in the 'Baron' in Merseton Rd, I'd just sat down with a treble scotch, when in walks this birra stuff lookin' like Diana Dors," he described, forming an hour glass figure with his hands.

"What date was that?"

"The fifteenth."

"Mmm, and all this was about two years ago eh Sam?"

"Why yeh - that's right Bill, but how did you work that out so quickly?" asked Sam with surprise.

"It was about that time that a certain little ram called Billy Jarvis - you remember 'im don't yer - God's gift ter women, or so 'e seemed ter think."

"Yeh, go on Bill."

"Well yer see Sam, Billy 'ad kidded Rosy over how much he was worth. 'E promised her marriage an' a big 'ouse ter go with it, if she'd 'elp 'im over is bad patch. While he was on the sick, I think she was the only one who didn't know 'e adn't worked since 'is first divorce ten years before. He started givin' 'er one regular an' lettin' 'er buy all 'is booze, until she come out of work and the cash dried up. Next thing yer know, she's in the puddin' club an' looking for a mug ter make an honest woman of 'er. That's when you came along - tailor made ter fit the bill. Yer know all the rest don't yer?"

THE MACE GOES IN

"Well flamin' 'eck, why didn't yer tell me all this before Bill, yer could 'ave saved me a lotta trouble?"

"Sammy?" Bill stormed, "are you serious, what d'yer think all yer pals was tryin' ter do two years ago, when we took yer for a stag night? Yer nearly didn't make it the next day did yer. If it 'adn't bin fer Rosy's Mam waitin' outside the club in 'er car, you wouldn't of made it ter the Registry Office on time."

"Yeh Bill, I remember now, yer did do yer best ter put me off 'er didn't yer, only I thought I was in love with 'er didn't I," he confessed. "Yer know Bill, it's a true sayin', there's no fool like an old fool, is there?" Sam thought for a minute and suddenly said, "But what can I do about all this."

"Well mate, d'yer think yer'd 'ave any trouble banjoing Billy, or d'yer want me ter do it?"

"No chance Bill, I'll do it, I'm going ter enjoy this. I've never liked that little beggar-ever, and I'll make 'im sorry 'e ever 'ad any truck with Rosy."

"Now 'ang on Sam, do it the right way, threaten 'im with a broken nose or a few teeth ter make 'im cough up to admitting it is his kid, an' signin' an admission to it, yer could ger a solicitor ter witness it couldn't yer - even if nuthin' comes of it, you'd 'ave the alimony squashed wouldn't yer?"

"D'yer think that'd work Bill? I mean..."

"Course it would," Bill emphasised, "yer know 'ow 'e poses in front of the mirror, the last thing 'e wants is 'is features changed."

"Bur 'e's outer collar, 'ow could 'e pay?"

"'E couldn't but the National Assistance could, and they'd make sure that they claimed it back off 'im. Then the shoe'd be on the other foot wouldn't it? He'd be the one doin' Brown Uniform, collectin' the 'lucky bags' at (human refuse) Walton nick!," with the 'andcart.

"I see what yer mean," he concurred happily, "I'll do it Bill, in fact I'll do it now," he mouthed with glee.

"Ang on Sam, 'ave a bevvie, it's Sunday yer know, what would they think about yer threatenin' folk on a Sunday? Better leave it till termorrer dinner, yer'll catch 'im in the Baron's'bar at one o'clock won't yer?"

"Yeh Bill, yer right mate, we'll 'ave a bevvie now an' worry about that later."

"By the way Sam, 'ave yer still got that old coal wagon what yer had last year?" he asked.

"Course I 'ave, why d'yer ask Bill?" he queried.

"Is it still taxed?" Bill probed.

"Nar, bur it's still runnin' well, I uses it fer the ole rags an' tats and as our "'Arry does the 'bawlin', I just crawl along fer 'im ter load up. We don't do so bad, bur it's gettin' a bit slack now - what 'ave yer got in mind?" he posed.

"On the top o'the 'ill at Thamestmor, there's a Plumber an' steel fabricators, now keep this under yer 'at,"- he lowered his voice to a whisper- "Me an" Del cleans the skip out every month for the steel bloke. But unbeknown to Del, I talked the Plumber into sellin' me all 'is boilers. Pure 'eavy copper they are but the snag is, I've gorra ger up there before Tuesday, otherwise Del'll probably see 'em, an' wanna mace 'em," he urged.

"But what's up with macein' 'em Bill?"

"Nuthin' really Sam - 'ceptin' yer can't go back again, an' anythin' as good as that, is worth goin' back for time an' time again," he exhorted.

"Say no more Bill," he said, winking his eye. So you think I can 'elp out with the transport arrangements?"

"Exactly that mate - what d'yer say? Fifty-fifty down the middle mate?"

"Yer've got yerself a deal Bill, by the way 'ow much d'yer think yer can get 'em for?"

"You leave that side o' the business ter me Sam an' we'll take it out o' the weigh-in, okay?"

"Sounds okay to me Bill," he assured, "where and when d'yer want me ter pick yer up?"

"I'll come down ter your place Sam at half past seven Monday morning and we'll go from there, 'ow's that grab yer?"

"Bang on mate, bang on," his friend approved.

Bill drank all afternoon with Sam and even drank a few scotches,

THE MACE GOES IN

but only till early evening, reminding his friend of the need to be early, the next day.

Monday morning saw both of them driving along the Wrexham Road at 8.10 am making good time and negotiating the left turn to Thamestmor, which lay at the brow of the hill. They arrived at the Plumber's yard and Bill motioned Sam to remain in the cab.

The door opened just as Bill was about to enter with the secretary removing the key from the inside.

"Can I help you sir - do you require Mr. Jenkins?" she asked politely.

"Oh yes," he nodded, adding, "Tell him it's Bill Foggit from Newtown."

Bill sat waiting for a few minutes in the passage before the man arrived, reminiscing the events of the last week.

"Mr. Foggit?"

He looked up and answered, "Yes sir, that's me, I came here about a month ago to negotiate a price for your scrap boilers?" he reminded,

"Oh yes, and I asked you to return, hmm, you've just come at the right time it seems Mr. Foggit, we've run out of storage space to keep them. Tell me, are you prepared to take this light stuff away as well?" he searched.

"What kind of light stuff is it sir?" asked Bill.

"Come and take a look," he indicated, as he pointed to the inner door, which led to the rear of the workshop.

Bill walked forward toward the copper boilers which lay about everywhere, wondering where the light stuff lay.

"That's it," said the man, "what can you offer me for this lot?"

Bill was confused but thought the man had made a mistake so he played along with him by replying, "Hmm, let's see how many of these light boilers are there," and he commenced to point his finger counting: "3,5,11,14,17,24 and ten that's 34 and...have you any more?" he asked.

"Of the light ones? No, I'm glad to say, well what can you offer me?" he asked hurriedly.

"Is there any other stuff besides this sir?" Bill probed.

"Yes but I want to sell this light stuff first," he pressed.

"Well, I'd be willing to give you £80 per ton on this so let's see now, 34 divided by 4 equals 8 ½ hundred weight which is er, er.

"Sixty eight pounds Mr. Foggit, yes, I'll accept that - now I'll show you the heavy gear, follow me."

Bill trailed obediently behind and the man who opened the rear store door to reveal, an absolute fortune in thick gauge copper pipes, 9inches diameter with ¾" thick copper flanges.

Bill almost choked and was unable to speak as his eyes beheld the gleaming array.

"Now then Mr. Foggit, all of this is not scrap, as you've probably guessed? Most of which you see here has got to be re-cycled at the paper mill at Feniscowles, but a lot of it is just rubbish, and couldn't be used again. That's why we need the main workshop clearing of all those light boilers."

"Funny, I was in Feniscowles only on Saturday, a bit of business,'" he lied as he thought of Cathy.

"Really?" voiced the man trying to show interest, "anyway, getting back to this Mr. Foggit, I can promise to have it ready in two weeks time if you'd like to call to put a price on it."

Bill reached into his wallet for the money and upon saying, "A pleasure to do business with you Mr. Jenkins," he shook the man's hand adding, "could you open the main doors for my driver to back in sir? Thank you. And oh, could you sign my receipt book sir – er proof of my purchase."

So the man did and then said, "Goodbye Mr. Foggit."

After loading Sam's wagon, he climbed into the passenger side saying, "Take the Mold Rd home Sam, there's less Scuffers on it."

Sam drove out of the yard and the boilers rattled and clunked at the rear.

"Two pound a piece I gor 'em for Sam, we'll make a flamin' fortune on 'em!" he enthused, "thirty four of the beggars we've got, now let's see, I thought they'd be about a quarter cwt each, but lookin' 'em over, we've got mostly big 'uns so that means we've got about 15 'undred weight, which isn't bad for 68 quid is it mate?" he

THE MACE GOES IN

lied - actually Bill had speculated on at least 18 hundred weight - and felt a little uneasy because he'd kidded Mr. Jenkins about the weight, lied about the purchase price to Sam, and was about to perpetrate a mace of three hundred weight from him also.

Sam between driving, reached into his inside pocket for his so-called 50-50 split with the outlay of £34 and Bill promptly pocketed it with, "Oh ta Sam, now we're quits. Oh, by the way mate, how much diesel d'you think you've used?" he asked.

"Oh, about 4 or 5 quid Bill," he speculated.

"Here's what we'll do Sam, when we get the money off the weigh-in, we'll take a fiver out eh mate? - no, better still, I'll give yer two pound ten shillin' now and that'll be quits won't it mate?"

Sam nodded his approval and drove the wagon into Chester to 'Canal Metals' which came into view.

"I'll go and negotiate a price Sam, you watch the load!" Bill instructed as he leapt from the wagon. He entered the yard and made a bee-line for Freddie Boxman the owner.

"Freddie, 'ave I gor a load fer you?" he voiced excitedly, "but listen mate, I'll 'ave ter 'ave the receipts done with three 'undred weight short on the one - you know the mace job?" he winked knowingly.

"What's in it for me Bill?" Fred demanded.

"Oh, go on, I'll give yer a fiver back fer yerself," he promised.

"The things yer 'ave ter do ter make a livin'," Fred rued with disgust at the deception, but agreed to the ruse eager to get the custom.

"Back the motor in Sam - they're goin' ter give us top bat," Bill assured.

After the boilers had been weighed, Bill jubilantly handed the receipt describing the bulk of the copper to Sam who read out approvingly, "Fifteen hundred weight, totalling £225 in cash. The 'maced' receipt he kept in his wallet.

"Happy Sam?" he smiled.

"Yer, I'll say Bill. oi, it says 'ere that it come ter fifteen 'undred weight at £300 per ton. Blimmin' 'eck that's too much... oh no, I forgot about the quarter," he corrected himself. "Well now, let's see, if I take £112/10 out fer meself and knock of f £34 outlay for over 'eads it leaves me with a profit of £80-7/6' ter the good. That's fantastic mate, it's nearly 200% per cent profit! You'll do me Bill, anytime yer want transport fer another drop-give us a shout? £78 for a morning's work, I still can't get over it!" he enthused with joy.

Bill said nothing but just chuckled. He wasn't very happy with himself. He had the other receipt tucked safely in his wallet for the remaining £90 and felt sick inside.

Yes, Del had really got to him with his dirty tricks of the 'mace' as it went against the grain of his almost submerged principles. His conscience bothered him so much that he prayed to God in his mind. After some deliberation, he deducted the £2-10/- he had paid Fred and decided to donate the remaining cash figure to Doctor Barnardo's Homes, to appease his conscience. He made an excuse to Sam to detour in Chester and drop him off at Northgate Street where the charity was based. He waved goodbye and Sam was gone.

Slipping into a Midland Bank alongside he procured a cheque for the set amount and delivered it to the charity secretariat who thanked him and gave him a receipt.

After giving the bankers draft to the charity, he left Chester in a taxi, completely rejuvenated by his action and able to live with himself once more. Arriving back at the flat, he removed the day's profit from his pocket. He noted the time, it was 2.35 pm, "Hmm," he murmured, "if I put a sock in it, I'll just have enough time to make the bank."

As he entered the Riverton bank, the manager made a noticeable effort to serve him before the other tellers arrived.

"Mr. Foggit, how are you? It"s very good to see you sir. Allow me to thank you for that tip you gave me. As a result of it, I was able to transfer all of my Unit Trusts' and make a practical fortune."

"What, oh yes I remember, the bullion investment," Bill recalled, happy that he was able to help.

"I'd like you to add this to my deposit account please," he requested handing in the money. The manager readily complied furnishing him his receipt. Bill felt accomplished with the day's

THE MACE GOES IN

progress and decided he'd go for a drink in the old serviceman's club.

After sampling the brew, he wished he hadn't. The bitter tasted like soda. They obviously hadn't cleaned the pumps with enough fresh water and the customers now bore the brunt of the indiscretion. Most of the regulars were drinking bottled stuff out of disgust for the brew, But Bill decided to go home. On his Way out he bumped into an old friend Henry Baker,

"Whoops, I'm sorry mate," said the man.

"Oh 'ello 'Enry 'ow are yer?"

"Bill? Bill? Champion mate, where've yer bin lately?"

"Oh round an' about 'Enry - yer know 'ow it is?" he said.

Henry took on a serious note and informed him,

"I need the advice of somebody like yourself Bill, what d'yer think of this Arthur Fogg can 'e be trusted?"

"Well 'Enry, 'ow far can yer throw 'im?" he asked.

"I thought you'd say that Bill, I've been worried about 'im all week. I've got this birrofa contract clearin' the EVCO chemical plant out an' there's a lotta bronze and copper ter come outer the job an' I was wonderin' if I could leave 'im to it, while I negotiate this 'ead cherang fer the platinum points." he explained.

"When are yer doin' the job 'Enry?"

"Bin on it all week mate, tell yer the truth, I could do with an extra hand - are yer workin' at all? I'd pay yer four bluies (£20) a day ter watch them other three as well as work - interested?"

"As much as that eh 'En' - will the job stand it?"

"Course it will Bill, if you'd seen 'ow much stuff there was yesterday, you'd be amazed…"

Bill thought for a moment before replying:

"Trouble is 'En', Del's comin' back on Tuesday mate, so if anythin', I could only do termorrer," he emphasised.

"Well, okay Bill that should do it, but don't tell that crowd o' Lachichoes that yer only there fer just one day, no, as far as they're concerned I'll tell 'em you'll be there till the end o' the job. That way it might deter 'em from nickin' anythin' from the plant - what d'yer think mate."

"Okay 'Enry, I'll give it a whirl, give me the address - oh and by the way, who are these other two you've got workin' for you?" he queried.

"Er, I was hopin' yer wouldn't ask Bill."

"They can't be that bad 'Enry - or can they?" he probed. "Come on now, who are they - out with it?" he commanded with a voice of authority.

"Oh all right, it's Knight and Day Salvage," he finally relented.

"Oh 'Enry, yer bloomin' silly sod, yer mean ter tell me I've got ter work alongside those two gaol birds? They're the biggest pair o' thieves in the town. Yer must o' bin 'ard pushed to 'ire these baskets," he emphasised.

"Oh they're not that bad Bill, p'rhaps just a bit light fingered, but apart from that they're good grafters, and that's what we need right now."

"I'll pay yer £20 - 'e says," Bill mimicked, "no chuggin' wonder? Workin' with Blackie Knight and Sonnie Day, I'll 'ave ter keep checkin' me pockets with these two around me. Oh go on 'Enry, I'll do it then," he relented, "Where shall I pick 'em up?"

Henry furnished Bill with the address of the Chemical firm adding: "Pick 'em all up at the corner o' Westminster Rd at 7.30 am termorrer. By the way, Frederick Engels is the name of the chief engineer who will instruct you and the men what to do Bill. Any questions mate?"

"Yeh, after 'earin' about Knight and Day and now Frederick Engels, I'm 'alf expectin' Karl Marx ter come creepin' out of the woodwork, ha ha," he joked at Henry's expense.

Henry smiled and said, "See yer at the plant Bill, tarah!"

Bill decided to get as much done that day regarding his shopping for shirts and shoes. The shirts which he favoured of the short collar style then prevailing and proving to opt for black Gibson shoes to match his dark suits, Burton's the tailors' manager was quite happy with Bill's order which he proceeded to pay with cash to clinch the sales.

"Thank you sir, come again," voiced the man, obviously pleased with Bill's recent choices which Bill removed from the shop and placed in his car. He then proceeded to drive back to the direction of the Old Serviceman's Club, where upon he locked his car and entered in.

"Pint o' bitter Agnes," he requested adding, 'and chalk it up!"

"Hiya Bill, haven't seen you 'ere for ages, been away 'ave yer," nosily, inferring prison.

"Aye that's right," he replied, "I've 'ad a lorra business lately, by the way 'ow's the beer trade?" he enquired.

"Not so good Bill, we don't seem ter sell a lot of it just lately," she complained.

Bill felt just a bit insulted by Agnes quote of 'been away 'ave yer' which inferred a gaol term.

"I'm not surprised Aggie, judging by the way yer pulled this pint."

"'Ow d'yer mean?"

Ignoring her request he further remarked: "Aye, yer'd sell a lot more beer if you took my advice!"

"Sell more," she mimicked, "How then smarty pants?"

"Fill the scutching glasses up," he replied adding, "Just look at this glass o' mine what yer've given me is ¾ of an inch off the top," he criticised, "fellas won't put up with this Aggie! I realise that yer've got ter 'ave a bit o' fiddle ter make the job pay, and if yer keep a bit o' beer back every time, it means that yer can pocket the price of a couple of pints every session but you 'ave ter use yer loaf when it comes ter the fiddle," he emphasised. Judging by the look on Agnes' face, she obviously didn't like Bill's counsel and went up to the boss to complain about his criticism.

"Gorra trouble maker 'ere Cecil."

Upon hearing Agnes' complaint fully, he commenced to tear off a strip at Bill's expense, who retaliated with, "Listen Cecil, I only asked her ter fill me glass up - where's the 'arm in that?" he pleaded.

But Cecil was adamant with him and further added insult to injury, by ordering Bill to drink up and remove himself from the premises.

Bill was aghast and retaliated with, "What d'yer mean Cecil - get out?" he reasoned. "Listen mate, I'm an old serviceman, I'm a paid up member o' this club and entitled ter stay 'ere, and neither you nor anybody 'ere as the right ter stop me drinkin'," he exclaimed.

Cecil was taken aback slightly, but felt that he'd stuck his neck out and to avoid losing face, felt the need to assert himself by replying, "As steward of this club, I can use whatever discretion I like- that's my prerogative, I want you out, and that's the end of it!"

Upon the delivery of his daring speech, he took hold of Bill by the shoulder, re-iterating his intention by saying, "Now Mister," in a bid to hurry Bill's removal.

Bill completely ignored Cecil's demonstration and commenced to drink his beer slowly, which proved to agitate the manager even further. Bill knew the law, the manager had no right to lay hands on his person or forcibly remove him at all and although he could have quite easily downed the man with a few deft punches in the right places, he decided to teach this arrogant upstart a lesson.

"Take your hand off my shoulder Cecil - you're committing common assault," he warned. But Cecil seemed to become more agitated by this, and continued to wrestle with Bill, who shouted to Charlie Ellis who owed him money: "Charlie tell Cecil he can't do this!"

Cecil by now was struggling with Bill, who was straining to obstruct the man's attempt to remove him. Also, Charlie responded by saying,

"Hey Cec, Bill's right yer know, yer can't put 'im out forcibly, yer can only ask 'im ter leave!"

"You keep outer this," warned the steward, "or you'll be goin' as well!"

Charlie looked at Bill with his hands open gesture. He obviously wasn't prepared to lose his own membership as well, until Bill commanded him, "Charlie, I need you as a witness mate."

With this, Charlie who was interested in staying in Bill's good books particularly due to his debt owing - responded by walking out toward the outer doors, in the bid to witness the proceedings from a vantage point.

Bill sussed what Charlie was up to and continued with his refusal to leave by, "I've got my rights Cecil, I fought in the war for the likes of you!"

THE MACE GOES IN

This struck a sore point with Cecil who had made no secret about being a conscientious objector in the war but this felt like an insult. He grabbed Bill by the arm and forcibly ejected him out of his seat still with his pint glass still in his hand, from which the contents spilled over the floor, where eventually the glass followed.

By this time Bill retaliated only by struggling and further insulting the man with, "Yeller conshie," which proved to infuriate the manager who threw a punch right into Bill's right eye. Followed by another on to Bill's nose, which commenced to bleed profusely. Bill smiled - this was just what he wanted. He noticed that Charlie who was hiding behind the stone pillar, had observed all of this and as Bill was man-handled out of the club by Cecil, he was quickly followed by Charlie who ensured that Cecil had gone back into the club before he re-joined Bill.

Bill allowed his nose to bleed holding his head to left and to right directing the blood onto his shirt and suit, which looked like he'd been beaten up badly.

Charlie produced a handkerchief and gave it to Bill who made his way to his car.

Charlie accompanied him as Bill started coughing and pretending to choke.

"Aagh cough cough cough heer-hagh," he sounded, as he attempted to clear his throat.

"Blimmin' 'eck Bill, yer need ter get ter 'ospital, 'ere I'll drive yer," worried for his health.

Bill made no resistance to this gesture and sat in the passenger side of the Morris Minor. Charlie took the key from him and started the car which he entered into gear and drove toward the Chester direction.

"Listen Charlie, I want yer as a witness - are yer game?" he quizzed between coughs.

"Course I am Bill, I saw it all!" Willingly

"That's good mate," said Bill, 'cos I want yer ter pull in ter the cop shop!"

"'Ave an 'eart Bill, I've 'ad a few scoops. They'll do me fer drunken drivin'?" he pleaded.

"Use yer loaf Charlie - park the car at the 'Barons'," he reasoned.

"Oh aye yeh, I never thought o' that."

Charlie parked the Morris and both he and Bill arrived at the police station.

"I want to report a., cough, cough, 'an assault," said Bill, as the blood started to drip over the station floor, encouraged by his earlier action of blowing his nose as he entered the building.

"Strewth," said the sergeant, "wha' happened?"

Bill tried to explain and suddenly experienced real difficulty in speaking as the intermittent blood dripped down the back of his throat causing him to choke. Charlie whacked his back which helped and his friend commenced to explain the circumstances, which Bill agreed with for it put him in a good light.

"So he just man-handled you provoking your resistance sir?" asked the sergeant standing by.

"Ye, yes that's right, I told hi - him he was breaking the law bu' bu' but Cecil just grabbed me and hit me twice as you can see," pointing to his nose and eye."

"Didn't you retaliate in any way sir?" asked the sergeant, who was not entirely convinced of the story.

"I w' was te' tempted serge," Bill stressed, "but felt that because of my specialist training in the army, I might 'ave ended up doing something I would regret."

"Oh what mob were, you in sir?" he queried.

"I was an assault trooper sergeant in the Royal Armoured Corps," he replied, honourably.

"Hmm…I see Mr. Foggit, perhaps in view of the circumstances, you did the right thing. Well sir, I'll send a constable down to see this Cecil er…"

"Cecil Arbuckle is his name," Charlie retorted.

"Don't worry sir, we'll sort it all out," he assured, "would you care to leave your full name and address before you go. I'd say sir, that by the look of your face you could do with seeing a doctor?"

"I'll take him up to the 'ospital serge," said Charlie.

After the paper work was completed the sergeant asked the inspector if he should go to investigate and his superior replied, "Yes

THE MACE GOES IN

Jenkins, you get the particulars right now before closing time, whilst Mr. Ellis takes Mr. Foggit up to the casualty," he commanded.

"By the way Mr. Foggit, in view of the unusual circumstances, I honestly believe that Mr. Arbuckle will probably give you an apology in view of what has happened. What you have to remember sir, is that in pubs and clubs there is a certain element of trouble to be expected from some patrons and quite often preventative measures need to be taken. In this case, perhaps Mr. Arbuckle misinterpreted your actions and contemplated further trouble. This would probably explain his later actions sir," he offered.

"But he hit me for no reason?" Bill emphasised.

"Unfortunately this does tend to happen when a manager uses his discretion, depending upon the circumstances," he further stressed.

Bill was quite exasperated by this approach and countered it by, "I want to press charges," he said firmly.

"Let's see what Cecil has to say first Mr. Foggit. You get your hospital treatment and we'll be in touch," he promised.

"I'd rather sign the statement now," said Bill firmly, adding, 'or we'll see what my solicitor has to say!"

"You do as I advised Mr. Foggitt and I'm sure you'll feel differently by tonight."

"Okay, but if I don't, I'll be around to make that statement," warned Bill.

Arriving from Chester Hospital at 7pm, Bill told Charlie to slow down at the wine store for a half bottle of scotch to drink and kill the pain. After its acquisition, he started to glug down the contents then passed the bottle to Charlie. Within ten minutes they had downed its contents, with Charlie arriving at Bill's flat and invitation to take a further drink.

Charlie's snores awoke Bill at 9.30 pm and he arose from the easy chair with a real eye-shiner and swelling on his nose. Suddenly Bill realised that he couldn't possibly go to work for Henry Baker now after all.

He descended the concrete steps and inserted a sixpence into the phone of the foyer ringing Henry's number.

"You can't? Aw heck Bill, an' I was countin' on yer!" Henry voiced disappointedly,

"I'm sorry for yer gerrin' that punch on the nose mate - make sure yer get 'im ter pay won't yer," he warned. "No don't worry mate, I'll be able ter manage - it can't be 'elped. Thanks for ringin' me anyway. Yer never know, we might yet work together in the future? Take care of yerself mate- an' keep smilin', tarah."

"Why couldn't Del be that reasonable Charlie!" asked Bill thoughtfully.

"Cos 'e's a con artist Bill, and 'e thinks everyone's out ter take 'im fer a ride."

"E's back termorrer Charlie, and me with a flamin' shiner," Bill chuckled.

"Well, it'll give 'im a good topic ter talk about won't it?" said Charlie chuckling also.

They both broke out in chorus laughing.

Bill reached into his drinks cabinet and pulled out his stock of spirits which included: gin, rum Vodka and whisky to which he offered, "Name your poison mate," and they both drank well into the early hours.

The alarm sounded at 10.30 am and Bill awoke and shut off the key, going back to sleep until 12.15pm by which time, both he and Charlie had arisen to answer the knocking at the front door.

As Bill opened the door to his surprise he saw Cecil standing there looking very sorry for himself.

"Can I come in Bill?" he asked in a soft voice.

"Well I dunno?" replied he, watching the manager squirm.

"Please Bill, I've come to make amends," he pleaded.

"Just a moment," said Bill and flew back into the living room, "Arbuckle's here to make a deal," he enlightened his friend quietly, "Look, you nip in the bedroom just so's 'e doesn't suss out what's goin' on Charlie."

Charlie complied adding, "I'll keep my ear to the door Bill, to witness anythin' 'e sez."

With that, Bill returned to the front door inviting Cecil to enter.

THE MACE GOES IN

The apologies through Cecil's complete change of attitude, which he witnessed via the bedroom door ajar, convinced Charlie that Cecil was remunerating Bill for all the physical distress he'd caused him. The conflabbing took almost half an hour by which time Charlie had smoked three roll ups when Bill finally closed the door behind Cecil.

"Tell me the worst," he voiced eagerly and Bill commenced to enlighten him:

"You remember how snooty he was when he was tryin' ter kick me out?" said Bill.

"Yeh, yeh?" said his friend with anticipation.

"Well, yer could 'ave knocked me down with a feather by the change of 'is attitude of:

"Hello Bill, how are you?"" he mimicked in a posh voice, "I've come to tell you how shocked and ashamed I feel about the way I so wrongly treated you. It was Agnes who told me that she thought you said she was a part-time prostitute. Naturally I jumped to her defence - to protect the name of the club of course. P'rhaps I got a bit carried away? It's not like me to become violent at any time," he insisted. "It was only when the sergeant came down, did I realise just what a stupid insensitive thing I'd done," he cried remorsefully.

"What did yer say to 'im Bill?" breathed Charlie.

Bill replied, "Well mate, I didn't say anythin' at first. I decided ter wait for a few seconds before I spoke - ter make 'im sweat so's to speak."

"Ha ha haa," Charlie retorted fully enjoying the scene.

"Then when I thought he was ready ter start cryin', I said to 'im I've been advised by Hymie Jacobs the solicitor, ter take it ter court an' 'ave yer summoned,' I waited fer the result as his face paled and I thought he was 'avin' an 'eart attack," he related gravely.

"Whar 'appened then?" Charlie probed.

"Well 'e suddenly cried out, "Bill, Bill yer can't mean that mate - I'd lose me job, the club'ed lose its license. We'd 'ave ter shut up shop. What would Annie and the kids do then? Sellin' beer is the only thing I know," he wailed remorseful like. I realised that it wasn't Annie and his kids 'e was worried about - but 'is bit on the side Agnes," he implied.

"Oh, I gerrit, that's why Cecil got the 'ump after you told 'er she was fiddlin'. She musta said somethin' about their relationship, ter get even with yer for insultin' 'er...no bloomin' wonder 'e came at yer like a roarin' bull?" he confuted. "But you knew about their 'avin' it off already - didn't yer, yer crafty begger," he reasoned. "In fact Billy Foggitt you set the 'ole thing up – didn't yer, even at the risk o' gerrin' a black eye?" he challenged. "Yeh, you crafty begger, you engineered the whole provoked assault, right from the start!"

Bill started to chuckle nodding and commenced to pour out two cups of neat scotch, handing one to his friend.

"I can't kid you can I Charlie? Yer worked it all out faster than most fellas I know," Bill commended.

Charlie took a big gulp of the whisky and felt the warm glow enter his body, "Aye Bill, I think I know you pretty well after all these years," he said proudly. "Anyway Bill, did yer ger' anythin' out of it all?" he enquired.

"Well now Chas, 'ow does wipin' me £30 slate clean sound? Not ter mention a compensation of £30 for all the pain an' aggro' I suffered," he replied tongue in cheek.

"As much as that? Phee'w," his friend whistled. "Hey Billy!" Chas suddenly growled, "What if I'd o' gorra black eye, yer didn't think o' that did yer? I could of ended up without most of me teeth," he rued. "Yer put me ter risk there without even considerin' my feelin's, or even me good 'ealth for that matter - what then eh, eh?" he argued angrily.

Bill realised at once just what Charlie was up to, it was obvious his friend wanted a cut in the profits of the day. He relented to this need by playing up to it with, "Is it £9 yer owe me or £8 Chas?" he reminded.

"Surely yer not gonna ask me fer that back are yer Bill? After the risk I took fer yer gerrin' involved. Not ter mention the threat of me membership under fire, since I stood as witness at the cop shop?" he reasoned.

"Oh aye yeh, I see what yer mean," amicably nodding with agreement.

"Yeh, yer right o' course Chas, I should really share half of the

£30 with yer. 'Ere y'are mate, 'ave these three fivers," he offered and his friend readily fingered the blue notes.

"Now that's somethin' more like it Bill, I always said yer were a good 'un," he voiced with pure flattery.

Bill was chuckling inside and couldn't contain himself and started laughing at the deceit, which really was quite funny.

Cecil had actually given him, not £30, but £300 to agree not to prosecute and Bill had signed a letter typed out by Cecil to confirm it, indicating that he'd actually sustained his injuries falling down the steps of the club, for which he was duly compensated by the club's cover. Charlie was unaware of any of this and as Bill commenced to chuckle outwardly, he did it with a certain ruse, to put Charlie off the track.

"Ha ha haa, ha ha ha," he chortled mirthfully, "and ter think I let 'im off with £30," he rued falsely, "tut tut tut," he added.

"What's that Bill, what are yer on about?"

"I've been a blimmin' fool Chas, I could've took 'im fer a scutchin' fortune," he said, convincingly.

"Ow's that?" puzzled Charlie.

"Well mate, when I think about it, I 'ad 'im over a barrel with a witness an' everythin', and 'ere I am - goes an' signs a statement which says I fell down the flamin' stairs. I must a' bin flippin' drunk to 'ave bin so daft!" he rued, putting on a good act.

"I see what yer mean, mind you Bill, yer did come out of it £60 better off didn't yer, an' that's not too bad is it?" he encouraged.

"£60 - don't yer mean £45?" he corrected.

"Well £45 then. Where would yer get £45 for a black eye an' a snotty nose?" he asked, anxiously fearing Bill would ask him for his money back. Suddenly he said, "Is that the time Bill, half one? Shoot, I'll be late fer the probation officer - an' 'ere's me smellin' of whiskey. Quick, 'ave yer got any mints Bill?" he pleaded.

"Er yeh, I've got a packet of Polo somewhere?" he replied, frantically searching his pockets, "Oh aye, 'ere we are!" he retorted, handing the tube of mints to his friend.

"Ta Bill, thanks for the scotch- I'll 'ave ter go!" he determined, stuffing the sweets into his mouth., "I'll see yer in the town sometime mate," he promised, donning his jacket - still forcing the mints into his mouth now overloaded with the sweets.

Quickly Bill opened the door, enjoying the charade saying, "I hope you get there in time Chas, I'd run yer there, bur I'm full o' whisky - yer know 'ow it is, don't yer?" he emphasised.

"Thanks Bill, fer everything Tarah mate I'll see yer?"

After which Charlie made a beeline for the door and was gone.

"Ha ha ha ha haa," echoed Bill, obviously tickled by Charlie's deceptive ploy to leave.

"Ow," he said, changing his tune as the pain from his nose returned. He felt his nose, no it wasn't broken he thought, 'and where would a fella get 300 nicker for a bleedin' nose- Heh heh heh!"

He renewed his relationship with the whisky bottle and drank himself into oblivion, sleeping all of the day and right throughout the night, with the gas fire turned up to ensure he was cosy.

To You Bill, £50

CHAPTER 19

"Bang bang bang, rat tat tat tat, bump, bump, bump, bang bang, bang..."

"Okay, okay, I'm coming," Bill replied arising from the couch, "ooh,ooh," he commented feeling his forehead. The pain in his head confirmed the hangover over all hangovers. He couldn't remember actually having a hangover with a headache at all, for he was such a seasoned drinker, but the advent of the black eye, he surmised, probably had a lot to do with his present condition.

Bang, bang, bang...

"Stop that flamin' racket!" he screamed, agitated by the noise.

He reached the front door only to be met by Del whose first words were, "Ave yer any idea what time it is Bill? It's flamin' ten o'clock!" said his partner, "and we're still in the town. "Hell Bill what 'ave yer been doin' - playin' cards all night?" Del queried as he came through the door - oblivious of Bill's condition. "Got any tea Bill?" adding, "me mouth's very dry."

"I'll shove the kettle on Del 'ang on," said his pal, taking the pot to the stove. "'Elp yourself to a scotch Del while I just put the tea in. 'Ow many sugars?"

"'Two please mate an' I'll 'ave a piece o' toast if yer've gorrit," he added.

"Toast it is!" complied Bill, as he removed the rounds from the wrapper, to the toaster.

"Pheeeeeeeee," sounded the kettle, so he turned off the electric and commenced to pour the water. By which time the toaster had popped up the slices, which he started to spread with butter.

Carrying the teapot and empty cups he added the toast to the tray also and upon arrival into the living room, offered the toast to Del, who gratefully commenced to chew the bread.

"Mmm, yer can tell this is butter - not that margarine rubbish eh mate," he voiced appreciably looking up at Bill. "Haven't yer 'ad a wash yet Bill? Yer've gorra black mark on yer face mate, an' flippin' 'ell, what 'appened ter yer nos?"

"It's a long story Del an' I don't wanna talk about it. Did yer 'ave a good 'oliday?" he probed attempting to change the subject.

Straightway Del thought about Delvene's onslaught, but then put on a smile and replied, "Ah lovely weather Bill, but it doesn't last does it? Yeh, Beth's had ter go back to Cornwall but, she'll be back termorrer. Her Dad took a turn for the worst an' she doesn't want ter leave 'im - yer know 'ow daughters love their Dads - don't they?"

"Yeh yer right Del, I know what yer mean."

"Anyway Bill, what were yer sayin' about that shiner?" he probed.

"Oh all right Del, I'll tell yer - yer'll probably find out about it eventually and I want you ter gerrit right from me. Don't laugh; promise me yer won't laugh if I tell yer," he searched with a serious note.

"Course I won't, you know me Bill," he replied seriously.

"I only got drunk, an' fell down the steps of the Old Serviceman's Club didn't I, an' I don't want yer ter breathe a word of this ter anyone."

"Aah ha ha ha ha haaa," smirked Del.

"Yer promised not ter laugh - yer rotten scoundrel," voiced Bill with derision.

"I heh hehe, ca' can't help it, heh heh, yer mean yer fell all the way down them concrete steps? Heh heh heh h,h,h,h. I'm sorry Bill, I couldn't 'elp me self, heh. Anyway mate, you were very lucky only ter ger a black eye an' a banged up nos - eh, very lucky. I meantersay yer could o' broke yer flamin' neck, couldn't yer?"

"I suppose yer right Del, now let's forget it eh?" he commanded.

"Right Bill, listen, pour a drop o' scotch in this tea will yer - an' hair of the dog?"

"That bad eh Del?"

THE MACE GOES IN

They both washed down their piece of toast each and Del removed a packet of cigarettes, Full Strength, handing one to Bill.

"Oh ta Del, by the way, where did yer 'ave in mind fer terday?" he queried.

"A bit late ter go anywhere now Bill, still I s'pose we could go out on safari ter make some new contacts," he relented.

After they had puffed their cigarettes, Bill signalled Del and they both moved toward the door.

"Er, I've brought the wagon - just in case we'd decided to go out Bill."

"The Perkins?"

"No the Bedford," he replied.

"Aye it's a lot cheaper ter run isn't it mate?" Bill drooled.

"Ey, dearer yer mean don't yer - it's petrol y' know," he insisted.

"Frightened o' the Perkins are yer Del?" mused Bill.

"No it's not that Bill," he replied colouring up, "It's just that I'm used ter the old girl," he assured unconvincingly.

Bill gave a silent chuckle, due to Del's non verbal communication, giving the game away.

The landscape rolled by as Del gave it the clog and speeded up as the last vestage of the town disappeared from view.

"What's the hurry Del?"

"Nothing Bill, really!"

"Listen mate, I haven't seen you clog the pedal this much, since we 'ad that cheese factory job," he determined, "by the way, isn't it time we went back there?"

Del looked at Bill with anger, "Oh all right mate, I'll tell yer what the 'urry is... yer remember 'Enry Baker 'oo 'ad that big seven tonner, what 'is Dad left 'im in 'is will?" he related.

"'Enry? Ooh aye yeh," he pretended to recall. "Wasn't that 'im what had ter pay out all that compensation fer criminal negligence that time?"

"That's the bloke," Del retorted.

"Yer 'aven't thrown in with 'im 'ave yer Del?" he asked.

"Why, what's wrong...with 'im? 'E's all right Bill, he's the one 'oos goin' ter fix us up with a load o' stuff fer nuthin', so he can't be that bad can 'e."

"Well purrin' it like that, I don't think I could moan about anythin' mate," Bill resolved, "I mean, a fella that gives yer a load of scrap fer nothin' at all, can't be that bad can 'e?"

"Well…there was one thing 'e 'as asked me ter do, we've gorra…"

"Oh 'ere it comes - I knew it, we've bin took fer a ride 'ave we?" he criticised.

"Now 'old on Bill, all we 'ave ter do is watch that pair of snakes what's workin' fer 'im!" he rationalised.

"Don't tell me - Knight and Day Salvage?"

"Ow the –flamin' 'ell d'you know that?" he fumed. "Oh, I gerrit, you're the bloke what let 'im down, that's right innit Bill?"

But Bill was chuckling to himself, enjoying putting Del on the spot. "You know me Del, I only work with one feller at a time."

"I appreciate that Bill, but when 'Enry rang me last night I promised 'im we'd be up there today," he reasoned.

"After me tellin' 'im I couldn't make it with a bad 'ead, yer've wrangled me 'ere after all, mind you, yer weren't ter know I was hurt, but that stupid 'Enry ought to 'ave known better," he cursed.

"Well anyway mate, here's what 'e wants us ter do," he directed to change the subject. "Y'know the factory, what the stuff is actually in - yeh?"

"Oh aye?" Bill queried following the direction.

"Well in that part of the plant, there's a lorra phosphor bronze valves, that need comin' out. They've already been dismantled, just waitin' for us ter collect 'em, but Blackie Knight is hoisting them out - chiselin' 'Enry out of most of 'em. That's where we come in. 'E wants us ter get as many as we can loaded on ter our wagon, but first 'e wants us ter locate just where Knight and Day 'as the main cache hidden," he indicated. "So I've bin thinkin', if I keep 'em talkin' an' occupied doin' the strippin', it'll give you a free hand, locating where that pair's stashed the booty, won't it mate?" he drooled proudly.

"Hmm," Bill grunted. "It is just like Del innit? 'e 'as all the easy stuff, an' I gets all the 'ard collar, he thought. "I suppose you'd like

THE MACE GOES IN

me ter load the wagon up, if and when I find their hidin' place "eh Del?"

Del nodded in agreement adding: "If and when yer find the stuff, don't put it on the wagon - not until yer've shoved 'alf a dozen pavin' slabs on first, then tare off on the weighbridge," he directed.

Bill was way ahead, "Yer crafty sod, that'd mean the wagon was about 'alf a ton 'eavier than the true tare - meanin' we can chisel 'Enry out of the load. I get yer drift!" he mouthed excitedly. "Okay mate, I'll see yer later then," he said, as they arrived at the plant, where Bill drove in and allowed Del to drop down onto the pathway, leading to the factory building.

He then drove the wagon in the direction of the plant's building section.

"Sheesh, that Lachicoe's done it again - 'e's got me to do all the 'and ballin'. It was then, that he decided to use the building section's labour force to help him to load up, remembering the plant manager's name spoken of by Henry Baker, he put it to good use. "Mr. Engel's sent me ter collect six 3 foot x 18" pavin' slabs," he told the man in the yard.

"Mr. Engel, oh certainly sir - who are they for exactly?" asked the man.

"Oh I forgot to mention - 'e doesn't want perfect ones, they're to be used to prop up the pipes, we're taking out for The Baker Contract," he lied.

"Well in that case sir, I'll get the lads to throw on the chipped ones - hey Georgie come 'ere will yer? Put six of those cracked flags on this wagon son, an' get Wally ter help yer."

Complete with the slabs, Bill drove the wagon out of sight of the men and dropped down to search for the loot. He surveyed the area first and thought to himself, where the 'ell would anybody, hide a load of valves? He could see the factory building to the right of the Bedford and the pipe gantry to the left. There was no conceivable place to hide anything. Perhaps Henry had been wrong, perhaps Del had also jumped the gun. He made a sweep of the whole area on foot, but every place he looked, even in the hollows of the embankment, he couldn't find anything. So he decided to search further a field and even went through all of the waste bins in all of the areas, but to his dismay, was only able to locate a few brass turnoffs. Half an hour had passed, without proving to be fruitful.

"I'd better get back, Del will be wondering what's happened?"

Quickly he drove the Bedford to the gatehouse weighbridge, to discover that with the slabs on board, the tare weight had now an increase of 10 cwt to 2 tons 13 cwt. Upon arrival back he was met by a fuming Del, whose hands already showed signs of manual labour.

"Where the 'ell were yer?" he raged, "I've been 'ere for an hour pullin' me tripes out."

Bill looked on sheepishly saying, "What is it yer want doin' Del?"

"Yer can throw them silly slabs off now - that is if yer've got the tare?" he instructed.

Bill had almost completed clearing the 674 interceptor line of pipes and was busily stripping the bronze valves from them, when Blackie who was collecting the valves in a wheelbarrow, came by to borrow the Stilson wrench. Bill gladly parted with it, as it gave him an excuse to roll a cigarette. He rolled one for Del also, who was just as tired as he.

"Thanks Bill," Del murmured appreciably and inhaled the welcome fumes of the tobacco.

"Where's that Blackie gone with the barrow Bill? I've gorra big pile of copper pipes up on the top. We might just as well put 'em on with the bronze. It'll save comin' back for 'em twice won't it?" he reasoned.

"Where's the iron 'Enry's givin' us Del?" he asked.

"Blinkin' 'eck Bill, yer don't think we came 'ere for iron do yer? Use yer loaf, we've gorra cover the cost of the motor 'aven't we, an' besides that, I owe Peter Strate £300 from the strap 'e let me 'ave a fortnight ago," he cried.

"Well that's YOUR problem Del, now being your partner, I don't expect ter honour your debts as well!"

"There again Bill, I've just thought o' summin', if I were ter take that load of number 2 iron and chuck it on the motor, to get it outer

THE MACE GOES IN

the way, so's ter speak, we could always smuggle a birra bronze an' copper underneath," he exclaimed.

Bill nodded his head. He had to agree, Del had a point, "I'll take these copper pipes then Del and chuck 'em on to the bottom first," he offered.

"That's the spirit Bill, but don't let Sonnie Day spot yer - yer know 'ow 'e grasses everybody," Del warned.

Bill looked around fer Blackie's partner, who didn't appear to be anywhere in sight. He scooped up the pipes in his arms and proceeded to walk to the Bedford. Upon arrival he caught sight of Sonnie who was too pre-occupied to notice anyone, as Bill ducked behind a chemical waste skip.

Sonnie appeared to be climbing up the side of the Bedford, with what Bill thought were two pieces of iron and so he waited for him to climb down and depart, before jumping onto the petrol tank to gain access to the top of the wagon. To his surprise the wagon was bare,

"Well, what the 'ell was Sonnie doin'?" he thought aloud. He decided to climb higher to push down the piping which had proved to be obstinately stuck up in the air. He pulled himself up the empty stillages alongside and as his hand lay on the wooden boards he felt something cold. Out of thoughts for his own safe grip, he turned around, only to be met by a wonderful sight.

The second stillage up was crammed completely full of bronze valves. Upon this discovery, he almost let out a cheer, and had to re-adjust his grip, in order to avoid falling from his position.

He couldn't believe his luck, here was that very cache, that both he and Del had sought. Quickly he reconnoitred his position, and when he was quite sure that none of the scrap men from the Baker contract were present, he commenced to empty the stillages - tossing all of the valves into the awaiting Bedford.

He had to be very careful for as the weight was removed from the three high stillages, they threatened to topple over. Carefully, he leaned against the wagon side to prop his weight against the stillage to counteract the imbalance.

Finally after what seemed like twenty minutes, he had loaded the

Bedford full of bronze artefacts,, then carefully climbed down and ascended into the cab. He drove the wagon further a field, to ensure that no-one could investigate its contents, without obvious motives. He couldn't wait to see Del. He climbed down onto the road and ducked into the factory, where he located a number of corrugated sheets, which he collected two at a time and ascended the side of the Bedford to deposit them to mask the load up, thus intending to deceive the weighbridge man later in the day.

Quietly, he enlightened Del of his discovery.

"You've got what?!?" Del mouthed with surprised greed, which overtook all of his thoughts as he scanned his brain on where they could locate more iron, to completely mask the load.

As if in answer to their problem, Henry Baker suddenly appeared on the scene.

"Oh, so yer were able ter ger 'ere after all Bill?" he voiced with surprise.

"Yeh 'En'," he assured, "yer can't keep a good man down!"

"'Ave yer come across that iron yet Del? I've marked it all fer yer over 'ere," he indicated.

"Oh - so that's where it is? No flippin' wonder we couldn't find it Bill, it's on the other side!" Del moaned sarcastically scolding Henry with, "oo's a naughty boy then?" smiling as he said it.

"I'm sorry if I misled yer Del, anyway, I am payin' yer fer the day ain't I?" he assured.

"Well purrin' it that way, I suppose it's all right - what d'yer think Bill?" Del replied.

"Yerse, that's fine 'Enery - you're the boss!" he affirmed.

"This is it 'ere," he pointed at the mess of pipes piled high adding, "there's a lorra cast iron 'ere Del - should be a coupla ton at least. It might take yer a coupla trips. Anyway, yer've got all week yet, an' I need yer ter clear the walk ways first."

"We'll load all these awkward pipes first 'En, this'll clear the pathways, then we'll come back fer the cast. No sense in cockin' the load up with this light stuff," Del stressed.

"Oh aye Del, that's favourite, then yer can get the best price fer the Heavy cast what's left 'ere. There's no flies on you mate!" he commended.

This was just what Del and Bill wished Henry to think. Whilst their wagon had number 2 scrap iron-oversized- sticking out of its, rear, the weigh-bridge-man would assume that the load contained just general scrap and would book it out accordingly. Thus enabling them to retreat with their booty of contraband bronze. Quickly, they unitedly threw out the pipes onto the roadside and upon completion, Bill hurriedly rushed to the parked Bedford and commenced to move it to the spot..

"Give us an 'and ter chuck this on, will yer Del?" he shouted.

Del ambled over and concurred with the need, actually hand balling the thin steel pipes over the side into the Bedford.

When both men considered that enough of the light iron was high enough, together they conferred, and Bill commenced to take out the wagon and then drove it again over the weighbridge.

Later across the scales at Rivkits, he discovered that the amount of bronze he ended up with -after the removal of the light iron- totalled 2 ton 14 cwt from which he was amply rewarded.

He returned to the job - still assuming the 10 cwt additional weight of the paving slabs, to ensure that the weigh-bridge-man at the EVCO plant that the tare was still 2 ton 13 cwt. Upon arrival, he gave Del his share of £426/16/8d

Del nearly fainted with surprise, "W,w,w what was it fetchin' Bill," he asked finally.

"Three hundred and twenty two pound Del," he answered proudly confident, due to his newly acquired honesty. He could see that Del was attempting to work it out in his mind, for he asked Bill what the final weigh in actually totalled, after which a smile suddenly appeared on his face and Bill knew that Del was confident, that he hadn't been 'maced'.

They both continued to strip the remainder of valves from the piping. After a few hours, Henry came around to direct Del to where the iron lay he had promised him.

Del whispered a few words to him out of earshot of Bill and then commenced to accumulate the pieces of cast iron into one pile. He beckoned Bill to assist him and they both hurriedly started to load up the Bedford.

"P'rhaps we could weigh this lot before the yards close Del?"

"I'm way ahead of yer mate," he retorted adding, "why d'yer think I'm loadin' this so fast?"

"It's twenty past three Del - we'll 'ave ter 'urry if we're gonna catch Ma Finlay's yard open?" Bill prompted.

His friend motioned him to connect his side of the wagon's tailboard, and together they secured the motor for safety, before Del bade Henry goodbye and then they were off to the factory weighbridge.

Ma Finlay's yard loomed up, into which they entered.

"Sixty pound even Del," the silver haired old woman pronounced, as she handed him the receipt.

Del read out the weight, "Two tons eh Bill,?" he remarked, "well mate, I suggest we put this money into the tank fer termorrer - what d'yer think?" Bill nodded and drove down the New Chester Road to the nearest petrol station. Bill filled up the tank taking the cash from Del and returning with the remainder. "There's £56 left, so I'll 'ang onter this Del, so's I'll 'ave enough left for the week's petrol and emergencies."

"Eh, what - oh all right Bill, you're the driver," he conceded, anxious not to invoke Bill's anger, any more than he dare. He hadn't forgotten the earlier incident in the George.

They arrived in Newtown, and instead of calling into their local, Del mentioned that he'd promised Beth he'd pay the electric bill and so after parking the wagon in Oakfield Terrace, he told Bill he'd take the wagon back home. This suited Bill for he needed to get to the bank to deposit his money.

He arrived at the bank but to his horror realised he'd left it too late and cursed his bad luck. Then he remembered the pawn ticket in his wallet from Cohen's Hock shop. He decided to claim the stamp to which the ticket pertained.

The old man produced the article in a cellophane container upon receipt of the stub adding, "Oy yoy yoy, mine poy, you haff got a bargain here! Another 42 hours and it Vould haff been too late - too late," he repeated, "yes my friend, you haff fallen onto your feet all right!" the usurer voiced. "It's been a pleasure to do der business viz you!"

Bill watched the man counting the money and to his surprise, the old man handed him back a fiver saying, "Vot are you trying to do - up der price?"

Bill took the money back saying, "Thanks Mr. Cohen, it's nice to meet an honest man in this day and age."

The old man smiled chuckling to himself. Bill left the shop in a good mood and put the one penny red Cape of Good Hope triangle into his wallet.

As he turned to go home, his eyes noticed a diamond solitaire lady's ring mounted in a box in the 'pop shop' window.

He took an immediate fancy to it, for the huge stone which must have weighed at least three carats, reflecting the whole colour spectrum from its professional polish.

Upon his request, Cohen removed it from the window commenting, "A good stone it is Bill, zey don't make zem like zis any more you know," the old man emphasised, "just look at zis platinum mounting – can't you see zer craftsmanship in zer setting? None of that silly glue holding zis piece of ice. Vy, it's all been specially made to house such a beautiful stone. I'll be so sorry to see it go. It reminds me so much of zer old country, zose ver der days you know, ven ve Ver paid for our craftsmanship, ven zer money vast no object!"

"Okay okay Effie, just tell me what your price is on it and we can do some 'agglin', said Bill.

"It vould cost der earth to pay for such a ring with zis setting and…"

"Never mind that Effie, what's your price on it?" Bill asked getting perturbed.

"Vell, it's hard to say..."

"I'll give yer twenty quid an' chance gerrin' bit," Bill ventured pushing the boat out.

"Twenty quid - twenty quid? Zat's an insult, I loaned zer Voman £40 usury on it three months ago, and she didn't even haff zer decency to come back again. I don't know Bill, you do somevone a favour and zey valk all over you!" the old man emphasised with open hands gesture.

Bill weighed the situation up at once. For instance, if the ring was all that Cohen said it was and that he did allow £40 usury on it, then it must have a market value of at least 400 pounds. There again, he wondered if the old man had been completely honest about the transaction? But then the incident with the fiver earlier convinced him that for all they say about pawnbrokers, this one was the exception to the rule. He decided upon a snap decision.

"What's your price on it Effie?" he asked brashly.

"You really interested Bill, or are you just vasting my time?" asked he.

"Well now, I've thought about it, and I've come to the decision that I need a good looking ring. There may come a time in my life, where I need to pop the question to some female. It may be tomorrow, there again, it may never come to this, but if and when I do, then the ring I do it with, has to be a good 'un. Now then Effie, it could be this ring or one out of another poppin' shop, but the price as to be right - if you catch my drift."

"Vell Bill, I know exactly vot you mean, and I think zat you vill find zat my price is right," said the old man, eager to retrieve his money and show some return on his investment. The old man looked Bill up and down, trying to assess what colour Bill's money really showed. Judging by Bill's apparel, it was apparent that he was no eccentric millionaire, made obvious by the callouses on his hands. The ruddy weather beaten face- no, this man was a typical hard working man, who knew a bargain when he saw one. The recent acquisition of the stamp would probably net him at least a couple of hundred profit. Suddenly the old man felt cheated, out of the opportunity to sell the stamp and decided there and then to make this awkward customer pay for the privilege of having the ring. He therefore made a hurried decision of £40 usury plus the £200 loss expected on the Cape triangle.

"Right Bill, I'll give you a price right now," he determined

Just as if Bill had read his mind, he interjected saying, "Don't say it Effie, I can't afford the price you're going to ask, but first let me tell you something," he proffered. "If I had just allowed £40 usury on

THE MACE GOES IN

an article in my shop and then the pawnee had failed to return, I'd just mark that item up as £40 owing, and at least 100% return on my money, to cover the time the item had lain in the window, and all, the insurance I have to spend on it, to cover its safety in the shop before its final sale - am I right?" he asked.

Effie was exasperated, "Who vast zis gentile - born out of zer covenant- telling me how to run my shop - zis 'shiska' who doesn't even credit zer contempt of a goy?" he thought with derision. "And yet...he does appear to know zer ropes-zat's it. I'll bet he's Jewish really and doesn't vant anyvone to know him. Yes, zat's it, he is Jewish, and as von Jew to another I need to be honest," he determined.

"To you Bill, £80 vizout argument, zis ist zer price!"

It was if Bill had heard every thought, for he put his hand into his wallet and removed 16 fivers altogether and placed them onto the table saying, "A pleasure doing business with an honest man."

Effie was aghast and quickly removed the fivers to a safer place ringing the till and giving Bill his receipt along with the ring, which he enclosed in its container.

As Effie watched the countenance of Bill leave, he offered up his prayer to his maker thanking him for the inspiration to stay honest. It made him feel ten feet tall.

Bill had also received a good feeling in the shop and savoured his love for the human race, "A pity we can't all be as amicable as that?" he thought philosophically.

He arrived at his flat and placed both ring and stamp, in the old vase at the end of the sideboard. He then lay on his sofa after turning on the gas fire for forty winks before his belated lunch.

Cottage

CHAPTER 20

At 6.30 pm he awoke and felt completely Refreshed. He switched on his television and immediately became engrossed in 'Coronation Street'. It reminded him of his origins with all its hardships and kitchen sink dramas.

All too soon the programme faded out and he was brought back to the reality of his surroundings.

He picked up the 'Liverpool Echo', for the sake of something different and browsed through the wanted ads in the hope of making some more cash. Nothing he could find suited anything he owned, so he delved even further into the centre of the paper.

Finally he fluttered through the real estate agents pretending he was a prospective buyer:

The ad read: Original condition end terrace cottage with hot water, gas cooker and easy access to shops - £1,750 or nearest offer.

"Ha ha haa," he mused, some people have a lotta gaul – expectin' ter get that much for an ole' buildin'. He continued to flick through the page and the further he went, the more expensive the homes appeared to become.

"Cor, houses are dear now, what the 'ell 'appened?" he thought quite alarmed.

He scanned the page to find the cottage once more and thought: 'Ere I am payin £3 a week for a council flat in Newtown, which must cost me at least one and a half 'undred a year. I could 'ave me own drum for about 10 years' rent, an' not 'ave ter worry about any more rent in me old age would I?" he thought.

He noticed that the cottage was situated between Newtown and

THE MACE GOES IN

Chester, and with a flash of inspiration put on his coat and made his way to his car.

Compton, Compton and Bygraves, advertising the domicile, were having their usual late night extension in Canal Street, Chester, when in walks Bill with around £500 burning a hole in his pocket.

After a few enquiries through the woman at the desk, the manager appeared with his usual beaming smile to enlighten Bill of the best aspects of the cottage to which Bill had enquired.

"Yes sir, let me take your particulars. Do you have any form of identity with you sir?"

"Listen, I only want to see the place first."

"It's only a formality sir, you do understand - don't you?" he assured him, "I need to know just exactly who we are lending our keys out to."

Bill had a hate of gobbledygook and any form of red tape bureaucracy, but decided to show his driving license and services disablement card, to satisfy this unreasonable young man, who stood in the way of his unison with a home of his own. He left him with the required deposit of £110.

After arriving in Frontmere, he located the lane at the address of the house and looked hard at its exterior, there wasn't much to be admired. Its bricks were that porous they had crumbled in many places and showed bad signs of erosion over most of their area. In fact, the 'cottage' was more like a crumbling barn side with no damp course built in and upon Bill's entry into its interior, large patches of damp engulfed its walls. Not only that, but the windows looked as if they hadn't seen paint since their construction.

Further investigation revealed more bad news; the rear door and casement proved to contain wet rot, along with the Elizabethan styled windows. In fact, the whole house downstairs appeared ready for demolition. Bill felt completely disillusioned. After coming all this way also, a sheer waste of time. He had had such high hopes of the prospect of owning his own home but all this was now out of the question. "Hell," he exclaimed, "I need somewhere to live - and pretty quickly too." He looked at the price tag of the cottage once more and considered it had been far too much for good value. He weighed up the other options he had: Either he could return the keys and forget all about the cottage and enquire about something else, or he could forget about home ownership completely and return to his £3 a week council flat. The latter seemed the most viable and he turned on his heel to go.

As if fate were to play a hand in his decision, he happened to look through the rear door aperture which lined up with the kitchen window. Outside lay the rear garden, to which he couldn't discern exactly where it ended. Amid the complete disarray, there appeared to be rows and rows of apple and pear trees, with fruit briars of all descriptions.

He could remember something in his childhood recall, where he and his friends had witnessed such an orchard as this upon their school working holidays in the depression of the late 1920's. They had all enjoyed themselves immensely with the choice of all of the fruits to eat, as they picked them.

It was this epic which influenced him now to withdraw the kitchen door bolts, which held access to the rear of the property. What beheld his eyes when he stepped outside, fulfilled all of his childhood dreams of living in a home with a garden, and what a garden this was. It was easy to see amid all the weeds, which had appeared to have recently overtaken the back, at some point earlier, the occupant had been a creature of tidiness and order, judging by the evidence of borders of flowers so neatly set out. Yes, this garden looked like it had real prospect. It did in fact remind him again and again, of the ideal home he had envisaged and prayed for as a child. He noticed also that because it was the end of a block of four, there now could be provided garage space. He even had a mental picture of driving his own wagon through into the rear of the garden.

Immediately the prospect of owning the cottage, became closer to reality and added expense of the windows replacement, proved less and less relevant.

He ventured up the stairs and became aware of the existence of two fairly large bedrooms, but no bathroom, yet even this was no disappointment. He thought he could install one down stairs somewhere or other and dismissed it from his mind. He couldn't wait to get back to tie up the loose ends. He wondered if anyone else had been interested in the house and hoped not. Feverishly, he ransacked his pockets in order to secure a deposit and discovered he had almost £400 remaining. He then re-bolted the rear door and returned through the front to which was attached a Yale lock which could be slammed shut.

Driving back to Comptons he had visions of all night parties at the cottage, without the objection of old Mrs. Bellow who would bang her ceiling directly below his flat and the intervention of Barry Simkins who was placed next door. "Yes," he thought expectantly, "It'll be great, I could even bring my Judy back without waggin' tongues…"

He arrived back at the estate agents with just barely enough time, for the secretary and manager were jointly engaged in locking up and securing the shutters.

"Mr. Foggit, how did you like the house sir? Isn't it an absolute steal? Yes sir, you'd go a long way before securing something as nice as that for such a low price," he emphasised with his usual sales patter.

Bill, although he was delighted at the prospect, suddenly remembered his bartering instincts and replied with, "What about the windows rotten an' all that?"

"But sir, this is why the price is so low. If they were perfect, we would be asking in the range of three thousand," he stressed.

"And the crumbling bricks," Bill added with sarcasm.

"Er, ah well, perhaps that was an oversight sir, if Mr. Ranger the owner would agree then I'm sure he'd come down a bit on his price - by the way Mr. Foggit did you have an offer in mind?"

Bill thought for awhile and motioned the manager into the rear of the shop.

"Is this leasehold or freehold?" he queried.

"Freehold of course sir, didn't you see the ad," he replied.

"Well £1,750 is a bit steep. Namely, it would probably cost me about £500 to get it into some semblance of order," Bill argued, "and so I decided in all fairness, £1300 would be my bid for this lot."

Before the manager could speak Bill pulled the bundle of fivers and tenners from his hip pocket stating that he would be willing to leave the £390 odd as deposit, making a total of £500.

"I'll ring my client right away sir, by the way, how d'you intend to pay the remainder?" he asked excitedly.

"In cash by tomorrow lunch," Bill replied.

The manager dialled the number and closed his office door to ensure Bill couldn't hear.

He didn't have long to wait however for less than a minute later, he emerged to enlighten Bill of the result.

"Mr. Ranger was most adamant about the price, but I reminded him of the exterior condition and he immediately knocked his price down to £1600 but after I told him about the rotten windows, he decided that £1500 was the lowest he could go," said he, searching Bill's face for approval.

Bill weighed it up in his mind and thought about whether he should or shouldn't take up the offer, even hesitating, wondering if really he was doing the right thing, but then the thought of picking his own fruit in that beautiful huge rear garden, overshadowed all of his fears as he found himself saying:

"Well...yes, perhaps I could raise that amount, yes, I'll have it here for you by noon tomorrow."

At once the manager re-dialled the number and affirmed it with the owner, who was more than pleased with the outcome and promised to arrange with his solicitor to later in the week sign the contract.

Bill was given a receipt that night and assured that the water in the cottage would be turned on, in time for his subsequent acquisition of the deeds. Bill was on cloud nine as he left the estate office and couldn't wait to return to his partner with the good news.

He drove back intending to enter the George with, "Who's bought himself a house then?" But then something prompted him to say nothing at all, and he fought strongly an inner battle with himself to be completely discreet about the whole thing. He entered the lounge and ordered himself a pint of bitter and took a seat near the pumps.

THE MACE GOES IN

"Hiya Bill, are yer comin' over or what?" asked Del. Bill picked up his drink and moved to his partner's table.

"Pick any winners tonight Del?" he asked for the want of conversation.

"Yeh, I did very well Bill - yeh, even managed ter square up Peter Strate's account," he said with pride.

"About temorrer Del, are yer still goin' ter 'Enry's contract or not?" he queried.

"Naw Bill, I think we'll give 'Enery a miss - don't you, I meantersay, there's only old iron left isn't there?"

"But I thought we were doin' 'im a favour watchin' Day and Knight?" Bill reminded.

"D'you honestly think that's why we went mate? That was just a con, so's we could nick the stuff ourselves and besides, 'ow d'yer think Sonnie will feel when his stuff's gone out of them stillages, 'e'll know it's us - won't 'e?" Del reasoned.

"Oh aye yeh, I'd forgotten about that," Bill lamented.

"Drink up mate," said Del, "we'll go on 'safari' in the mornin'!"

"Ooh me: achin' 'ead, what did yer put in that cocktail last night Bill?" Del lamented.

"It was only a bit of gin, oh and some whiskey, and rum…, vodka and the like - mind you, Sarah did go a bit overboard with all that Tabasco sauce," he lied, chuckling under his breath.

"Tabasco - yer've gorra be jokin'! Yer not jokin'! I'll kill 'er. Me ulcers'll be playin. me up all week," he moaned. Del started to hold his stomach imagining his pain already and with all his stress, actually started to experience discomfort there. He reached for his dyspepsia tablets and washed three of them down with his tea.

Bill was apparently enjoying seeing Del squirm, as he leaned back on his chair against the cooker where Beth was turning the eggs.

"How many sausage Bill?" she asked smiling.

"Two's smashing Beth, and one egg."

"How about you Del?"

"Two raw eggs Beth without the yeller," he moaned holding his middle.

"Now listen here, Vandel Bovis," she stated sternly, "you haven't got ulcers –and you know it!"

Del looked up sheepishly, still trying to convince her that he really did have pain there, pleading, "But it really hurts Beth – honestly."

"Now Del, you've really let the side down by this negative thought –remember what the doctor said about it all being in your mind?" she suggested.

"Well…" he half reasoned.

"Think positively Del, think: I am healthy, I am healthy!" she indicated determinedly.

Del repeated it in his mind a few times and then, verbally, "I am healthy, I am healthy, I am…" He could feel the pain leaving his stomach, slowly but surely he started to feel fit once more and even relished the idea of breakfast. As if a miracle had occurred, the pain left him completely and half a minute later, he was feeling on top of the world. He had psyched himself up once more, where even the suggestion of pain anywhere, would have been out of the question.

"I'll 'ave two eggs and four sausages Beth, an' a bit o' kidney if yer've gorrit? He mused.

"Now that's the way I like to hear you talk," she commented happily.

They decided to take the Wrexham road as they travelled through Chester, if only to sample fresh fields of trade.

"Know anybody up this direction Bill?" asked Del.

"Er, it's been a long time mate, but I used ter know a widow who used ter, 'ave a small holdin,' but I dunno whether she'd still be there or not?"

"'Ow far down is it?"

"Oh it's not far now - make a left on the next junction. Yer never know, she might 'ave a bit of old cast, off that old manor 'ouse that was fallin' down, the last time I was 'ere?"

"This the turnin' Bill?" asked Del, as the signpost loomed up.

"Aye, left 'ere," agreed his friend.

Del turned the Bedford into the lane and asked, "Say when Bill?"

"Go about 'alf a mile Del, then left again till yer come to a fork -

THE MACE GOES IN

then a quick right,"

Del followed this instruction until he arrived at the fork, but turned left.

"Right Del, not left mate," Bill corrected.

Del Stopped the wagon and jumped from the driver's seat.

"Oh aye, a nature call eh?" Bill smiled, but the smile faded as he noticed Del open the gate which led to the field.

"Where the 'ell are yer goin'?" he screamed, but Del ignored him completely. His attention was aimed at an ominous shape in the field.

Exasperated, Bill left the motor, shot through the gate to join his friend, who was busily hitting with a stone what resembled an antiquated water pump. The kind Bill remembered well, in the Royal Armoured Corps.

"What the 'eck are yer doin' ter that old pump, it's knackered - can't yer see, the fly wheel's shaft's broken off," he affirmed.

"Course it is - course it is, d'yer think I'd be after it if it was serviceable? Use yer loaf Bill, anyway, if we can find out 'oo's it is, we'll be on for a bomb."

"What for an' old scrap pump?" he echoed with mirth.

"Blummin' gun-metal Bill - gold," cried Del.

"It's not - is it? By 'eck, yer right mate, it must be worth a flamin' fortune, let's gerrit on the wagon quick." he stressed.

"Really Bill, yer jokin' aren't yer, y'know I don't do any nickin' - in broad daylight? Tell yer what, let's see 'oo owns this field, an' we could mace it off 'em, what d'yer say?"

"Oi, what's all this then?"

Both the men swung around to be confronted by a Holland and Holland twelve bore gun barrels, carried by a ruddy faced bearded fellow with a determined look. "What are you two doing in my field - out with it, and make it snappy," he demanded.

"We're looking for Marjorie Williams place, and we seem to have lost our direction," Bill revealed.

"Put that gun down will you old chap it's likely to go off," ordered Bill with authority.

When the man realised that Bill showed no fear, he lowered the gun saying, "You can't be too careful these days, what with all that's goin' on…Marjorie Williams you say? Hmm."

"D'you know if she still lives at the Manor House?" asked Bill

"Er yes, she still lives there, but you may not recognise it now, it's been modernised by her brother James, y'know," the man stated. "By the way do I know you, your face seems very familiar?"

Bill looked hard at the man but he couldn't recognise him in any way, but then said: "I'm Bill Foggit and this is my partner Del Bovis. We're machine dismantlers. Here's our card, and I'm sure that I've seen you before, somewhere?"

"It's me - James, James Williams, don't let the beard fool you," the man stressed.

"James, I don't know any - 'ang on, not young Jimmy, him 'oo 'ad is Dad's loot, an' spent it in Australia?" Bill probed, noticing a frown appear.

"Well, it wasn't quite like that, I had a run of bad luck actually, mostly a cash flow problem. Anyway, I came home with most of the money left and invested it into Marjorie's place when our Dad died."

"Oh so Marge did make a go of the place then?" queried Bill.

"Yes she did…so to speak. Mind you, that husband of hers, I wouldn't give much stock to."

"Who did she marry anyway?" asked he.

"Oh nobody you know mate, 'pears his father was a gentleman farmer - big man in the city. Trouble is he doesn't know a piece of clay from a sod. This is the reason why he's bought all that damned new machinery."

"New machinery?" Bill echoed.

"Yes," he elucidated, "spent all of Marge's money doing it. Of course Marge didn't object, she's so madly in love with him, she'd allow him to do anything.

"Didn't you try to stop him?"

"Silly begger he is, why he allowed all those salesmen to talk him into it. Probably been shooting his mouth off in the pub on how good a farmer he was," Jim assured.

They walked back out of the field and as Del re-entered the motor's driving seat, Bill stopped for a moment to speak with Jim who said, "Are you coming up to the house to see Marjorie, Bill? I

THE MACE GOES IN

know she'd be happy to see you again. It must be all of seven years since you were last here."

Bill nodded in approval saying, "I'm sure Del wouldn't mind half an hour of his time – we're business partners y'know Jim. Yes, hop up into the cab and we'll drive you in, mind you, we'd better park at the rear of the manor, I wouldn't like to offend Marjorie's husband," he searched.

"Of course Bill you're right, take it alongside the stables."

This suited both Del and Bill, for it gave them the opportunity to survey the area for potential scrap metal.

Bill pointed the way out to Del and they commenced to drive up the rough road. Ahead loomed the manor, its original design was influenced by Christopher Wren and emphasised greatly that era of building style. Bill had always liked the house, for it held 'majesty' of its very own. If ever he had experienced visions of grandeur, this house echoed his private fantasy and always would. At their approach of the home, he instructed Del to make a turning left, in order to miss passing by the front of the house. The stables came into view, and Del steered the motor to the side of their gable, unobtrusive to the access.

"Guess what Marge? Bill's here again. He's brought a friend along," called Jim.

"Bill, Bill," she echoed, "Not my Billy? It's been years," she exclaimed happily, "Oh do come and sit down love," she welcomed. "Claude, leave that accounting now and come and meet Billy," she motioned.

The enormous figure of a man arose and approached Bill. His face and body echoed riotous living. His eyes were full of bags and lines and his neck sported three separate chins. His hair balding - to reveal a sweaty brow and pate which brought instantly to Bill's mind a picture of Dickens' 'Beagle' out of 'Oliver Twist.' Even to the shape of his stomach, for which his clothes had been particularly tailored to accommodate.

Marjorie made the introductions and Bill did likewise.

"So you're Billy eh...not that army feller are you- eh, eh?" he quizzed, "Marge has told me so much about you," he enlightened smiling.

Bill smiled back, wondering just what Marjory had said to him, finally replying, "Yes, Claude is it? It must be what? Oh, seven years since our last meeting Marge. I can remember it like it was yesterday."

"Yes Bill," she replied, "If they hadn't shipped you back to Nicosia, you'd probably still be re-building that old T Ford. It's still in the barn y'know. Anyway, speaking of old crocks, Claude is at present restoring an Italian Frasheeny!"

"Not an Isotta Fraschini?"

"You've got it old boy,' he said proudly, "I've taken pictures before I started, and recorded each sequence in order," he beamed going over to his bureau to pick up an envelope, "Here we are Bill, have a glance at these. Now, here is the original condition of it, and here as you can see are the stages I took to restore it."

Without giving Bill chance to reply, he further enlightened, "You should have seen the rust and rot to the wooden floor it was shocking..."

Bill smiled with feigned interest, but his mind was not in the world of veteran cars but how to make his daily wages.

Marjorie noticed Bill's plight and interrupted with!

"Claude don't go on so, I'd like to talk to Bill also," she reasoned.

Claude suddenly got the message, for he frowned slightly and replied, "But of course Marge, I got a bit carried away."

"Bill?" she motioned, "come and have a look at that barn you designed before you left."

Bill followed her out of the room, and Del cottoned on immediately that Bill needed some time alone with her for he suddenly said, "Gosh Claude, did you really do all of this work yourself, or did you have some help with it?"

Right away, Claude lost all interest in Bill and turned his attentions on Del with: "No, I'm proud to say that I've done it all myself. It was quite a challenge at first, but by disciplining myself each day, I've been able to cope with most of the under-body an…"

THE MACE GOES IN

Bill reached the barn and entered in walking to the side and moved behind the hay stack. As Marjorie entered, he suddenly took her in his arms and gave her a brotherly hug and a kiss on the cheek saying, "Gosh love, it's good to be back."

She returned his gesture with a firm kiss upon his lips purring, "I've missed you Bill, you don't know how much?"

"P'rhaps I shouldn't have left so quickly Marge, but I was falling madly in love with you, and let's face it, I am fifteen years your senior," he rued.

"Bill, Bill, that didn't make any difference love, we loved each other - and you knew it - didn't you? Times haven't changed, I still feel the same way about you even now," she assured him.

"But Marge, you're married love?" he emphasised.

"Only a marriage of convenience Bill, Claude came to the rescue with his money, why he doesn't know the first thing about agriculture - and hasn't even the slightest interest!" she cried with tears.

Marjorie stood there looking on adoringly, her black hair blowing in the slight breeze. Her fair complexion, her lythe figure standing there so proudly and her sensuous lips pouting to gain sympathy.

Bill relaxed on a bale of hay and she lay next to him as they commenced to caress each other's hands...

Surely this isn't really a genuine 'Fraschini is it Claude?" voiced Del, "I meantersay, most of these models disappeared by the late 1920's, and any which did survive, were merely mongrels of similar models," he searched.

"Not this one Del, everything is original."

Where have you got it parked then?" he queried, (trying to get Claude outside so that he could survey the area for scrap iron.)

"Come I'll take you there, it's only around the corner," he assured.

Del followed him excitedly as Claude led him out of the manor.

Before long, they arrived at the rear of the stables, where a longish garage was placed.

Claude took out a key and unlocked the door. Beyond it stood a 1914 Isotta Fraschini type - TM. It was a magnificent specimen with its 6.2 litre engine gleaming under its partly open bonnet. The colour of post office red immaculately coach painted, with its sparkling chromed radiator and lamps reflecting the sunlight, caused a slight envy in Del, but then something else distracted his gaze: He couldn't believe his eyes. It wasn't the gleaming car which now took his view, but the abundance of heavy guage copper tubes which littered the area.

"A fortune - a blinkin' gift," he thought with avarice.

"Gosh Claude you're a very talented fellow to have restored this car so well. I'll bet you're very careful not to scratch the paint, in fact I'd be willing to assume that with something like this you'd want to cover it up with sheets, to protect it from falling objects," he enthused, adding, "here, let me take these old bits of piping away, so's they won't endanger the bodywork," he suggested.

"Which pipes? Oh those!" he exclaimed. "I'd completely forgotten about them."

Del commenced to move carefully the heavy piping out of the shed asking, "Where on earth did you get this lot from Claude?"

"The old man," he voiced with disgust.

"Old man - not Marjory's dad, but what did he need with it?"

"Really Del, didn't Bill tell you? I thought it was common knowledge, about old man Williams' distillery," he enlightened.

"A still?" Del smiled chuckling with disbelief.

"But of course Del, he drank that much, he just couldn't get enough of it. He did in fact use this garage for his illicit brew," he said with derision, " he made a rotten mess of the roof too with his chimneys."

"D'you mean to say he actually sold it for profit?" Del probed.

"Oh no no Del, he only used it for himself and private parties - in fact, that was what led to his undoing. He lost all interest in agriculture. It started, I suppose when he failed to plant his 'catch crop' in July, and I feel that from there it went from bad to worse."

"That bad eh?"

"Yer, it got so bad that Seth kept falling from the tractor in his permanent state of inebriation and well, Marjorie couldn't always be there to drive it for him. I mean, you can't expect a mere woman, to

THE MACE GOES IN

take on a man's job can you?"

"So I suppose you'll want to get rid of this bad memory as soon as possible eh?" Del edged pushing the boat out.

He acted at once, and with this incentive, started to carry out the copper piping from the shed.

Claude didn't even argue, but felt a sudden relief as the tubing was thrown onto Del's wagon. Del came back with the Bedford and backed it up to the door. As quickly as he could, he continued to eject from the garage the main cache of copper tubing, which as he did it became clear that he had under estimated the amount, for what

seemed like a few hundred weight, now proved to be closer to half a ton. He had developed quite a sweat in his handling of it and showed signs of fatigue, but the thought of the price it would bring edged him on, until finally he had accounted for every piece.

"This boiler to go Claude?" he asked. Noticing a frown on Claude's face he quickly said, "Cor, smells like a blinkin' brewery."

Claude's doubt soon faded as he remarked, "Take it all out Del, get rid of it, the sooner the better."

Del couldn't quite lift the Mathieson boiler, which he resorted to roll toward the wagon.

"Give me a lift would you Claude?"

Claude seeing Del's predicament had acted already and was busily placing two twelve foot scaffolding boards against the rear tailboard. Del observed this as he arrived with the boiler and manoeuvred the drum to negotiate the boards.

"One, two three-eeee," he barked as they both pushed the copper up the bridge. It started to roll back and Del held it shouting, "Jam a stick into it!" Claude replied by bending down to pick up a tongue and grooved board, which he deftly jammed under the drum.

"You've done this before, haven't you?" Del commanded as Claude levered the drum upward, enabling it to drop over the tailboard.

Claude smiled as he removed the scaffolding boards and re-entered the garage, enlightening Del with:

"Ever heard of 'Dalton's Metals' Del?" he quizzed.

Del thought for a minute before replying, "Didn't they go out with a bang over that scrap in the Middle East scandal?" asked he.

Claude coloured up saying, "It wasn't really like that Del, the papers exaggerated the story right out of proportion."

Del suddenly realised who this Claude was; this was the son of Algie Dalton who had blown his brains out. To avoid government confrontation, by selling arms to Egypt at the time of the Suez Crisis. The actual Crunch had come when Algie had attempted to retrieve the salvage, which had cluttered up the banks of the Suez Canal. The newspapers had had a field day, and poor Claude had been left to face the music, no wonder he was so obese, Del thought, poor devil, probably tried to drink himself to death.

His thoughts were interrupted by Bill and Marjorie, who had just arrived back from the barn.

A contented look on Bill's face assured Del that his partner had mixed business with pleasure. Claude hadn't noticed the change on Marjorie's face for his thoughts still rested on the past.

"Oh Claude, Bill's been telling me how much he admires the way you handle the business so well," she lied for the sake of something to say.

Claude mentioned that Del had loaded up the wagon remarking: "Del's kindly taking all that copper away for us, 'aren't you mate?"

Del nodded smiling, but the smile began to fade as Claude continued, "How much d'you think we'll get for it Del, I know Marge needs the money?"

Del's face dropped, he had felt like the cat's whiskers up to this stage, but the thought of actually having to pay for the load knocked the wind out of his sails.

Bill smirked at the latest turn of events and caught Del's eye. He was furious.

Yes Del was so livid he couldn't reply straight away. He clutched at straws for a reply and then suddenly the brain child.

'Mace' will pay for it!" he exclaimed, looking for approval from Bill who frowned and replied with horror.

"Oh no Del, don't you remember, Mace went bankrupt last month?"

Del smirked, obviously enjoying seeing Bill squirm, this'll teach

THE MACE GOES IN

'im ter make love in business hours!

Bill replied once more, "How much is there Del," as he climbed up onto the rear wheel.

"Hmm, there must be at least five hundred weight," he lied quoting: "At the present rate, that should bring at least er £30 a cwt times five hmm, £150 sounds pretty good what d'you think Marge?"

"That's fantastic Bill will you be able to pay us now?" she purred.

"Hang on a minute Del," Claude indicated, "there must be at least seven hundred weight on your wagon by now?"

Claude was no fool, as Del soon realised which caused him to interject with, "Now Bill, Claude's right, there's more than 5 cwt there. Mind you Claude, I'd say at a guess there's no more than 6 cwt if that!" he determined.

"Well perhaps you're right," the man relented, "anyway Del, that now makes it £180 you do have the cash don't you?" he queried.

"Now 'ang on Claude, £180 worth it may be, but that's the price that we get as bonafide dealers. The buying in price that we pay is half of that," Del enlightened.

"D'you mean that we'll only get £90 for it?" cried Marjorie with dismay, "Oh Bill, how could you build up my hopes like that?"

Bill coloured up and replied, "Wait a minute Del, I've known Marge a long time and well damn it mate, we could give her at least £120 - I mean she does need the money badly doesn't she, and it's not as if we're that desperate are we?' he emphasised.

"I see what yer mean Bill, aye, yer right o' course, well £120 it is then," he concurred.

"Here Bill, take this £60 with yours and pay Claude," he indicated handing him the wad. Bill passed the £120 collectively over to Claude who received the money happily, commenting: "Feel free to inspect the rest of the place for any metal you may take a fancy to, since my marriage to Marge, I've disregarded all those obsolete machines which have lain here for donkey's years," he assured them adding, "We have all new plant ones now."

After weighing in at Chester, Bill and Del stopped off at the 'Ring O' Bells' for some liquid refreshment. Bill ordered two pints of bitter and Del paid for two pork pies for them both. Handing one to Bill saying with disapproval, "You and yer flamin' generosity, - "Yes Marjorie - dear heart - we'll give you £30 extra for your copper, flamin' con artist if you ask me?" Del mimicked sarcastically,

"Wasn't it you who put the copper on the wagon Del? I mean, you could have stuck to old iron, but no, it's gotta be non ferrous or nuthin'. 'Pears ter me mate that you're the one 'oo's bin conned, some people, she-eash!"

"Speakin' of old iron Bill, don't get too flippant 'cos we need ter get back there for the steel, so's we can make it pay," he reasoned.

"Make it pay, we're £35 each ter the good aren't we?" Bill confuted.

"The pump - the water pump, you remember," he growled with exasperation.

"I'm way ahead of yer Del the 'Grampton Hydro', clears drains in half the time," Bill connoted.

"Right, now I'm not concerned about its silly efficiency Bill - only its composition," he fumed at his tomfoolery.

An hour later they upended their glasses and re-entered the motor, driving in the Wrexham direction. The all too familiar entrance to Marjorie's place appeared and Del suddenly pulled over to the gate where they'd first encountered James. Quickly he left the cab and took the hessian sack from behind the driver's seat.

"Bring the 14 pounder Bill," he voiced urgently.

Bill reached by the rear of his seat for the big hammer and followed Del who was briskly walking in the direction of the bronze pump.

"Hell's bells," Del remarked as he surveyed the area. The pump had sunk almost into the earth where there was evidence of land erosion as one third of it was obviously buried. Del hated the idea of any additional manual labour and so instructed Bill to remove the earth from around the object.

Bill concurred but broke two large sticks from a bush nearby and handed one of them to Del with, "To dig with Del," he indicated.

Del looked aghast, but realised that he would only incur Bill's labour, on the condition that he himself got his finger out. Both of the men proceeded to dig down to reveal more of the pump's casting.

The work proved to be quite hard, causing each of them to puff and blow, making large amounts of sweat peal from their faces.

Off came their jackets, as they set themselves to task even harder than before. The greed of the value, had overcome their worries of getting dirty and before long, each had mud on his clothes and cut hands from the rough terrain. Del seemed to be carried away with his newly found dignity of labour and commenced to move Bill out of harm's way before bringing the 14lb hammer down hard upon the pump's casting which after relentless blows by him proved to crack and break large lumps from its exterior.

One piece in particular flew out and caught him on the shin, "Aaarrgh," he howled, but this added torment only proved to be a further challenge as he disregarded his wound and flailed a further barrage of blows out at the pump.

Bill couldn't believe it, here was Del, - as unobtainable as the Scarlet Pimpernel, whenever work threatened, but here he was actually working, and working like a real grafter too.

Before long, Bill had rolled two cigarettes and handed one to Del, who had succeeded in completely demolishing the old water pump, which now resembled nothing of its original design.

"Sit down mate an' 'ave a fag," Bill gestured.

Del was a fountain of sweat. His face was completely running, his arms and shirt. Entirely drenched, as he reached for the weed which he puffed at appreciably, as Bill held out the lighter.

Del breathed out the smoke. A smile on his face as he enjoyed the smoke on his palette. This was a cigarette with a difference. He sat down on the grass and then lay down breathing and puffing enjoyably.

"Cor mate, yer've made short work o' that 'aven't yer?" said Bill, admiring the result. He reached down with a hessian sack and commenced to fill it with pieces of gleaming gun metal, filling up the old coal sack almost to the brim, to which he tied around the neck a piece of cord from his pocket.

"Flamin' 'ell it's 'eavy Del, must be a couple of 'undred weight 'ere mate."

But Del continued to lie on the grass, almost oblivious to Bill's comments, as he savoured the butt end of the cigarette, which had almost burned away. He arose after first taking a last drag at the stump, which he threw down saying, "Come on, Bill cop for tha' end, we'll take this to the wagon." His friend complied and they both lifted together, but the sack proved heavier than they could carry.

"Oh su-sugar, what are we gonna do now?" voiced a disgusted Bill.

"Take some out mate," Del reasoned, "'Ere, I'll show yer." He started to untie the neck and then removed half of the metal and retied the neck. "Ow's that?" he asked.

Even with half of it removed, the bag still proved to be a challenge, but they managed to carry it and half drag it, across to the truck. Bill dropped down the tailboard, and they both struggled to lift up the load. Bill then jumped up onto the rear and upended the sack after untying it.

The repeat performance over the field and upon return, saw them retrieve all of the remainder. Even after the gun metal, they continued to travel overland to collect the steel insides of the machine.

After a reconnoitre of the field, they resumed their quest for a quick load to round off the day but after starting the motor, realised that they both were not young men any more and proceeded in the direction of the scrap yard. Bill drove into Myrtle Pearsons yard, with barely a half an hour to spare before closing.

Both he and Del dropped the tailboard and attempted to carry the bronze to the non ferrous scale.

"I'll bet this was a mace Del?" Myrtle remarked knowingly.

"Er no love," he replied adding, "We 'ad ter work fer this!" telling the truth for once.

"Three 'undred weight, one quarter," she smiled, "that do yer then?"

"Ow much are yer payin'?" queried Bill.

"It's 'ad an 'ammerin' this week - it's down ter £600 pound a ton!" she informed them.

THE MACE GOES IN

"So that's, 30, 60, 90, - er £90 an' 'er 7¾ quid for the quarter - right Myrt?" said Del.

"Right first time boy," she complimented adding, "you know the score Del boy, 'ere's yer cash." She handed him the money observed by Bill who was mindfully working out his share.

£48/7/6d is exactly 'alf Del."

"Aye okay Bill," said Del handing him his share. "Now with the £56 yer've got left, yer can fill up the motor again can't yer?"

Bill nodded thinking, "That Del, gorra mind like an elephant - never forgets anythin'...!"

On the way home, Bill put six pounds worth of petrol in the lorry whilst Del looked on, and then drove to his flat where Del took the keys and drove home.

Bill arrived into his flat and suddenly it struck him - the bank. "Hell's blinkin' bells, it's six o'clock," he fumed helplessly. "I've done it now - 'aven't I, and no grand ter clinch the deal?" Thoughts of the cottage crashed down around him as he held his head in his hands with despair. "I can just see Comptons now, purrin' 'er up fer sale again, an' me with all that dosh in the bank an' no flamin' cash flow." He reached for a drink and was just about to throw the contents down when he thought, "I wonder where George Leadbetter lives?"

Out of the yellow pages he received some phone numbers pertaining to the Riverton Bank, which he feverishly wrote down including the one which indicated after hours. He ran down to the hall phone and was at once connected to the bank. "Hello, yes, Mr. Leadbetter? Right sir I'll see if I can contact him sir," the voice assured him.

Bill was putting in more and more coins as he waited for the result when suddenly a familiar voice came on, "Mr. Foggit? Oh hello sir, it's good to hear from you,"

Bill replied, "Gerald, is it all right to call you by your first name?"

"By all means Mr. Foggit," he relented.

"Gerald I'm in a spot of bother," said Bill.

"How can I help sir?" asked the man.

"You know I have quite a large amount in your bank," Bill reminded.

"Yes sir, you're a good customer."

"Well Gerald, the position is this: due to an oversight, on my part today, I left it too late to collect £1000 of my cash from the bank and the problem is, I need it right now- desperately!"

There was silence for a time until the man replied: "Would a cheque suffice sir, I'm sure we could help in that direction, as all the cash has now been replaced in the time vault."

Bill was over the moon and listened, as the manager asked him if he could go up to the bank at the side door in half an hour.

Bill agreed and at once replaced the phone and hurried up the stairs to change his attire. He arrived at the bank directly on time and knocked on the side door. A security guard accompanied the manager, as he appeared and handed the envelope containing the cheque.

"Just sign here Mr. Foggit," he instructed and Bill complied. He shook the man's hand and departed overjoyed.

Bang Bang

CHAPTER 21

He arrived at Comptons, who also had security men awaiting his arrival with the 'cash' he had promised, but after hurried words with the estate agent manager, resulting in smiles all around.

"Get Mr. Foggit the keys once more Janet." the man instructed.

"Oh no Mr. Kitchen that won't be necessary," said Bill, "I'll wait until the bill of sale is signed tomorrow," he picked up the schedule and noted the time 2.30pm Thursday.

Bill returned home and poured himself that promised glass of scotch, which he now threw down his throat and quickly replenished triumphantly. He felt accomplished truly and drank until he fell sound asleep.

Eight thirty with the alarm clanging, awoke him bleary eyed as he reached up for more scotch, but to his disgust noticed the bottle lying on the settee, almost empty.

He arose and ran the bath which was quite hot, considering his gas fire boiler had only been on 2 hours whilst asleep.

He climbed in and just lay there allowing the added salts he had inserted, to permeate his back limbs. "Ooh yeh, that's better," he mused and almost fell into the realms of sleep.

Bang bang, bang, sounded the door knocker, "To hell with 'em," he cursed.

Bang, bang, bang, bang, bang, bang,...

"Bill - it's me, Mary!?"

"Mary, Mary who?" he queried to himself, "I don't know any Mar....not Mary Valesque?"

At first his mind told him to ignore her pleas, as she continued to shout through the letterbox.

"Bill, oh Bill - please open the door?"

He could stand it no longer and almost flew out of the bath to get to the door, but then realised he was nude and so cried, "Okay, hang on, just a minute," hurrying to don his dressing gown.

He opened the door and sure enough, there stood that dark eyed brunette beauty facing him.

She entered into the flat commenting, "Nice place you have Bill, been here long?"

"Where the hell have you been?" he questioned angrily.

"Been? But you know where I've been love. By the way, the money didn't appear," she cried, "I've been home for three days, but neither Dad or Dinny have appeared, and I'm beginning to worry about where they are?" she wailed tears emerging.

"I don't believe this! Does she think I've just come down the river on a boat?" He thought. "How did you know where I lived?"

"You left your driving license on the floor of the bedroom, the last time you slept there," she enlightened adding, "Here it is love," as she handed it to him from her purse.

Everything was just too pat for Bill, "No," he thought, "something smells here." He decided to play along with her to discover the REAL reason for her visit and replied, "Oh thanks love, I've been looking all over the place for this."

He gave her a hug, to convince her he had fallen for the explanation. "I don't have any idea where they are love, the last thing I remember is bumping my head after slipping on a silly banana skin in the kitchen, when Dinny came down to get the Swiss account number. I must have suffered concussion from it, because I don't remember anything after that, until waking up two days later," he lied convincingly.

"Then you didn't actually come to the main meeting the same day?" she asked confused.

"Meeting, what meeting?" he enquired adding, "By the way Mary, my Morris Minor, mysteriously turned up again back at the flat. I still can't figure out how. Could you throw any light on this?" he quizzed.

THE MACE GOES IN

Mary looked perturbed answering, "There's a lot of strange things happening Bill," she sobbed, resting her head on his shoulder hugging him.

Bill felt like a heel, Mary really didn't know what had happened - how could she? She had been waiting patiently in Switzerland, for a non-existent account number. There again, it was just too well explained he reasoned.

"Oh hell, I don't know what's reality and what's fiction any more!" he muttered under his breath.

He took hold of her hand and led her into the lounge. "Sit here love, I'll get you a nice cuppa," he motioned. He switched on the gas fire saying, "I'll go and put the kettle on." After lighting the stove, he added a small scotch to her proposed drink! "Are you alright love?" he asked, concerned for her welfare.

"Yes love," she replied in a weak voice giving evidence of her recent tears. 'Pheep,' sounded the kettle and Bill hastily removed it and poured the water, adding four tea-bags.

"How many sugars love?"

"Just the one Bill," she replied beginning to recover.

He put everything on the tray with a packet of biscuits, and took it into the room.

"Shall I be 'mother' Bill?" she pouted.

"Are you alright love?" Bill asked again.

"I - I'll be okay love," she replied tearfully, making him feel worse than what he already did.

"You've given me the wrong one love, yours is the one with the scotch," he assured her.

"Oh really love?"

"I'll get the bottle," he gestured and commenced to pour in the whisky.

"Enough Bill, you'll have me drunk!" she warned laughing.

After which Mary went for a rest on the bed and Bill sat in front of the gas fire – both fell asleep for an hour.

Bill awoke on the couch and went into the bedroom to awaken Mary. He looked at her with love in his heart and leaned down to gently kiss her brow.

The smell of bacon and eggs filled Mary's nostrils causing her to awaken, just as Bill made his timely entrance into the bedroom with the tray on wheels, loaded with the hot supper and pot of tea with the accompanying bottle of scotch. They both tucked into the fare with relish, before Bill endowed her with his stories of his army escapades, which occupied most of the night.

Eventually he said good night and retired in front of the gas fire in the lounge.

Thursday morning came almost too soon and with a gentle word of assurance and comfort from Bill, gave Mary the confidence she needed to await his return home to the flat.

Bill drove his Minor up toward Del's home and knocked on his door.

After entering, assumed the same ritual of accepting his usual breakfast, without even the hint of Mary, who now occupied his own home.

"Yerse Bill, this is jut what you need - a little dolly ter cook fer yer, ter get yer up in the mornin' with a cuppa an' ter make sure the paper always comes through the door fer the racin' of the day. 'Ave yer ever thought of takin' the plunge?" Del queried adding: "A lot do - yer know, and it 'asn't done them any 'arm."

Immediately Bill thought of Mary back in his flat, and wondered if Del knew a little bit more than what he was admitting.

"What are yer looking at me like that fer Bill? I was only trying to help yer," said he clutching at straws.

"Take Beth 'ere, but fer me, she would of been doomed to a world of opera. I came along an' saved her from it all - didn't I love?" he stressed changing the subject.

Beth's face coloured up, she was furious. "The less said about that the better," she fumed.

"'Ave yer had enough tea Bill? Well we'll ger' off then mate," voiced Del with urgency.

Bill was quick to take the hint and replied with, "Well, where to today mate?"

Del walked up to the cab of the diesel Ford, climbed in and sat

THE MACE GOES IN

down. He started rooting underneath the parcel shelf, for his log book of calls, and upon acquisition of the article, proceeded to flick through its pages.

"Ah," he exclaimed, "I was sure it was 'ere, and 'ere it is!" Just as Bill joined him in the cab to investigate this new discovery.

"'Ere Bill get yer peepers runnin' over this lot," he directed, handing his friend the open book. Bill took it from him at the open page, upon which was scribbled, Jefferson Sanitations Ltd. He looked at the address and noted it was almost on the borders of Riverton.

"So it's Jefferson's is it mate, what can they possibly have that could interest us?" he asked sarcastically.

"We won't ever know, if we don't visit 'em will we Bill?"

"Perhaps yer right Del," he agreed, as his friend started the engine.

The oil sites road loomed up ahead and quite soon, they had drawn up outside Jefferson's main gate.

Del drove the Ford into the road and almost immediately, was confronted by the gate-man, whom he told he was clearing up the site for the main contractors.

"You'd get away with bloomin' murder Del!" Bill commented with adoration.

They both guffawed in chorus, as Del drove the wagon even faster once inside the gate.

"Check that demolition Bill, while I go an' see Franky Spooner!" he instructed.

Whoever this Franky was, Bill was only too glad to know of, for at least they were working, and with the prospect of a good day's cash for return.

Del stopped the motor and made his way toward the factory, allowing Bill to drive the wagon over to the derelict building.

'Anglo Scottish Steel Co. Ltd' was stamped on the R S J's, which were scattered about on most of the field surrounding the ruin.

"Hmm," he thought, "must be at least three tons here, a pity there's not more, perhaps Del will ger a bit of stuff from over there?" he reasoned, as he further inspected the scene.

Across the field lay an abundance of empty forty gallon steel drums with clamps around their tops, which out of sheer curiosity Bill examined relentlessly every one, in a bid to discover something of value - but to no avail.

"Hell, this is no good Del," he thought aloud, but his friend couldn't hear him.

Del was engrossed in conversation with Franky.

"Anyway Del, yer still 'aven't paid me fer the last load o' scrap what yer had last August 'ave yer? So I can't really see me givin' yer any more till yer coughs up can I?" he confuted.

"Bu? Frank?" he pleaded.

"No buts, either you have the cash ter give me, or yer get no scrap -as simple as that!" he determined.

"Aw, Franky, yer know I'm goin' ter pay yer - don't yer me ole mate? It's just that the wagon's been off the road till yesterday."

"No cash - no scrap!" he replied

"Ang on Frank, 'ave yer gor anythin' on this job ter sell me terday?"

"Thought yer 'ad no dosh then?"

"Er me driver's gor a few bob in the float what we carry fer diesel. P'raps we could come ter some arrangement - eh?" returned Del, pushing the boat out further.

"It's quite possible – that is if yer've got the readies, that some deal could be set," he hinted.

"I'll get Bill, 'ang on there Frank, I'll be right back with the cash."

"So this is all there is eh Bill?" Del queried, "just these few girders?"

Bill nodded adding, "There's load of steel drums Del but we can't flog them can we?" he reasoned.

"By 'eck we can," Del replied saying, "Ow much dosh 'ave yer got Bill?"

"Only the £50 for the diesel mate, and we daren't touch that 'cos the tank's runnin' low."

"Don't worry about that mate, we'll pinch some o' their pink industrial stuff. The main thing is mate, that we've got a few bluey's ter barter with."

THE MACE GOES IN

Bill got the gist of what was needed by handing over the float to Del, who at once marched back in the direction of the factory.

Bill patrolled the area once more as Del re-negotiated with Franky, who further enlightened Del about the availability, of other scrap on the site, which could be had for a price.

Pieces of old cast iron railway line chairs and even the actual rail track appeared to be lying in various locations of the site, noted by both Del and Frank, as they walked briskly about.

"Okay Del, I've shown yer enough - now then, 'ow much are yer offerin' - no better still, 'ow much 'ave yer got on yer?" he probed.

Del opened his wallet to reveal £30 of the £50 he had received from Bill and he handed it to Frank who immediately thumbed it before pocketing the roll.

"Yer've cleared me out Frank," Del lied, trying to discover if Frank was forthcoming.

"Okay Del, seein' as yer've given me all yer tank, yer can 'ave everythin' around yer can see, but I really must insist on one thing," he stressed.

"Anythin' mate," Del assured him delighted by the prospect.

"Don't - I repeat - don't leave a ruddy mess, if yer takin' the 'eavy, then take the light as well, savvy?" he emphasised.

"Certainly Frank," Del promised. "In fact, I'll start by loadin' all these drums first before I even touch the girders. Bill, Bill, ger over 'ere will yer?" he waved.

Bill hurriedly moved toward his partner. "What's up Del?" he asked.

"Listen mate," whispered Del, "ger about eight of them 40 galloners on the deck o' the wagon sittin' up, but make sure that the rim clamps are with 'em" he emphasised.

"Okay Del but....?"

"Trust me Bill will yer - eh?" he pleaded.

"Right mate, I'll do it right away," he assured.

Del rolled a cigarette, proceeded to smoke it, but then realized that it was a non-smoking area, so he stubbed it out on his car ash tray, as he headed toward the motor pool. After a short conversation with the storekeeper, he re-appeared with a length of rubber hose, to which he attached to the outdoor water supply. After a few minutes rolled by, Bill appeared with the wagon complete with eight 40 gallon drums.

"Right mate, now what's the 'crack' with all of these?" he enquired. Del handed Bill the end of the hose and instructed him to three quarter fill each of the drums with water, then secure the rims with the clamps.

"But but bu- oh you rotten macing begger, you don't mean to say that..? You do don't you?!"

Del was nodding his head chuckling.

"But, we'll never get away with it Del, I mean what about when he inspects the load, how are we goin' ter stop 'im clockin' the water?" he reasoned.

"R S J 's Bill, we'll cock the load up with a few girders on the top an' 'ell never suss it out! He confuted.

"Only somebody as depraved like you, could think o' somethin' like this. Yer just naturally bent aren't yer? Yer couldn't sleep straight if yer tried."

Del just smiled, but knew that a little bit of cheek always paid off and pay off it did, for Bill drove the wagon to 'Shelley's Metal', where Charlie 'one eye' climbed upon the wagon's rear wheel, to inspect the load. The smirk on his face tipped Del to argue for the best price.

"Ow much will yer give us then Charlie?" he quipped adding, "It's number one yer know!"

"It would be if it was under four feet long ter fit the smeltin' pot Del," he reasoned trying to lower the price.

"Smeltin' pot – SMELTIN' POT? this lot's not fer the smeltin' pot Charlie, this is all prime salvage yer could sell this lot through yer brother Billy's yard for extensions, for local builders use of these girders, fer ten times what yer pay me?" he reasoned.

Charlie coloured up realising that Del was aware of the value of the load, which spanned almost the full length of the lorry and decided to pay a price he considered fair.

"I'll give yer £28 a ton for the girders, Del," he offered.

Del spat on his palm and shook with his left- in typical Diddie Kye fashion assuring Charlie that he had a deal.

THE MACE GOES IN

"Shove 'em at the far end o' the yard, mate then we'll tare yer off!" he directed. Del winked at Bill repeating Charlie's words and including some knowing winks and mouth gestures, which instructed Bill just what to do.

He reversed the motor back as far as he could, all of the time looking forward with urgent glances, to ensure no intervention from yard workers, and when he was sure he was out of sight - threw off the girders as quickly as he could over the wagon sides. He then dropped the tail board after furtive glances back for when he thought the coast was clear - preceded to de-clamp the drums and upend them, allowing the precious water load to escape into the yard. He stacked the drums back into place and put all of the clamps inside the cab to avoid noisy clanking at the rear. He then re-sealed the tailboard and when he was happy with the truck's safety, returned to the weighbridge.

"Three ton even Del, come an' sign the book," beamed Charlie.

Del was counting out the money just as Bill arrived.

"Everythin' okay Bill?" he whispered.

Bill smiled nodding, saying, "And the load - 'ow much Del?"

For once Del decided to play it straight and handed Bill the receipt, "Forty two each eh Bill - by the way 'ow's the diesel?"

"Oh...shu-sugar, I almost forgot!"

"Flamin' 'ell Bill, gerrit up to the Esso station quick! Shove the four quid in to be on the safe side - er I'll see yer then Charlie,!" he hailed waving good bye. The Ford was beginning to falter as they made it to the station's forecourt.

"Sorry I can't switch off," Bill apologised profusely to the woman as she entered the diesel pump. She was aware of the plight of diesel engines and smiled saying, "Oh all right - just this once then, but don't make it a habit to get this low again," she warned, "I've got to think of the danger of fire."

Bill received the change and gave it back to her saying, "Get yerself some fags love- yer saved me life there."

She refused to take the five shillings, but after Bill insisted, she decided to accept the gesture. Bill waved to her in respect as he steered the wagon back to Jefferson's.

The repeat performance was made in Forester's Salvage and finally at Rifkits, where both Del and Bill were amply rewarded for their efforts of guile and deceit with bundles of dirty oncers.

"Home James," quipped Del, "let's leave a bit fer termorrer eh mate?"

Bill concurred with a nod smiling, "Home it is," he agreed, driving the truck back to Del's where he left his partner.

After leaving the Morris in the street he ascended the stairs leading to his flat.

He knocked on the door to await Mary, who opened it and flew into his arms crying uncontrollably.

"Bill, Bill, aw hawgh, hawgh," she blurted.

"What's up love - what is it?" he whispered.

After hugging her and holding her - he coaxed her to tell him.

What she did tell him then, made him truly feel like a heel and hoped the ground could swallow him up.

"Dad and Dinny are in prison, some one's shopped them - turned Queen's Evidence ahuh, ahuh, ahawgh," she sobbed.

Bill felt so low that he couldn't look her in the eye, "I wonder who it could be?" he lied, "I haven't seen them for weeks," he said, trying to convince her of his innocence.

"The trial's due in less than three weeks. I've got to go and visit them - I must!" she sobbed.

"No, you mustn't go anywhere near," he warned, "if they're both locked up, going there would only connect you with them - No Mary, you must stay well away for fear of retribution."

Distressed though she was, she knew that he was right and cried even louder.

He allowed her to nestle her head on his arm as he re-assured her asking, "Where is your passport love, you'll need to leave whilst it all blows over," he warned.

"But I can't just go?" She reasoned, "It's my Daddy, and I love him!" she pleaded irrationally."

"So because you love him, you want to go to gaol for him do you?"

"Oh Bill, how could you even think that, no Bill, I don't - oh, I don't know what to think anymore," she sobbed hysterically.

"Look love, you go ahead and cry - let it all out, it'll do you good!" he said lovingly.

It must have been a good half an hour, before Mary cried herself to sleep and Bill carried her in to the bedroom and carefully covered her with the blankets, before returning to the lounge, where he decided to drink himself into oblivion.

Seven thirty pm caused the alarm to suddenly awaken him, he'd forgotten to disconnect the buzzer.

"Oh well," he thought, "maybe it's just as well. Oh - no, I've missed it, the signing up. It was supposed to take place at 2.30 pm. I wonder if they're open now." Frantically he leapt down to the end of the hall and dialled the number.

"Hello, Comptons here, Kitchen's the name. Can I help you?" queried the voice.

"Thank Goodness I was able to catch you," he breathed, "is it too late to sign up?" he lamented.

"Is that Mr. Foggit - it is but of course not sir, we were worried about where you were. Fortunately the solicitor works late on Thursdays over here at the estate office. If you'd like to come sir he will be here until nine o'clock but really he can't stay later than that Mr. Foggit."

"That would be fine," Bill replied excitedly, "I could come now it'll only take me about half an hour," he assured.

Bill looked in on Mary who was sound asleep. Leaving a hurried note for her, he had a quick face and hand wash to spruce up and took off as fast as he could.

"That completes the last detail Mr. Foggit, here are the keys for the cottage, you can expect the final details to arrive anytime from now," assured the solicitor. "We'll instruct you to come in to collect the deeds."

Bill thanked both men for their co-operation and bade them goodbye. He was on cloud nine as he travelled back to his flat.

A lot of thoughts started to enter his mind - namely the past events of the Manchester Flying Squad's swoop on George Valesque's mob, caused the most panic to him (especially the prospect of having to stand up to give evidence against the gang) for Freddie Holly. To be able to secure the pinch and return George to gaol. It was this particular thought, which prevented him from revealing his new acquisition to Mary.

He decided to play it by ear for the present, and worry about future events when they occur.

Mary greeted him at the door as the aroma of Greek styled cooking wafted across his nostrils.

"Been at my herbs - I see," he commented,

"Yes Bill, why didn't you tell me you were into cooking, I found a wonderful recipe in one of your cookbooks for this meat dish," she commended.

She served up the roasted kebabs laced with eastern herbs of many descriptions.

He stuffed the food into his eagerly awaiting mouth commenting, "Cor - absolutely marvellous, how come my kebabs don't taste like this?" he praised.

Mary smiled saying, "What you need William Foggit, is a little woman to look after you," she hinted, smiling, and Bill had to admit she was right.

Bill took Mary out that night, for the late night showing and premiere of a new play at the Solent Theatre in London Road Liverpool, which held his interest almost to the end. It had been written by an old comrade who'd commenced writing whilst working on the docks. Its content had reflected most of the man's own exploits in life, for he knew that's how Bertram had based it. It was really quite funny in places, for it reminded Bill of his acquaintanceship with Trooper Keats in Malaya. Mary also was greatly amused and also most of the audience, who echoed their enjoyment of its humour. It brought the house down with cries of 'encore', as the actors took their final bow, with patrons clamouring onto the stage to meet the author.

Bill gave up any hope of re-contacting his old comrade at arms, and walked Mary out of the theatre toward the car.

They both laughed as they recalled the script they'd just heard. Bill entered the tunnel and drove quite briskly through, soon arriving in Birkenhead to pay the toll.

"One and six this is now, gosh Mary - everytime I go through this flippin' big hole in the ground, it seems to go up another threepence," he complained.

"Yes Bill, inflation seems to have taken a bad hold now doesn't it ~ of course I blame the Beatles."

"The Beatles, what the heck have they done?" he challenged protectively.

"Well, it's simple when you think about it, because of the Beatles, everybody is aping their dress, haircuts and style and anything to do with Liverpool, is attracting tourists by the score. The tunnel staff can't cope and are having to employ more staff to cover the increase - hence your increase of entry is passed on to the consumer, namely the tunnel user."

Bill was exasperated by her sense of reasoning and gave out a large long laugh, but after a while reasoned that perhaps this little woman had more to her, than he'd first perceived.

"Oh you men - you think you know it all," she fumed.

"No honestly love, it was the way in which you said it, it appeared so funny, but on further recap I realise that perhaps there's truth in what you say," he said smiling.

She appeared satisfied by his explanation and snuggled up to him, as he drove down the New Chester Road.

"Turn right here Bill," she suggested, as he passed through Bromborough village.

Bill obeyed her and steered the Minor alongside her home, where it lay beside the woodland.

"Let's go and have a cuppa," she offered.

Bill complied to this request and they entered the house.

After they had drunk of their cups, Mary set about vacuuming the hall way.

"Cut that out Mary? Look at the time," he scolded, "we'll have to get back."

"No Bill, I shall be staying here," she determined, "to keep the home ready for Daddy and Dinny," she said loyally.

Bill could do nothing to change her mind, and felt that he didn't have that right anyway.

With mixed feelings he bade her farewell and left for home. Arriving back he sorrowfully, took out a fresh bottle of scotch from the cabinet and proceeded to drink it from the bottle.

Sergeant Griffiths

CHAPTER 22

"Cut that flamin' din out," he moaned, as he fell out of bed in his attempt to reach the front door. Bill arose with a head like lead, but managed to get to his feet to reach the front door and draw back the bolt.

"D'yer know what time it is mate?" Del screamed, "It's flamin' ten o'clock - where've yer bin? Beth's goin' mad, she's ruined 'er pan tryin' ter keep yer eggs warm!"

"Oh I'm so sorry Del, I've bin 'ittin the bottle again an'."

"Yer don't 'ave ter tell me mate - woman trouble, I know, you've got that pained look, in yer eyes again," said Del knowingly.

"But how?" he asked.

"Listen Bill, yer looked exactly like yer do now, when that birastuff from Leicester left yer fer that big Dutch seaman, I've seen ir all before," he related.

"I'll 'ave to 'ave an 'air of the dog Del," said Bill, reaching for the drinks cabinet door. Flippin' 'eck there's nuthin' left!' He searched frantically knocking over the glasses within, but located only tonic water.

"Got any on the hip Del? I'm desperate, spitting feathers."

"Come on Bill get a wash an' 'ave a shave then we'll 'ead back for Jeffersons ter pick up the rest of the stuff."

"But Del…"

"If yer lucky, there might just be a drop o' rum in that bottle what I keep in the dash - for medicinal purposes o' course," Del hinted.

Bill breathed a sigh of relief and hurriedly changed out of his previous night's attire, donning his everyday gear after his wash and shave. He dashed ahead of Del toward the cab of the Ford wagon and entered the cab frantically to reach the dashboard, but to his horror - the compartment was locked.

"The key - the key Del, chuck us the key?" he pleaded.

"Oh I don't know Bill, d'yer think yer should, I mean s'pose the officers stop us an' ask yer ter walk the white line?" He joked, enjoying seeing Bill squirm.

"For the booze, yer rotter - not fer drivin'," Bill fumed.

"Heh, heh, 'ere yer are mate," he replied handing him the ignition keys.

Bill snatched them from him and fumbled with the lock. He took out the bottle of Lamb's Navy, and downed almost all of the half filled contents with one gulp, causing him to cough uncontrollably.

Completely oblivious to this, Del took back the keys and started the motor just as Bill was recovering. In a short while the Ford was outside of Jeffersons. Del steered deftly back into the RSJ area, "'Ere we are again mate, yer know what ter do - don't yer?" he gestured but Bill was fast asleep and dead drunk, past caring about temporal needs.

"Oh shu-sugar!" Del cursed, "what the 'ell did I give 'im that rotten key for? Now I've gorra do all the 'and balling," he fumed.

He opened the cab door and stepped down leaving Bill sleeping soundly in the passenger seat.

Quite painstakingly, he gathered bits of RSJ's and pieces of old railway lines for what took him almost an hour due to his work-shy condition, and now regretted past strokes of conning Bill, to do all of the raunging.

Somehow, he managed to make the hose-pipe from the motor pool reach the now upstanding forty gallon steel barrels in the wagon, which he filled by means of the lever valve. Going overboard a bit, he misjudged the levels in his panic and over-filled them, causing himself further problems in securing the clamps on the lids which just proved to leak out over his clothes,

"Bill - Billy," he screamed, "give us an 'and will yer?" But Bill was dead to the world and no longer aware.

Del was now beginning to regret taunting him, and vowed under his breath to treat Bill with more respect.

THE MACE GOES IN

It was only this past hour's struggle on his own, which made him realise just what an asset to their partnership Bill was, which made him attempt to try and waken his partner.

"Bill - Bill, for cryin' out loud." Then the brainchild, "I'll wake the begger up!" he fumed and climbed out the wagon's rear clutching the hose which he fixed point blank at Bill's face.

"Wh, w, wha, eargh h h gerroff yer soft beggar - I'm all wet. Whar are yer playin' at Del, 'ave yer flipped yer lid or wha'?" he wailed as he left the cab.

"A lorra good you were in that drunken stupor, while I've been pullin' me scutchin' tripes out," he reasoned.

Bill started to chuckle although he was soaked through. He could see the funny side even in his condition.

"Come on Del, let's load the old girl up with some number one!"

Del had to agree and complied happily, now that he'd received the offer of help. Together above the water filled drums they strategically placed short rail lines and girders, which spanned across the drums masking their shape upon which they then piled crossways- more girders, to form the framework to support the small castings, which lay about the fielded area. Gathering them proved slightly harder than they thought, but succeed they did and upon completion, Del jumped down from the rear, handing Bill the keys, instructed him to drive the motor out of the factory site. As he did so, Del approached the factory extension, where Franky Spooner sub-contracted his labour through the main building contractor. "What d'you want Del - not after more scrap are yer? I'm in enough trouble tryin' ter explain why yer wagon's 'ere terday," he raged.

"No Frank I'm 'ere ter pay me dues," he replied saying, "'Ere mate, I've gorra tenner 'ere with your name on it," he proffered.

Frank just couldn't believe his luck, and wondered just what future favours Del would capitalise on. He only trusted Del as far as he could proverbially throw him.

Del left him holding the tenner without even a goodbye, but congratulated himself on his honesty toward Bill. Yes the turn of today's events had taught Del to trust people.

He re-joined Bill in the motor and Bill started the engine, "Where to Del?" he asked. "Charlie Shelley's," he replied, as they drove through the main gate.

As Bill reversed in Shelley's yard, Charlie was determined to keep his eye on Bill for some reason, forcing Del to use a new tactic.

"Charlie don't turn around mate, there's coppers watchin' us."

Charlie froze in his tracks and instead of watching Bill he pretended he wasn't even affected by saying, "Coppers, well mate, if they want ter buy summat, they know where ter come don't they?" He immediately retreated into the large building and feverishly commenced to throw rubbish over, what appeared to be bright copper wire presumably weighed in by previous law breakers (Cable thieves).

Del was diplomatic by staying just outside of the office, pretending he wasn't aware of the subterfuge. The temperature quickly dropped due to the sudden wind bringing a light shower, which threatened Del causing him to edge into the warehouse near to Charlie, who suddenly espied him with a worried look and turned his back on him with a feeble excuse:

"That idle swine Cecil 'asn't put this rubbish away, 'e'll be causin' an accident with all this muck stickin' out."

"Cecil?" queried Del.

"Yeh - you know that bloke the dole sent us last week? By the way Del, can yer see 'im in the yard. Give 'im a shout ter give your driver an 'and ter throw the iron off will yer."

"But yer 'aven't seen it yet Charl?"

"Oh aye yeh," he agreed and quickly climbed up the rear wheel, glancing furtively from side to side. He perceived the rails and RSJ'S and smiled saying, "Yer'll get top bat fer this Del!" adding with haste, "Urry up - tell Cecil."

Del nodded and walked out into the yard pretending to comply with Charlie's request, but this was farthest from Del's mind. His main concern was to allow Bill to complete his task without any outside interference. The thunder in the sky caused Del to make a snap decision, "To hell with the rain," he thought, braving the torrent, which by now was really heavy. He almost ran to help Bill, who by now had succeeded in restoring the drums in their upright position as Del reached the wagon and climbed on the rear wheel to inspect.

Bill was just about to return the clamps to the cab when Del spoke, "Everythin' okay Bill?"

"Strewth, pheugh, hell Del, yer scared the life outer me!" he raged. "Don't creep up like that on a bloke - I thought it was Charlie?"

"Don't worry about 'im, 'e thinks the coppers are watchin' 'im, heh heh heh."

The hand on Del's shoulder froze him to the spot. He almost fell from the rear wheel.

He turned round to see Sergeant Griffiths of the CID standing on an engine block facing him.

"Had a good weigh-in have you Del boy?" he probed enjoying his stance.

"Oh 'ello Mr. Griffiths, what can I do for yer? It's terrible this rain, isn't it?"

Bill pretended he wasn't aware of the policeman's presence and commenced to clear the debris from the wagon's flat by brushing it out through the rear. He then climbed over the side and replaced the tailboard.

"Oh 'ello, Barry isn't it?" he queried addressing the sergeant; "Ave yer got yer stripes back since Nicosia?" Bill probed sarcastically.

Barry's face was brilliant. It was easy to see he was trying to put a name to Bill's face. The blank look told Bill that he'd got him to an advantage and the frown on the officer's face, only fired up Bill to have some sport at the man's expense.

Up to this point 'Barry' had appeared to have held Del in some form of hold, but Bill's onslaught had suddenly humbled the man and catching him off guard, to such a degree, that he changed his attitude to Del completely and instead of exerting typical CID pressure tactics suddenly asked, "How are things Del, is your gout still acting up?"

The concern seemed even genuine, for Del replied, "Well, the doc's put me on some pills ter retard me kidneys, from producing' too much…uric acid, I think 'e called it, an' thanks to 'is insight, the swellin's 'ave gone down."

"Good, good man, I'm so glad," he encouraged, in the nicest Welsh accent he could muster. Hurriedly he sped off towards the yard office to avoid more flak from Bill.

"What was all that about Bill? Is 'is name really Barry?" he asked, "and 'ow come you know 'im so well?"

Bill gave a low chuckle, "Is 'e REALLY a copper Del?" he said, puzzled.

"Yeh an' a real bad-un at that - he'd shop 'is own mother if 'e could," he said convincingly.

This revelation took Bill aback, "Ow the 'ell 'e ever got on the force beats me Del?" he voiced, shaking his head.

"Ow d'yer mean mate?"

"Well,'e was the 'Big Daddy' of the kit fiddle. 'E 'ad sappers workin' for 'im in an' out of the - Q's stores. He made about £500 a week in the 1950's. 'E even got that cocky, 'e'd openly flaunt his wallet full of dosh in the NAAFI."

"Yer kiddin' me Bill?" Del chuckled disbelieving.

"Kiddin' yer – kiddin' yer? The only feller what's kiddin' yer is HIM. If not fer 'is end of service, they'd have taken 'im ter court then, but because of all the diplomacy over Archbishop Makarios an' the army, not wanting bad publicity at the time, Barry got away scot free with an' 'onerable discharge.

"But I thought yer said 'e'd lost 'is stripes?" Del confuted.

"Listen Del, before leavin' the army I was a copper in the SIB, an' I saw the charge sheet with the recommendation on it, just prior to 'is release. We made 'im return all of his loot, with full intentions of drummin' 'im out with a light prison sentence ter foller, but it seems that the powers that be, saw fit to want England to appear honest ter the core, ter give credibility ter Makarios 'oo was takin' over," he explained.

"Well, stone the flippin crows Bill, who'd of thought that Griffiths 'ad been a villain? Wait till I tell the lads, 'is name'll be mud."

"No Del, don't tell anybody, anythin'!" he commanded.

"Why the 'ell not - he deserves ter be blown up, just look at the

THE MACE GOES IN

way 'e makes people squirm."

"Think of it Del, what it would be like to 'ave an ally in the local plod?" Bill suggested.

"Aye, yer right mate, we'd getaway with murder. Yer know Bill, sometimes I think that yer missed yer callin' in life-. Yer'd o' made a really good politician y'know," he voiced in admiration.

Del, upon reaching the yard office once more - there appeared to be no more sign of Griffiths who had apparently taken flight from the premises.

Charlie had re-appeared and now seemed more calmer, having completely hidden the bright copper wire, told Del he'd like to be sure they'd placed the RSJ's in the right place, for he was convinced that somehow he was being hoodwinked on the true weight of the consignment.

"How come Del, that everytime you come to my yard, your scrap is always wet?" he criticised sharply.

"Probably because it's always rainin'," Del retorted.

Charlie felt like he'd been shot down in flames. There was nothing more to be said because he couldn't argue with the weather, which was apparent even now.

Bill was motioned by Del and drew up back to the motor scale"

"Three ton three quarters Del," said Agnes out of office, "by the way what was it?" she asked.

"RSJ's and a few rail lines," he enlightened.

"Oh in that case, it's the special salvage price, Charlie did tell me yesterday, "er, 'erm,"

"Twenty eight pound a ton," Del quipped.

"Yes, that's right," she concurred, "could you come and sign this please, if you would, it's for 3¾ ton salvage steel £28 a ton which totals £100 exactly."

Del signed the book, but then a puzzled look covered his face, "Hey, that can't be right, £16 isn't ¾ of 28, more like £21. I think you'll find that it should read £105 instead?"

The girl, started counting and suddenly said, "Give me back that advice note please, you're right, I'm truly sorry." Feverishly, she changed the last zero for a five and handed Del the £105.

He smiled and divided the money into two parcels, handing one to Bill adding, "Put the fiver in the tank Bill and we'll 'ead back for 'ock country."

The Esso garage was being tanked up with supply renewal when they arrived and both had to wait.

"I'll be in the 'Broken Stirrup'," said Del, "D'yer fancy a drop o' top shelf stuff?"

"Yeh yer could do," Bill agreed saying, "is that 'Garden Gate runnin' at Newbury terday Del?"

"Where 'ave yer 'eard that then Bill?"

"Ere, shove us a bluey on the nose will yer - I've gor an 'unch it'll make it!"

"Okay mate £5 it is," he agreed as he took the note.

Bill ambled into the garage shop to view the wares, just as the girl came in from out the back. She was quite a dame he thought. About mid - forties he imagined and good looking too. Something familiar about her - but of course, she had been there, when he'd almost run out of diesel the day before.

She looked him over as he inspected the products, and he became suddenly aware of her eyes upon him. He turned around and she was aware, that he'd seen her looking. She coloured up and pretended not to be interested, but Bill had already seen the sign of her eye pupils' dilate, which she couldn't disguise. Her long brown hair was really her main asset, for it shone in the bright sun and her brown eyes with a faint hint of make up. Her rose red lips completed a perfect balance of face, and Bill suspected that she'd had modelling experience.

"Will the diesel be long luv?" he queried.

"Only about ten minutes sir, are you in a hurry?" she asked.

"No luv, really - it's alright, I need to relax anyway. What's it like here at night in Chester, are there any places of interest I could ask a good looking girl like yourself out? P'rhaps you could show me the sights. I'm unfamiliar with Chester and having recently bought a small cottage here, I'll be one of the residents by the end of the week and need a better knowledge of the place."

"Where is it located?" she edged.

THE MACE GOES IN

'Barrat's Lane, I think or is it of Carrot's Lane? - no more like Barrats in Frontmere," he finally enlightened.

"Oh - yes, it's very nice up there. Quite recently I spotted an end terrace cottage with a beautiful orchard within, but they wanted too much…1750 I think, but what potential if only…"

Quite purposefully Bill dangled the keys of the cottage number and address written on the brown tag saying, "Isn't this a coincidence, here I am talking to an absolute stranger in a strange city, about a strange cottage, which I've just bought, that even SHE has considered buying, I'd say that this was more than just coincidence -wouldn't you?"

Her eyes met his full on with pupils dilated and she made no attempt to turn away. It was as if he had been destined to buy the previous day's diesel. "What's your name love, if I'm to come here for my fuel, I'd like to call you something?" he asked smiling.

"Well I don't know - really?" she pouted, unwilling at first to reveal her title.

"Well, I'm William Foggit, at present reside in Newtown but soon to live in Frontmere at Backford, Salvage dealer by profession. There that's me taken care of, now luv, who are you?"

"You have a way of putting things don't you?" she smiled finally relenting, "Okay then, I'm Alice, Alice Wordsworth, fashion model between appointments…"

"I knew it, I knew somehow you'd been a model," he smiled.

"Is it that obvious?" she fished.

"It's your lithe figure and the way in which you walk. It's as though you're balancing a book there, most of the time," he said smiling.

She laughed happily interceding, "I hate to say this William, but the diesel pump is free once more."

Bill looked toward the wagon with urgency. Del would be waiting for him. "Excuse me a moment luv," he said, as he left for the pump.

After filling up the tank he returned and gave her the fiver which she marked up in the till.

He hung around which she knew he would, and began to check the retail list.

"A'hem, well, I'd better be going," he hinted.

"Eh, hm, alright goodbye William," she murmured.

"But before I go I'd like to be able to take you out sometime."

"Oh - William," she spoke disapprovingly.

"Only to familiarise myself with Chester - but with good looking company to boot," he complimented.

"Alright, seeing as you've put it like that - yes, you do have a car don't you?"

Bill nodded.

"Then pick me up on the corner of Thames Palace in Hough Green."

Not wanting to sound uneducated about where Hough Green was, or this Thames palace place, he just agreed.

"At what time?"

"About seven would be ideal," she hinted, "we could take in a film and then perhaps I could show you the best restaurants in town - are you game?"

"But of course - see you then," he promised and smiled as he walked to the wagon.

With this Alice, Bill felt a certain Je ne sais quoi.

"Where the 'ell 'ave yer been Bill, I was startin' ter worry about yer. 'Ere mate, I got yer double scotch an' there's a couple o' pints too, what the lads 'ave sent over fer yer. Georgie Woods 'ad ter go, 'e sends 'is regards and Albert Leason left one as well."

Bill took the two pints over to the table in the snug and swallowed large gulps of the bitter. It was really welcome, and just hit the spot. The first pint he didn't really taste, but followed it with the scotch and then commenced to sip the second. Del looked in a philosophical mood. He was quiet and locked in thought.

"A penny for 'em," Bill offered.

"Eh?" Del grunted almost oblivious.

"A penny for yer thoughts Del, - yer know."

"Ohhh, I was just re-cappin' on the events of these last two days an' thinkin' maybe somebody up there likes me after all?"

"Up there?" Bill guffawed.

THE MACE GOES IN

"Yes, 'ave yer ever thought just 'ow protected we've been - gerrin' away with this 'mace'?" he asked.

"We've been lucky Del."

But Del was most emphatic, saying; "Take fer instance 'ow we've never been discovered with the water fiddle - an' even terday when Charlie almost sussed it out about the wet scrap, it started rainin' ter cover our tracks?!" he confuted. "Ever thought that the Lord might 'ave 'ad an 'and in it? Yes Bill the Lord looks after his own," voiced Del tritely.

"So does the devil Del, haha haha."

"What's so funny Bill?" he questioned.

It's you Del with your platitudinous remarks, it's so unlike you mate, you're usually so insipid."

"I 'ave got feelin's yer know Bill. There's somethin' else an' all Bill, I put a pony on that hot tip yer gave me just now fer Newbury an' it come in at 15-2 which means I stand ter gain 187 pound 10/- plus me £25 back. Your bet will net yer £37 plus yer fiver back. Now then, 'ow is it, that you 'oo never backs a nag can suddenly pick a winner right out o' the blue?" he demanded.

"Easy, I 'eard it on the wireless this mornin', an' it was his first race, so I thought I'd 'ave a flutter and that's all there is to it."

"'Ere Bill, I'll get the drinks!" Del offered completely out of character.

"Oh well if you insist Del."

Bills winnings lay on the table, which he quickly counted and placed in his wallet.

When Del returned, Bill told him about his date and said, "Now if anything was meant ter be - that was. If somebody up there likes me or thee, then p'raps today is our day."

"Aye Bill, yer've got somethin' there, the gods are on our side today all right."

"Ow much 'ave yer 'ad ter drink Del? Are yer safe ter drive?"

"Maybe you'd better steer it 'ome Bill, in fact I'll put yours in this pop bottle, an' yer can drink it when we get back ter the 'George'."

With this suggestion, both men arose and after some accounting with their money, ambled toward the cab outside. The drive back took only 20 minutes and Bill directed the Ford to the rear of their local. They descended from the cab and Bill glugged down the bitter beer from the pop bottle.

"I'll see you on Monday Del, I've gorra bira business on terday mate."

"Yer not goin' already Bill, yer me good luck charm?" he pleaded.

"Sorry mate, I've gorra be awake ternight an' I wanna get me 'ead down."

"Oh aye yeh, yer right mate - well, I'll see yer Monday then, ta-ra!"

Bill marched towards Del's home and within minutes he was in the Minor and driving back to the flat. After arriving back, he turned his gas fire on to full, lay on the sofa and set his alarm for 5.30pm.

After four straight winners in a row by Del, a worried Peter Strate looked on in despair.

"You did say £60 win didn't you Del?"

"Correct," he replied as he was handed his ticket.

"Lashin' out aren't yer Del?" asked Strate.

"I can't go wrong today Pete, my guardian angel is around," Del smirked confidently.

"Six to four on Del, doesn't give you much return, now if I was you, I'd back one of the newcomers in the field like 'Lachicho' at four to one, something to give me a decent return?" he reasoned, eager to put a brake on Del's record of wins. Every bet so far had proved to romp home. There were ten minutes left before the race, when suddenly Del got a terrible forboding about his latest bet, and try as he may he couldn't shake the feeling off.

Peter Strate was still quaking - trying to hedge Del's bet to the bigger companies but without success due to less than quarter of an hour before the race, so when Del asked him what the present odds lay on Lachico, he jumped at the chance to try and dissuade Del from his present one.

"Seven to one Del, but personally I could guarantee the tote and keep it at seven especially for you, if you're the gambler I judged you for?" he offered.

THE MACE GOES IN

Little did Peter know that Del had cold feet anyway.

"Seven to one, that much Pete?" he probed.

"Yes Del, sevens it is."

"In that case Pete, I'll transfer my recent stake onto Lachico, but make it each way - okay?"

"Done, you've got yourself a bet Del. Give me the ticket back and I'll give you a fresh one."

Peter breathed a sigh of relief chuckling, "There's one born every minute!"

Del returned to the George and celebrated, by buying himself a hock and washed it down with two pints of bitter. He was so happy with his spiritual high, that he didn't even bother to check whether it won, and at three o'clock, when last orders call was made, he arose from the table and walked home.

Somehow Del knew that today was a special day. He even gave Beth all of his cash to hold, upon his return to the house.

"I want yer ter ger a new outfit Beth."

"But Del we can't afford..."

"Never mind Beth, you get one anyway, money's made round fer goin' round, an' I feel I've been neglectin' yer these past months, so now I'm makin' up fer lost time!" he asserted, pressing £80 in crisp fivers into her hand., "Anyway love, d'yer feel up ter drivin', 'cos we're goin' out this affo' ter buy yer that small upright pianna yer've always admired."

Beth just threw her arms around Del, and bear hugged him for all she was worth.

Meanwhile Bill, who had awoken for no apparent reason, glanced at his watch which read 3.25 pm and decided that he had slept long enough.

He put on the gas fire boiler heater for a bath to ease his arthritis, and a general clean up in the bargain. Something caused him to get out the vacuum and commence generally tidying up the flat. After five minutes of vacuuming the carpets he discovered that it was long since due. The filth appeared from everywhere, as he discovered that the cylindrical model needed emptying. After which he found the job tolerable and continued in his quest for dust. He even found items of interest, which he had long since thought lost. It made him realise that if and when he were to move into the cottage at Backford, then he should at least have some form of cleaning woman to keep it tidy.

Straightaway the memory of Alice entered his mind, and he fantasized being married to her living there, with both of their interests being served. She with the orchard, and he with the sought after residential preference.

Under his bed he pulled out an old inset box accommodating all of his old photographs, which he studied with fondness. He smiled in the memory of his brothers, whose faces showed on the family snap, and his mother, who had struggled so hard through two world wars to ensure enough food for all of them. Bill had been the youngest of a family of six, one girl and five boys. He had been born just prior to his father's death - due to a family feud and left with mother Alice to rear as best she could.

As far as Bill knew, his father had been a native of Chester, whose immediate family were fairly well respected in the community of butchers, who had monopolised Lower Bridge Street at the turn of the century, and who still pre-dominated in that line of trade.

He had often seen the Foggit shops as he'd driven through Chester. Strangely enough his Father's name Louis was above all of the shops.

As a boy, Bill had always wanted a gran and grandad, but his mother had cut herself off from them, and not allowed him even any connection with them. He had only found out by accident, that he was even connected to them.

Tearfully, he replaced the snaps into the box. His soul cried out for the kinship he had never experienced, for the war years had taken their toll and separated all of them after the death of his mother, whose own immediate family had disowned her due to her marrying 'common butchers'. Not respected by her landed gentry father Roger Fitzsimmons who's family had been connected to the lineage of Henry the Eighth. Bill looked back on his life with dismay, his first and only marriage had ended abruptly ten years before in Malaya where he was stationed. His wife had been having an affair with a

THE MACE GOES IN

planter, before finally suing for divorce. He had no-one to leave his worldly goods to, no sons or daughters and this feeling of insecurity had driven him - he thought - to hard drink. "Perhaps Alice could be the one for me?" he thought with hope. He ran the bath water and found it to be quite hot, so he turned and switched off the gas fire and commenced to retrieve a clean shirt and vest from the wardrobe, with a complete change of smalls.

He entered the bath giving groans of pleasure, as the water permeated his aching zones.

"Yeh, give me the simple things in life," he said aloud and lit up a full strength.

It's Not An Hotel

CHAPTER 23

Bill, to his surprise, had managed to find a sign post pointing to 'The Thames Palace Hotel' in Hough Green. He attempted to find it but to no avail. So he back tracked and parked next to the sign he found earlier. He sat in his Minor around seven o'clock and in anticipation, started reading a Liverpool Echo, to control his avidity. He had to fight off a temptation to just call it a night and go for a belly full of ale.

"No," he said to himself, "Alice is worth the wait, now if I could only find where this Thames Palace is? Why oh why didn't I say her, I don't know where her house is." Bill in his thoughts decided to just sit tight and ask anyone who passed by, if they knew. To his dismay, nobody did.

Alice, who dressed really well for her date, was clad in a 'Coco Chanel' original dress of bluish purple lacelike material, which was supported by two loops on her shoulders, tailored to fit her trim waist. Three quarters the way down, it evolved into three separate layers of blue set on a purple base, which flared out past the waist.

She donned black tights, onto which she wore patent black leather stilettos. She was determined to wow Bill, and wore her mascara quite thickly blended upon blue eye shadow, to match her dress with pale red lipstick and her hair put into a pony tail. She viewed herself in the full length mirror, before she allowed herself to go.

Alice, now ready, looked at the time, it was getting late - 8.00 pm.

THE MACE GOES IN

She looked out of the window but Bill's car was not there.

"He should 'ave been here already," she thought. "I know what it'll be, he probably doesn't realise that he is still in Saltney not Hough Green. She grabbed her car keys and left the house to go and locate him.

At 8:10pm, she finally spotted a car parked under the 'Thames Palace Hotel' sign post, she drew up in her Mini and stopped in front it. She could see that the car was occupied and so got out, walked over to it and knocked on the window.

As the window of the car started to roll down she asked, "Excuse me, have you seen a man in his fifties around here at all? And then she realised, "Oh it's you Bill, what happened, couldn't you find the house?" she asked in a caring voice.

"I followed the sign but I couldn't find it, I went round in circles," he said feeling slightly embarrassed.

"Oh Bill, I forgot you don't know Chester do you? This is Saltney up to the railway bridge and then after that, heralds the start of Hough Green!" she said.

"But the hotel?" he reasoned.

"Oh Bill, it's not an hotel - it's a house, and I live in it."

"How could I be so silly, I must be getting old," he rued.

"Oh it's easily done Bill, tell you what, follow me down in your Minor, and I'll leave my Mini at home. That way you'll always know how to find the place," she hinted. This made him feel better, and he started up the car and followed her Mini half a mile down the road. Up loomed Thames Palace, a strange Victorian type of house, this silhouetted against the darkened stormy sky. It had a roof of twin gables pitched at sixty degrees, in beautiful green Welsh slate, with dormer type windows in the front elevation, which accommodated Georgian small window panes with sliding sashes. Its decor was black window sills with white exterior walls, and bronze handles on the door, which glinted in the lamplight.

"What a beautiful house Alice, have you had it long?" he queried with interest, as he stepped from his car.

"Actually it belongs to Mum, she's always lived here since her childhood. It was bequeathed her in her father's will," she informed him, locking up her Mini,

"Right love," he said, as he held the door open for her to enter, and they sped off towards the Dee roundabout.

Crossing over the bridge he asked, "Where to love?

"It's a bit late for a film William, but we could go and eat somewhere, I know a lovely little place recently opened which serves truly glorious food."

"What's it called?" he queried.

"The Beanfeast."

"That's a strange name for a restaurant?" he remarked, but she offered no explanation.

"You can park the car off Frodsham Street William, it's quite near to the place."

"Give me the directions as we enter the town Alice - by the way, is it okay if I call you Al?" But before she could answer he quipped, "You could call me Bill!"

"Certainly Wi- er, Bill? Al would be fine."

He followed her instructions and finally parked his car. A sixpence piece secured a display ticket, from a meter alongside his car window, which he then stuck onto the dashboard.

Hand in hand they then strolled briskly to the restaurant.

Upon entry to the eating house, he became aware of the most luscious aromas, which caused his taste buds to fill with saliva.

The waiter directed them to a table, and Alice immediately picked up the menu as she sat down. Bill looked around at the decor. It reminded him of the foliage he'd observed in the Malayan jungle.

Apparently someone had gone to a lot of trouble to create a green vista, and had succeeded completely for it was most soothing to the eyes as Bill observed.

"Hmm, corn and asparagus flan," she pondered.

Bill suddenly was aware of reality and picked up a menu. He browsed through it condensing the content: Potato omelette, corn and asparagus flan, oaty cheese quiche, Gooda cheese pie, Pipesade.

He was perplexed, "Alice, what are all these main dishes love, I've never heard of chakchouka or wholewheat pizza?" he lamented.

"PEETZA!" she stressed.

"Eh?" he queried.

"It's pronounced PEETZA - not piiizza," she corrected, amused at Bill's ignorance.

"Pe, peetza?" he ventured.

"That's it Bill - you've got it," she commended adding, "I think I'll commence with a slice of melon for an appetiser followed by minestrone, what are you having?"

Bill panicked, he needed to show her he was in command of the situation by making a snap decision. The melon he didn't fancy, his taste buds were used to years of bitter drinking, so he answered with, "Er, toasted grapefruit with brown sugar looks good."

"How about minestrone Bill, would you care for a portion?" she asked supporting.

"Mini...?"

"The soup Bill," she encouraged, smiling.

"Oh yes, Al, that will be fine," he replied relieved that she could help.

The melon came on a large plate in slices with two separate dishes, where Alice motioned Bill to follow her actions as she helped herself to a slice, then so did Bill.

She used a spoon to extract the yellow flesh, but Bill just picked up his slice and started to guzzle it slurping and sucking like a babe with a bottle.

Alice looked up with humour and chuckled to herself.

Bill slurped and slurped commenting finally, "I think I'll have another slice - it's good."

Alice just nodded in agreement chuckling.

Bill was really enjoying himself now and even at the threat of looking greedy, he continued to sample even more of the fare.

"Don't you want your grapefruit Bill?" she teased.

"Grapefruit?" Bill wasn't even sure what it looked like.

She recognised his perplexity and pushed the item in question toward him.

"Oh that," he pretended and took it from her.

He took it in his hands at first but then realised that he'd need a spoon. Alice was selecting the appropriate tool which he took from her smiling to hide his embarrassment.

The taste of the first spoonful almost fractured his tongue with its sharpness.

"Good is it Bill?" she encouraged.

"Lovely," he replied smiling in an attempt to hide his loathing of it.

He quickly dug out all of the flesh and forced it down his throat to be rid of it, just as the minestrone arrived. He quickly put down the fruit and picked up the soup spoon, to rid his mouth of the offending taste.

"Mm, this soup is good Bill," murmured Alice appreciably.

Bill was too busy slurping his down, to hear what she was saying. He reached for the wholemeal cob, which lay at the side to dip it in the soup. He put it to his mouth and with astonishment put it back down, "Hell, this bread is harder than a goat's knee," he said, looking at it perplexed.

"But Bill, cobs are supposed to be like that, it's the wholemeal which causes that beautiful crispiness - why that's the added feature," she stressed.

Bill looked on smiling taking it all in. His main concern had been to impress Alice of his knowledge of this new cuisine, but due to later events, his confidence was wavering.

He decided on a new approach and took up the menu once again to order a main course.

"Perhaps I could try a whole wheat pizza?" he ventured- this time pronouncing it correctly.

"Ah yes Bill, I think I'd like the same," she cooed.

The pizzas arrived served upon a large dish and armed with the large knife supplied. Bill attacked it vigorously and laid a large slice on his plate.

"Now this is something like it," he voiced, but even the chopping of it into pieces proved difficult. Bill had never before encountered Mozzarella cheese, and experienced great hardship in his quest, to reduce it to smaller pieces.

THE MACE GOES IN

Alice was quite amused at Bill's antics, but with great tact pretended not to notice, but expertly cut her slice into small pieces to enable her to fork it into her mouth.

Gradually Bill got the hang of it and almost expertly polished off the last two pieces from his plate, "Think I'll have another slice," he stated. "Never thought I'd ever enjoy cheese as much as this?"

"I've ordered two stuffed artichokes Bill, have you ever tried them?" She fished.

"Er, no, I don't think I have - ever," he admitted.

"Well love, the ones they served here the last time, were roasted at a low heat primed with olive oil, then mushrooms added with cauliflower and a small hint of garlic, parsley added with onions, butter and finally whole wheat breadcrumbs surrounded all the inside. Believe me Bill, once you've sampled one, you'll just have to eat another."

In came the globes which were served separately with Alice first, then finally Bill. He dug in his fork to extract some of the fillings but Alice waved her forefinger in a half circular motion, "No Bill, don't dig it out - cut into the globe and it'll release its taste."

"Oh I see," he replied, as he inserted the knife and sampled it, 'mm, it's absolutely out of this world, tell me Alice, how is it that I haven't had the need for salt or pepper, with any of these dishes? Generally, I smother everything with tomato sauce before I can taste it."

"Well Bill - what can I say, perhaps tonight is the first time you've ever sampled vegetarian cooking?" she offered.

Bill nodded in agreement as Alice continued, "I think one has to allow one's taste buds to appreciate good food. So often these days the population just eats what it's offered, without question, irrespective of what's been done to the food."

"I know what you're referring to love, tinned stuff has been boiled for too long, with all those additives put in, that it loses all semblance of its original condition," he said knowledgeably.

"You amaze me Bill, you're the only fellow that I've ever met, who's aware of the problems in our food," she said, in appreciation.

"Me?" he laughed, not sure if she was putting him on.

"Yes you, the average fellow just eats what's put in front of him, but you - I can see, take your time to review each situation. Take for instance our coming here today; I could tell at a glance that you'd never once experienced vegetarian cooking, but even that didn't daunt you. Oh no, you just fell in and sampled it, even though it was alien to you. I think really that it wasn't your intention to offend, for you're such a caring person," she commended, "and it's wonderful to discover someone of the opposite gender - so considerate, anyway Bill, from what I've seen of you, I like very much," she said honestly.

Bill completed the artichoke commenting, "You're right Alice, I do feel like another one." He signalled the waiter who came at once, and received his new order with a smile.

Bill decided on another one each, and asked Alice if she had room for a corn and asparagus flan.

"Yes Bill, that would be most appropriate," she agreed. "D'you think we should end the meal with a sweet? The Pavlova looks good!"

"Pav-lova?" asked he bewildered.

"Yes love, it's meringue and cream, but if you didn't fancy that, perhaps a chocolate gateau?"

"Why don't we have both, and if you're still peckish, we could try some fruit salad?" he offered.

"Absolutely, tip top Bill," she remarked diplomatically.

He smiled, happy that he was in command of the situation.

After half an hour, they both were finishing off a cigarette each and a glass of wine which Alice had chosen.

"Mm that was good Bill," she mused appreciably.

"Shall we go then Al?"

She nodded returning a smile, as Bill signalled the waiter for the bill, which arrived on a silver platter.

'Fifteen pound seventeen and sixpence,' it read and Bill dug into his wallet mistakenly for a fiver but on further examination discovered the true quote which almost made him faint, "Fi, fifteen pound, se, seventeen an' six. I can't believe it?" he rued under his breath.

"Everything all right Bill - wait a minute," she directed as she glanced at the bill, "I don't remember having Piperade or the spinach and ricotta cheese if it comes to that," she disclosed. "I think some mistake has been made here, could we see the manager please?"

Soon the manager appeared.

"Everything alright sir?" he queried.

Before Bill could get the words from his mouth, Alice saved him the trouble.

"Overcharged, that's what's wrong," she emphasised.

"Really?" he replied looking perplexed, "Could I see the bill please?"

Alice took him to one side saying, "Really Cecil, this is a bit of a cheek you know - charging Bill for two extra selections. This isn't the way to promote new custom you know. I'll bet Marjorie would pop her cork if she could see what's happening?"

Bill looked on amused at what he'd heard, and the apparent familiarity of Alice with the manager. The conversation carried on for a short time longer, with Alice rejoining him with a new bill totalling £11-6-4d which she presented to him proudly. Bill smiled, although he was still angry, but managed to convince Alice that he was happier.

"It's a good job you were there Alice," he said, "I wouldn't have known whether I'd been rooked or not?"

"Well love," she piped, "Cecil is all right normally, but he has a terrible staff shortage and it's very hard to find workers with a good head for figures."

"Speaking of figures, you seem to be blessed with a good one, how d'you keep so beautifully slim?"

"Now then Bill, flattery will get you nowhere," she replied laughing.

Bill paid the waiter standing by giving him £11-10/- with a gesture to keep the change and hand in hand, walked Alice into the street.

Above them hung a pub title called, 'The Grottie Straw' which caused Bill to laugh.

"What's so funny love?" asked Alice.

"Ha ha ha ha, it's this, the Grottie Straw - what does it mean?"

"Oh that, well Bill, apparently the name of this pub goes back quite a long way. It must be at least two-hundred years old."

"Yes but the name - wha?" he reminded.

"I'm coming to that love. Around about 1768, Chester was a thriving farming district, with markets everywhere and the 'Grot' in Grottie, was a mildewed ear of wheat, which when shaken and thrashed by hand, proved not to release its grains. Finally when it did release them they had a tendency to mar the taste of the flour, when ground and so you can see how important it was to thoroughly inspect the produce, to avoid this unhappy situation."

"Mmm, I reckon you're right love. Is history your favourite subject then?"

"No Bill, not at all, I'm merely a Cestrian, who's proud of her heritage," she smiled adding, "actually they teach this in most of the schools anyway- even the history of the Roman occupation."

"Well now, you learn something every day. D'you fancy a tipple then Alice?" He motioned with a hand waved in the direction of the pub.

"Why not?"

Bill opened the door for her and they stepped back into the past, with its old fashioned peg furniture of the 18th century, and the horse brasses which adorned the walls. A post horn hung over the bar, and a mixed collection of muskets and flintlocks. Most of the customers seemed to be drinking from pewter pots, although at the bar hung an assortment of heavy glasses.

"I think I'll have a half," he voiced diplomatically, adding, "what d'you fancy Al?"

"Would you think me awful, if I were to ask for a half of bitter?" she searched.

"Not in the least love, I was about to supplement mine with a drop of scotch, do you fancy trying the same?"

"Really Bill, you'll have me drunk before the night's over....but, oh well, go ahead, nothing ventured, nothing gained."

Bill brought a tray containing the four glasses over to Alice, who had sat with her back to the wall, in order to inspect the collection of artefacts displayed over the bar.

"Thank you love," she said, taking the bitter and quaffing it halfway down, "needed that."

"Just hit the spot, eh love?"

"Mm," she murmured, "by the way Bill, just have a glance at that carbine on the wall, it looks so much like my late husband's pair of Khybers."

Bill whirled around and arose from his seat to inspect the rifle. The numbers engraved upon its' side confirmed what Alice had inferred much to his amazement.

"You're only right love," he agreed pondering about what she'd just said.

"Are you a widow then Al?"

"Yes Bill, I'm afraid I am, Mortimer's widows fund doesn't pay very much, this is my reason for returning to the modelling field."

"Is he buried in Chester then?"

This brought tears to Alice's eyes who lamented, "They couldn't find Mortimer's body after the bomb blast."

"Oh no - not a bomb? I'm sorry Al."

"Those extremists from Bahawalpur were responsible. I was lucky not to be at home at the time. The whole bungalow including three servants were blown to pieces."

"You have a good cry love."

Tears streamed from Alice's eyes and Bill handed her his large whisky glass motioning her, "Drink this straight down Al, you'll feel better."

Alice took the glass with an inexperienced palate and swallowed hard, causing her to cough and choke but after the liquid had gone down, filled her with a glow and an inner happiness. She reached for the glass once more but to her disappointment discovered it empty.

Bill perceived her need and offered her the single scotch sitting on the tray.

She smiled as she took the glass from him and commenced to sip its contents.

"'Thank you Bill, for being so understanding, I'm all right now, I think - oh look, greedy me, I've gone and drunk your scotch."

"I'll get some more love," he answered and arose, heading for the bar.

He returned soon after and involved himself with the usual small talk attractive to women, always ensuring that he built her up in the nicest light he could muster, careful not to flatter her too much, and even being critical at times in order that whatever they spoke about, they were equal to each other, as he was quite a bit older.

There was something about Alice which he admired. He couldn't put his finger on exactly what it was, but she was very unassuming and modest too, a rare commodity with most of the women he'd met.

He found himself comparing her with Mary Valesque. His thoughts raced to Mary whom he'd left in Bromborough earlier in the week. He hadn't heard from her and wondered why? Perhaps she had found out about her father and discovered that Bill was responsible? He hoped not.

"Bill, BILL, you're not listening!" Alice said firmly bringing him back to the present.

"Oh, er, I was miles away."

"Perhaps we could go for a walk on the Roman walls?" she hinted, "the fresh air might do us both good?"

Bill somehow felt that he was being directed, but replied, "What a good idea Alice," in order to play along with her - after all it was close to closing time and he hated being on the road when full of drink, due to the dangers of driving under the influence. They drained their glasses and arose walking out. They gained access to the wall by means of a sandstone flight of steps, alongside the cathedral. Their conversation consisted of many aspects of both of their lives. Her marriage to Mortimer and their courtship throughout their teens. Their subsequent lives in India where Mortimer was based, until that fateful day...

Bill interjected at this point encouraging Alice to go on with the story, "Get it all off your chest love," he consoled.

She continued tears streaming from her eyes as she did, but determined to get it out of her system and carried on the explanation right to the bitter end…

Bill came in at this point commending her with, "There you are love I told you you'd feel better, I'm proud of you!" She smiled at

THE MACE GOES IN

him as he continued, "You know Alice I was married once also..." he related to her about his wife's promiscuity and explained how lucky Alice had been, to have had a happy marriage.

"You know love, it's my belief that we meet each other more than once on the other side, when it's our time to go, so don't worry. Think of all the happy times you had together. Conserve these thoughts for the rest of your days. To quote William Shakespeare; 'Parting is such sweet sorrow'."

"Yes Bill, I do believe you're right. I've never really looked at it like that before. Yes, I think that this is the first time I've felt happy about anything connected to India."

"By the way Alice, I think that soon I'll be able to move in to that old cottage I told you about," he revealed.

"Oh?" Looking surprised.

"Yes love, and I wondered if you'd care to come along to make some suggestions on the decor, I really haven't got much idea where to start," he said, with his open palm gesture.

"I'd be very glad to Bill, when are you expecting to take possession?" she enthused.

"Oh, I've paid the last payment earlier, all that remains is to order some new windows, to replace those fiddly little things in there," he said proudly.

"Not Georgian windows - oh Bill, don't get modern windows - please, you'll take away its whole character," she pleaded.

"Trust a woman?" he thought regrettably, "she wants to dominate me already and we're not up the aisle yet."

"Listen Bill, perhaps the windows are not as bad as they seem? I'll tell you what I could do, old Mrs. Jenkins' son Larry is an apprentice Joiner who lives next door to us, and I'm sure if I asked him nicely, he would help us out quite cheaply for his services," her squeezing his hand.

He thought of what she said, "US," he recalled it once more, "US," he breathed. "Could this Alice, be contemplating - our marriage?" The thought wasn't entirely disagreeable. He rather fancied the idea of Alice for a wife - especially since she was cultured and full of etiquette. Any future business he'd got planned with a customer, whom he'd have occasion to entertain at his home, would guarantee immediate success with her around.

"A Joiner you say, that's a great idea, Al, in that case, I think that by the end of next week, I may be moving in," he envisaged.

"When d'you think we could go around then Bill?" she asked with obvious interest.

"According to the note from the electric people, I'll be connected back up on Wednesday."

"Then Wednesday it is, what time Bill?" she asked delightedly.

"About 7 pm okay?"

"Wonderful Bill, oh, I can't wait to get there."

They hurried almost back to the steps leading to the car park with Alice remarking; "Oh it's been such a wonderful night, first the meal, then the drink, and now the great news that you have the cottage."

They arrived at his Minor and entered. As he put in the key, Alice put her arm around him and gave him a hug saying, "Oh Bill you've given me so much pleasure tonight."

He reciprocated by taking her in his arms, for he'd seen her pupils enlarge. They kissed romantically and almost forcefully, as both of their temperatures arose.

After what seemed like many minutes, Bill was able to subdue his feelings, and break from the clinch but Alice commenced to shower his neck with kisses.

Bill put the key in once more and this time turned the starter, which responded immediately, giving the engine life causing Alice to sit up once more.

He looked at his watch which read 11.30 pm and wondered where all the time had gone.

"Well Alice, I must say that tonight has been one of the most memorable nights I've experienced in a long time. You have awoken many feelings in me, which have lain dormant for many years."

"I too have felt happy Bill, I don't think I've ever seen so much happiness in my life before?"

Bill smiled appreciably and drove outward toward Hough Green, gently squeezing her right hand with his left.

Thames Palace suddenly appeared as he turned right, and drew the car alongside the house. Bill got out of the car and went round the car, opening the door on Alice's side.

"Would you like to come in Bill and meet Mum? I know she'd love to see you?"

Bill wanted to get home, he'd got a thousand things to organise for his new move-in.

"It is very late Al."

"Oh come on love, she won't bite you," she teased.

Against his better judgement he smiled and nodded affirmation, but promised himself to stay chaste, whatever temptation was put his way. He liked Alice greatly, and thought that perhaps it was love he had for her, and so decided to hold onto his precious feeling and not regard Alice as a commodity.

In reply to Alice's full push, the large polished oaken door opened smoothly on a well oiled hinge. A woman in her early seventies beckoned them to enter, just after Alice had remarked, "Mum I'd like you to meet Bill. Bill, this is Mum!"

The old lady put out her small hand, and Bill gripped it with half his usual grip.

"Hello," he said, "I'm Bill - Bill Foggit."

"Helen, Helen Wentworth," she greeted, "I'm very pleased to meet you."

Bill walked down the hall after Alice into the dining room, and Alice pointed to an easy chair.

"Coffee for two?" asked Helen.

They both nodded and smiled.

Bill lay back in his chair, "Wow, the height of this ceiling," he remarked impressed.

Alice just laughed explaining, "Probably due to the large fires in the grate Bill, it is a very old house, but I love it."

"I suppose you're right love, it must be nice to be educated," really impressed.

Helen appeared with the percolator and poured out the contents.

"Gosh Mum, you were quick," Alice remarked.

"Had it almost on the boil when you arrived, I had contemplated the time you would arrive. Cream Bill?" asked she.

"Please, that's fine," he stopped her as she poured.

"Help yourself to brown sugar, it's in the bowl," she pointed to it, adding, now to her daughter, "Well, Alice, I really must be off to bed, got to get my beauty sleep you know. You young ones have got all this to come," she joked bidding them a diplomatic goodnight.

"Your Mum's very courteous."

"Yes Bill, she's very understanding."

He dipped into the biscuits and cheese and crammed them into his mouth, which were very welcome, which he washed down with his coffee.

"More coffee Bill, I can see you're enjoying the cheese?"

"Thanks love," he replied and held out his cup.

After they had dispensed with their dishes, Alice took them away on a tray and reappeared with a bottle of gin and two glasses.

"Mum gets this sent over by my brother Jonathon - the flyer of our family. He works for World Airlines and quite often sends us a bottle of 'Boar's Head' Export, duty free of course. It tastes so much better than the standard stuff sold in England."

After Bill had tasted it he was inclined to agree with her. Although he was a whisky drinker, he even found this new brew palatable. So much so, he helped Alice to polish off almost all of it, well into the night, before she suggested he stay and sleep on the couch.

He - not wanting a brush with the traffic police in his present condition readily agreed.

He awoke fully refreshed discovering that Alice had covered him in a hand knitted blanket and candlewick coverall, which he was quite loathe to leave, but after his watch revealed 10.30 am, he felt the urgency to arise. He folded the covers in strict army fashion and placed them on the dining table where he discovered her note which read: 'Good morning Bill, I've had to dash off for the shopping for Mum, also at 11 am, I have a modelling appointment. I hope to see you before you go home. If this is not convenient, please give me a ring wherever you are. This is my number: 4239. I feel very happy in your company, you are good for me, I like your humour too. Lots of love, Alice, xx'.

He walked through the house into the kitchen where he located a bar of soap and freshened up. Suddenly he heard the dining room door shut, it was Helen.

"Had a good sleep Bill? I didn't disturb you because I knew you'd want to snooze," she commented, "My husband always had a lie in on Saturdays."

"I was very comfortable," he replied gratefully, "Helen, I need to go back to Newtown today to give notice of acquittal of my flat to my landlord, so will you give Alice my regards? I have your phone number - 4239 which I'll ring as soon as I've sorted out my business problems," he revealed.

"Do ring her Bill, won't you? I haven't seen Alice looking quite so happy as she was this morning. You're good for her you know, and she knows it."

He took Helen's hand and said, "Thank you Helen for making me so welcome. I've really enjoyed myself here in Chester. You've got a good honest lass in Alice, and I certainly want to see her again if I may?" he asked earnestly.

She gave his hand a squeeze saying, "You know Bill, you're just like my son Jonathon, you have that same sweet spirit."

Bill was touched, but replied, "Well I've got to go Helen, and thank you again," he repeated as he walked toward the front door. She held the door as he walked down the path to the car. Turning around he said, "Don't forget to tell Alice I'll ring her as soon as I'm through?"

"Right Bill," she assured him, "will do!"

He entered his car, waved goodbye and he was off.

Condition Purple

CHAPTER 24

"And so you see Mr. Burns, I'll be able to vacate my flat next Friday. Now then, do I need an inspector of works to ascertain that it's still in good condition before I leave or what?"

"Yes, you're quite right Mr. Foggit, your flat does need an inspection before you go."

"Right then, when can your man - er inspector pay me a visit?" he stressed.

"Wednesday afternoon," he offered.

"Right then Mr. Burns I'll take a day off work on that date in order to meet him."

'THE WRIGHT WAY TO REMOVE' read the sign of the local furniture shifters. Bill stepped into the office and made the date for Tuesday afternoon in which to transfer all of his worldly goods to the cottage.

"Okay Mr. Kipling I'll expect you by one o'clock?" he affirmed, having left the new address.

Bill felt like the cat's whiskers by now and decided to return home to prepare the packing of his goods.

He arrived back at his flat and retrieved all of his mail from off the hall floor. Most of it was 'junk' mail which he quickly collected and threw into the waste bin. Then he saw it, it was in Mary's handwriting. Although he'd got mixed feelings about ever seeing her again, he hurriedly tore open the sealed envelope to discover its' message:

THE MACE GOES IN

Dear Bill,

I've contacted Daddy's barrister and he wants me to go to see him to explain about the whole affair of Daddy's venture, in order to form a plea of mitigation for him. He also wants you yourself to accompany me at his office in Liverpool, to explain just what connection you had in the conspiracy.

Could you please give me a ring as soon as you arrive back at your flat, so that I can come down and escort you there?

Please, please, do help me to enable Daddy to get bail. I'll always love you Bill, Mary, xxx

Bill almost ran down the steps to the phone, when suddenly he stopped himself in horror and reasoned:

"How did she know that I was away from the flat?"

He retrieved the envelope and for the first time noticed that the 2½d stamp was not cancelled. Which meant, Mary had been there and discovered his absence.

"A clever ruse," he thought, "and I almost fell for it. He started to worry about his safety. He remembered his 'Sweeny' friend, Freddy Holly from Manchester police, had told him that lots of people were probably involved and still at liberty.

A knock appeared on the front door, and Bill suddenly dropped to the floor to avoid disclosing of any sight or sound which might reveal his presence in the flat.

Further horror came to him as he realised the appearance of his car had made the culprits aware of his presence. He hardly breathed in case they were listening.

The knocking grew louder and a male voice was heard, "Mr. Foggit, are you in there, I've been sent to chauffeur you to Miss Valesque's home!"

The letter box slammed shut as the man finally decided that Bill wasn't in his flat. Bill lay on the living room carpet not daring to move for at least half an hour. He was petrified and in fear for his very being.

He thought back to earlier events, "Anybody desperate enough to pump me full of heroin to make me sleep for a week will stop at nothing!"

His mind raced to the thought of their witnessing the removal of his furniture, and also the council inspector knocking on his door on Wednesday. Any fool could see where he was moving to, they only had to follow the shifter's van to find out.

"I need to contact Freddie Holly," he determined, but how?" All of the exits were obviously being watched. He reached for the scotch bottle but quickly changed his mind. "No, I must keep my wits about me if I'm to survive this lot."

He lit a cigarette and gratefully took big drags of the welcome smoke which, due to his lack of smoking - caused his head to spin, but it was something that he could handle. He needed this stimulant, in order to give himself time to think. "That's it," he exclaimed, "I'll wait for dark and nip out of the attic window."

He commended himself for his solution and decided to clean himself up. He set the immersion heater in action for a well deserved bath, and picked up the newspaper from the hall, but on further thought put it back on the floor with the bills also. He collected the junk mail from out of the bin and carefully placed it along with Mary's letter on the hall mat unopened.

"If anyone does look through the letter box, it will appear that I haven't arrived yet?"

He checked the bath water, and after deciding it was hot enough, entered the bathroom to turn off the switch and ran the bath.

He had just finished his soaking and was about to don his clothes as the door sounded once more, rat tat tat tat tat, rat tat tat tat, "Mr. Foggit?" sounded the voice once more. It was him again.

Bill didn't move as he craned his neck to hear.

"Mr. Foggit, are you in there?" the voice called.

He could hear more than one voice mumbling, "Silly basket must be kaylied - does he drink much Mary?"

"Mary, was Mary with them?" he thought, convinced now that she was aware of his part in the raid earlier. He quickly donned his clean underwear, shirt and trousers and shoes and crept toward the kitchen to where his boiler suit was kept. He put this on over his clothes and stealthily made his way to the inner hall where the attic

THE MACE GOES IN

ladder was situated. After all of the shouting had stopped, he carefully pulled down the ladder as slow as he could to avoid the noise, and when it was fully extended, he climbed into the loft pulling it back by means of its cord which after its restoral and satisfied that the attic trap door was back in place, he lay down to relax his body. After a couple of minutes still convinced there were no sounds, he proceeded toward the small attic window which after some difficult manoeuvres, he was able to open. He climbed out onto the flat roof, which was obscured from view of the road. If Bill had been in his flat, he would have had heart failure, for they had now gained access to his abode and were making judgements as to his whereabouts.

"Silly blighter's gone out," the first man said.

"No, I doubt whether he's ever come in?" the other voice ranted.

"Oh you idiots, you couldn't catch a cold in the north sea nude?" Mary exclaimed impatiently. "Mind you Harry, I think you're probably right, perhaps he hasn't yet arrived - there's my letter still on the mat!" she confuted supporting him.

Bill decided that the time was ripe to make his move. He shinned quickly down the soil pipe at the end of the concrete building, to which he gained access to the floor below through an opening, which turned onto the lower landing. He dropped onto the floor and absconded the staircase on the far side of the flats.

Looking over toward his car, he noticed a man with a newspaper weighing up the vehicle and decided against going for it.

He quickly made himself scarce and only when he was two streets away from the scene did he enter a public house, 'The Shrew' to disrobe his overall.

"Just put this under the bar," he bade Monty the barman, 'and 'ave a drink mate, I'll 'ave a double scotch - you 'ave what yer want," he offered handing the man a pound note.

"I'll collect it a bit later on, okay?" he searched.

The man nodded replying, "Okay Bill, I'll 'ave a glass o' bitter," handing him the change.

Bill quaffed the drink and was gone. He caught a bus into town and made straight away for a phone.

"Hello, is that Freddie Holly?" he questioned.

'Er, no sir, it's not. Who shall I say is calling?" the voice replied.

"'Sergeant Foggit'," Bill answered.

"Sergeant Fogg..." the man suddenly became active-"Get Freddie quick," Bill heard.

"Won't keep you long sir, we're trying to locate him on the other side of the station - here he is sir, Fred, your pal."

Freddie picked up the phone, "Bill, BILL, I've been trying to contact you all day, Listen Bill, I've got to see you at once mate. Something new has come up!" he enlightened. "Where are you now? Wherever you are, go to the nearest police station and mention the codeword: CONDITION PURPLE, they'll know what you mean, but do it as

quickly as you can. Promise me Bill - will you do it?" he pleaded.

"Okay, okay mate - condition purple?"

"Yes that's it Bill, now then mention my name and Trafford Park Station and you'll find out why. Don't forget -condition purple - and do it now!"

"Right Fred, I'm at the corner of Lomax Street in Newtown, I'll head for Gilbert Street Police Station. I should be there by eight o'clock. How soon can you be there? I need to see you," he determined.

"I'll be there in an hour Bill, now don't move from there will you?"

"Okay Fred - will do!" he put the phone down.

No sooner had he mentioned the words 'condition purple' to the desk sergeant, when two uniformed bobbies suddenly converged on him and frog-marched him to the cells.

'Trafford Park Police Station,' he screamed, 'Freddie Holly-Flying Squad' but this only seemed to cause more fervour for they forcibly ejected him into one of the cells and one of them stood guard as the other went to warn the rest of the force.

Bill couldn't believe it. Here he was locked in a cell where minutes before he had been free as a bird. He screamed out for an explanation but nothing was offered and for the best part of an hour he was forced to sweat it out, before Freddie Holly finally arrived and

THE MACE GOES IN

entered his cell.

"Hello Bill, sorry about the reception committee, but all the stations have been warned. The gang has got wind of your part in the pinch and are determined to silence you whatever the cost."

"Oh no!" Bill lamented.

"Don't worry mate, you're in protective custody, you'll be all right."

"All right – ALL RIGHT? D'you know what's happened since I last saw you, I've met a wonderful girl with whom I've fallen madly in love. I don't want to involve her in any way."

He took Freddie in his confidence and mentioned Alice and how he felt, also how Mary had suddenly appeared with two professionals to annihilate him.

Freddie enlightened him of the latest development and new date of the trial, which had been brought forward nearly three weeks up to the Monday following, pending the contact of Bill and his evidence to follow.

"Oh Fred, how am I going to explain all of this to Alice? I promised faithfully to ring her, as soon as I could to arrange a further date - and now this has to happen. What can I do?"

Freddie thought for a while and replied: "Well, no-one knows you're here, listen Bill, if I stick my neck out and allow you out on Sunday, you wouldn't do anything foolish would you?" he pleaded. "Like doing a bunk!"

"Oh Fred, you know me mate?"

"Only too blummin' well, listen Bill, I'll ask my men if they'll give you a couple of shadows to allow you to take out this bird although - goodness knows why - I could lose my pension if anything goes wrong!"

"Please Fred, do it, and I promise that I'll do whatever you say - that is if I don't end up getting' done myself?"

"No, Bill, you know you'll stand to gain a lot of reward money for this - leave it with me till Sunday and I promise you that you'll be able to take out this, er, Alice is her name? Yes, you can take her out in an unmarked police car driven by one of our drivers, to take you wherever you want to go, but to return you back to Chester main police precinct for late Sunday night, how's that grab you?"

"Well, I suppose it's the best I could expect judging by these circumstances."

From the police station he rang Alice excusing himself with a rather large lie, but convinced her that he would pick her up on Sunday night and she became satisfied with the explanation.

He slept the night in the cell which was unusually comfortable, to awaken to a large breakfast served by the constable.

"Good as a five star hotel is this," the man remarked who left him the 'News of the World' and a packet of twenty full strength. He was also left a safety razor, with which he was allowed to shave and wash up. The day wore on and into the night when appeared three plain clothes men - who introduced themselves as Harry, Jack and Roger. One of whom ushered him to the Rolls Royce, whilst the others followed in Morris Minors.

Sometime later he knocked on Alice's door and was welcomed in.

"Wait there would you Roger?" he ordered curtly.

Alice's mother Helen was very impressed and guided him into the house to wait for Alice who immediately descended the stairs to meet him.

"Hello Bill," she welcomed, "glad you could come," she enthused and took his hand.

Bill gave her a kiss on the cheek saying, "I missed you Al. I've had this terrible load of business to cover and tonight is the only time I can get off, then it's back to the grind on Monday. Flipping contracts, I can't get away from then," he lied convincingly.

She looked at him adoringly and gave him a long hug saying, "Let's not talk about it anymore then love - let's just enjoy ourselves shall we? I thought that we might be able to see that new play at the Royal Theatre tonight, if you think you'd like it love," she suggested.

"What's its theme?" he asked.

"Well" love, it's an old message really, the urgency of loving in the war torn years of the forties, when no-one knew whether they'd make it back from bombing raids etc."

"What time does it start?" he further enquired.

"Oh, seven-fifteen first performance Bill, so if you like, we could take a light meal before?"

"Hmm, I could do with a T bone," he pondered. "D'you have any objection to meat eating Alice, or are you really a strict Vegan?"

"Oh no Bill, there's nothing I like more than a good medium rare steak. I love the juices infused with the right herbs."

"Then it's to Alfies steak bar, we can go - okay?"

"I'm looking forward to it," she drooled.

Once back outside, he escorted her to the Rolls, where Roger, complete with grey cap sat waiting patiently. His eyes lit up as they approached for he saluted as he opened the rear door, "Where to sir?"

"Lower Bridge Street, Roger, and stop outside of Alfies's steak bar."

Alice by now was truly convinced that Bill was some kind of business executive, as she reclined back in the plush velvet seats which suited Bill, for he adopted an executives' attitude with the chauffeur all the way to the restaurant, by the emission of orders, through the microphone at the rear.

"This car must cost you a fortune to run Bill?" she probed.

"Oh just one of the perks of the job, I always use the company's Rolls' when I'm out to impress someone," he assured her jokingly.

'ALFIE'S STEAK BAR' loomed up ahead, and Roger drew the large car up alongside it.

"Will you require me later sir?" he asked subserviently.

"Go and park the Rolls Roger, then come back here and wait in close vicinity of the bar, I may need you to take us elsewhere."

Roger nodded touching his cap, aware that Bill was observing close security regulations.

Bill escorted Alice into the restaurant, which was quite full of hungry expectant people, sitting at tables with others in the process of eating and talking.

A light background music lent a contrast to the clicking of knives and forks and the lighting which was dimmed in green lights, gave the illusion of peace and refreshed your eyes as you entered.

Bill studied the menu which was steak oriented, and ordered the largest T bone available, just as Alice did the same. Also a light vermouth to appetise the palette before the meal, then sat back in his chair and commenced to chat about topical events, until both the meals were served.

"I'll never be able to eat all of this Bill?" she pleaded, "what about my figure?"

"You'll never notice the difference love - there's no fat on it at all, so you've nothing to worry about."

Nervously, she toyed with her knife and sliced off a small piece of the meat, which had a slightly pink hue. Putting it into her mouth, she couldn't really disguise the fact that she wasn't really a meat eater at all, but had agreed to accompany Bill if only to try to understand his needs.

Bill hadn't overlooked the situation, but pretended that it didn't exist for the sake of her feelings.

He hurriedly hacked up his meal, and voraciously caused it to disappear, commenting, "Gosh, that was good, I could just eat that again!" Then to save her embarrassment with her struggle to despatch her steak commented, "Come on Alice, I'll be attacking your meal soon- I've got this terrible hunger."

Nothing could have been more welcome than Bill's diplomatic hint. She concurred with, "Okay love, I think I can let you have some- if you're really that hungry?"

She took the serrated knife and hurriedly began to halve her meat dish, allowing Bill's side the part without the 'T' bone.

"There you are," she said jubilantly, as she passed the large portion to his awaiting plate.

He poured two glasses of Vermouth as she did so, and raised his, to wash down his earlier meal. Bill hacked and hewed at his latest acquisition and relished the aromatic taste of the herbs and tomato puree garnishing their meal. With deft slices and servings, proved almost to annihilate the fare? But seeing Alice struggling with hers he decided to slow down and put on a pant and pretended to perspire, 'Seems my eyes are bigger than my stomach," he lied, anxious that she didn't think of him a glutton.

She was relieved and replied, "Really Bill, I did have something before I came out," as convincingly as she could, "I don't seem to have an appetite at all!"

Bill glanced at his watch. It read 6.45 pm so he made show of looking saying, "What time is the performance again love – sevenish? It's a quarter to now."

Alice was relieved and hinted that perhaps they call the waiter for the bill adding, "I got a special discount in restaurants Bill, particularly this one," she enlightened, George Foggit who owns this place is a particularly good friend of mine. "Oh, here he comes now."

From out of the kitchen area in walked a tallish man in his late forties who almost resembled Bill except for his limp, which caused him to stoop slightly.

"George, how nice to see you, we were just going," she quipped, "could you give us our bill?" she stressed, "we're in a hurry." It was then that she noticed the resemblance, "D'you know, you two could be brothers, you both have the same features, and the same name?" she remarked.

Bill was in too much of a hurry to notice, and tendered a £10 note from which George rang up the till.

Bill pocketed the change thanking the man as they left the bar.

"You know Alice, I've been thinking...."

"About what Bill?"

"Well it's about you and me."

"Ooh?" she exclaimed.

"Yes love - us. D'you believe in deja vu?"

"We - ell, yes, I suppose in some cases, I do," she admitted, adding frivolously, "you meant that you've met me somewhere before - don't you Bill?"

"But how could you possibly have known what I was thinking?" he asked incredulously.

"Well Bill, I'll tell you how, since the very first moment that I saw you, I felt I knew you from somewhere before, so much so, that I even consented to that invite to show you around Chester. A thing I would never dream of doing at anytime since my husband's demise," she said fervently.

Bill was quite taken back, "You're a flippin' witch!" he voiced astonished.

"Ha, ha, ha, a lot of people have told me that before."

Bill could see Roger hovering in the background trying to intrude to reveal the Rolls' whereabouts and so Bill gave him the thumbs up sign with a gesture to bring the car.

"You know Bill, the feelings you have for me, are not dissimilar to those I have for you, and I know that sooner or later we'll both realise that we have something special."

Bill looked at her with adoration, "I wonder if she can perceive my thoughts?" he pondered.

"Bill, I know you think I'm some kind of a mind reader, but I feel that this special bond we have for each other has grown since we first met," she said with a serious look.

"In what way love?" he replied, taking her hand.

"When we went to the 'Bean Feast', I noticed that although you hadn't experienced vegetarian cooking before, that you laboured on and tried to appreciate - in order not to offend - what was being offered.

Bill at this point felt a little foolish and coloured up as she continued:

"You also began to enjoy the food just to please me, and it was this gesture which touched me the most," she admitted, tears running from her eyes. "Also tonight when I experienced difficulty in consuming that medium rare steak, you came to my rescue immediately and removed the awkward part, enabling me to keep my cool. Yes Bill Foggit, when they made you, they broke the mould," she commended giving him a hug.

The shadow of the Rolls suddenly blocked the light and Bill located the door in front of them.

"Step in love," he directed, then he got in behind her.

"Where to sir?" Roger bleated.

"I'll tell you in a moment, just drive around for a bit till we decide!"

This suited Roger, for Bill was too easy a target sitting still in the back, stationary.

The car moved off and Bill took in the scenery of the ancient city

THE MACE GOES IN

dominated by Tudor buildings.

"By the way Alice, how did your modelling interview go, everything okay?"

Alice's face showed him that something was amiss, "They said I was too old," she choked, trying to compose herself.

"Don't worry love, you don't even look old. Who were they, I'll go and sort them out?" he gestured.

"Oh no Bill, that would only make matters worse," she bleated, "I still have my part time position at the garage. I'll get by, and Mum has her pension - no, we'll both be all right- believe me!" she replied convincingly.

"Alice, after tonight I have quite a heavy work schedule, which points me toward a rather large commitment, which may take days to complete, even weeks, I'm not sure, it's a matter of extreme urgency, from which I might not come out of unscathed. I know that you've arranged for that joiner fellow to inspect those windows for me, but I don't really know if I can get away from all of this to be there. However, I'd like you to take this key, which unlocks the front door of the cottage - here is the address, if you would do the honours for me in my absence?"

Alice took him in her arms saying, "I'll do anything for you Bill, but what is this undertaking you have, is it dangerous? Promise me that you'll stay out of danger love, I wouldn't want to lose you now that I've found you." She showered him with kisses as she spoke.

Bill perceived her sorrow and realised that he must have reminded her, of the circumstances in which Mortimer had met his end. "It's nothing like that love," he assured her.

"Like what?"

"Like what you're thinking," he lied, "no love, it's merely a matter of an affidavit being signed by me and defended," he confided.

"Oh no Bill, you're not a witness in a murder case are you?" She said with a frown.

"She's a bloomin' witch,' he thought. "Can I say this to you Alice, when I come out of all of this, we'll be quite comfortably off…"

"We?" she asked.

"Yes love, we. I suppose - you being a witch, would not find it hard to perceive the thoughts I'm planning on my return from all of this?" he ventured.

"I'm way ahead of you Bill," she retorted, taking him in her arms once more and hugging him.

"Drop by the 'Pig and Whistle', Roger," he said after sliding back the separation window.

"Oh not that delightful little pub in Waverton?" she drooled.

"That's the place," he concurred.

"A bottle of Bubbly, and could you bring it over to the corner please?" Bill asked the barman.

"There'll be a certain tottage charge sir," the man explained.

Bill gave him the two pound note saying, "Keep the change," bringing a smile to the barman's face.

"Mm, this is good stuff Bill, what is it called?" she enquired.

"Er," replied he. He couldn't read French so he retorted, "Chateau-de-pi, plonki"

Alice started laughing in appreciation, as he replenished both of their glasses for which Alice seemed to have a never ending swallow.

Bill signalled the barman collecting empty glasses, and ordered another bottle of the same. The man returned and de-corked it leaving it standing in the ice pale.

Bill paid him and they continued in their quest for inebriation. Bill was aware of a tightness appearing over his forehead which caused him to sway slightly and put his hand to his head.

"Are you all right Bill?" she cried with a worried voice.

"Er,.." but Bill was far from all right.

He closed his eyes just as the barman arrived, his head slumped backward.

"It takes some people like that," he stressed, "d'you have a car Madam or shall I call a cab?"

Roger hurriedly made his way over to the table. He had accompanied them both into the pub without their knowledge.

"I'll take him home Miss," he offered, taking charge of the situation.

Between them both they managed to walk him to the car with

Alice trailing behind.

Roger tipped the barman for his trouble and drove the car away with Bill's head nestled upon Alice's arm lying across the back seat. Alice slid back the glass, "Bring the car up to my place Roger, Bill wanted to stay the night here tonight."

"Okay ma-am," Roger responded and made a right turn toward Hough Green.

Bill was aware of a choking feeling, he struggled to get his breath but was unable to. He coughed and choked in an attempt to take in air but found it impossible. He could feel a great weight on top of his shoulders. He struggled in a last wild attempt to take in air, but collapsed and fainted into unconsciousness.

"Here's your share Audrey, and here's Rita's," the man pointed as they took the envelopes.

Audrey examined hers with a cry of dismay, "You promised me £2000, there's only £1000 here."

Rita quickly examined hers, "You've withheld £200 of mine also. What's the idea Charlie?"

"I've got to ascertain if he's truly dead?" he determined.

"Follow me!" Rita ordered.

The man complied as she led him to the yard.

"Under that mound of earth lies a slab of stone pinning him down," she pointed. "Now then, if anybody could live after eight hours of that, he'd have to be superhuman wouldn't he?" she confuted.

But the man still wasn't satisfied. He at once shovelled the earth away from the stone, a few moments after Bill had come to and heard every word.

The man rose up the slab to find Bill motionless, but aware of what was transpiring.

Although Bill was confused at these latest circumstances, it didn't take him long to realise, that he must play dead if he was to survive at all. He took in a small amount of air and held it as the man lifted him up.

Satisfied that he was 'dead' he dropped him down again. Bill's head flopped forwards before hitting the earth and he managed to cradle his mouth and nose by his forehead down on the freshly dug earth.

The man replaced the stone onto Bill, who braced himself in order to form a small archway to trap the air, as the man proceeded to emit shovels of earth over the slab.

Finally when he was satisfied that the 'body' was covered, he patted the earth down, which was really a blow for Bill, whose mouth came into contact with the earth once more.

He passed out again.

"Here's the rest of the cash, George didn't want slip-ups from you, but seein' as everythin' is okay, mum's the word. You'd better make tracks from 'ere quick, before it's eight o'clock, or that chauffeur'll be back ter collect 'im," he warned.

"I'll be there in a moment, first I've got my accounting to do."

"Accounting?" he sniggered.

"Now then let's see?" she queried as she pondered over the figures, "there was the East Dee scam which cost £15 to set up with £280 return. The double blonde congesting £18 for wigs, cabs etc., which netted £175 and the Racecourse caper, with the use of Thames Palace to pull it off - which, incidentally produced £500 from the turf in the month it took to set up. Let's see now, that night after Bill Foggit dropped me off and you contacted me here which cost practically nothing to set up, except the hire of the Mini, ha, ha, that's almost £2000 for him," she chuckled, "and all for a day's work," she stated proudly.

"Don't forget the £40 for the Thames Palace," quipped Rita.

"That doesn't count, we charged this to the race course caper."

"Oh yes," she agreed, "well how much does that come to?" she enquired excitedly.

"Erm, £265 plus £158 and £460 and finally £1965, let's see," she commented as she totalled the figures:

£1965
£460
£158

THE MACE GOES IN

£265
£2848

"That's £2848 to the good - not bad for a month's work eh Rita?" she voiced rubbing her hands with avarice.

The man looked up saying: "That's good going love, but we've really got to go, see you around then - Bye."

Both Rita and he were gone.

Audrey followed soon after.

Bill could hear Alice's voice, but even in his half twilight world, he knew that Alice had put up the whole charade. His hearing had picked up part of the conversation between the man and Alice and Helen, filled him with despair. Perhaps this really was the end, nothing mattered any more, first it had been Mary's treachery, and now Alice's. He felt that he should just give up the ghost and resigned himself to that fact, just as Alice made the last cutting remark:

"Poor sap, he was going to ask me to marry him. Me-marry a scrap dealer, 'eaugh." she remarked in disgust.

She walked over his 'grave', in a last gesture of contempt for him, as she left for her car.

Rita following bleating, "Wait for me Audrey."

Roger was hammering on the front door in a bid to raise a reply which was not forthcoming.

His partner who had been trailing them undercover, quickly left his parked car and accompanied Roger who was still pounding the door. "I'll go to the rear," Harry indicated. "By the way where's Jack?" asked Roger.

"Isn't he with you? He was supposed to trail you and Bill to ascertain the address. "Well he's not here," Roger determined. "Right, I'll search the rear," said Harry.

He moved quickly away and located the back gate, which having discovered it locked, climbed over to gain access to the rear.

He landed on the path and regained his balance, in order to creep around the house to locate the resident.

He ducked down below the window, but after viewing through

from over the ledge, discovered no one.

He looked for a way in and located a double door, on what appeared to be a small wooden extension, sticking obtrusively from the building. He wrenched at the doors which just flew open, to reveal a cellar with a number of furniture items cluttering up the area. He searched for a way into the house and noticed the shape of a man further back. Further examination revealed a small chair upon which the man sat - it was Jack.

"Jack, so this is where you've been hiding? You've given us both a fright; we thought something had happened to you!" He touched Jack on the shoulder and the sudden movement, caused him to fall to the floor. Jack was cold. Harry recoiled in horror.

"I, I, eh," he choked almost heaving. Gathering his wits about him, he decided that Jack had been killed long ago, and that he needed to tread carefully if he were to avoid his colleague's fate. He decided to report back to Roger and sped off to locate his pal.

"Jack's dead as a doornail, I'm going to report in," he indicated. Both of them returned to Harry's Minor to contact headquarters who immediately assigned photographers and a coroner to the scene. Upon arrival, an ambulance stood by as the area was cordoned off with uniformed constables.

Freddy Holly arrived ashen faced, "I knew I shouldn't have let him go," he lamented, head in hands as he thought the worst for Bill's fate. "Where is Bill?" he asked finally as he composed himself.

"We haven't as yet located him, or Alice, his girlfriend, sir," Roger enlightened.

"Oh blast, has anybody searched the house yet?" Showing frustration in his face.

"We haven't yet been able to gain access sir!" Roger replied.

"Then it's about flamin' time somebody put their shoulder to the door—Bill could be dying," he urged.

He ran to the rear of the house in a bid to break down the door. The rear gate was open and the cellar doors agape. The coroner was already instructing the constables, to take out the stretcher holding Jack.

THE MACE GOES IN

The adjoining door to the kitchen above the stove steps, was also open with policemen hurrying up and down. Freddie quickly ran up toward the kitchen.

"Anything - anybody been found?" he urged.

"Not a sausage sir, the place is empty - except for its furniture there's nothing else here."

Freddy sunk his head in his hands with anxiety. He slowly descended the steps leading to the cellar. Two constables stood either end of the stretcher and looking down he saw Jack lying motionless.

"Poor beggar, what can I tell his wife Betty, and all those kids. Blast, it's all down to me, if only I hadn't agreed to let Bill out..?"

Freddy's tears were running unashamedly down his face from seeing his dead colleague and friend. He reached for his cigarettes and pushed one into his mouth. He lit the lighter in his grief, with his hands shaking as he walked toward the gate. The lighter dropped and he was unaware at first, but then returned to retrieve the object. It moved. He stooped to pick it up - it moved again.

After all the turn of events, he recoiled warily before making a further attempt.

He was just about to reach for it when: "Freddy, Freddy Holly!"

He looked up to espy his superior, the head of the Manchester Crime Squad, Samuel Peel.

"Where's that feller Foggit?" the man boomed.

Freddy swallowed hard. How could he explain this lot? "Well, er, erm, er, you see sir, Foggit isn't around here to let us know what plan of action he has," he bleated.

"Have you searched the house?" he probed.

"Yes sir."

"What about the grounds - come on man, have you searched the gardens? What the devil's that?" he pointed.

It was Freddy's lighter, "It's my Zippo sir," he told him as he reached for it. It moved again.

Freddy clawed at the soil, completely forgetting the lighter and the petulance of his superior. He cut his fingers as he dug down deep, but was oblivious to any pain.

Suddenly he located the stone slab and shouted, "Ger old o' this

Sammy quick!"

The crime chief ignored Freddy's lack of respect, for he also felt the urgency of the situation and almost clawed at the slab jointly with Freddy. As they raised it they each saw Bill's shape.

"Is he alive?" Sammy screamed, as he clawed Bill's body to turn him over.

Freddy put his ear to Bill's chest. He'd got hold of his wrist at the same time.

He started slapping Bill's chest to start his heart.

"He's got a pulse, oh thank heavens, Bill, Bill, don't worry mate, everything's going to be all right."

Sammy was running for the coroner, who came immediately to give Bill the kiss of life. He was about to when Bill's eyes fluttered, "Ooh," he moaned.

"Blankets quickly, the coroner shouted - in the ambulance and something to drink." Sammy dashed back with the blankets and put them around Bill who started to regain consciousness.

"Here sip this."

"Fred…, Freddie…," he croaked in recognition.

"I'm here Bill, it's alright me ole mate, you're goin' ter be all right now."

They put him on a stretcher and took him to the ambulance, where within in, on the other side lay the body of Jack covered up. The vehicle drove off to the West Cheshire Hospital where the emergency team awaited.

Bill was placed in a bed pre-heated with hot water bottles, which warmed him immensely and soon he was breathing normally once more.

"After only an hour, but it's eleven o'clock, no Inspector, I'm afraid that you really can't take him away, no, I'm sorry sir, but you'll have to leave him, at least overnight!" the doctor stressed.

"But you don't seem to realise doctor, this man is an important witness in a case of national importance…"

"And I don't think that YOU realize Inspector, that if this man were moved now, he could die of shock. He's been buried alive, it's a wonder he's not dead already?" he exhorted loudly.

THE MACE GOES IN

"Oh what's the use," said Roger, "I'll get the chief," and ran back down to the reception.

Freddy entered Bill's room and said, "Hello me ole mate, how are yer?"

"Leave us will you doctor? I have national security to discuss," he requested as he produced his authority. Against his better judgement, the doctor signalled the nurse to accompany him out, and as soon as they had left Freddy enlightened Bill of the urgency of the day, explaining that Bill himself must sign himself out of hospital, in order to get to court, assuring him that a team of doctors would be on hand, should the need arise for medication. For the security at the hospital would not suffice against an onslaught from the Valesque supporters.

Bill seemed convinced of this and upon the doctor and nurse's return, requested the form.

"You chaps think that because you represent the establishment, that you can get away with anything!" voiced the doctor with derision. "Well let me tell you Mr. Chief Inspector, you've not heard the last of this - no not by a long chalk!" he raged.

Freddy by now was oblivious to the threats, for his impending retirement, assured him that Sammy Olivier would carry the can, if anything did stir up from this action.

After the night in the police cells, with full protection and under the care of two doctors and a nurse.

"Right then Bill, time for the court, up ya get." Said the inspector.

"Calling Mr. William Foggit," ordered the prosecution.

"Call Mr. William Foggit," pealed the clerk of court.

"Get Mr. Foggit," the sergeant instructed, and the constable stepped down toward the police cell, where Bill awaited with the doctors.

"Mr. Foggit sir, we're ready for you now," said Constable Hughes.

Bill arose, followed by two doctors, who accompanied him to the courtroom, where he was instructed to hold a Bible and take the oath of promise.

The doctors sat in the front row in readiness should he need them.

He pronounced the oath and the prosecuting barrister proceeded to question him.

Bill looked across in time to perceive, the horror on George Valesque's face with Geraldine, who appeared to share all of his fears as they sat in the defendant's seating.

Bill was determined to get his revenge on all the trouble they'd caused him.

He searched around, but there was no sign of Mary. Then just as he commenced to answer the questions, he noticed her accompanied by two WPC'S at the rear.

He related all of the events in fine detail, which were recorded at the source.

It was at this stage that George and Geraldine's barrister, advised them to change their plea to guilty, due to mitigating circumstances and throw themselves upon the mercy of the court, in a bid to avoid further charges of conspiracy to the murder of Jack and himself.

Up to this point Alice/Audrey and Helen/Rita had not been apprehended and so the Crown was forced to accept both of their pleas but the added charge of possession of dangerous drugs, and the illegal administration of them to Bill, without care to his welfare. This was accepted - reduced from the original charge of Dinny's attempted murder of him. Through a huge dose of herion she'd administered.

They were both sentenced to twelve years each hard labour - without remittance or parole- and Bill was commended for his undercover action.

After the trial, Freddy shook his hand saying, "Well Bill, George and Dinny won't be getting out for quite a while. Next month I retire, so let's see what we can do now about that reward money."

"Never mind that Fred, what about all the lesser minions, will they get porridge too?"

"Oh yes Bill, their trials are already started - listen you can go and sit in the public gallery if you like?" he offered.

THE MACE GOES IN

"I didn't see Malcolm Johnston at the court?"

"Oh, he's already been given probation for his part in this. The local plod helped him out when he gave a confession to them."

"How did you convince them about me then?" he further enquired.

"Oh that was easy Bill, when you're undercover, anything goes."

Bill was happy once more and answered, "Okay Fred where do I sign?"

"That's my boy Bill," Fred chuckled.

As they left the 'Castle' courtroom, Freddie motioned Bill to the car awaiting them for the police station.

Later Bill filled out all of the forms assuring Fred, that later he would cut the reward 50-50. As he arose from the chair Fred stopped him and said, "Bill, we decided that not all of those concerned were to be charged with anything."

He instructed the constable to open the office door alongside and gestured to Bill with open hand to enter.

"Mary," he breathed, "I thought you'd tried to kidnap me?" he queried turning to Fred.

"No Bill, Fred replied, "it wasn't how you thought," he explained. "Mary smelled a rat at the beginning, when her father's barrister instructed her, to bring you to his office. She contacted us at the local station, and we in turn lent her a couple of our best body guards, to go and protect you from George's men, who were trailing her everywhere she went. So you see Bill, she really loved you through it all," he commended tip - toeing out to give them privacy.

"But what about George, Mary, how could you do it to him?" he queried astonished.

"Well Bill, it was when the prosecutor had told me, that you had worked with the police from the beginning, that I knew that lies were being told, and that Daddy was only using emotional blackmail, to convince me that YOU were the enemy. Having got to know you Bill, I was convinced that their allegations were just not true, and that if Daddy came out of this scot-free, he would be up to his old tricks again. No, Bill, he's better where he is. He'll be re-habilitated in prison and when he comes out he'll be a better man for it," she decided.

"Say no more," he instructed her, holding her and kissing her, saying, "How could you ever forgive me for judging you like that?"

"I love you Bill," she replied tearfully.

He hugged her and kissed her, holding her strongly to him.

"Are you two taking up home here?" Fred interrupted, as he re-entered.

Bill took her hand with adoration, smiling to Fred who opened the door to let them out.

The awaiting taxi took them back to Bill's flat, which he entered with Mary following.

"I'll put the kettle on love," she offered, as Bill raced up the hall to the vase which held the ring.

As she entered with the tray, he waited for her to pour the tea and then told her, "I've got something for you love," he motioned, handing her the object.

With excitement, she opened the small ring box…………

ABOUT THE AUTHOR

Lles Noiz, born in Bebington, Wirral, England, 1938.
He worked in construction as a carpenter and joiner.

Although in construction he always had a passion for writing; works of fiction, non-fiction and poetry, drawing upon insights from many of his personal journals and life experiences.

Originally 'The Mace Goes In' was written by Lles, in the early 1970's as a biography, where he was inspired by the antics and legendary exploits of an infamous scrap metal dealer. Stories of whom, he would often hear, being told in his local pub over a few pints. This sparked the idea for 'The Mace Goes In' and a premise to write this work of fiction .

It may have taken time but he got there in end.

2020 released for print and kindle.

Printed in Great Britain
by Amazon